'Sweet and lovely. I guarantee you will fall in love with Heidi's wonderful world' **Milly Johnson**

'Wise, warm and wonderful – a real summer treat!' ***Heat***

'Sparkling and romantic' ***My Weekly***

'The most delicious slice of festive fiction: a true comfort read and the perfect treat to alleviate all the stress!' **Veronica Henry**

'A fabulous feel good read – a ray of reading sunshine!' **Laura Kemp**

'Sprinkled with Christmas sparkle' **Trisha Ashley**

'A story that captures your heart' **Chrissie Barlow**

'Fans of Carole Matthews will enjoy this heartfelt novel' **Katie Oliver**

**Heidi Swain** lives in Norfolk with her family and a mischievous black cat called Storm. She is passionate about gardening, the countryside and collects vintage paraphernalia. *Poppy's Recipe for Life* is her eighth novel. You can follow Heidi on Twitter @Heidi_Swain or visit her website: heidiswain.co.uk

*Also by Heidi Swain*

The Cherry Tree Café

Summer at Skylark Farm

Mince Pies and Mistletoe at the Christmas Market

Coming Home to Cuckoo Cottage

Sleigh Rides and Silver Bells at the Christmas Fair

Sunshine and Sweet Peas in Nightingale Square

Snowflakes and Cinnamon Swirls
at the Winter Wonderland

Heidi Swain

SIMON & SCHUSTER

London · New York · Sydney · Toronto · New Delhi

A CBS COMPANY

First published in Great Britain by Simon & Schuster UK Ltd, 2019
A CBS COMPANY



1 3 5 7 9 10 8 6 4 2

Simon & Schuster UK Ltd
1st Floor
222 Gray's Inn Road
London WC1X 8HB

Simon & Schuster Australia, Sydney
Simon & Schuster India, New Delhi

www.simonandschuster.co.uk
www.simonandschuster.com.au
www.simonandschuster.co.in

A CIP catalogue record for this book is available from the British Library

Paperback ISBN: 978-1-4711-7438-4
eBook ISBN: 978-1-4711-7439-1
eAudio ISBN: 978-1-4711-8042-2



Typeset in the UK by M Rules
Printed and bound by CPI Group (UK) Ltd, Croydon, CR0 4YY

Poppy's
Recipe for
Life

*To*
*Emma Capron,*
*with love and thanks*

# Prologue

I was curled up on my sofa, tweaking my 'chuck-it-all-in chutney' recipe and dreaming about preparing it in my new kitchen in Nightingale Square, when my mobile rang. It wasn't the first time it had interrupted my evening and I snatched it up, fully prepared to tell my best mate Lou that I was absolutely certain that an evening in the pub celeb-rating Halloween was not the way to prepare for packing up my flat.

'I haven't changed my mind,' I announced, accepting the call without checking the ID. 'You and Colin will have to manage without me.'

It was just a week until the move and I couldn't risk wasting precious packing time nursing a Creepy Cocktail-induced hangover.

'Poppy?'

'Mum?' I jolted upright, scattering my notes and recipe cards far and wide as I squinted at the screen.

'Poppy?' came her voice again.

'Yes,' I said. 'I'm here.'

'Good, because I need to talk to you. It's urgent.'

My heart sank. Mum and I didn't have the sort of relationship where we kept up with each other's lives. In fact, we didn't have a relationship where we kept up with each other at all. Her call was completely unexpected and I knew from past experience that it wouldn't be littered with idle chit-chat. I only hoped it wasn't about my brother.

'It's about Ryan.'

My heart slumped further. Ever since Ryan's father, Tony, divorced our mother three years ago I had been wondering how long she would be able to cope. Tony was still very much on the scene, but with Mum severely lacking in the maternal instinct department it had always felt like just a matter of time before the testosterone-charged teenage bomb detonated.

'He got surprisingly good GCSE grades,' she shocked me by saying, 'and now he's studying for his A levels.'

Perhaps the urgency wasn't of the negative variety after all.

'But I'm not sure he's going to be able to keep it up,' she continued. 'In fact, I know he isn't.'

But then again . . .

I braced myself for impact.

'The thing is, Poppy,' she went on, sounding more whiney with every word, 'I just can't afford it.'

'What do you mean, you can't afford it?' I snapped, cutting her off, the second I sensed trouble.

'Well,' she said, 'we moved house in June. Straight after Ryan's last exam.'

I wasn't at all fazed by this announcement. She had moved before and neglected to tell me until I had been forced to text after Ryan's birthday card, marked 'return to sender', had landed on my doormat. Had I not put my own address sticker on the back I never would have known.

'We're just on the outskirts of Wynmouth now.'

That, I was not expecting. Wynmouth was on the north Norfolk coast and only an hour or so from my patch in Norwich. Suddenly she was a little too close for comfort.

'Sorry,' I said, forcing myself to remain focused on her words as opposed to her uncomfortable proximity, 'but I don't see how you living near Wynmouth means Ryan can't afford to study.'

'He's enrolled at Norwich city college and has to commute every day and it's not just that, there's the equipment he needs and money for trips, not to mention the new laptop he'll have to buy to keep on top of everything. It's got to be a specific one, apparently.'

'But surely Tony will help out with all of that,' I said bluntly.

He had never shirked his parental responsibilities before. I couldn't imagine he was exactly thrilled that Mum had moved Ryan so far away, but he wasn't the sort of bloke to throw his toys out of the pram over something like that.

'Tony's will hasn't been sorted yet,' Mum shot back, every bit as bluntly. 'There's some complication apparently . . .'

'Tony's *what*?'

'Will,' she said, louder this time.

I didn't say anything.

'You know,' she carried on as if I hadn't heard of a will before, 'the legal document that shares out your worldly goods when you die. Do keep up, Poppy.'

'Are you actually telling me that Tony's dead?' I gasped.

'Yes,' she said, an edge of frustration creeping into her tone. 'He had a heart attack just after Easter and never recovered. That's the reason why we moved. To help Ryan move on.'

I didn't for one second believe *that* had formed any part of her motive for packing up but it wasn't the time to mention it. I was still reeling from the casual way she had dropped Tony's death into the conversation.

'Ryan said he was going to let you know,' she carried on.

Why she thought that grim task should fall to him, I had no idea.

'Well, he didn't,' I stammered.

'I thought it was a bit strange when you didn't turn up for the funeral.'

'But not so strange that you thought you should call me?'

She ignored the question.

'But it's all done now.' She sighed, as if the situation had exhausted her. 'We're just waiting for the money— Ryan's money,' she hastily corrected herself, 'to come through. Should there be any, that is. But in the meantime, I was wondering if there's any chance you could help tide us over? Tide Ryan over, I mean.'

I hated the thought of Ryan having to give up his education when it must have been so difficult for him to carry on with it, and I didn't allow myself to think about why he had been within spitting distance of me most days over the last few weeks and not been in touch. The ball was in my court now and I was going to have to make amends. I wanted to make amends.

I grabbed a scrap of paper as Mum relayed her bank details, all the while wishing that I'd gone out with Lou after all. A creepy cocktail was probably just the thing for treating shock.

# Chapter 1

Winter determinedly matched my mood and for seemingly weeks the city was held tight in the clutches of what the media called another Beast from the East. Having had to shelve my plans to move into my beloved Nightingale Square, I had avoided the place, along with the community garden attached to it and Kate, the lovely lady who owned the house I had so longed to rent, as much as possible.

Instead of hankering for what I had lost, I focused my attention on trying to build bridges with my brother, but my enthusiasm to rekindle our relationship was never reciprocated. In fact, Ryan had bailed on every single get-together I had pushed for and he kept communication between us firmly confined to occasional texts and the odd stilted and extremely brief call. He had never thanked me for the money and I didn't feel comfortable mentioning it.

*

'Poppy!' called Harry, my boss, one afternoon in early March. 'Customer!'

There had been a sudden change in the weather since the calendar had flipped from February to March and I was grateful for the reappearance of the sun. Not only because it meant warmer weather was on its way, but also because it meant that Greengages Grocers, the shop I had worked in since dropping out of university six years ago, was busy again.

'Coming,' I called back, snapping my laptop shut.

Harry had asked me to start investigating the possibility of Greengages going plastic-free. Customers had been asking about it more and more and he considered me the person best suited to finding out whether it was a viable option for his business. I had been using every spare minute to research the idea and was excited about what I had found so far. It wasn't going to happen overnight but it was looking feasible long-term.

'Oh,' I said, as I stepped from the stockroom and on to the shop floor.

I had expected to find Harry swamped but there was only one customer.

'Kate.' I swallowed. 'How can I help?'

I retied the bow of my apron and looked everywhere but at her. I still felt awkward about letting her down at such short notice, especially as I knew the tenants she had then hastily taken on had turned out to be less than ideal.

'I'm hoping I might be able to help you actually.' She smiled, stroking the head of her baby, Abigail, who was cosily nestled in a fabric sling across her chest. 'It's about the house.'

I felt my face begin to flush.

'I heard your tenants had another humdinger of a party last weekend,' Harry tutted.

My cheeks flared even redder. Had I moved in when I was supposed to, Kate's pretty little property wouldn't have had to endure the tenants from hell.

'Yes,' she said with a sigh, 'they did. It's hardly any wonder that the other new resident in the square doesn't want anything to do with any of us, is it?'

I hadn't met the chap myself, but I knew he had moved in just before Christmas and had made a point of keeping his door firmly shut. Hardly surprising given who his closest neighbours were. Everyone else in Nightingale Square was lovely but his first impression of the place would have been far from impressive.

'It can't be easy for any of you living next door to folk like that,' said Harry, before disappearing through to the stockroom.

'I take it he still hasn't visited the garden?' I asked, finally finding my voice.

I knew that if I had moved to the square as planned I would have never been out of the place. In fact, it had been one of the main reasons why I was so keen to secure the property. The thought of utilising all that fresh produce in my pickle and preserve recipes still set my heart racing, but it was too late now.

'Nope,' said Kate. 'He hasn't so much as set foot in the grounds of Prosperous Place.'

Prosperous Place was the Victorian mansion house across the road from Nightingale Square where Kate now lived with her partner, Luke, stepdaughter Jasmine and their beautiful baby Abigail. It also happened to be where the garden was located.

'Truth be told, he's a right old grumpy so-and-so,' she carried on in a low voice. 'He keeps himself to himself and you're lucky to even get so much as a mumbled hello out of him ... but he's not what I wanted to talk to you about, Poppy,' she went on as Abigail began to stir.

'Okay,' I said.

'As I said, it's about the house.' Kate smiled, rocking her baby from side to side. 'And please don't look so worried whenever I mention it. I'm sure you had your reasons for changing your mind last year.'

Well, my mother had, but Kate didn't need to know that.

'I just wanted to tell you that it's available again. The tenants from hell have decamped.'

Her words were music to my ears, but the melody was less than tuneful. Thanks to Mum's inability to balance her budget I had even less available in the bank now than I'd had before.

'It's in a bit of a state,' Kate continued, 'but they're gone and that's all I care about. There's nothing a decent clear-out and a deep-clean won't sort and I wanted you to be the first to know. I wanted to offer it to you.'

I shook my head. I wished I had started saving again, but

I hadn't for one second thought the house would be available so soon.

'That's very kind,' I said sadly, 'especially given everything that's happened since I let you down last time round, but I can't take it, I'm afraid.'

'Have you got somewhere else in mind?' Kate frowned.

'No,' I said, 'no, it's not that. I just can't afford it. What with the deposit and everything, I'm just not in a position to move anywhere right now.'

The simple life I strived to lead was perfect in my eyes, but on rare occasions like this a few reserves in the bank would have been most welcome.

'Oh, good grief,' said Kate, shaking her head. 'Sorry, Poppy. I'm not explaining myself very well, am I?'

'Aren't you?'

'No,' she said, laughing, 'I'm not. What I should have said is that I want *you* to take it and I'm not going through the letting agency again, not given the fiasco I've already been through. I love that little house and I want to move someone in who will treasure it every bit as much as I do.'

'But what about the deposit and everything?'

'I'm not worried about that,' said Kate, waving the mention of money away. 'I would far rather secure the right tenant than worry about cash up front.'

'Really?'

'Really.' She smiled. 'Please tell me you'll take it. You can move in as soon as I've had it cleaned and polished.'

*

'So,' demanded Lou when I met her and our other friend, Colin, in his bookshop along the road later that day, 'spill the beans, Pops! I've shut up shop early as requested, so whatever it is you have to tell us better be worth the loss of custom.'

'Do you think I should shut up too?' suggested Colin, looking around the dark and dusty shop he had inherited from his uncle the year before, along with a stocky little French bulldog called Gus.

'I don't think so,' said Lou, frowning. 'I can't imagine you're going to be inundated now, Col, can you?'

Colin's shop couldn't have been more different from the vibrant retro emporium, Back in Time, which Lou had opened in the new year. Her place was never without at least three browsers, even during the worst the winter had thrown at us, and they rarely left empty-handed.

'Hardly,' huffed Colin. 'To be honest, I've forgotten the meaning of the word "inundated". I've had one person through that door today. One!'

'And did they buy anything?' I asked, picking Gus up and stroking his silky ears while Lou made cups of instant coffee in the makeshift kitchen corner of Colin's office.

'No,' said Colin, blushing. 'They only came in to ask for directions.'

I looked down at Gus's little face. He looked every bit as miserable as his new master. I was certain the pair of them were still missing their beloved Uncle Alowishus. How the old guy had stayed in business was beyond me and I feared for the future of what was now Colin's shop.

'Oh Colin,' said Lou, flapping into full mother hen mode. A role she adored, by the way. 'This can't go on.'

'I know,' said Colin, relieving her of the coffee tray and looking down at her with adoring eyes, 'I know it can't.'

'But,' said Lou, completely unaware of his affectionate attention, 'we can't worry about that today. We're here for Poppy, remember? Please don't tell me your mother's back on the scene again, Pops?'

'No,' I said, 'this has absolutely nothing to do with her. Although' – I grinned, thinking of the text I had sent Ryan earlier suggesting he could come and visit now I was going to have more room – 'what I have to tell you might mean I can finally form some sort of relationship with my brother.'

The pair looked at each other and shrugged as I took a sip of my drink.

'Kate came to see me at work today,' I told them, refusing to allow the bitter tang of the cheap coffee to sour the moment. 'She's offered me her house again and I've said yes. I'm finally moving into Nightingale Square!'

# Chapter 2

I'd never really understood what it meant to be floating on cloud nine, but the next couple of weeks were an education in the art. Kate had insisted that I could visit the house as many times as I wanted before the big day, but I had been dreaming of the layout for so long that there was no need – and, more to the point, there was no time!

I had so much to do that my feet hardly touched the ground, and as moving day drew nearer I began to realise that Mum's phone call hadn't been such a disaster for me after all. Yes, I might have spent the winter harbouring less than friendly feelings towards her, even though I knew my money had gone to a good cause, but was there really a better time than spring to be moving house?

A change of residence offered the opportunity for the ultimate spring-clean and as much as I had enjoyed living above Greengages and was grateful to Harry for giving me the opportunity, I was ready to spread myself out a little further and move on.

Change was in the air and I was delighted to be a part of it. Harry was gearing up to embrace the plastic-free ethos, my new seasonal recipe cards were flying off the shop shelves as fast as we could print them and from what I could make out from Lou's mysterious midweek request to meet her in the pub, she had something up her sleeve for Colin. I knew it wouldn't be what he hoped, but I was keen to hear about it nonetheless.

The Dragon was the tiny pub my mates and I had frequented for more years than I would care to mention. A tucked-away, low-ceilinged little place, it was cool in the summer and cosy in the winter, the perfect amalgamation of Rowling's Leaky Cauldron and Tolkien's Prancing Pony.

'Here,' said Lou, calling me over as I pushed through the door, 'I've got you a drink already.'

'Thanks,' I said, flopping into a seat at our familiar table next to the door. 'I could do with a stiffener.'

'Have you finished packing?'

'Almost,' I said, nodding, between gulps of the refreshing bitter that was brewed by the microbrewery that managed the pub. 'There are just odds and sods to finish now.'

Lou nodded and waved to Colin, who had walked in with a reluctant Gus in tow.

'Silly sod didn't want to leave the shop,' he told us as he settled the dog under the table. 'I swear he's getting more depressed.'

'Can dogs get depressed?' I asked, ducking down to look at the sad expression on Gus's face.

'Look at him,' said Colin.

'Um,' I conceded. 'I see what you mean.'

Head on paws, Gus huffed and closed his eyes.

'So, where's the fire?' Colin asked Lou. 'You said it was urgent. Everything is still all set for moving day, isn't it, Poppy?'

'Yes,' I told him, 'no worries there.'

Clearly, he was as in the dark about Lou's summons as I was.

'So, what's the deal?' he asked her.

'Well,' she said, taking a deep breath and spreading her hands out on the table. 'I've been thinking about your shop, Colin.'

'Right,' he said, sounding wary.

'Even the name's a duffer,' she announced. 'The Reading Room. It sounds positively Victorian.'

I shuffled in my seat, not sure how Colin was going to react. He could be very defensive about the legacy he had been left.

'I see,' he said.

'To be honest,' Lou pushed on, 'the place probably looked exactly the same when Dickens was scribing.'

That much was true. The bookcases were built from the darkest wood and they were high, packed and imposing. Only the tiniest pinprick of light made it to the back of the shop. Had it been an antiquarian bookstore the image would have been spot on but the Reading Room had contemporary stock and a children's section and I knew Colin was keen to encourage young readers. If only he could get them to cross the threshold.

He frowned. 'What's your point?'

'My point is,' said Lou, not unkindly, 'that in a year's time, probably less, you'll be shutting up for the last time if you don't do something soon.'

Colin mulled this over but didn't contradict her.

'What are you suggesting?' I asked.

It was obvious she had something in mind.

'I want to give the place a makeover' – she grinned, her eyes lighting up with excitement – 'and I want you, Colin, to come up with a new name.'

'What's wrong with Colin?' he muttered.

'Not for you, you idiot,' Lou guffawed, 'for the shop, of course.'

'So,' said Lou as she gazed around my rapidly emptying flat with her hands planted on her hips, 'what did you think of my idea about giving Colin's place a makeover?'

'Loved it,' I told her truthfully. 'Personally, I think it's a great idea.'

'I'm pleased you've said that.' She nodded, throwing me one of her *I knew I was right* expressions, 'because for some reason he's still dithering and at this rate he's going to leave it too late.'

'Oh, please don't tell me she's on about the makeover again,' puffed Colin as he wheezed his way back over the threshold and caught the end of our conversation. 'I've said I'll think about it and I am.'

Lou selected a heavy carton from the small pile of boxes that were left and thrust it into his outstretched arms.

'I'm only trying to help, you know,' she told him, her trademark pout fixed on her crimson-stained lips. 'I just want to see your business thrive, Colin.'

'I know you do, Lou,' he said, jiggling the box to get a tighter grip. His tone softened as he looked down at her. 'But seriously, if I have to hear it all even just once more today . . .'

'All right,' she relented. 'I'll leave it, but you can't put off making a decision for much longer.'

'Come on,' I said, quickly stepping between them as my eyes made one last sweep of the now almost empty rooms, 'let's get on. The sooner we're out of here, the sooner you pair can get back to work.'

'And don't forget you promised us lunch,' called Colin over his shoulder. 'I was hoping for another taste of your piccalilli later on, Poppy.'

'Oh hello,' Lou said, sniggering childishly, 'is there something you two want to tell me?'

Poor Colin went bright red and turned his attention back to the stairs and I dug her sharply in the back with the corner of the box I was carrying.

'Hey,' she yelped. 'Watch it. This frock's vintage, you know.'

'I was actually rather proud of that last effort,' I sighed, thinking of the piccalilli. 'It was tantalisingly tangy with just the right amount of crunch.'

It really had been piccalilli perfection and I hoped I was going to be able to make another equally exquisite batch as soon as I had set up my new kitchen and unpacked my precious pots and pans.

'I've almost finished setting out the recipe card for that one, Colin,' I told him as we emerged from the stairwell at the back of the shop and into the bright spring sunshine. 'I'll save you one if you like and then you can make your own.'

Given how fast the cards were flying out of the shop, I would soon have to increase the number I had printed. They were proving so popular, I was hoping that by the end of the year I'd have the entire neighbourhood pickling and preserving their own seasonal harvests as well as utilising the local produce we stocked in the shop.

Now the move was really happening, I had finally allowed myself the indulgence of getting excited about using the fruit and veg from the community garden in my cooking. The thought of using produce I had actually had a hand in growing was thrilling – and there were hens in the garden too. Perhaps I should try my hand at baking again. Surely I couldn't have got any worse at it, could I?

'Thanks, Poppy,' said Colin, 'although if it's all the same with you, I'll pass on the DIY option. I'd rather just eat yours. I'd get in a right mess with all that peeling and chopping at home.'

'Me too,' Lou agreed.

This was no good at all. I was going to have to get the pair of them in the mood for making their own otherwise I'd never have enough left over to keep my own larder stocked.

'Well, we'll have to see about that,' I said, tossing Lou the keys to her old van, which was acting as my removal vehicle for the day. 'I'm sure you'd both enjoy making it if you entered into the spirit of it and weren't so worried about the mess.'

Colin looked doubtful.

'Perhaps.' Lou smiled, capitalising on his apprehensive look. 'I mean, it would be the perfect opportunity to get Colin into one of those floral aprons that I've just taken delivery of, wouldn't it?'

Colin rolled his eyes.

'Never mind that,' I tutted. 'Hadn't we better get on? The morning will be gone at this rate.'

'Yes,' agreed Colin, 'I really need to get back to the shop.'

'Scared you'll miss your one and only customer of the day?' Lou teased. 'If only you could tempt more readers in, Col. You really need—'

'A makeover, a book club and a new name,' he batted back in a sing-song voice.

'A book club,' Lou gasped. 'Why didn't I think of that?'

'I told you I'd think it all over,' said Colin for the hundredth time. 'And I am.'

All he needed was a bit more time to come round to the

idea, but Lou was all for licking him into shape in record time. Personally, I couldn't help thinking that if she backed off a bit she might find him more malleable.

'We'll talk about it on the way,' she said with a grin, climbing behind the wheel and turning the key. 'You sure you'll be okay walking round?' she asked me as she revved the engine to encourage it to keep running.

'I'll be fine,' I told her. It was only a short walk, after all. 'I'll drop the flat key with Harry and then I'll catch you up. The fresh air will do me good and I need to get some bread. I'll see you both there.'

The April day was wonderfully warm and, as Lou's van disappeared from view, I lifted my face to the sun, feeling grateful that the sharp sting of winter had finally gone for good. My plans to move into Nightingale Square last autumn might have been unexpectedly scuppered, but now all was firmly back on track and I had every intention of grabbing this new beginning with both hands.

'You all set then, love?' asked Harry, as I pushed open Greengages' shop door. 'Did you get all your stuff in Lou's van?'

'Yes.' I frowned. 'Every last bit of it packed into just one load. Not much to show for well over two decades' worth of living really, is it?'

It hadn't struck me before, but I hadn't accumulated much in the way of material possessions during the few years I had lived above the grocers.

'Well, I shouldn't worry about that,' Harry chuckled as he set about restocking the boxes of bright spring greens. 'You'll soon make up for it now you've got more space to fill. Although,' he added with a wry grin, 'knowing you, I daresay you'll be more interested in buying new jam pans and Kilner jars than the knick-knacks most women go in for!'

He was right, of course. The prospect of a new jam pan did set my pulse racing perhaps a little faster than was generally considered acceptable for a woman in her late twenties.

'Funny you should say that . . .' I began and Harry laughed all the harder.

I didn't know how I would have managed without him over the last few years, but then I'm not sure how he would have managed without me. Harry had just been widowed when I arrived on the scene and had soon become so much more than an employer to me; he was always willing to help, right from the moment when I had burst into tears during my interview after he had, quite reasonably, pointed out that I was really rather overqualified for the job. I think he had been expecting to attract applications from school leavers rather than someone who had abandoned studying for a degree. We had both shed tears by the end of that afternoon but we had formed a bond and our friendship had gone from strength to strength as a result.

'Seriously though,' I said, swallowing hard as I handed over the keys to the flat, 'thank you, for everything.'

Harry wouldn't hear a word of it and waved my thanks aside with a dismissive sniff.

'I know,' I continued nonetheless, 'that you always maintain you'd do the same for anyone in a tight spot, but you have made me feel like *someone*. Someone who actually counts. I haven't had many people in my life who have bothered to do that.'

Harry began to look a little misty-eyed, but I wasn't going to stop. The shop was almost empty and I knew I might not get the chance to say this to him again. It wasn't as if I was leaving my job as well as the flat, but I knew Harry would go out of his way to avoid having to listen to me sing his praises and I was determined to let him know how grateful I was that he had taken me under his wing when I had been so desperate not to have to move back home.

'You,' I told him, 'are my family.'

He nodded and wiped his eyes roughly with the palms of his calloused old hands.

'I know,' he croaked.

'And Ryan, of course,' I quickly added, thinking of my elusive brother.

The poor little sod had been an afterthought in every way since the day he had been conceived. I hoped, if I could get him to turn up, I might have a chance of making him feel as good about himself as Harry had made me.

'And what about your mother?' Harry ventured.

'Hey now,' I said sternly, trying not to imagine what Ryan's life stuck with her was like, especially now he didn't have Tony to escape to. 'Let's not go there, shall we? Today is supposed to be a good day.'

'Sorry.' Harry smiled ruefully, taking my rebuke on the chin.

I gave him a swift hug and headed back out into the spring sunshine. As always, I could smell the comforting scent of freshly baked bread wafting along the road from Blossom's Bakery even before I had opened the door.

'Poppy!' called Mark, who was now going to be my neighbour as well as a pal. 'How's it all going? Have you unpacked? Are you ready for visitors yet?'

'Give the girl a chance,' said Blossom, laughing. 'You said yourself not ten minutes ago that Lou had only just headed round to the square in her van.'

I looked at Mark and raised my eyebrows.

'I might have been keeping an eye on proceedings.' He blushed.

'I haven't had so much as a cottage loaf out of him all morning,' scolded Blossom good-naturedly.

'Oh, good grief, it's going to be like living next door to Miss Marple, isn't it?' I groaned. 'I won't be able to leave the house without someone signing me in and out.'

'You have no idea!' Mark giggled. 'And if you think I'm bad, just you wait until Carole starts her curtain-twitching antics. Then you'll really know the meaning of neighbourhood watch.'

Fortunately, I already had an idea of what I was letting myself in for and, to be honest, I rather liked the thought of living in such close proximity to neighbours who looked out for each other.

'Anyway,' said Mark with a wink, 'I wouldn't worry about that too much if I were you. You won't be the sole focus of attention, not today anyway.'

'What do you mean?'

'Customer!' shouted Blossom.

I waited until he had finished serving and then asked him again what he had meant.

'Neil phoned,' he told me. 'He's working from home today, but he's having a job concentrating.'

'Why?' I frowned.

Mark's husband, Neil, ran his own business from home and tended to be rather too married to his work. I couldn't imagine he had any issues focusing when the day job called.

'What's happened to our oasis of calm to draw his attention?' I asked. 'You know I'm only moving in because it's so peaceful again now. Well,' I added, 'that and gaining access to the community garden, of course.'

'Apparently,' Mark confided, leaning his flour-covered shirtsleeves on the counter as he settled down for a good gossip, 'you aren't the only one moving stuff today.'

'You mean someone's moving out of the square?' I gasped.

'No,' Mark laughed. 'Who in their right mind would want to leave?'

He had a point. The place was perfect. Well, it was now Kate's former tenants had done a bunk.

'Your neighbour,' Mark confided, 'Mr Grumpy. He's moving stuff in. He's finally getting himself some furniture.'

'Did he not have any before?'

Mark shook his head.

'The day he moved in he had little more than suitcases and a couple of boxes. None of us have been inside of course, what with him being such a misery, but as far as we can tell the place must be pretty sparse. He's certainly not had any major deliveries. Not until today, that is.'

I felt rather sorry for the house and its current occupant. Nice neighbours were one thing, but having your worldly goods scrutinised by everyone around you was a bit much. I wondered if the intense interest might account for his belligerence, or if perhaps his bad temper had been fuelled by a lack of home comforts as well as the noisy folk who had been right next door.

'Why would anyone want to spend winter in an empty house?' I mused.

'Beats me.' Mark shrugged.

'Perhaps some new stuff might cheer him up,' I suggested.

Mark shot me a withering look.

'Well,' I said, 'let's hope Lou's van won't get in his way. The last thing I want is to stir up trouble before I've so much as plugged in my kettle.'

'I wish I could be there to watch,' Mark said with a frown. 'I'd been hoping we'd eke out any excitement and now it's all happening on the same day and I'm not going to be around to see any of it.'

Clearly, he took the unsatisfactory situation very much to heart.

'Unless I fire you for slacking on the job,' Blossom's voice boomed from further along the counter. 'If I let you go, Mark,' she said, 'then you can head home with Poppy and not miss a thing.'

'Point taken,' he said, rushing over to give her a make-amends hug, which she failed to fight off. 'Now, what was it you wanted, Poppy?' he said seriously. 'Are you here to buy something or have you just come in to get me into trouble?'

With the loaf I had gone in for, and some cream cakes I hadn't, tucked under my arm, I set off for the square. I didn't have much to unload but it was hardly fair to leave Colin and Lou to do all the donkey work.

'Text me when you catch a glimpse of Mr Miserable, won't you?' Mark called after me. 'Neil thinks he's quite a dish!'

Life was certainly going to be fun with Mark and Neil as neighbours. As I wandered along I imagined impromptu get-togethers, both in the garden and on the pretty green in front of our houses. Barbecues, beers and long sunny evenings stretched ahead and I couldn't wait to throw myself into life in the square.

My blissful bubble of idyllic imaginings didn't last long, however, as I had barely set foot in the square before Lou's dulcet tones met my ears. She didn't sound happy. She didn't sound happy at all.

'But for how much longer?' I heard her shout. 'You aren't the only one on a tight schedule, you know.'

The schedule she was banging on about was news to me, but then she and Colin did need to get back to their shops. Lou caught sight of me and came rushing over.

'Would you look at this!' she shouted as the man she had been 'talking to' retreated back inside his house. 'Have you ever seen such selfish bloody parking?'

The situation was far from ideal. My neighbour had a huge delivery lorry and a truck outside his house. They were both completely blocking the road and as a result Lou's little van couldn't get through.

'I've told him it's a one-way system so I can't go round the other way, but he says there's nothing he can do.'

'Well, he can't just let them block the road like that,' I said, as Colin came over to join us. 'It isn't safe.'

'Exactly,' Lou butted in, 'what if the emergency services need to get by?'

It didn't seem particularly likely, but she did have a point.

'I hardly think . . .' Colin began, but Lou glared at him and he stopped.

'I'll go and have a word,' I said, handing over the bags from Blossom's. 'Why don't you two go and find the kettle and get it on? Kate messaged me earlier to say there's fresh milk in the fridge.'

Lou didn't seem particularly keen to relinquish the horns of the dilemma, but as soon as Colin mentioned the cream cakes he had spotted in one of the bags she followed him over to mine and I went next door to see what I could do. I didn't want my first encounter with my new neighbour to be confrontational, so I determinedly moderated my tone.

'Hello!' I called through the front door, which stood slightly ajar.

The hall smelt musty and there was a general air of neglect about the place, but perhaps things were set to improve if new furniture was finally being introduced.

'Hello!' I shouted a little louder. 'I'm Poppy. I'm moving into the house next door today!'

'I've already told your gobby girlfriend that my delivery guys are going as fast as they can!' a man's voice bellowed back from one of the upstairs rooms.

I wondered if this was the guy Neil had already decided was a 'dish'. If it was, then he was going to have to be nothing short of a Roman god in human form to balance out his belligerent tone. Not that his appearance would have much impact on me. I was far more interested in determining someone's attraction by their personality and the way they treated others than by their looks. So far, this chap was looking very ugly indeed.

I opened my mouth to apologise for interrupting him on what was obviously a stressful day, but I didn't get the chance.

'I can't do anything until they're finished, can I?' he roared again. 'You'll all just have to wait!'

He obviously wasn't going to bother to come down to introduce himself and I had no intention of crossing his threshold to risk being shouted at in close quarters. I knew settling in somewhere new could be stressful but there was no need to let what he was going through ruin my experience. I was actually feeling rather chilled about my move. Or I had been.

'Sorry to have bothered you,' I called back up, snuffing out the creeping edge of sarcasm that I could feel infiltrating my voice. 'I was just going to ask if you would like to join us for tea while we wait, but I'll leave you to it.'

# Chapter 3

Just as I had suspected, there really was no need for the drama and shouting. More often than not, in my experience, there isn't. It was Lou who spotted the delivery team coming back out of the house next door, but I was the one who rushed out to have a quiet word, as she was still too wound up from her encounter with the so-called 'dish'.

'If you could just drive round the square again,' I suggested, after I had explained to the driver that I was supposed to be moving in, 'then my friend will be able to get her van through.'

'No need for that love,' said the guy, who was swinging a big bunch of keys. 'We're done. Once we've bagged up some of the packaging we'll be off.'

'Great.' I smiled, relieved that the situation had been so easily sorted.

'I'm sorry if we've held you up,' he said, looking back at the house. 'Did you speak to old misery-guts?'

He could only be talking about my neighbour.

'I tried,' I told him, 'but was bawled out before I had a chance to offer him so much as a cup of tea.'

'There now,' he tutted. 'I wish I'd known there was a brew going. He's not offered, even though I've whistled "Polly Put the Kettle On" at least three times.'

I couldn't help but laugh. We were set to carry on chatting but were interrupted by Mr Grumpy, who started hollering again.

'Are you lot going to get rid of this bubble wrap or what?' he shouted from somewhere inside his house.

He sounded like a bear in his cave, one with a very sore head, and I hoped this aggressive tone wasn't his default setting. I was, for the most part, a happy-go-lucky type of person who kept my life simple and as stress-free as possible. I didn't much want a near neighbour who was prone to throwing his weight around and shouting the odds.

'I better get on,' said the chap, 'the sooner we're out of his hair the better.'

I thought fur would have been a more appropriate word.

It didn't take Lou, Colin and me many minutes to shift my boxes from the back of the van and into their allotted rooms. Not surprisingly, most of my things were destined for the kitchen, but I wouldn't be unpacking them until I'd given the room a good scrub.

When Kate had first offered me the house she had been planning to employ the services of a professional cleaning team, but I had said I'd be happy to do it myself and between us we had struck a bargain. I was going to sanitise and set the place to rights and she was going to waive the first month's rent. I had always found cleaning surprisingly therapeutic, so it was a win-win situation as far as I was concerned.

I had made it my mission to have the place back up to speed by the end of the week, which happened to be the Easter bank holiday weekend. A Prosperous Place garden party was planned for the Saturday and I wanted to have my chores list empty by then so I could relax and enjoy it, as well as lend a hand with the cooking and setting up.

'That's certainly not my idea of what a spring break should be,' said Lou, tutting, as she rifled through my big box of eco-friendly cleaning products after I had explained my plans. 'Why didn't you do a clean before you moved in? Surely that would have made more sense. You've got to work around this lot now.'

I wasn't usually prone to superstition, but my carefully made plans had been sabotaged before and I hadn't wanted to bond with the house in case anything had gone wrong this time round. As far as I was concerned it had been worth the wait. 'I'm not exactly inundated with boxes,' I pointed out. 'It won't take me long.'

'And are you're sure you don't want us to help?' asked Colin, twitching my new feather duster along the highest kitchen shelves and dislodging a sprinkling of dust. 'Lou did say she has the perfect apron for me.'

'No,' I told him, 'thanks for the offer, but I can manage. I'm actually looking forward to it.'

Their faces were a picture.

'I've never had a whole house to myself before,' I reminded them. 'All this space just for me is a treat.'

The flat above Greengages was borderline claustrophobic rather than cosy and I was looking forward to filling up the extra rooms.

'But before you go back to work,' I said, clearing a space on the table and dousing it in my home-made anti-bac spray, 'I promised you some piccalilli sandwiches, didn't I?'

We ate our lunch sitting on a rug on the green and washed it down with yet more tea and the last of the cream cakes.

'Coming to the pub later?' Lou asked me as Colin pulled her to her feet and she brushed the crumbs from the skirt of her dress.

'Not tonight,' I said, stretching my hands above my head and moving my neck from side to side to release any tension. 'Maybe tomorrow.'

I picked up the depleted lunch tray, turned my back on the bear cave and then waved my friends off before closing my front door and exploring every one of the rooms in my new home.

I didn't realise the rest of the day had slipped by until my rumbling tum alerted me to the fact that I needed to start thinking about dinner. I looked out of the front bedroom window and found the square quite devoid of traffic. Both the delivery lorry and van were long gone and everything was as I had imagined it would be. I let out a slow breath, relieved that my plans to move here had only been temporarily scuppered, and then spotted Kate and another neighbour, Lisa, heading in my direction. I tapped on the window and waved before heading downstairs to let them in.

I had expected to open the front door and see the pair of them standing there, but what I actually discovered was a wall of bright spring blooms with a pair of slim legs sticking out below them.

'Surprise!' cried Kate, laughing, as she lowered the hand-tied flowers and peeped over the top. 'Welcome to Nightingale Square, Poppy.'

'Oh, my goodness,' I laughed, taking the flowers from her. 'Thank you so much. These are beautiful. I can't remember the last time someone gave me flowers.'

Which was sad really, because they happened to be one of my top five favourite things in the whole wide world. I know I could have gifted them to myself, but that wasn't quite the same, was it?

'They're all from the garden at Prosperous Place,' Kate proudly explained, 'so no air miles have been involved in getting them here, which I know is just how you like things.'

Kate had clearly taken a lot on board about me in the short time we'd known one another. Wherever possible I was a seasonal and shop-local enthusiast – another reason why having the community garden right on my doorstep was such a draw.

'Come in,' I said, opening the door wider to welcome my new landlady inside. 'I'll put these in water and get the kettle back on. It's been on the boil all day.'

The beautiful bunch of flowers was predominantly made up of different varieties of daffodils and narcissus and there was lots of vibrant fresh greenery as well. It was sweetly scented spring in a jar. Or three jars, to be precise. I didn't think I'd ever owned a vase. It seemed such a waste to buy one when I was rinsing out and recycling any number of bottles and jars every week.

'There,' I said, standing back to admire the arrangements before fussing over finding the best spot to show them off. 'Perfect.'

'Lovely,' agreed Kate.

'Wasn't Lisa with you when you crossed the green?' I asked, only just remembering. 'Or did I mistake the flowers for her?'

'She's just nipped next door,' Kate explained, stifling a yawn as she stirred her tea.

I hoped she meant to see Harold, the elderly gent who lived on my other side, rather than Mr Grumpy.

'Are you still not getting much sleep?' I asked, no doubt stating the obvious.

Kate was usually so full of energy that it was easy to forget that she had baby Abigail to look after, as well as her little stepdaughter, Jasmine.

'Not as much as I'd like,' she admitted, 'but it's getting easier.'

'And what about Heather?'

Heather and her husband Glen lived in the first house in Nightingale Square and she, Lisa and Kate had become the firmest of friends since Kate's arrival. Not only did Heather have her toddler Evie to keep up with but also six-month-old twin boys, James and Jonah. Lisa had three children of her own and quite often the green looked like a crèche rather than a place to unwind with a glass of wine at the end of the day, but that was part of its communal charm.

'Does the word "teething" mean anything to you?' Kate grimaced.

'Ah,' I said, wincing at the thought of potentially three sets of rosy cheeks to contend with as opposed to one. 'She and Glen should buy shares in Calpol and frozen teething rings.'

'I'll suggest that,' said Kate, laughing, as the front door opened and closed again. 'Here's Lisa,' she added, with a wink, 'barging in as usual. You know you'll have to keep that door locked if you want to keep her out.'

'What an absolutely ignorant bloody sod,' Lisa ranted as she marched into the kitchen and pulled me into a hug before stepping back and taking my face in her hands. 'Welcome to Nightingale Square, my lovely, and good luck with that git of a neighbour.'

'Thanks,' I said, puffing out my cheeks when she finally released them. 'Tea?'

'Yes please, and I better have a bit of sugar in it to sweeten me back up again.'

'I take it he didn't invite you in for a coffee and a catch-up then?' asked Kate.

'No,' said Lisa with a sniff, 'he certainly did not.'

'He doesn't make the best impression, does he?' I smiled. 'First or otherwise.'

'No,' Lisa said again, 'he certainly doesn't, but Neil's right, he is a dish.'

I was surprised Lou hadn't commented on my neighbour's supposed good looks – she'd seen him at closer quarters than I had – but then she was no doubt still too riled up about the way he had talked to her to have processed what he looked like.

'Another dish, eh?' I mused. 'How are you coping with two in such close proximity, Lisa?'

She wrinkled her nose and took a sip of the lightly sweetened tea.

'Luke is stunning,' she said, and Kate rolled her eyes, 'but I've kind of got used to him now so he doesn't really count.'

'I was actually referring to John,' I teased, 'you know, that rather wonderful bloke you happen to be married to!'

Lisa blushed and we all laughed. Living in the same post-code as Luke Lonsdale had distracted everyone for a while. Formerly one of the world's leading male models, he had jacked it all in to reclaim and renovate his ancestral home, open up his garden to the Nightingale Square residents and fall head over heels in love with Kate.

'Yes, well,' Lisa gabbled on, 'that goes without saying, doesn't it?'

'Right,' said Kate, slipping off the stool she was perched on, 'I better get back. Abigail will be due another feed soon.'

She looked around the kitchen and then back to me.

'I hope giving the place a spring-clean won't be too much of a chore, Poppy.'

'Not at all,' I told her. 'I'm actually looking forward to it.'

'I do love this place,' she said fondly.

'Did you ever track down your tenant?' I asked.

'Nope.' She sighed. 'They fell behind with the rent and then did what my mum calls a moonlight flit after that last party. I've heard nothing from them since and I don't expect to now, but at least they cleared out their stuff when they went.'

'Good riddance to bad rubbish,' said Lisa, rubbing her friend's arm.

We both knew how much Kate loved her little house and I was looking forward to taking just as much care of it as she had.

'Exactly,' I agreed. 'I'm just sorry that I couldn't move in last year as planned. It would have saved you all this heartache and inconvenience.'

'Well, never mind.' She smiled. 'You're here now and we're looking forward to seeing you in the garden, not to mention sampling anything you happen to cook up.'

'Talking of the garden,' joined in Lisa as she drained her cup, 'come on, Poppy. I told the happy chappie next door to meet us on the green about now, so I can fill you both in on what we have planned for it this year.'

I didn't reckon much for her chances of getting him to leave his lair.

'Oh yes,' said Kate. 'I forgot Poppy doesn't know about any of that.'

'About any of what?' I quizzed.

'Wait and see,' said Lisa, tapping the side of her nose.

It was a mild end to moving day and Lisa and I sat on my blanket on the green, soaking up the last of the warmth before the grass turned damp while we waited to see if my neighbour was going to appear.

'Do you know what his name is?' I asked as I tore up a handful of grass and looked back towards his house. 'Someone must. He's lived here long enough.'

'Not a clue,' said Lisa.

'I can't imagine it really is Mr Miserable or Mr Grumpy, although both do seem to suit him.'

'You're not wrong,' Lisa huffed.

'Look out,' I hissed, catching my first proper glimpse of him. 'Here he comes.'

With his arms rigid by his sides and his shirt untucked, he strode over to where we were sitting and glared down at us. I squinted up at him and saw that the lines etched across his forehead and around his dark eyes were every bit as deep as the creases on his unironed shirt. Clearly he'd had a rough time recently, and I felt an unexpected pang of sympathy for him.

He was far younger than I had assumed and his whole aura

was pulsing, but not in a good way. His shoulders were practically touching his earlobes and, given the physical evidence in front of me, I thought perhaps I shouldn't take his earlier rudeness to heart. I sometimes forgot that not everyone was as chilled about life as I was. A deep tissue massage would have no doubt done him the power of good, but I wasn't going to suggest one.

'Hello.' I smiled warmly, dropping my handful of grass.

I was determined to get off on the right foot with him this time round.

'I'm—'

'Hi,' he interrupted with a scowl. 'Look,' he continued, addressing Lisa, 'it's Lisa, isn't it? I know you weren't listening earlier, but I meant what I said. I really don't have time to exchange pleasantries with neighbours and, given the last lot I had to put up with, I don't much want to either.'

I thought it was a bit harsh that he had judged me on first sight and assumed that I was the same as them. I felt Lisa bristle beside me.

'I'm Poppy,' I said before she could launch, kneeling up and holding out my hand. 'Pleased to meet you.'

He looked back at me and bit his lip. He was taken aback that I had ignored his rudeness and that I was going to be civil even if he wasn't going to make it worth my while. I felt rather pleased to have wrong-footed him.

'Jacob,' he said in a clipped tone, finally taking my hand.

I grasped it tightly and levered myself into a more

upright position so he had no choice but to help pull me to my feet.

'Pleased to meet you, Jacob.' I smiled, still holding on to his hand. 'I understand you've had pretty rotten neighbours recently?'

I let his hand go before it felt too awkward, but kept my eyes firmly fixed on his, my eyebrows raised in expectation of an answer.

'That's putting it mildly,' he said darkly, thrusting his hands deep into his trouser pockets, no doubt fearing that I would try to make contact again.

'Well, I can promise you that everyone will be in for a quieter time now.' I smiled again.

'Good.'

Clearly, he wasn't in the mood to chat.

'So,' I said, swallowing, 'apparently Lisa here has something exciting to tell us.'

The look he gave me was withering.

'I very much doubt it,' he muttered.

'Haven't you, Lisa?' I said, urging her on.

I was keen to find out what was in store for the garden even if Jacob wasn't and something told me this little tête-à-tête could spiral even further away from friendly if I didn't keep Lisa focused and on track. Jacob obviously wasn't the sort of guy who would take to reclining on a blanket, so I pulled my friend to her feet – and then what I naively thought was an inspirational idea struck.

'Look,' I said, 'I know it's early, but I've got some fizz in the fridge. How about I run back to get it and then we can toast . . .'

The words died in my throat as Jacob rubbed his eyes and let out a long breath.

'I really have nothing to celebrate,' he said sharply.

Clearly the fact that I had didn't enter his head.

'And if it's all right with you, I just want to get back to my micro meal and go to bed.'

For a moment I had thought some fizz would loosen him up a bit, but he had knocked the wind out of my sails and I didn't have the heart to fight for it – or share my beloved bottle with someone who'd prefer to sit and eat his sad little dinner alone and without the addition of bubbles.

'In that case,' Lisa began, 'I'll cut to the chase and let you scoot off, Jacob.'

'Thank you,' he huffed.

'Okay, so the news is about the garden,' she said, smiling at me, 'obviously. Now that it's been up and running for a year, we've decided—'

'Which garden?' Jacob cut in, looking about him.

'The community garden,' said Lisa. 'In the grounds of Prosperous Place.'

Jacob sighed again.

'Don't tell me you don't know about it,' said Lisa with a frown. 'I've put flyers about it through your door myself.'

'And I've ignored them because I'm not interested in it,' Jacob scowled back. 'Did you not get the message after Christmas when I didn't take up your offer to *dig in*?'

Lisa looked outraged.

'You should at least take a look, Jacob,' I chimed in, trying to defuse the tension. 'It's a really special place. Everyone from Nightingale Square plays a part in helping out and maintaining it.'

'Except me,' he cut in.

'There's a rota,' I carried on, 'and, in exchange for the hours you put in, you can take a share of what's produced. A chap called Luke Lonsdale owns it.'

'*The* Luke Lonsdale?' Jacob frowned.

'Yes.'

'It's a wonderful space,' said Lisa, sounding somewhat mollified. 'Rob, the chap who lived in the house before you, Jacob, was part of the team.'

'We're all part of the team,' I reminded her.

Pride swelled in my chest knowing that I was now an integral part of the community who ran the garden rather than an occasional visitor who just popped in.

'Well, I'm sorry,' said Jacob, sounding even grumpier than before, 'but you can strike my name off your list of unpaid workers.'

'What?' Lisa and I chorused.

'I'm not interested,' he told us firmly.

Surely he didn't mean it?

'And I'll stick to buying my food, thanks.'

'Are you serious?' I gasped.

The thought of him living on a diet of microwave meals literally turned my stomach.

'Deadly serious,' he told me, 'and I'm not interested in socialising either, so you won't need to waste your time issuing invitations in my direction.'

'Well,' said Lisa.

For once she was lost for words.

'Well, what?' Jacob demanded.

He sounded as if he was almost willing her to contradict him or try to cajole him into changing his mind. He was the angriest person I had come across in a very long time. He was spoiling for a fight. Thankfully, Lisa decided not to rise to the confrontational bait being paraded in front of her.

'Well, do you have a partner?' she eventually asked him. 'They might be interested in coming along.'

'I can assure you that you needn't worry about that either,' he told her. 'Now if you don't mind—'

'At least stay and listen to what Lisa has to tell us,' I said quickly. 'It might turn out to be something you consider worthwhile thinking over.'

He shrugged but didn't move, so Lisa carried on.

'There's a competition that's just been launched,' she explained. She sounded less excited now and I was annoyed that Jacob had stolen her thunder. 'It's to find the most community-spirited garden in the area. The council are particularly interested in unusual places where folk have pulled together to create green spaces to grow and socialise in.'

She was describing our garden to a T.

'Is this part of the campaign to highlight the mental-health benefits of gardening?' I asked.

The topic had been hot news for months now and I was all for doing whatever I could to help keep the momentum going.

'That's it,' said Lisa a little more enthusiastically. 'And there's going to be some funding available for the winner to spend on setting up another project somewhere else, like in a nearby school or youth centre or something.'

I risked a quick glance at Jacob. He still didn't look even remotely interested, which was a shame because I was sure getting his hands in the earth would be just the thing to help soften his sharp edges.

'What a fantastic idea,' I said, ignoring his sour expression and wondering how I could encourage him to change his mind.

'Ideally,' Lisa continued, 'in order to make the entry really stand out the whole community that has access to the space should be on board.'

'Well, I'm sorry, ladies,' Jacob muttered, taking a step back and looking every bit as belligerent as before. 'Manipulation, subtle or otherwise, isn't going to tempt me to join in.'

'I wasn't trying to manipulate you,' Lisa snapped, drawing herself up to her full, but still not very impressive, height. 'I was merely explaining our plans.'

'Of course you were,' said Jacob, smiling for the first time, although it wasn't a very striking effort.

I really couldn't see why everyone thought this guy was in any way attractive.

'I was,' Lisa reiterated.

'Well, good luck with your entry,' he said, turning

properly away. 'I'm sure you'll all be able to manage to pull it off without my help.'

Lisa looked at me open-mouthed.

'And as you're so environmentally minded, Lisa,' he added as a parting shot, 'you can save yourself some trees by not shoving any more flyers through my letter box.'

# Chapter 4

The weather continued to be glorious and I was more than happy to shut myself away and give the house the thorough spring-clean it was crying out for. Suddenly, not having much in the way of material possessions was a godsend rather than a concern; I was able to give the place a really good going-over without having to shift too much around, meaning Lou's concerns had been unfounded.

The square's resident male blackbird woke me just after five every morning and I was happy to thank him with a handful of raisins before throwing open all the windows and getting to grips with the grime.

Snow White had nothing on me, but I knew domestic chores would eventually lose their charm and my thoughts strayed across the road to the exciting ingredients I knew were growing there, which I would soon be able to incorporate into a whole host of new recipes.

'I can't believe you still haven't been over there,' said Lou, laughing, when she called to tell me that I had better get back to the pub with her and Colin if I didn't want to give up my regular spot. 'Have you not been tempted at all? I thought it was what you moved to the square for.'

'Of course I've been tempted,' I told her, 'sorely tempted, especially when I can practically see the place from my bedroom window, but I haven't wanted to rush. I want to take my time and enjoy everything here first.'

'Even cleaning the windows?'

'Even that.'

'And what about your mysterious brother?' she asked. 'Has he been to visit yet?'

I knew Ryan's continued absence had my friends doubting he even existed.

'No,' I said sadly. 'He hasn't. I'm still waiting for a reply to my last text.'

Our always infrequent text messages had become even more of a rarity and I had to admit, if only to myself, that my plan to establish a sibling connection after Mum's request for finance had failed miserably. I had tried to offer my support but it had been ignored and now I didn't know whether to back off or push harder.

'And what about Mr Grumpy?' Lou carried on, unaware of my confusion. 'Have you seen anything more of him?'

'Haven't seen him,' I told her. 'Haven't heard him. I don't think he's been out since the day I moved in. He's probably terrified Lisa's going to accost him with a trowel.'

'You're wrong there,' said Lou smugly. 'I know for a fact that he has been out.'

'Has he?' I asked. 'And how exactly do you know that?'

Aside from the details I had given her about the disastrous 'getting to know you' moment on the green, I didn't think Lou knew anything about him, other than him being a miserable bugger, that is – but perhaps I was wrong.

'Come to the pub tomorrow night,' she said before ringing off, 'and I'll tell you.'

Colin had bagged our usual spot and already got a round in by the time I arrived the following evening, but there was no sign of Lou.

'Well, that's about right,' I huffed, having kissed Colin, accepted a drink and squeezed myself into the seat between the wall and the table. 'She demands I come out and then she doesn't show.'

'She'll be here,' he said, 'but it's good to know that I was worth the walk.'

'Oh, you know what I mean.' I smiled. 'What's she up to?'

'Some chap has driven down from Yorkshire to take a look at that pinball machine she's been trying to flog to free up more floor space.'

'He must be keen,' I said, thinking how sorry I would be to see it go. 'That's quite a trek.'

I had whiled away many a lunch hour playing the thing and had been almost tempted to put in an offer for it myself when I moved into the square, knowing I now had the room to accommodate it.

'Keen on Lou no doubt,' said Colin glumly. 'I offered to act as chaperone but she said I'd be better off here entertaining you.'

'Does she need a chaperone?' I frowned. 'Don't tell me she doesn't know the bloke?'

I didn't like the thought of her meeting a stranger after hours, even if she had graduated top of the self-defence classes she'd dragged me along to last year.

'Oh, don't worry about stranger danger,' said Colin, taking off his glasses to clean them. 'She knows him. They met at some trade sale last year, apparently.'

'Well then,' I said, a little impatiently, 'I'm sure there's nothing more to Lou dismissing you, Colin, than her wanting some space to strike a decent deal.'

Lou was always keen to share the details about any bloke she was interested in and I had no recollection of her blathering on about a Yorkshireman, so Colin was fretting over nothing. Clearly this guy wasn't a threat on any front. Although he might be in danger if Lou got her hands on his wallet.

'But you really do need to stop mooning over her, Colin,' I said robustly. 'If you suddenly lost interest she'd probably fall straight for you. You know what she's like.'

Colin put his glasses back on and I took a pull at my pint.

'So, what have you been up to then?' I asked, keen to change the subject. 'How's business in the Reading Room?'

'Slow,' he said, nodding, 'although I have had a few unexpected sales this week, but Lou said I should wait until she gets here before I tell you about those.'

'I'm intrigued,' I said with a laugh, 'and pleased for you. I know you've been worried about footfall.'

'I still am,' he said taking a deep breath, 'so I've decided to screw my courage to the sticking place and go with the makeover idea she keeps harping on.'

'That's fantastic!'

Colin flushed and shrugged his shoulders.

'Well, whatever happens business can't get any worse, can it?'

I smiled. 'I very much doubt it.'

I was really pleased he had finally come round to the idea. I was sure lightening the decor and adding some sofas and the top-of-the-range coffee machine Lou had been championing would make all the difference.

'Lou has drawn up some plans,' Colin said, grinning, 'and I have to say, they do look amazing. She's even on about using some of her stock to help make book-themed window displays.'

'That's wonderful.'

'The idea she had for *A Christmas Carol* was inspired,' Colin carried on, 'and as you know, I have plenty of copies of that to shift. She thinks an improved shop layout and rearranged displays will appeal to a completely different clientele.'

I looked at him over the top of my glass. He relented. 'Not that I have a specific clientele at the moment, of course.'

I leant across and gave his shoulder a squeeze.

'And I'm even thinking about starting a monthly book club or reading group,' he went on. 'Maybe even a writing circle if there's any interest. I thought I could ask Lisa what she might think of that, now she's about to be published.'

Lisa was poised to realise her dream of becoming a published author and was the toast of the square.

'My goodness, Colin.' I laughed, feeling slightly taken aback. 'You really have been busy.'

'It's all down to Lou,' he said shyly. 'She's the one who's got me fired up.'

We were all well aware of that.

'What's all this?' said the woman herself as she rushed in, sending the door flying. 'I'm sorry I'm late,' she carried on before either of us could answer, 'but I've just made *the* most amazing sale.'

'The pinball machine?'

'Yep,' she said, her eyes shining with excitement, 'it's heading up to Yorkshire as we speak and, thanks to my cut-throat negotiating skills, I've made a healthy profit on it. Cheers, guys!'

'So,' I said, once we had toasted her success, 'what's all this about Colin's mystery sales and you being in the know about what my new neighbour has been up to this week?'

Lou put her finger to her lips and shook her head.

'What?'

'He's right there,' hissed Colin. 'Did you not see him when you came in?'

I glanced over his shoulder and spotted a man I guessed could be Jacob sitting alone at a table with his head tucked behind the local newspaper. There was an empty plate and a half-full pint glass set to one side and the guy looked as if he'd been ensconced for some time.

I wasn't sure how I felt about my neighbour, if indeed it was him, moving in on my turf. It no doubt shouldn't have mattered, but I went to the pub for a laugh so I hoped his humour had improved.

'Are you absolutely sure that's him?' I squinted.

I still wasn't convinced, but I did recognise the leaflet on the table next to him.

'Of course, it is,' said Lou. 'I met him when he was in the Reading Room yesterday.'

'Was he your mystery buyer?' I asked Colin as I began to put the pieces together.

'Yes,' Lou said on Colin's behalf.

'And was he in a happier mood then?' I ventured.

Surely he had to be. Surely it couldn't be possible for him to maintain such a miserable mood for so long, could it?

'Well, he wasn't rude,' said Colin, 'but he wasn't the life and soul either. I barely got six words out of him, but he was civil enough.'

'He didn't apologise for bawling me out though,' said Lou, before thoughtfully adding, 'but I don't think he recognised me. I tried to get him to chat but it was like trying to get blood out of a stone.'

I was surprised she hadn't gone out of her way to help

him remember who she was. When it came to settling scores and making waves Lou could have given Lisa a run for her money. I hoped I wasn't going to end up acting as the calming go-between for the pair of them. If that was the case I would have to enlist Colin to the cause.

'What did he buy?' I asked, before Lou had the opportunity to feel further outraged about Jacob's poor memory and lack of conversational skills.

'Practically every book in the young adult section,' Colin whispered.

'Personally, I would have thought blood-curdling crime and dark thrillers would have been more up his street,' said Lou, looking at him over her shoulder, 'but there's no accounting for taste I suppose.'

It was a surprising choice and stirred my interest in him a little, but for now I was more concerned about how I was going to try to get him on board when it came to joining in with the garden. I knew Lisa wouldn't relax until he had a hoe in his hand, and I felt my tactics might be a little subtler than hers.

'I'll be back in a sec,' I told my friends as I drained my glass and quickly levered myself out of my chair and round the table before I chickened out.

'You aren't going to talk to him, are you?' gulped Lou.

'Assuming it is him,' I whispered, 'you know, I think I am.'

I took my empty glass with me to make it look as if I was actually heading for the bar, and the subterfuge would have worked had Lou not noisily scraped back her chair on the wooden floor and drawn his attention far sooner than I was ready to receive it. It was definitely him. His eyes met mine before I had made it even halfway across the tiny room and I raised my arm in an awkward sort of salute.

'Hi,' I croaked, knowing it was impossible to veer off and ignore him now.

He reluctantly raised his hand in response and then returned his attention to the paper. Clearly, he had no such qualms about ignoring me.

'Hey, Jacob,' I said as I got nearer, trying to sound casual. 'I thought it was you. How are you?'

Nothing.

'I see you're familiar with the best pub this part of Norwich has to offer.'

'It's certainly the smallest,' he said without looking up.

I wasn't sure if he was stating a fact or criticising the place. Either way he still didn't sound much happier.

'And I can also see that you've got the leaflet that Lisa posted through the door earlier today.'

I couldn't help but admire her dogged determination. The leaflet was an invitation to the Easter garden party that was happening on Saturday, as well as a reminder that we would be looking through the competition paperwork. I hoped the fact that Jacob had bought it with him to The Dragon was perhaps an indicator that he was at least a little interested in joining us at the party and taking a look around.

'Yeah,' he said, giving it a cursory glance, 'I meant to put it in the recycling bin as I walked by but I forgot.'

Not even the slightest bit interested in coming along then.

'Right.' I swallowed. 'I see.'

I looked back at Lou, who was waving her hands about, urging me on, and Colin, who was shaking his head and shrugging. He had 'lost cause' written all over his face and I couldn't help but think that out of the two of them he was right.

'Well,' I said, licking my lips before giving it one last attempt, 'it would be lovely to see you there. I know you said you don't want to get involved with it—'

'I don't.'

'—but the garden took a lot of work to get up and running and entering the competition means a lot to us all, so if you do happen to be about on Saturday and could just put in an appearance for even a couple of minutes, that would be great.'

His head snapped up and he stared at me from under his floppy dark fringe. Just for a second, I thought he was going to either shout at me or get up and leave, but he did neither.

'If I say I'll come will you leave me alone?' he asked.

He didn't say it quietly and I was horribly aware that the folk closest to us were listening. I hadn't realised my interruption had been such an unwelcome intrusion or would warrant such a terse response.

'Yes,' I said. My voice came out in a tiny squeak and my face was burning bright.

I didn't think I'd ever felt so embarrassed. I could feel sweat uncomfortably prickling the back of my neck. It had been my intention to open up a little dialogue, not subject myself to abject humiliation. The guy at the next table sniggered and I looked Jacob in the eye, bitterly regretting that I had felt even an ounce of sympathy for him when we first met.

'Yes,' I said again, a little more confidently this time. 'If you promise to come over, I will definitely leave you alone.'

'I don't do promises,' he muttered, turning his attention back to his paper.

'Well,' I said, addressing his bent head, 'I'll leave you alone anyway.'

Quite possibly for good, but I didn't say that out loud.

# Chapter 5

'Good morning!' called a voice from an upstairs window as I walked past Neil and Mark's place early on Saturday morning. I was on my way to help set up for the Easter party.

'Are you not working today, Poppy?'

It was Neil.

'I'm still on holiday,' I called back. 'So I'm off to the garden.'

'In that case, hang on a sec and I'll come over with you. You'll need the code for the gate, unless you've got it already?'

'No,' I said, shaking my head. 'I forgot all about that.'

The garden at Prosperous Place was open to all Nightingale Square residents but the house was also home to Kate, Luke, Jasmine and baby Abigail, so there had to be some security in place. Norwich was in no way a crime hotspot, but the house and grounds were private property nonetheless.

'Chilly, isn't it?' said Neil as he locked his own front door and frowned up at the cloud-heavy sky.

'It's supposed to clear later,' I told him, 'according to the local report anyway.'

'Well, as long as it's dry,' he said, pulling a jumper over his head, 'that's all we're really bothered about. Luke and Kate have offered us the use of their kitchen if it rains, but it's not quite the same, is it?'

'No,' I agreed, 'not really.'

I would have been sorely disappointed if wet weather had ruined my first garden gathering as a bona fide resident.

'Is Mark at work already?' I asked.

'Yes, he's been gone for hours, but Blossom has given him the afternoon off so he'll be back in time for the lunch.'

I was pleased to hear he still had a job to go to. Blossom must have the patience of a saint to put up with him and his antics. Perhaps I wasn't the only advocate of living life to the full in the neighbourhood. I only hoped I didn't induce as many eye-rolls from our mutual neighbours, friends and colleagues as Mark managed to elicit.

'Carole and Graham are getting on already,' said Neil, checking the road before we crossed, 'and this,' he said, pointing to the keypad that was almost completely hidden under a tangle of scrambling ivy next to the garden gate, 'is the code to get in.'

I watched as he punched in the sequence of numbers and wondered how many failed attempts it would take until I remembered it.

'Stick it in your phone contacts somewhere,' Neil advised. 'That's what I did until I knew it off by heart.'

The grounds were every bit as beautiful as I remembered. Thanks to the late winter and its snowy onslaught a few things were a little behind, but they would soon catch up. The drifts of daffodils were in full bloom, though, and swayed in time to some unheard melody in the gentle breeze.

The walled garden was a hive of activity and the addition of every kind of container imaginable, filled with spring flowering bulbs, made up for the temporary halt that Mother Nature and her snowstorm had put to proceedings in the ground. I stood in the brick archway and drank the scene in. It smelt as good as it looked and I knew it was all going to taste incredible.

Many of the raised beds were full of produce that was ready to harvest and others had fresh green tips showing through the dark crumbly earth. Both the big garden shed, which the residents referred to as the bothy, and the greenhouse were crammed with trays of seedlings that would soon be ready for potting and then, eventually, planting out, along with other plants that had been overwintered inside for extra protection.

Unbidden, my mind skipped back to Jacob prowling about in his dark den. How could he not want to be a part of this? Gardening and growing was good for the soul and given his continuing bad temper I couldn't help thinking that his soul was in need of a little tending. However, having been on the sharp end of his tongue I was more than happy to leave someone else to order some R and R. Perhaps Lisa would step in again to try to tame the beast.

'Poppy,' exclaimed Carole, rushing over. 'At last! I'd all but given up on you. What have you been doing with yourself this week? Graham said you haven't been over at all. I would have called round to see you myself, only I've been busy helping Heather with Evie and the boys.'

'That's all right,' I told her. 'I've been spring-cleaning. I told myself I wouldn't come over here until I'd got the house back in order. It's taken all week but it's as clean as a whistle again now, just how Kate had it.'

'I wish I'd known,' she tutted. 'I would have lent you my Karcher. It's a whizz on grimy grouting.'

'Well, thank you anyway.' I smiled. 'This is all looking lovely. Is there still a lot left to get ready?'

Thankfully there was and I enjoyed getting stuck into hanging the bunting and arranging the tables in preparation for when everyone else arrived a little later. Originally the party had been planned for Easter Sunday, like the year before, but almost everyone had commitments elsewhere and so the arrangements had been altered.

'Every event here is a movable feast these days,' explained Graham, 'and with so many little ones being born these last few months it's had to be.'

'That's right,' said Carole. 'Kate and Heather are still doing what they can, but obviously it isn't quite so easy to get out here with little ones in tow. And Lisa has been hard at it, busy writing her new book.'

'That's one of the reasons why we were all so pleased to hear that you were moving in after all.' Graham beamed. 'We know how keen you are to get involved, Poppy, and we're hoping your new neighbour will join us at some point.'

I didn't have the heart to tell him that was never going to happen.

'We're all doing our bit,' Carole carried on, passing me some daffodil-filled jars to arrange along the tables, 'but new pairs of hands are just what we need to keep the place on track.'

'Well, I'll do my best,' I promised the couple, who clearly loved the project every bit as much as I did.

'Which is more of a commitment than you'll get out of Poppy's neighbour,' announced Lisa as she arrived with her family and set to, filling in the others on the latest details about Jacob that I couldn't bring myself to share.

A little later, once everything was arranged and in place, I headed home, bags brimming with bounty straight from the garden. Graham had dug up some of the new potatoes, which, although they were a little on the small side, I was going to cook with fresh mint, then toss in butter and take back, along with a few jars of my piccalilli and spicy salsa. I'd also knocked up a peppery salad made from the rocket, radishes, spring onions and watercress.

By the time I had prepared the food, showered and changed, the clouds had cleared and the sun was back in full force. It was far from hot, but the gentle warmth and light would add its own spring flavour to the party and was much appreciated.

As reluctant as I felt about doing it, I decided to make

one last-ditch attempt to get Jacob onside and remind him that he had made a commitment, if not a promise, to come over at some point and have a look around. I knocked and knocked but he didn't answer and, with his windows shut and downstairs curtains closed, it was impossible to tell if he was at home or not.

'He's not there,' came a voice from the far side of the green. 'He's gone out.'

It was Harold, the octogenarian neighbour who lived on my other side. We had met many times before as he had always been holding court when I happened to visit the garden. He was a sprightly character who had lived his whole life in Nightingale Square.

'I saw him head off well over an hour ago,' he further explained as he zipped along the pavement on his mobility scooter to where I was standing.

'Hello, Harold,' I said, stooping to kiss his cheek. 'It's wonderful to see you again. How are you?'

'Blooming, my dear.' He smiled back at me. 'Now, what have you got there? It smells absolutely delicious. Is it mint?'

I gave him a brief rundown of the dishes I had prepared, loaded up the basket on the front of his scooter and together we set off back to the garden. I couldn't help feeling furious with Jacob. He'd gone back on his word – even though I had cajoled him into giving it – and now it turned out I had been made to look a fool in the pub for no good reason.

I told myself he never had any intention of coming to the party and that he was most likely back in The Dragon. No doubt he'd picked out some shadowy corner to hide away in until it was all over. Well, that was it as far as I was concerned – both him and his hostility could bugger right off.

'Look who turned up just after you left,' said Lisa in a low whisper as she ushered me into the bothy to deposit my culinary contributions. 'He's been here for ages. I'm surprised your paths didn't cross when you went home earlier.'

I peered out of the window and was amazed to see Jacob, mug in hand, standing with John, Lisa's husband, at the barbecue.

'What the—' I began, but then stopped before I fell into the trap of sounding every bit as rattled as he usually did.

After all, I had wanted him to come, had been made to look a total idiot as I tried to convince him that he should, so it would have been a bit off to be annoyed that he'd made the effort, wouldn't it?

'He's been a real hit with the kids,' said Lisa as she popped a piece of potato into her mouth. 'Oh wow,' she said, groaning with pleasure, 'these are delicious.'

I liberated the container from her grip. They were also few and far between.

'What do you mean he's been a hit with the kids?' I frowned.

'They all think he's wonderful,' she laughed.

Why was she not in the least bit concerned that a man we knew absolutely nothing about had turned up more or less unannounced (yes, he had been invited, but no one had *really* expected him to come), and set about charming the local children? Was that not just a little bit weird?

'But they don't even know him.'

'Well, they do now.' Lisa carried on smiling. 'When he arrived, they were all getting bored so he sat them down and told them a story.'

'You mean he read to them?'

'No, he didn't have a book. From what I could tell, he just made it up.'

I looked back out of the window and narrowed my eyes at the rear view of him. I couldn't really picture him as some modern-day Pied Piper, but then again what Lisa was telling me didn't sound like the version of Jacob either of us had been subjected to either. Perhaps he had a twin? Perhaps the nice helpful one had shown up today and the evil one with the gruff bark was back in the lair, brooding in the dark—

'Poppy?'

I almost jumped out of my skin.

'What? Sorry.'

'I said: do you want a drink?' Lisa repeated.

'No,' I said, 'not yet, thanks. I'm good.'

I slipped back outside and began unnecessarily lining up the cutlery, moving surreptitiously round the table to try to listen in on John and Jacob's conversation. The merits of gas versus charcoal for outdoor cooking didn't sound particularly incriminating . . . but then I remembered how my neighbour's ears had pricked up the day we moved in and he realised that Luke Lonsdale owned Prosperous Place.

What if he was some paparazzi hack looking for a story? Granted, buying a house, moving into the area, hibernating for the winter and then charming the local kids was quite an effort to go to, but none of us were still any the wiser as to what his job actually was. I knew that Luke had been pestered by the press before and wondered if I should warn him that we may have an impostor in our midst.

'Grub's up!' bellowed Lisa before I had the chance, and everyone rushed to the table.

The feast laid out before us was nothing short of spectacular and everyone tucked in with gusto. It was a combined effort from everyone: John had cooked the meat (and done it to perfection), Mark had supplied the bread from Blossom's and the salad, potato and pasta dishes were courtesy of me and some of my neighbours. Carole had lined up the sweet treats, including rhubarb crumble made with tangy tart stalks plucked straight from the garden.

'Surely this has to beat your microwave meals, Jacob?' Lisa winked as my neighbour helped himself to another lamb chop and a dollop of my rapidly disappearing salsa to accompany it.

'It certainly does,' he told her.

He looked different, more relaxed. His shoulders weren't quite so close to his ears as they had been before. He wasn't the dish some of the others had suggested, but he did look better. I only hoped he wasn't going to turn out to be someone he shouldn't.

'Poppy made the salsa,' Lisa carried on, 'and the piccalilli.'

'It's nice,' he said, not looking at me.

Crikey, my cup runneth over.

'You're very quiet today, Poppy,' observed Luke from his seat at the head of the table.

'I daresay the move has taken its toll,' said Heather, who was being fed cut-up mouthfuls of food by her doting husband, Glen, while she somehow managed to discreetly feed both her baby boys at once. 'Things like that are so draining.'

This from the woman who was successfully wrangling three tiny children on less than four hours' sleep a night.

'I think it's far more likely that she's still smarting over the fact that I've been astonishingly rude to her every time we've talked,' said Jacob unexpectedly. 'I'm probably the last person she wants to be sitting down to celebrate Easter with.'

He was looking at me now, but his expression was completely unreadable. I got the feeling that he was happier talking about me than to me. I hadn't been thinking anything like what he had suggested, but as he'd mentioned it . . .

'From what I've heard you've been astonishingly rude to everyone,' I blurted out before I had time to stop myself.

'Now that is true,' said Lisa, laughing behind her napkin as everyone else gasped. 'You do have to admit you have been a bit of a miserable bugger, Jacob.'

'Lisa,' tutted Kate, covering Jasmine's ears, 'the kids.'

Lisa shrugged and I looked back at Jacob to see how he would react. He just carried on eating.

'But the kids love him,' I said, deciding now was the time to air my concerns, 'don't they, Lisa? And Jacob, you clearly know more about us than we know about you.'

'What do you mean by that?' he said between mouthfuls, frowning.

'Well, you obviously knew who Luke was when his name was mentioned the day I moved in,' I said, watching him closely, 'and you apparently have a way with words, or story-telling at least. You aren't a journalist by any chance, are you?'

'God no!' he laughed, making us all jump.

His eyes crinkled at the corners but I couldn't enjoy the change in his demeanour because I felt, knew in fact, that he was laughing at me rather than with me. My suggestion must have been wide of the mark.

'He's a teacher, Poppy,' said Kate. 'A primary teacher.'

Okay, very wide of the mark.

'And he recognised my name because I was a part of the school panel who interviewed him for a job a couple of weeks ago,' said Luke.

So, that'll be me not just wide of the aforementioned mark but in a completely different time zone to it, then.

'He's going to be Jasmine's new teacher,' joined in Lisa. 'Sorry,' she added, shaking her head, 'I should have said.'

Yes, that might have quelled my suspicions before I made a total arse of myself. Again.

'I only found out just before you and Harold arrived,' she went on.

'Right,' I said. 'I see.'

'No wonder you looked a bit weirded out when I said he'd come in and started telling the kids a story.'

'Did you think I was an impostor?' asked Jacob.

He was laughing at me again.

'I didn't know who you were,' I said haughtily as I began clearing plates.

So much for my chilled attitude and *c'est la vie* approach to life. He'd got me well and truly rattled now. 'I still don't, but so long as everyone else does, that's fine,' I continued.

An awkward silence descended and I looked to Carole for some support.

'Oh yes,' she said, finally catching on, 'now, who fancies some of this delicious crumble and cream?'

# Chapter 6

Carole's delicious crumble was the perfect antidote to the earlier awkwardness and the adults sat replete and relaxed while the kids, those who were old enough, tore about burning off the calories they had just ingested seeking out the dozens of foil-wrapped eggs we had hidden earlier.

'So, what does everyone have planned for tomorrow then?' Harold asked.

'We're off to Wynbridge,' said Kate. 'Mum's been asking us to go for ages, so we're heading there for a couple of days. Jasmine is back to school on Tuesday so we'll be home some time Monday afternoon.'

'I'm guessing Tuesday will be your first day in your new job then, Jacob?' asked Neil.

'It will,' said Jacob.

'And we've got my family coming over,' said Glen when Jacob didn't add anything else. 'We told them it would be easier if they came to visit us this year.'

'And you're cooking for them all?' I asked, the thought distracting me from Jacob's monosyllabic response.

I knew Glen had a large family – Heather was a real-life Wonder Woman, but cooking a meal for so many with the three little ones to tend to was surely too much.

'No way,' said Heather, as she burped one of the boys over her shoulder. 'The food is coming with the guests. We're simply providing the location.'

That sounded like a far more sensible proposition.

'I'm spending the day with Carole and Graham,' announced Harold.

'And we're off to your parents,' said Lisa, nudging her softly snoring husband to bring him back into the conversation. 'Aren't we, John?'

'I'm not asleep,' he mumbled, 'and yes, we are.'

'What about you guys?' I asked Mark and Neil.

'We're seeing friends,' said Neil.

Mark flushed and squeezed Neil's hand.

'Our friends Toby and Matt have just adopted a little girl, Leila. We're going to meet her tomorrow.'

'You sound broody, Mark,' said Heather with a smile, handing over her freshly burped baby.

'You have no idea,' he sighed happily.

'I'll be a surrogate for you if you like,' jumped in Lisa. 'We won't be having more of our own, but I'll happily hatch one for you guys.'

Suddenly John was all ears again.

'And what about you, Poppy,' asked Kate, before Lisa got

carried away with the idea and swept Mark along with her. 'What are you up to? Any plans to see your family?'

Had she known anything about my family dynamics she wouldn't have asked that.

'No,' I said lightly, 'nothing like that for me. We don't really get along.'

I thought sadly of the massive chocolate egg I'd splashed out on for Ryan that was never going to fulfil its Easter destiny. I had planned to give it to him in person but he'd cancelled on me again and it was too late to post it now.

'But that's fine,' I hastily added, 'friends are the family you choose and I'm spending the day with my mate, Lou.'

'And Jacob, what about you?'

'Oh, I'm the same as Poppy,' he said dismissively.

I didn't know if he was referring to having family he didn't get along with or being happier in the company of friends. Truth be told, I wasn't sure his family weren't better off without his grumpy presence and I couldn't imagine he had many friends.

'What a shame,' cried Lisa. 'I think it's sad the pair of you won't be with relatives.'

'Well, obviously I can't vouch for Poppy,' muttered Jacob, 'but you wouldn't be saying that if you knew anything about my family, Lisa.'

We might not have shared the same happy-go-lucky attitude towards life, but apparently my neighbour and I did have something in common after all. I watched as Lisa shifted a little closer to the edge of her seat, no doubt in the hope that he was about to explain why he and his family didn't hang out, but he clamped his mouth shut and went back to swigging the beer John had handed him earlier.

'You'd be more than welcome to come to us if you'd like to, Jacob,' offered Graham. 'Even if you just popped in for lunch.'

'That's kind of you, Graham, but I'll pass,' he replied. 'I've still got a mountain of planning to do so I need to get on with that, but thanks for the offer.'

He still wasn't the conversational life and soul, but at least he'd stopped biting everyone's heads off.

'It can't be easy moving schools at this point in the academic year,' I commented. 'It's quite unusual, isn't it?'

'Not really,' he snapped. 'It just depends when vacancies come up. I'd taken a few months off and then this job happened to become available. Nothing unusual about that.'

Apparently I'd hit a nerve and his snappy ceasefire was abandoned as quickly as it had been instated. It hadn't been my intention to rile him again.

'Well,' said Lisa, as my face flushed with embarrassment, 'I do hope you'll consider coming back over here to help out now you've seen how beautiful it is, Jacob.'

'I doubt I'll have the time,' he told her.

'But teachers have loads of holiday,' I butted in, determined not to let him get the better of me again. 'I'd imagine you'll have more time than the rest of us put together, especially during the summer.'

'She's got you there, lad,' chuckled Harold.

'I'm going to be volunteering at the youth centre whenever I can,' Jacob told me tersely. 'The place is falling apart and I've been asked to help out.'

No doubt that was where Colin's books from the young adult section were destined to end up, then. If the place really was in a mess it could be the perfect project to benefit from the competition prize money. It was ironic that Jacob wouldn't be part of the gang working towards turning the garden into a winner and therefore – if we did pull it off – potentially helping the centre, but I thought it best not to say as much.

'But even so,' said Carole, 'surely you could spare us just a few hours?'

'Yes,' joined in Lisa. 'It'll keep your mind off whatever it is you moved here and took some time out to forget.'

Jacob looked as if he wanted to crawl under the table and I realised that Lisa's astute observations were about to slip to the unsavoury side of meddlesome. Clearly the bear amongst us was on the run from something and I wasn't the only one who'd picked up on it.

Something had happened in his life, something monumental that had forced him to hide out in Nightingale Square, but he really didn't seem like the type of guy who would be up for baring his soul to a table full of strangers – and who could blame him? Had I been in his position, had anyone asked me about my unpleasant past, I was sure I would have been sporting exactly the same closed expression as him.

'Do you know,' I said, jumping up, 'I've gone and forgotten the biscuits I got for the children. Jacob, would you mind coming back and helping me with them? There's rather a lot to carry.'

We walked back over to the square in silence. I didn't feel I could bring myself to open my mouth for fear of saying the wrong thing again. Where Jacob was concerned that seemed to be a habit.

'I'm just going to nip in for a sec,' he told me when we reached his gate.

'You are coming back though, aren't you?'

'Of course,' he tutted. 'You just get these biscuits you can't manage to carry and I'll come over to yours in a minute.'

He didn't seem to have any idea that I had been trying to free him from Lisa's clutches.

Thankfully there really were biscuits to take back to the party. Stacks of them, but they weren't home-made. I was something of a failure when it came to baked goods. These were undecorated vanilla Easter egg-shaped biscuits from Blossom's. I had planned to embellish them that evening and then deliver them, Easter-bunny style, early the next morning. However, going out of my way to prise an oblivious Jacob from Lisa's prying had denied me the little project and I figured the children might enjoy decorating them themselves anyway.

'So, you really do have biscuits,' said Jacob as I loaded him up with a variety of tubs containing icing ingredients and natural coloured gels.

'Of course,' I snapped. 'Didn't you believe me?'

'I wasn't sure,' he said. 'I just thought maybe you were looking for an excuse to leave.'

He really was dense. My motivation for leaving was to save him, but he was still completely clueless about that.

'But why would I?' I asked.

I hoped he didn't think I was trying to get him all to myself!

'Because it's a bit full-on over there, isn't it?' he grumbled. 'Everyone knowing everyone's business' – he shuddered – 'and Lisa's the worst—'

'I think you'll find,' I interrupted before he had a chance to say something that would really make my blood boil, 'that actually she's the best, even if it might not always be obvious. Everyone looks out for each other around here and for those of us who aren't close to family,' I added pointedly, 'that's no bad thing.'

Jacob snorted and I set off after him at a brisk pace around the green.

'If you hate it so much,' I asked, staring up at him, 'then why are you bothering to come back with me?'

'Because either you or Lisa, or both of you, will keep trying to drag me over there if I don't give it a decent go today.'

I wasn't sure I would.

'Look,' he said, as he stopped dead in front of me, 'I didn't move here to join in.'

That much was obvious. He'd managed to stay home alone for months.

'I didn't move here to make friends or get to know my neighbours.'

Funnily enough, that was exactly the attitude Kate had initially moved to the square with, but somehow I couldn't imagine Lisa was going to find Jacob as easy a nut to crack. I certainly wouldn't be going out of my way to try to smash through his emotional armour.

'I don't want to grow my own row of radishes in the hope that it will make me feel better,' he went on.

'About what?' I cut in.

Apparently, my curiosity wasn't as easy to switch off as I would have liked.

'And I certainly don't want to enter some busybody, let's all pull together, community competition. That's not why I moved here.'

'So, why did you move here then?'

Jacob looked down at me and bit his lip.

'Come on, you two!' Lisa called from the garden gate before he had a chance to form an answer. 'We're waiting to go through these entry papers.'

Predictably, my neighbour refused to have anything to do with the competition details, so he was left in charge of the children, who were decorating the Easter biscuits with the bits and pieces I had supplied.

As I watched him from afar, I thought he looked like a completely different beast in the company of kids. He was helpful, patient, tender and kind. He was also covered in a rainbow of icing and he didn't seem to mind at all. I was in no doubt that he was a great teacher. He just wasn't a great adult, not around other adults anyway. I wondered if he would prove to be as capable with the teens at the youth centre as he was with the littlies. Given his comments about his own relatives I didn't think family mediation would be his forte.

'He is a dish, isn't he?' said Lisa, sidling up and following my gaze.

'Who?'

'Mr Grizzle, of course.' She grinned and gave a nod in Jacob's direction.

I was pretty certain she wouldn't still be thinking that if she was aware of how he had spoken about her. Although in assigning him the new name of 'Grizzle' she was pretty accurate, even though Mr Grumpy had been fitting as well.

'You can't call him that,' I hissed back. 'He might hear you.'

'So,' Lisa frowned. 'Why should that matter, it's his name, isn't it?'

'Is it?' I gasped. 'He's actually called Jacob Grizzle? I don't believe it.'

'He is,' Lisa giggled, plucking at my elbow like a silly schoolgirl. 'It's too perfect, isn't it? He's just like a bear emerging from its cave in the spring!'

'He certainly has the temperament of one,' I said, taking a deep breath to stave off the unexpected giggle I could feel rising. It was uncanny and really rather hilarious that her thoughts about him had matched mine.

'How are you getting on, Mr Grizzle?' Lisa called in his direction.

He looked up and stared at us from beneath his fringe and I tried to arrange my features into something that resembled serious.

'I'll have to go over now,' I told Lisa out of the corner of my mouth, 'otherwise he'll think we're taking the mick.'

'Go on then,' she said, shoving me along. 'I'm sure he'd love to talk to you of all people.'

'What's that supposed to mean?' I frowned.

'Well,' she said, grinning. 'We've all been trying to get him over here for months with no success and then you move in and here he is.'

'Oh, be quiet,' I tutted.

I knew for a fact that Mr Grizzle was no more interested in me than I was in him.

'But don't be long,' she added. 'I want you to read the last of these forms.'

Thankfully, Jacob didn't watch me walk over – that would have turned my face an even brighter shade of giveaway red than it already was – but instead went back to helping Jasmine place the eyes on her bunny biscuit.

'What do you think?' She beamed, holding it up for me to admire.

'I think she's beautiful,' I told her seriously.

'It's a he,' she said, sounding a little disappointed.

'Sorry,' I apologised. 'I thought because he was wearing a pink ribbon . . .'

'Boys can like pink as well you know,' she told me, 'it's only a colour. Isn't that right, Mr Grizzle?'

'Absolutely,' he agreed, 'I happen to be wearing a pink T-shirt myself today.'

Jasmine didn't look as though she believed him, so he lifted the bottom of his shirt to reveal the hem of a bright pink T-shirt.

'See,' she said to me, before rushing off to show everyone else what she had created.

'I can operate a washing machine, but a very red sock got mixed with my whites,' Jacob confided, with a shy grin that took me aback. 'I have a whole drawer full of pink clothes now.'

It was the most amusing thing he'd ever said and I wasn't sure how to react. Having a sense of humour didn't fit in with everything else I had worked out about him.

'Are you still pissed off with me?' he asked, lowering his voice so the children couldn't hear.

'Well, you were mean about Lisa.'

'I was talking about during lunch,' he elaborated, 'when we were all at the table. I know you were annoyed, although I was impressed that you were so on the ball and had the kids' backs, just in case I was a wolf in sheep's clothing.'

I wasn't sure if he was laughing at me again or not.

'I am sorry I've been so rude,' he continued. 'But it's hard to be civil when you're living through the worst time of your life.'

Perhaps he was being serious after all.

'Do you think it might help to talk about it?'

'No,' he said, almost reverting back to his gruff self. 'Definitely not. I'm just apologising for being a prick. I haven't always been like this.'

I was relieved to hear it.

'And as I've done what you asked by coming here today, I hope you'll forgive me.'

He didn't add that he had done it to get me off his back, but that was the implication again.

'But have you enjoyed it?' I asked.

He shrugged, not looking overly impressed.

'Well, don't go mad,' I said.

'I'm not going to lie,' he told me, 'or pretend. I've already told you I'm not into this whole communal vibe thing you guys have got going on here, Poppy.'

'And there's absolutely nothing I can do or say that will make you change your mind about joining in?'

'Afraid not,' he said, turning his attention back to his bunny biscuit. 'As far as signing up and joining in with stuff is concerned, this ship has sailed.'

# Chapter 7

During the following week a new routine quickly established itself and I was in no doubt that I had made the right choice in pursuing my dream of moving into Nightingale Square. My commute on foot from home to Greengages was just long enough to wake me up in the mornings and I had plenty of time left over at the end of the day to pop across the road to help out in the garden.

My simple life was still as uncomplicated as it was possible to be, but was much improved by my new address. Everything had turned out to be just as wonderful as I had dreamt it would be and, in spite of my concerns about my shortcomings as a sister, I was incredibly happy.

I had taken to leaving the square in the mornings with Jacob, who was also settling into a new routine, and although he never seemed particularly pleased to see me he didn't seem to much mind my presence either. His lack of reciprocal chat meant that I wasn't sure if he was merely tolerating the few steps we took in tandem, but I wasn't going to waste time worrying about that.

'I thought teachers had tonnes of equipment to lug about,' I said with a nod to his empty-looking backpack, on the Friday morning at the end of his first working week. 'Marking and stuff.'

'Not me,' he replied, as if the very idea was mad, 'my planning is all on my hard drive and I don't come home until I've finished any outstanding marking and set everything up for the next day.'

That would account for why I hadn't spotted him at home in the evenings as I went to and from the garden, as well as why he'd turned down the two invitations to the pub I'd issued during the course of the week. Much to Lou's disgust.

'For someone who claims she doesn't have an interest in him,' she told me with a disgruntled sniff, 'you seem to be going out of your way to make an effort to include him.'

She was right. After his insistence that he wouldn't be helping in the garden and his unerring ability to always make me feel a fool in the presence of others (be it intentional or otherwise), I had decided to pretty much leave him to it, but for some reason, I couldn't seem to help myself. I was resolute that neither the absence of family nor his misguided determination not to join in with what was on offer should mar the pleasure of living in Nightingale Square for him.

'Oh Jacob,' I said, pretending to be appalled. 'You aren't a workaholic by any chance, are you?'

'No,' he huffed, 'I just like to be organised and as I don't currently have a car, I can't manage to bring much work home with me.'

I was surprised he hadn't got a car. Personally, I was quite happy with my bike or the bus if I had to travel further afield than to work, but Jacob struck me as a car person.

'Are you thinking about getting a car then?' I asked, trying to frame the question in the best possible way to elicit an enlightening answer and not aggravate him any more than I already had.

Conversations during our brief walks rarely crossed the line beyond small talk, so more often than not it was impossible to add any new information about him to the thin file of what I had garnered so far.

'Morning, you two,' called John as we reached his and Lisa's driveway. He was getting stuck into loading his van with tools for his working day. 'All ready for the weekend, are we?'

'Absolutely.' I grinned. 'I have plans to make a very fine circlet of flowers especially for the occasion.'

'Marvellous,' John chuckled. 'Glen and I were wondering if perhaps you'd help us get the pole up tonight, Jacob?'

'I beg your pardon?'

'The pole,' said John, 'for the May Day celebrations on Monday.'

Jacob looked momentarily relieved and then shook his head.

'I'm afraid I won't be able to come over to the garden tonight,' he said firmly.

John didn't miss a beat.

'That's all right,' he said, matching his wife easily when it came refusing to take 'no' for an answer. 'We celebrate the start of spring here on the green, so that's where the maypole goes. This particular party will be happening right on your doorstep.'

I might have missed out on the opportunity to find out if Jacob was in the market for buying a car, but his face after John had finished wrapping him up in maypole ribbons was totally worth the sacrifice.

'It's a good turnout this, isn't it?' said Lou, early on the sunny Bank Holiday Monday afternoon, when she arrived with a somewhat reluctant Colin in tow.

'I'm not getting roped in with the morris again,' was the only salutation he offered, before he wandered off to find where John was serving drinks.

'Poor Colin,' said Lou with a smirk, 'he really got quite a whack with that stick last time, didn't he?'

'He told me his knuckles haven't been the same since,' I smiled back. 'But I'm hoping the lure of wearing bells again will be too much for him to resist.'

Lou chuckled in response.

'I like this,' she said, reaching up to readjust the circle of flowers I had spent so long fashioning and which had slipped a little as a result of all the earlier dancing round the maypole. 'Did you make it?'

'I did,' I told her proudly. 'As it's my first year here as a resident I thought I should make an extra effort.'

'And what about your neighbour,' she asked with a nod towards Jacob's house. 'Has he gone to any bother?'

'Between you and me,' I told her as Colin came back with three compostable cups of Colin's potent home brew, 'I get the distinct impression that all the extra bodies here today are down to him and him alone. Well, the tanned and toned ones anyway.'

'What do you mean?' Lou frowned as she took a tentative sip.

'The yummy mummy brigade are mad for him,' I said, pointing out the group of sleek and stylish mums who had unusually turned out to embrace the square's pagan celebration. 'According to Kate, he's the hottest property in Jasmine's school.'

Much to my amusement, Jacob, who had been forcibly dragged from his den on the pretence of setting up tables, was now in the thick of things and completely oblivious to the preening going on around him. He was so engrossed in telling tall Beltane tales to practically his entire class, who sat enchanted on the grass around him, that he didn't have eyes for any of the women who were so keen to secure his attention.

'Well, would you look at that!' Lou laughed. 'I've never seen anything like it.'

'Me neither,' I agreed.

'I can't believe they're *really* keen for their kids to learn about fertility rights and fire festivals, can you?'

'Nope,' I agreed again, 'but we are!'

I handed our cups over to Colin and pulled Lou over to the pole to join in with another rousing dance that was just about to start.

By the time the local morris dancers had packed up their bells and the bonfire in the brazier had been lit, practically everyone other than the Nightingale Square residents had drifted away. It had been a wonderful day and even Jacob appeared in good humour when Luke teased him about drawing away the attention of certain women who usually homed in on him.

This revelation came, as I knew it would, as a complete surprise to Jacob, but the cheering from John, Glen, Neil and Mark soon had his cheeks glowing and I wondered, not for the first time, if there had ever been a Mrs Grizzle on the scene. And I wasn't thinking about Jacob's mother either.

As the evening deepened around us and I sat with my friends watching the flickering flames, drinking Graham's brew, which somehow tasted better with every cup, I knew that my life had never been more satisfying and I hoped that Jacob was beginning to feel the same way.

'Does this belong to anyone here?' came Carole's voice, slicing through the tranquil moment. 'It was in the grass near the maypole.'

No one took much notice.

She tried again. 'I picked it up this afternoon. It's a Samsung something or other.'

I obligingly patted the patch pocket on my skirt, just to be on the safe side, and realised that my phone was missing.

Usually I would have been aware of the weight of it but the beer must have dulled my senses.

'It might be mine,' I said, standing up to have a closer look.

She held it aloft and I instantly recognised the glittery case.

'Well, thank goodness,' she said, handing it over. 'Here, have it back. It's been driving me mad, buzzing away all afternoon.'

'Have you got it set to vibrate, Poppy?' giggled Lisa.

'I think someone's desperate to get hold of you,' Carole continued, ignoring Lisa's cheeky innuendo.

I looked down at the screen and squinted as it lit up.

'Oh yes,' I said, my heart picking up the pace. 'I think you're right.'

I apologised for ducking out early and reluctantly headed home so I could answer in private as yet another call came through.

'Mum,' I said, only when I was safely inside and the front door was closed. 'What's going on? Is everything all right?'

'I'm fine,' she said with a sigh, 'don't panic.'

I was concerned about Ryan, not her.

'Although I'm still cash-strapped because of this ridiculous will business.'

'I haven't got any more money,' I told her bluntly. 'You cleared me out last year and, as I'm sure Ryan will have told you, I've moved recently myself so I'm as strapped as you are.'

'I had no intention of asking for more money,' she tutted, sounding affronted. 'It's Ryan I'm actually calling about.'

My heart started beating rather more rapidly.

'What is it?' I demanded. 'I have tried to keep in touch with him. We got off to a decent enough start last year but now I'm lucky to get so much as a two-word text out of him.'

I had thought about going down to the college to try to find him, but I didn't think he would appreciate me just turning up.

'Nothing's wrong,' said Mum, 'well, not really. It's just that I'm going away for a few weeks and I've been called in to college to talk about his attendance. I've asked them to change the date but they've refused. They want it to be a fortnightly thing apparently. Can you go in my place?'

If the college were asking for fortnightly meetings then there was more to worry about than just skipping a few classes.

'What's wrong with his attendance and what do you mean, you're going away?'

'I'm going to Spain,' she said. I could tell she was smiling. 'With my new man.'

My mother, the self-obsessed man-eater, was set to strike again.

'His name's Roger and he's—'

'Never mind that,' I interrupted before the image of her as a hungry mantis clinging to some unsuspecting middle-aged man with a paunch and receding hairline became lodged in my poor brain. 'What about Ryan?'

'Well, he hasn't been invited to the meeting. It's just me—'

'No,' I interrupted again, taking a deep breath. 'What I mean is, what's wrong with his attendance to warrant regular meetings and what's he going to do while you're away?'

And more to the point, why was she in such a rush to go? Was it all to do with her new man or was there more going on with Ryan than she could handle?

'He's not been turning up as often as he should so they want to keep a more formal eye on him, that's all. And he's going to stay here while I'm in Spain.'

'On his own?' I gasped.

'Yes.'

'Unsupervised and underage?'

'Yes.'

'When you've just found out he isn't turning up for college.'

She flared up. 'Well, he has to grow up some time. It'll do him good to stand on his own two feet. He's been nothing but hard work since Tony died and I need a break. So, can you come to these meetings or not?'

# Chapter 8

The call didn't end well because Mum slipped into one of her customary sulks. This was her go-to modus operandi whenever she didn't get her own way about anything. She had assumed that concern for my brother would mean that I would jump straight in, say yes to attending the meetings, perhaps even offer to shuttle backwards and forwards to Wynmouth to keep an eye on him, but I hadn't so much as suggested I would do any of those things.

I wanted to of course, more than anything, but I knew that if I did then I would be letting her off the parental hook, so instead I gave her conscience a poke and rang off. Time would tell whether or not the message would sink in, but I wasn't holding my breath. I didn't know if she would come to the right decision and cancel her plans to jet off to the sun, but I had to give her time to step up.

I hung my flower circlet on the hook behind the kitchen door, made a cup of soothing camomile tea and then sat at the table and carefully flicked through my grandmother's packed recipe book as well as my own slightly less impressive effort. Hers was brittle with age and beautifully embellished. Granny had been a talented artist and a keen cook, a country woman who knew the benefit of stocking the larder with nature's bounteous glut, and she had passed on her knowledge, as well as her treasured tome, to me.

I spread out my own half-finished recipe cards, the newest ones I had been working on to give out in the shop, and set to with my pen, knowing that going to bed would have been pointless. It was nearer one than midnight when I glanced up at the clock, my neck and shoulders stiff with having sat in one position for so long.

I picked up my phone and scrolled through my contacts until I found Ryan's number.

*Mum says you haven't been turning up to college*, I typed before I could change my mind. *You aren't thinking of dropping out, are you?*

The second I hit send I realised I'd asked the wrong question. I should have asked if everything was all right rather than sent what, when I read it back, looked like a demand. Damn. Too late to change it now.

I jumped as a message pinged back.

*So? You dropped out of uni. It's got nothing to do with you, POLLY.*

I stared at the screen and bit my lip. Ryan's retort was confirmation that my enquiry had come across exactly as I feared. That said, I hadn't expected such a blunt response, and the fact he'd called me Polly really stung. It was what he used to call me, when he was in his early teens and full of swagger, but that felt like for ever ago.

'It's because I don't really know you,' he used to say with a self-satisfied smirk as he realised he was getting to me. 'I keep forgetting what your name is.'

I had thought we'd moved on from all that. The text messages I'd been getting from Ryan after Mum had finally told me about Tony's heart attack might have been brief, but they hadn't been anywhere near as blunt as this one. I knew I was partly to blame as I'd just sent him entirely the wrong tone of message, but nonetheless I hadn't been able to shake off the feeling that there was more going on with him than Mum had let on, and his snappy reply confirmed it.

It had suddenly become very obvious to me that Ryan needed more than just someone who was willing to turn up at college and tick all the right boxes.

I dragged myself into work the next morning feeling like death warmed up and it had nothing to do with Colin's potent home brew.

'Good night, was it?' Harry grinned.

'Good day,' I conceded. 'I've had better evenings.'

'Oh?'

'I had a phone call from my mother.'

Harry's face was a picture. He knew enough about her to know it wouldn't have been welcome.

'She didn't want more money, did she?' He frowned.

'No,' I said, just as the bell above the door chimed, announcing the first customer of the day. 'Not money this time.'

'What then? She must have wanted something?'

I shook my head. I still didn't know what I was going to do about the situation and until I'd decided I didn't want to discuss it.

'These new potatoes look good,' I said, focusing Harry's attention on the produce in a bid to distract him. 'Shall we make them pick of the week?'

It was a quiet morning, which didn't help to distract me or stop Harry asking if I was all right, but we did have one afternoon customer I wasn't expecting.

'Jacob.' I smiled, looking up from the local paper I had been reading in lieu of there being anything left for me to arrange, tidy or sweep. 'This is a surprise.'

He was the last person I expected to see, from what he'd said about his eating habits. I watched as he walked over to my elaborate potato display and picked up a spud barely bigger than a cherry tomato.

'Are you looking for something tasty and fresh to balance out those micro dinners you seem so fond of?'

'Not really,' he said, returning the potato to the teetering pile and sending another rolling.

I was going to have to simplify the mountain I had sculpted, otherwise Harry and I were going to have an avalanche on our hands before long.

'These,' I said, coming out from behind the till, 'are so

fresh that you don't even need to peel them. Just pop them in a pan of boiling water with a sprig of mint for about twenty minutes—'

'I know how to cook them.' He frowned. 'I just choose not to.'

'But why ever not?' I demanded. 'You'd save yourself a fortune by buying fresh—'

'It doesn't matter,' he interrupted, 'I didn't come in here for a lecture on my eating habits.'

'Sorry,' I said, feeling chastened.

'I just came to see if you're all right.'

'What?'

'This morning,' he said, fiddling with the apples I had also spent so long lining up, 'you weren't around when I walked to work and what with that and leaving the party early . . .'

'Oh,' I said. 'I see.'

I'd been so preoccupied by thoughts of Ryan's text and whether or not I should respond to it that I hadn't given walking with Jacob a second thought.

'So, are you?'

'What?'

'For pity's sake, Poppy,' he snapped. 'Are you all right?'

'Yes.' I swallowed, my eyes misting up a little as a result of his annoyance. I really didn't need him turning up and making me feel bad as well.

'No,' I said. I sniffed, blowing my nose on the tissue I had fortuitously stuffed up my sleeve. 'Not really, but I'll survive. Thank you for taking the trouble to ask.'

I supposed him going to the effort of coming to find out how I was suggested that he cared, but he did have a funny way of expressing it. It felt almost as if he was angry with me because we had a connection and annoyed that the connection had elicited from him something verging on a compassionate emotional response. He really was a conundrum.

'I'm supposed to be in school,' he said, looking at his watch, 'it's my PPA time.'

'PPA?'

'Planning, prep and assessment.'

'Oh, right,' I said, 'I see.'

'I better go.'

'Well, thank you for checking in with me.' I smiled. 'It was kind of you to come.'

He looked at his watch again.

'How did you know where I worked?' I asked. I didn't think we'd ever discussed it. In the mornings when we reached the road at the end of the square he went right and I went left. He'd never asked where I was heading.

'I popped into the bookshop and asked Colin. You were with him in the pub the other week, so I guessed he'd know.'

I nodded, but didn't comment. I didn't much want to think about how that particular trip to The Dragon had ended.

'Well,' he said, his tone lighter now he was at the door, 'that's all right then.'

And with that he was gone.

*

I kept myself to myself that week. I walked to work earlier to avoid Jacob, even though he had gone to the bother of checking up on me; I cancelled my midweek plans with Colin and Lou and was an infrequent visitor to the garden. There had been no further texts from Ryan, even though I had sent him plenty. Mum had shot a fair few in my direction too. I hadn't given her an answer about the meetings, in the hope that she would realise that she should be the one to go, but she was still all set for her sojourn in the Spanish sun.

Dug deep into a depressing fug, I couldn't believe how quickly my perfect new life had been derailed and, as I dumped myself down on the sofa for another evening of channel-hopping, I knew that if I wanted to get it back on track then I was going to have to get to the bottom of everything and do a darn sight more than try to curb Ryan's absenteeism. But what could I do? It wasn't like me not to know the answer and the brick wall I'd hit was making me feel even worse.

A heavy couple of thumps on the front door knocker pulled me out of my reverie.

'Jacob,' I said, wrapping my cotton dressing gown a little more securely round my scantily clad frame. 'Hi.'

'There you go!' shouted a voice behind him. 'I told you she was home.'

It was Mark.

'Hi,' said Jacob, ignoring Mark.

'Are you checking up on me again?' I smiled.

'Something like that,' said Jacob, examining his shoes. 'I've not seen you all week, and . . .'

'Yeah,' I said, clearing my throat. 'I'm sorry about that. I've just needed some space to think.'

'About what?' asked Mark, bounding up the path.

Jacob looked as if he wanted the ground to open up and swallow him.

'Come on, Pops,' Mark wheedled. 'A problem shared and all that.'

'It's all right,' I told him, feeling myself blush. 'It's all sorted now.'

Jacob left his shoe-gazing to look me full in the face. He clearly knew that whatever I'd been thinking about wasn't sorted at all but, not surprisingly given how fiercely he protected his own privacy, he obviously had no desire to pry. Mark, however, had no such qualms.

'Bullshit,' he burst out. 'Something's up. Lou said you've been hiding out all week so we're here to drag you to The Dragon.'

'You are, Mark,' Jacob amended. 'I'm not. I was all set for an early night until Lou collared me when I was in the bookshop.'

'She said we were to tempt you with the promise of chips, Pops,' Mark continued with a boyish grin.

Evidently Lou felt my self-imposed quiet time needed to come to an end. My stomach growled as I imagined diving into a bowl of the pub's home-made chunky chips, liberally sprinkled with salt and dipped in thick tomato ketchup.

'All right,' I told the dynamic duo, 'give me two minutes and I'll meet you at the end of the road.'

It turned out that Lou had backed up her potato plan with a generous dollop of Jacob on the side.

'Here they are,' said Colin, ushering me into my seat as Lou magically appeared and set down a bowl of the aforementioned chips and a pint of the usual in front of me and another for Jacob and Mark.

'Well done, Jacob.' She beamed. 'I told you she wouldn't be able to resist.'

'I helped too!' Mark added indignantly.

'Resist what?' I asked.

'A lost cause, apparently,' Jacob sighed.

'A lost what?' I frowned, furiously fanning my mouth because the chip I had bitten into was so hot.

'I knew' – Lou winked – 'that if old Mr Grumpy here extended the hand of neighbourly friendship—'

'And we offered chips,' chimed in Mark, leaning over to pinch one from my bowl.

'Hands off,' I warned him.

'. . . then there was no way on this earth that you were going to turn him down.'

She was right.

'And how did you work that one out?' I asked, deciding to let her enjoy her moment of glory.

'Because you want everyone to be as happy as you are, Poppy,' she laughed. 'The thought that Jacob isn't as content as you are living in Nightingale Square has been half killing you.'

She was right again, of course, but also blissfully unaware that my own feelings of contentment had taken a bit of a battering. Suddenly I was feeling more choked than cheery.

'And I knew,' Lou continued, 'that if he suggested coming out for a drink—'

'I suggested it actually,' said Mark with a wave.

'. . . then you'd jump at the chance in the hope that it meant he was ready to start socialising and settling in.'

'I'll never be ready for that,' grumbled Jacob.

'You're just so lovely and so giving,' Lou carried on, not noticing that I was about to start sobbing into my napkin, 'and that's why we've—'

'It was more you than anyone, Lou,' Colin butted in as I wiped away a traitorous tear.

'And that's why,' she carried on, 'I've roped the guys in to stage this intervention and find out what the heck has been up with you this week! You've never missed our Wednesday-night pub pick-me-up. Not once in all the time I've known you!'

She would have carried on, but Colin put his hand over hers and shook his head and Jacob, aware of the change in the atmosphere, suddenly became more interested in examining the liquid in his glass than joining in.

'What is it, Pops?' asked Mark. 'What's happened?'

*

They sat and silently listened as I explained that the one person in my life who I still hadn't found a way of helping was my brother. I don't think I would have got through the lengthy monologue had Colin not handed over Gus once I'd finished my chips. As I talked I fussed the little dog, who took it all in while I avoided making eye contact with my two-legged friends.

'Poppy, you are far from useless,' Jacob surprised me by saying the second I had finished telling them that I was a hopeless sister. 'From what I can make out, the reason you haven't been close to your brother until now is because your mother's such a bloody nightmare.'

'Hear, hear!' agreed Mark. 'And you have been trying to build a relationship with Ryan recently.'

'I suppose,' I said.

'Where family are concerned things can be far from straightforward,' Jacob continued. 'And given what you've just told us, I'm not surprised you've kept your distance for so long.'

'If I were in your shoes,' Mark told me, 'I don't think I could find it in my heart to even consider getting involved.'

'Really?' Colin frowned.

Out of all of us, I knew Colin would have the hardest time getting his head round that idea, because he and his relatives were super-tight.

'Really,' Mark said firmly.

'Not everyone is blessed with a lovely family, Col,' Lou reminded him.

'And in my experience,' Jacob carried on, 'relatives think they can get away with doing pretty shitty stuff to each other because you're bound to them by blood and Christmas dinners and crappy camping holidays.'

The rest of us exchanged a quick glance and sat stock-still, not wanting to interrupt his rare moment of sharing.

'If you fall out with friends you make new ones but when it comes to real family feuds that rip life apart, you lose everyone and it's not just the people you sacrifice. It's like your entire childhood never existed . . .'

His words trailed off.

'Is that what's happened to you?' Lou asked, wide-eyed.

I was every bit as keen as she was to find out but I would never have asked so bluntly.

'No,' he snapped back, suddenly refocusing on me. 'It's not, and anyway we're here to talk about Poppy and her family, not me and mine.'

'I know but—' Lou tried.

'So,' said Mark, tactfully shutting her down, 'do you really think there's more going on with Ryan than him just playing hooky, Poppy?'

'Yes,' I said, swallowing, 'I do and given what he's been through recently, and who his mother is, I can't say I'm all that surprised. I just don't know what to do about it.'

'At the end of the day, Ryan is your mother's responsibility, Poppy, not yours,' Colin said sensibly. 'She can't run away just because things have got tough.'

'But she will,' I whispered. 'I know she will.'

'And you'll step in to pick up the pieces,' said Jacob, a shadow of a smile playing around his lips.

'Will I?' I swallowed again. I could feel fresh tears gathering and tried to blink them away.

'Of course you will,' he said, smiling properly now, 'because it isn't in your nature to ignore someone when they're in trouble, Poppy. If you see someone struggling you can't resist lending them a hand and now you know that your brother really needs you, you'll find a way to reach out to him.'

Out of the corner of my eye I saw Lou nudge Colin and I wondered if Jacob was thinking about how I had nagged him into giving in and coming to the garden because I thought it would help him, but I didn't ask. His kind words had ignited a warm glow somewhere near my heart and I didn't want to risk snuffing it out.

'And now I think we should all have another drink and sleep on it,' he carried on. 'Lou was right to get Mark and me to trick you into coming out tonight. You've shared the problem and together we'll come up with a solution.'

I felt the glow heat up a little more as he said the word 'we'. I wasn't sure when the transition had occurred but apparently I had worn his hostility, if not completely away, a long way down and he now considered himself one of us. It was a good feeling, knowing that I'd somehow made that happen.

# Chapter 9

It was days since I had bared my soul in The Dragon and no one had come up with a solution to the situation. Mum hadn't given up sending texts and I knew time was running out. If I didn't get a wriggle on she'd be gone and Ryan would be impossible to get hold of. I needed to come up with a solution to suit everyone – and fast.

'What are your plans for tonight, then?' Harry asked as we closed up on Saturday evening. 'A night out on the tiles dancing, is it?' he chuckled, 'or a get-together on the green with your girlfriends?'

I had told my boss a little about the situation with Ryan, but I hadn't gone into details. If he knew that I was concerned then he would worry and that was the last thing I wanted. This was one problem Harry wouldn't be able to solve and I didn't want to burden him with it all.

'I'm on watering duty at the garden,' I told him. 'So, the only dancing I'll be doing is with the watering can.'

Harry laughed again and shook his head.

'You certainly know how to party, Pops,' he teased.

'Laugh all you like,' I told him cheekily. 'As far as I'm concerned, it's the perfect night out.'

My responsibility to help keep everything growing wasn't the only reason I was keen to get over to the garden. Not showing up to do my bit as regularly as I had been had made me feel pretty low very quickly. I was hoping that taking on a few more jobs and talking about the competition might free up enough headspace to help me untangle my family conundrum.

'At last!' cried Lisa, laughing, when I eventually arrived at the garden. 'We'd all but given up on you. Where have you been?'

'Trying to get in,' I told her, deciding not to elaborate on my personal problems. 'I forgot the code.'

Lisa shook her head.

'That's because you haven't used it enough,' she said, and tutted. 'Stick it in your phone,' she advised, just as Neil had done the first day we came to the garden together, 'that's what we've all done.'

I nodded and pulled out my mobile to follow her instructions. There was another message from Mum but I ignored it and added the code to my contacts list. All I needed now was to remember the name I had come up with to file it under.

'I'll get the watering underway,' I told her, 'and then look through the competition stuff with you if you like.'

'Thanks,' she said with a smile, 'that would be great. Many

hands make light work and all that. At least now we don't have to worry about how it would look to the judges if they happened to notice we were a neighbour down.'

'What do you mean?' I frowned.

Lisa pointed over to the henhouse.

'Is that Jacob?' I gasped, looking from the hen run to her and back again.

'Yep,' she giggled. 'It is. He was loitering around the gate when I arrived, so I let him in and now Graham's teaching him all about the pleasures and pitfalls associated with poultry care.'

I could hardly believe my eyes and wondered what had finally tempted him to come back. As far as I was aware he hadn't stepped foot in the place since our Easter celebration.

'I don't know what you've said or done to him, Poppy,' Lisa beamed. 'But he's been like a different man since you moved in.'

I nodded, but didn't comment. Lisa's imagination didn't need further feeding. I knew she would bend whatever I said to her will, so I deemed it best not to say anything.

'Are you a breast or a leg man, Jacob?' I called as I slowly worked my way along, watering the containers closest to the henhouse first before moving on to check the rest of the beds.

'Now, don't you start,' he groaned. 'I've had more than enough of that from Lisa.'

Whatever it was that had initially lured him over had clearly lost its charm because he didn't look happy at all. If he'd just popped over with the intention of having a look at the place again then he was bound to be disappointed; not even the most casual visitor got off that lightly. Not when there was always so much to do. I hoped Graham dragging him to the henhouse hadn't put him off.

'Ignore them both,' said Graham, firmly thrusting a hen under Jacob's right arm and picking up another himself. 'Now, if you don't mind, Poppy, we need to crack on.'

Jacob didn't look particularly relaxed with the squirming hen I recognised as Hetty inexpertly held under his arm. One flap of her wings and she'd be away.

'Just don't crack the eggs,' I couldn't resist saying.

The comment instigated the biggest eye-roll imaginable from my neighbour and a tut from his tutor.

'If you don't lay off the mickey-taking,' said Jacob, frowning, as Hetty made a noisy bid for freedom and he let her go, 'I won't tell you about the egg-citing idea I've come up with to solve your problem.'

'Oh, good grief,' Graham cried as he picked up another hen with his free hand and passed it to Jacob. 'Don't you start as well or we'll never hear the last of it.'

'Was that a joke?' I gasped, feeling genuinely surprised but determined to capitalise on the unexpected moment. 'Does moody Jacob actually have a sense of humour buried beneath those furrowed brows?'

'I'll have you know,' he said, expertly waggling his brows while wrestling to smooth the ruffled wings of Petal, the little lavender Pekin, 'I have an eggcellent sense of humour, thank you very much. It's just a little rusty from lack of use.'

I could hardly believe it. Two jokes in the same conversation. I mentally added up Jacob's recent achievements and wondered if he really did have a twin after all, because this new and improved version didn't tally with either the angry man I had met the day I moved in or the sincere but serious version I had feasted with at Easter.

In the last few days this guy had visited a grocery store, he'd played a part in Lou's plan to get me to the pub and now he was back in the garden, hen-wrangling and making jokes. Bad ones, but jokes nonetheless. Was the Nightingale Square magic finally beginning to find its way into his heart? The vision before me suggested he was in the midst of a transformation and I only hoped his problem-solving skills were as competent as his ability to miraculously loosen up.

'Oh my God.' I laughed out loud when I finally heard what it was that he had come up with. 'You have got to be kidding me.'

It was just the two of us left in the garden eating supper. Lisa and I had gone through the competition paperwork and painstakingly filled out the online entry form, including details and attachments that showed how the garden had been renovated and adapted over the last year as well as pictures of the celebrations and the learning that took place there.

Along with Graham's amateur poultry care course, there were the obvious seed-sowing, maintenance and harvesting lessons, as well as barbecue masterclasses from John. Carole was in charge of flower-arranging and I was hoping to contribute something myself soon.

To my mind the garden was already a winner, whereas this hare-brained idea of Jacob's . . .

'No,' he said, 'I'm not kidding. I think it's a wonderful idea and, given what you've told me about your mother, I'm certain she would agree with me.'

I didn't doubt it. What he was suggesting was liberating her from all responsibility. If she got wind of this then I wouldn't see her for dust.

'You said yourself he's already on a sticky wicket with the college,' Jacob continued, 'so this suggestion would sort that out in a heartbeat.'

That much was true.

'This could be Ryan's best chance to get back on the straight and narrow now he's having a wobble.'

'So, you think he is then?' I sighed. 'You think there might be more going on than cutting classes?'

'Yes.' Jacob nodded. 'Given what you've said, I think ducking out of his education might be an indicator of more problems than you know about.'

'But I don't *know* him,' I said, shaking my head. 'How can I ask him to come and stay with me when I don't know anything about him?'

Yep, that was the crazy idea Jacob had stumbled upon. He had suggested that I should ask my brother to come and live with me in Nightingale Square. Not permanently, just until he got his head straight and some of our mother's influence out of his system. Jacob thought that being so close to the college would help with Ryan's attendance too. If he didn't have such a lengthy journey to face then he was more likely to go in. On this point I couldn't help but agree, assuming of course that it was the travelling that accounted for his non-attendance.

'Look,' said Jacob, 'just think for a minute, really think about the reality of the alternative option.'

'About leaving Ryan to fend for himself when Mum goes to Spain, you mean?'

'Yes.'

It wasn't an idea that sat well with me. Ryan was still no doubt grieving for his father – who knew where his head was at right now? Simply agreeing to attend the meetings Mum had mentioned just wasn't going to be enough.

'Not a pretty picture, is it?' Jacob nudged after I had been quiet for a few seconds.

'No,' I answered, chewing my lip. 'Not pretty at all.'

'Just ask him to stay with you for a while,' Jacob went on. 'Perhaps until the end of the summer term. Get the college student support team involved, so he can properly work through his feelings.'

We had both agreed it was paramount that should happen.

'Then set out some ground rules and give him some boundaries, banish the tech, even set him to work here,' he continued. 'You said your mum has no patience with him and I daresay he's feeling pretty worthless and unloved. Now's your chance to undo some of that with her out of the way. You could really help Ryan turn things round before they get out of control.'

He made it all sound so simple – and was he finally admitting that coming to the garden helped? It was hardly the time to ask, but it sounded like it to me.

'But I can't,' I said feebly, 'I wouldn't know how to.'

In theory what Jacob was suggesting sounded amazing. It was a solution that had the potential to give my brother the space he needed to deal with the death of his dad and turn his life round again; but setting it all up and making it happen was a different story.

'I know you don't know how to deal with any of this, Poppy, but I also know that in your heart you want to and I think this is the best option you have.'

'I know.' I nodded. 'I know you do.'

'Don't make a decision straight away,' said Jacob, gathering our leftover bits and pieces into a pile before I sorted them out again to show him where to recycle them. 'Sleep on it.'

'I'll do that,' I said with a sigh, 'although I'm not getting much sleep.'

We cleared away, checked the garden gate was locked and crossed the road into the square. It was a chilly night but clear and in spite of the street lights in the next road along, I could just about make out the odd shining star.

'If it will help make your decision any easier,' Jacob told me as we reached my gate, 'I promise I'll help you out as much as I can.'

'Will you?' I gulped. 'How?'

'I could take him to the youth centre.' He shrugged, trying to make his kind offer sound low-key. 'It wouldn't make any difference to me. I'll be going anyway. We're setting up some counselling groups and one-to-one opportunities for those who want a bit more privacy.'

Perhaps it might help Ryan to talk to someone he didn't know.

'I think the place could make a real difference to a kid like Ryan,' Jacob elaborated, pushing his still-too-long fringe away from his face. 'And there are plenty of jobs to do there. The whole refurbishment is volunteer-led. It could give him a purpose and keep him occupied while you're at work and he's not in college.'

It didn't feel such a daunting prospect knowing that I wasn't going to have to face the situation entirely on my own. That is, of course, assuming Ryan agreed to come.

'Thank you,' I said. 'That means a lot.'

Jacob nodded and scuffed at the pavement with the toe of his shoe.

'I don't always mean to be a miserable bugger, you know,' he suddenly burst out, his voice cutting through the quiet. 'I've just had a lot of shit to deal with recently and it's taken its toll.'

'Well,' I said, smiling, 'not that it's really anything to do with me, but I think you're in the right place if you want to start over.'

'I'm not sure about that,' he said looking back to Prosperous Place. 'I hardly got off to the right start here, did I? What with the neighbours from hell and me shutting everyone out. And I'm not still convinced about this whole garden malarkey either.'

'But you enjoyed today, didn't you?'

'I did,' he sighed, 'but I didn't expect to get roped in to doing stuff the second I showed my face.'

'It's kind of how it works over there,' I explained. 'And keeping busy can take your mind off things. You just said as much when we were talking about Ryan.'

And given the nature of his job, teaching tiddlers, I was sure he was aware of that first-hand.

'That's true,' he agreed. 'But Lisa . . .'

'Can be a bit much,' I said, 'yes, I know. Don't worry, I'll try and tone her down a bit when she's in your face. You can trust me on that one.'

An unexpected flash of pain shot across Jacob's face.

'I'm sorry, Poppy,' he said, some of his former mask slipping back into place again, 'but I can't do trust. Not any more.'

'What's that supposed to mean?'

He shook his head.

'Trust and I have parted ways,' he muttered, the pain still visible in his dark eyes. 'I better get back,' he added, taking a step away as the shutters came down a little further. 'I hope I haven't made your decision about how best to help Ryan even more difficult.'

'You haven't,' I told him, quickly closing the space between us again and pulling him into a hug.

'Poppy,' he gasped, 'please don't.'

I knew it was a little on the awkward side, hugging a man you barely knew, but I was doing it with the best of intentions. I wanted to show him some reciprocal kindness and was desperate to send him home with a head full of thoughts that the evening had been a good one and that he had been a real help, both to me and in the garden. It was clear that he had been hurt, and badly, but whatever had happened in his life hadn't happened here. I didn't want him to associate Nightingale Square with anything negative.

'It's okay.' I smiled soothingly.

'No really,' he said, pulling away. 'Too late . . .'

For a moment I thought I had crossed the line and blown it, but then I noticed a stain developing around the pocket on his shirt.

'The eggs for my breakfast,' he said, looking down at the sticky mess. 'Graham said the shells were a little on the thin side.'

We exchanged a look and then we both burst out laughing and I knew that, for this evening at least, he really would be going to bed with a smile on his face.

# Chapter 10

I slept better than I'd expected, but I was still up early the next day. My mind was buzzing, and not just with thoughts of Ryan, but also because I owed my neighbour a breakfast.

'You're up early,' said Graham when I went back over to the garden almost before the sun was up.

'I could say the same of you,' I said, laughing, as I watched him collecting a huge bundle of rhubarb.

'It's thoughts of this stuff,' he said, shaking his head. 'We can't keep up with it. It's a shame to waste it but there are only so many crumbles, tarts and pies our freezer will hold. I thought we'd peaked a couple of weeks ago, but it just keeps coming.'

Mentally, I flicked through the pages of my recipe book.

'I'll take some if you like,' I told him.

'Will you?' he asked, sounding surprised. 'Are you sure?'

'Yes.' I nodded. 'In fact, I'll take all of that lot, if you don't mind helping me carry it home?'

'I can bring it back with me when I'm done here, if you like,' he offered. 'I'll chop the tops off and wash it in the big tin bath. That'll save you the bother, but only if you're sure you can find a use for it.'

'Definitely.'

'What have you got in mind?'

'Rhubarb chutney,' I told him.

'Rhubarb chutney?'

'Trust me' – I laughed as he screwed up his nose – 'it's delicious. The perfect accompaniment to have with cheese, pâté, all sorts of things.'

'And have you got all the ingredients you need to make it today?'

'Believe me, Graham, I might not have the latest designer bag or a wardrobe full of shoes, but my stock cupboard is second to none. Give it a month and you'll be tasting the result of a Sunday morning well spent.'

He looked suitably impressed and I was delighted to have the opportunity to chop, peel, boil and stir. I was in no doubt that by the time I was pouring the steaming concoction into sterilised jars I would have decided whether or not I was going to follow Jacob's advice or go my own way. And thinking about Jacob . . .

'Anyway,' I said, making for the henhouse, 'I only came to see if there are any eggs. Am I too early?'

'If the nest boxes are empty, there's half a dozen left

from yesterday still in the bothy. You're welcome to those,' Graham said.

'Two will be enough for today.' I smiled. 'Thanks, Graham.'

I had planned to knock and run, but on second thoughts, given our recent track record with eggs, I decided it was best to personally hand them over. Jacob seemed to take an age to answer and when I remembered how early it was, I knew the reason why.

'Sorry,' I was saying before he had even turned the key in the lock. 'I forgot the time. I didn't realise it was still so early.'

'What is it?' he asked, looking around me and out into the square. 'Is everything all right?'

He looked much younger with his mussed-up hair and bare feet. He was almost cute.

'What's wrong, Poppy?' he asked again when I didn't say anything.

'Nothing,' I said quickly. 'Nothing's wrong. Sorry. I've just been over to the garden . . .'

'Already?' He frowned, scratching his head and making his crazy bed-hair even crazier.

'Yes.' I smiled, holding out my hands. 'I owe you a breakfast, remember?'

'Of course.' He nodded, stifling a yawn. 'I was really looking forward to that fried egg sandwich.'

'And now you can have one,' I said, carefully transferring the precious cargo from my hands to his. 'Or two.'

I swallowed as the backs of my fingers grazed his palms. 'Assuming you have some bread.'

'Thick, white sliced,' he said, grinning, 'nothing but the unhealthiest loaf for me.'

'Spread with real salted butter, no doubt?' I tutted.

'No,' he said, 'I'm a spreadable type of guy.'

I didn't comment.

'The real stuff rolls the bread up,' he elaborated. 'Do you want to come in?'

'No,' I said, perhaps a little too quickly. 'Thanks for the offer but I have to get back. I'm expecting a delivery of rhubarb.'

'Of course you are,' he laughed.

I supposed it did sound a bit strange, even for me.

'Well, thanks for the eggs,' he said, holding them up.

I backed down the path, trying not to think about anything other than my morning in the kitchen, and certainly not about how warm and soft the touch of Jacob's hands had felt against mine. It had been a completely different sensation to the one elicited by the previous evening's eggy hug.

'Morning, Poppy!'

I almost jumped right out of my skin.

'Morning, Carole,' I called back, once I had zoomed in on her leaning out of an upstairs window, ostensibly to shake a speck of dust from her bright yellow cloth. 'Lovely day.'

'Yes,' she agreed. 'You're about early.'

Penny to a pound she was thinking she'd caught me making the walk of shame. Mark had warned me that she didn't miss a thing and was prone to putting two and two together and coming up with a whole lot more than four. At the time I had rather liked the idea of having someone looking out for me but now I wasn't so sure.

'Your husband said the very same thing about half an hour ago,' I couldn't resist replying with a cheeky smile.

Just a couple of hours later, the kitchen air was filled with the scent of ginger, cardamom, sugar and of course rhubarb. As the ingredients slowly simmered and I carefully mixed and stirred, I felt the tension in my shoulders easing. This really was the dream. The only question now was whether I wanted to invite my brother to be a part of it.

By the time the chutney had cooled I had made up my mind.

Ironically, after the barrage of texts I'd received (and ignored) from Mum, it then became impossible to get hold of her. Her messages ceased coming as abruptly as they had begun.

After days of trying both her and Ryan's mobiles, I finally got an answer on the house phone.

'Hello.'

'Hey.' I swallowed.

I hadn't been expecting Ryan to pick up and was a little thrown to hear his voice. He sounded different to how I remembered, but then he was practically a man now, so his voice was bound to have changed.

'Hey,' I said again, clearing my throat. 'It's me, Poppy.'

'Who?'

'Poppy.' My heart sank.

Clearly he had no intention of making this anything other than awkward and, given his previous *Polly* reference, I can't say I was surprised.

'I thought I'd just ring and say hello,' I went on.

'Hello.'

'So,' I struggled on, 'you haven't been answering my calls or texts.'

'I haven't had any calls or texts from anyone called Poppy,' was his speedy response.

'Look, Ryan,' I cut in. In spite of my determination not to, I was beginning to get riled. 'I'm just ringing to check in. I'm sorry I haven't called sooner, but if you'll just let me explain—'

'I'm not Ryan.'

'What?'

'I'm not Ryan,' the voice repeated, slower and louder as if its owner thought I was an idiot.

'Who are you then?' I demanded.

I hoped it wasn't Mum's latest man. She was living dangerously if it was. This guy sounded barely above the age of consent.

'I'm Kyle, I'm a mate of Ryan's.'

Oh, for pity's sake.

'In that case,' I snapped, 'can I speak to Ryan, please?'

'Who did you say you were again?'

'I'm Poppy, Ryan's sister.'

'I thought his sister was called Polly—'

'Look,' I interrupted, 'just put my mum on the phone, will you?'

'She's not here.'

'Okay,' I sighed, 'do you have any idea when she'll be back?'

'Not for a few weeks,' Kyle told me. He sounded very happy about it. 'She's gone to Spain with some bloke.'

'Already?' I squawked.

'Yeah.' Kyle sniffed. He was far too cocky about it all for my liking. 'Me and Ryan are looking after the house.'

'Put Ryan on.'

'He's not here either.'

'Where is he then?'

I doubted he was up the road from me studying at college, not with an empty house to fill with friends.

'He's just nipped out to get some more beers, I mean bread.'

Brilliant. So, he was home alone *and* he was drinking. Or was Kyle just winding me up? I couldn't imagine there was really anywhere irresponsible enough to sell alcohol to a lad of sixteen. Or was I being naive?

'He's not old enough to buy beers,' I pointed out.

Kyle didn't respond.

'Look,' I snapped, 'just ask him to call me as soon as he gets back, okay? On my mobile. He's got the number. Please,' I added, hoping a little belated courtesy might encourage the lad to at least pass the message on.

'Don't worry, Polly,' Kyle eventually answered, through a huge yawn. 'I'll tell him.'

He'd hung up before I had a chance to correct him and I had absolutely no expectations of hearing from Ryan any time soon.

As it turned out, Kyle did pass the message on and I did hear from my brother, the next day while I was at work.

'Sorry, Harry,' I said, as I pressed to answer the call. 'Could you please just serve this customer? I really need to take this.'

Harry stepped quickly behind the till and I ducked into the stockroom.

'Ryan.' I smiled as I said it, hoping my non-confrontational tone would transmit through the ether and he wouldn't see me as an interfering older sibling, but as someone he could talk to. 'Thanks for ringing back.'

'I didn't really have much choice, did I?'

He sounded just as sulky as I remembered him being at thirteen.

'I still can't believe Kyle told you Mum had buggered off.'

I let the profanity pass.

'For all I knew you could have reported her to the police. I've been waiting for social services to turn up and take me into care.'

'I'm not likely to let that happen, am I?' I said softly.

'I dunno,' he said, and I could imagine him shrugging. 'You've never seemed to bother much about me before.'

I could hardly refute the accusation, given the weight of evidence stacked against me.

'Well,' I said, trying to sound more in control than I felt, 'that's all about to change, if you want it to.'

Ryan snorted and I willed him not to hang up. I got the feeling that if I blew this conversation then I wouldn't get a chance at another one.

'I'm sorry I've been such a rubbish sister' – I swallowed nervously – 'and I'm sorry I left you to battle it out with Mum without any backup for so long.'

'So, what's going on then?' he demanded, ignoring my apology. 'If you say things are going to change, then tell me how. Are you coming to Wynmouth?'

'No,' I told him. 'I can't. My job's here in Norwich, remember?'

'Oh yeah.' He sniffed. 'I couldn't expect you to put yourself out for me, could I?'

I didn't answer.

'Go on then,' he muttered.

'Well,' I said, bracing myself to either hear the line go dead or be bombarded with bad language, 'I was wondering if you fancied coming to stay with me for a while?'

'What?'

'I wanted to ask you if you would consider coming here, to Norwich, to live with me for a few weeks.'

'I see.'

I could tell from his tone that my suggestion was the last thing he had been expecting. Truth be told, if someone had proposed it to me when Mum had called on May Day I would have sounded exactly the same.

'At least until the end of term,' I carried on, encouraged that he hadn't said no straight away. 'My place is only a few minutes away from college so you wouldn't have to face that journey every day. You could get your studying back on track.'

'I suppose.'

'It can't be easy having to travel that distance all week.'

'I haven't got lectures every day.'

'I know, but even so, it's a long way from Wynmouth. I was surprised when Mum said you were even doing A levels, to be honest.'

'You and me both.'

What did he mean by that?

'The place where I'm living now is much bigger than my old flat,' I told him. Not that he'd ever seen the old flat. 'And surely it's got to be better than living with Mum.'

'Not that I am at the moment,' he reminded me, 'not technically anyway.'

'That's true,' I conceded.

He was going to turn me down. I could feel him building up to it and I wasn't surprised. I mean, he was a sixteen-year-old lad who'd been left with a house to himself. He'd have to be mad to tell his older sister that he'd rather move in with her, wouldn't he?

'All right,' he said, 'I'll come.'

'Really?'

'Yeah,' he said, sounding suddenly wary. 'I mean, you do want me to, don't you? You weren't joking?'

'N-no,' I stammered, shaken by his sudden show of vulnerability, 'of course I wasn't joking. I just didn't expect you to say yes. I hoped you'd want to come but I didn't think you would.'

'Yeah, well,' he told me, 'cooking your own dinner every night wears thin after a while.'

'Mum's only been gone five minutes – and don't tell me she cooks for you,' I laughed. 'That I will not believe!'

'Nah,' he said, 'thank God. She's hopeless in the kitchen.'

As far as I was concerned she was hopeless everywhere.

'So,' I said, 'shall I come and get you at the weekend?'

'No,' he shot back, a little too quickly for my liking.

Surely he couldn't have trashed the house already?

'I can lock up here and then get the train to you. There's no point you coming all this way and then back again when I can get to Norwich myself.'

'Are you sure?'

'Yeah,' he said, 'I can manage.'

'All right.' I smiled. 'Try and get in after half three if you can. I should be able to duck out of work a little earlier than usual and meet you at the station.'

'All right,' said Ryan, 'thanks, Poppy.'

'No problem,' I replied, grateful that my real name had been reinstated, and then he was gone.

# Chapter 11

'So, Ryan's really coming?' asked Lou that evening in the pub.

'Yep,' I said, holding up my phone so she, Jacob and Colin could see the text for themselves, 'on the train this Saturday and arriving just before four.'

'I think you're mad,' said Lou, shaking her head.

'I think you're a wonderful big sister,' said Colin.

'I think you're in for a rough time,' said Jacob, 'but you've done the right thing.'

He hadn't made much mention of a 'rough time' when he came up with the idea, but there was little point in reminding him of that now. Ryan was coming and that was that.

'And Harry's given you another week off work,' said Colin, ignoring Lou's less than enthusiastic reaction and Jacob's cautionary one. 'How lucky was that?'

'I know,' I agreed. 'He really is the best.'

When I had reappeared in the shop after Ryan's call, Harry had asked if everything was all right and, when I explained that my little brother would be coming to live with me for a while, Harry had insisted I take the following week off to settle him in.

'You've worked for me for years, Poppy,' he had said when I told him I couldn't take more time, having only just had a week off after the move. 'And in all that time you've never called in sick. You made it possible for me to visit my family in Australia and, more importantly than that, you held the fort on the days when my grief got the better of me.'

That was all true, but I still didn't want to leave him in the lurch.

'I can manage,' he reassured me. 'You take this week to build some bridges with your brother.'

In the end I had agreed, grateful to have found such a generous friend in my boss.

'And next week is half-term,' said Jacob, 'so I'll be around too. Not that I want to interfere,' he quickly added.

'Says the man who didn't move here to join in or help out,' I teased, reminding him of his former mantra.

He had arrived at the pub with Mark and Neil, who had then gone on to a restaurant. I was pleased Jacob had decided to join us when they left. As far as integrating him into our little community was concerned, I felt we'd done a pretty good job, and even though Lisa was keen to put his transformation down to me I felt it had been more of a team effort.

'Yeah well,' he said, colouring slightly, 'I couldn't stay locked away for ever, could I?'

'Oh Jacob,' said Lou, beaming, 'is Poppy the Belle to your Beast?'

'She could well be,' he shocked me by saying.

It was a bus ride across the city from Greengages to the train station and, as the time ticked ever closer that Saturday afternoon, I couldn't believe how nervous I felt. I wondered if Ryan was feeling the same way. He had messaged again to say he was on the train and I had messed up two consecutive till transactions as a result. I was grateful to have the distraction of being at work, but poor Harry looked as though he was wishing he'd been able to talk me into taking the whole day off.

'You all set then?' asked Jacob as he arrived in the shop just as I was signing off from my disastrous stint on the till.

'Ready as I'll ever be,' I said, taking a swig from my water bottle and wishing I'd never let my relationship with my brother slide. 'I'm going now anyway. I'd rather be early than late. Have you been to the garden today?'

'Yes,' said Jacob, 'John asked if I'd give him a hand putting up the tripods for the beans.'

I grinned and Jacob shook his head. I didn't need to tell him that the place had sucked him in. He was well aware of what had happened and I couldn't have been happier for him.

'That's good then,' I said, 'because they need planting out. If anything, they should have been in already.'

'That's what John said,' Jacob told me. 'Apparently they'll

want all hands on deck tomorrow so everyone can have a turn planting something.'

'Including you? Planting something I mean, not being planted . . .'

'I guess,' he said, 'and you could bring Ryan.'

'Talking of my brother,' I said, checking the clock for what was easily the millionth time, 'I better go.'

'I thought I'd come with you,' he said, 'if that's all right? I thought you might appreciate the company and a hand with Ryan's stuff.'

I said goodbye to Harry, having made him promise to ring if the shop got too busy over the next few days.

'How are you feeling?' Jacob asked as I kept my eyes trained along the road for first sight of the bus. 'Nervous? Excited?'

'Nauseous and terrified,' I said honestly. 'I still can't believe you talked me into doing this.'

'Truth be told,' he said with a sigh, 'neither can I.'

'What do you mean?'

'Well,' he said, running his hands through his habitually untidy hair, 'I wouldn't give my brother houseroom and yet I've managed to convince you to embrace yours.'

I tore my eyes away from the road and looked at Jacob's bent head. I resisted the urge to run my own hands through his hair to try to straighten it out a bit and tucked them into my pockets instead.

'Have you been estranged for long?'

Just a couple of weeks ago I wouldn't have dared to risk

asking a question like that for fear of turning him back into the glowering beast, but things had changed.

'Not all that long,' he said gruffly.

Sensing the subtle change in tone, I decided not to pry too deeply.

'Is he older than you or younger?'

'Younger.'

'Oh,' I said. For some reason I had been expecting him to say older. 'So, the pair of you are a bit like Ryan and me then?'

'No,' he said, 'not really.'

'Right.'

'He's only two minutes and seven seconds younger.'

'Oh wow,' I gasped, 'you're twins!'

It was hard to imagine another Jacob walking about somewhere, even if I had sometimes wondered light-heartedly if he had a doppelgänger, due to his ever-changing personality. I wondered if his brother had tidy hair.

'Are you identical?' I rushed on.

'In almost every way,' he said, biting his lip.

'Crikey,' I said, 'that must make it even harder then.'

'What do you mean?'

'Not talking or getting along,' I elaborated. 'I went to school with twins, two girls. They were practically joined at the hip. They told me that they felt the other one was an extension of themselves, if that makes sense. I'm probably not explaining it very well.'

'No,' he said, pushing his hair back again. 'I get it. I know what you mean.'

'So,' I cautiously asked, 'does that make your separation harder to handle?'

'Nope,' he said, jumping up as the bus came into view, 'my brother has actually made it all very easy. I don't have a problem hating him at all.'

As the bus ground to a halt and we jumped on board there was no opportunity to ask what he meant and, to be honest, I wasn't sure I wanted to.

I was a bit of a mess by the time we arrived at the train station and I was extremely grateful that Jacob had offered to tag along. Not only did I not know what to expect in terms of Ryan's attitude and greeting, I didn't really have much of an idea as to who to look for either.

Mum had never shared photographs so, in my head, Ryan wasn't much more than a boy; a lad who was happy kicking a football about in the back garden if it kept him out of the house. This new version, deemed old enough (if only by our mother) to look after himself and with enough swag to bluff his way to buying beer, was going to take some getting used to.

'Is that him?' asked Jacob, peering along the platform from our vantage point beyond the barrier.

The guy he had pointed out was helping an elderly lady down from the carriage and then struggling to manage her wheeled suitcase along with his own luggage and what looked like a guitar.

'No,' I said, 'he's far too tall.'

'Well, he must have missed the train then,' said Jacob, 'there isn't anyone else.'

I squinted as the two unlikely travel companions made their way up the platform, and my breath caught in my throat.

'Oh God,' I gulped, reaching for Jacob's sleeve, 'it is him. That's Ryan, that's my little brother.'

But there was nothing little about him. He was easily six feet tall and as slim as the beanpoles Jacob had been putting up. His skinny frame made him appear even taller. It was a wonder he didn't snap under the weight of all that luggage.

'Thank you, young man,' said the lady, once he had assisted her through the barrier and handed over her suitcase. 'I hope you have a wonderful stay, my dear, and you tell that sister of yours that you're not going to be anywhere near the bother she thinks you're going to be.'

I looked at Jacob and raised my eyebrows.

'I will.' Ryan smiled. His sandy hair slipped to almost cover his eyes before he jerked his head and it fell straight back again.

Why did practically all the men in my life these days need a haircut? Although to be fair, my brother's was shaved short at the back and sides. It was just the top that was an unruly, and no doubt trendy, mess.

'I'm sure she'll be very relieved to hear it,' he went on.

'I'm sure she will,' said the lady before scuttling off to hail a taxi, 'I'm sure she will.'

I have to admit, I was rather comforted by her kind words.

'Hey,' said Ryan as he walked over to where Jacob and I were standing and dropped a large canvas bag at his feet.

'Hey,' I said, the word awkwardly squeezing itself over the lump in my throat.

I had no idea how to handle him and the bag he had put between us meant that a hug was definitely out of the question. Perhaps that was the intention.

'I'm so pleased you decided to come,' I said. 'I can't believe how different you look.'

'I'm not a kid any more, Polly,' he said, the shadow of a smile playing around his full lips.

'I can see that.' I nodded, deciding to let the namecheck go.

He was a good-looking guy, with jutting cheekbones and a strong jaw. I just knew he would be a hit with the girls. I wondered how many hearts he'd already broken.

Jacob cleared his throat and I realised I hadn't introduced him.

'Sorry,' I said, trying to laugh my surprise off. 'I'm a little lost for words.'

Ryan looked at me and raised his eyebrows and then held out his hand to Jacob.

'Hi,' he said, 'I'm Ryan, the not so little brother.'

'Jacob,' said Jacob, taking Ryan's hand and shaking it. 'Good to meet you. I've heard a lot about you.'

'Nothing good I hope?' Ryan asked, his eyes swinging back to me.

He seemed to have a far better handle on the situation than I had.

'No,' said Jacob, 'nothing good at all.'

'That's all right then.' Ryan nodded, his gaze still on me. 'I'd hate to be a disappointment.'

'I'm sure Mum has spent a lifetime making you feel like one of those.'

He ignored the comment and I instantly regretted it, knowing it was bitchy and perhaps not quite the thing to say about one's own mother. Even if it was true.

'So,' said Ryan, looking between me and Jacob. 'Are you two a couple or what?'

'No,' said Jacob, before I even had a chance to open my mouth. 'No. Absolutely not.'

Ryan began to smile.

'We're neighbours, just neighbours,' Jacob rabbited on. 'We live next door to each other. Don't we, Polly, I mean Poppy?'

Ryan's subtle mischief was playing havoc already. Perhaps I should pick a different name for him seeing as he seemed so keen to mess with mine. In that moment, Puck felt far more fitting than Ryan.

'Yes,' I said with a smile, 'we do. Although I was going to say we were friends.'

'Well yes,' Jacob rushed on. 'We are friends too. Friends who happen to be neighbours.'

'As long as that's clear then,' said Ryan, still smirking.

'Right,' I said, and reached for the bag, but Jacob got there first. 'Shall we get on? I bet you're gasping for a cup of tea, aren't you, Ryan?'

'I wouldn't mind a beer,' he said, hoisting his backpack a little higher and balancing his guitar.

'I'm sure you wouldn't—' I began, but Jacob cut me off.

'Shall we get a taxi back?' he suggested. 'It'll save the bother of struggling on the bus.'

# Chapter 12

My little home in Nightingale Square felt an awful lot smaller with Ryan inside it. Not only was he tall and with size ten shoes, his kit took up as much space as he did, in spite of his claim that he was travelling light.

'Right,' said Jacob, once he had seen us and the luggage safely inside, 'I'll leave you to it. I'm guessing you'll be going to the garden tomorrow, Poppy?'

'Definitely.'

'And what about the pub tonight?'

'I'm up for the pub,' said Ryan, stooping back through the door, in a move I guess he had got used to to avoid concussion.

'No,' I said firmly. 'We won't make the pub tonight, but we'll definitely come to the garden tomorrow.'

'I need a fag,' muttered Ryan, 'is it all right if I smoke in the house?'

'No, it is not,' I said straight away.

I had no idea he smoked.

'You'll have to go out in the garden. I'll show you where.'

Once Jacob had gone I gave Ryan a rinsed-out tin for his butts and pointed him in the right direction, then set about making us both tea and filling a plate with a variety of biscuits. As I carried the tray out I could see my brother expertly rolling a cigarette and hoped the habit was nothing more than a passing phase.

'I didn't know you smoked,' I said mildly as I set the tray down on the little mosaic-topped table and pulled out the chair opposite his.

'I daresay there's a lot you don't know about me,' he said, lighting up and taking a long drag. 'Like I said at the station, I'm not a kid any more.'

'I can see that,' I said, smiling, 'and I daresay there's plenty that you don't know about me either.'

'I daresay,' he shot back, hastily abandoning his roll-up when he caught sight of the biscuits.

Not that avid a smoker then, but a teenager with a healthy appetite nonetheless. The plate was soon half empty and I couldn't help wondering where he stored the calories. His thin frame didn't look like it held on to anything for long.

'So, how come you managed to afford to buy this place then?' he asked, once he had finally finished munching. 'I didn't think working in a shop paid that well.'

'It doesn't really.' I frowned, wondering where he had got the idea that my pretty abode belonged to me. 'This place isn't mine. I'm renting it from a friend.'

'Oh,' he said, 'right. Mum said she'd helped you out with a mortgage deposit.'

More like she had helped herself to my rental one. Even though I was seething, I didn't correct him. I wanted to welcome Ryan to life in the square and starting his visit off with a conversation to set him straight about all the lies our mother had spun would probably take longer than he was thinking of staying.

'She must have got the wrong end of the stick,' I said.

'She does that a lot.' Ryan nodded.

It saddened me to think that he was used to her mind games and half-truths, but at least he was some way aware of what she was really like and I was spared the unsavoury job of removing any rose-tinted glasses he might have been wearing.

'Talking of Mum,' I went tentatively on, 'did you get hold of her to tell her where you are? I still haven't managed to make contact but I've sent her an email, along with about a gazillion texts.'

Ryan shrugged.

'I left a note,' he said, 'and I did have a bit of a tidy-up.'

I resisted the urge to drill him about whether he'd turned the lights off, closed the fridge, locked the doors and shut the windows.

'Although,' he said, draining his mug of tea in three great mouthfuls, 'I think I might have left some milk in the fridge and some bread in the bin.'

'Oh Ryan,' I said, feeling momentarily dismayed. 'The

milk will stink and the bread will be a mouldy mess in no time.'

'Oh yeah.' He grinned, reaching for the last chocolate cookie. 'I didn't think of that.'

I smiled back and shook my head. He really was Puck to a T. I hoped his tricksy antics didn't get any more mischievous than forgetting to throw out the perishables.

'Well,' I said, 'not to worry, I'm just pleased you've come.'

He didn't say anything.

'I know things can't have been easy since you lost your dad.'

'I didn't lose him, Pol.' He frowned. 'He died.'

I couldn't keep up with him. One minute he was talking as though we were conspirators but the next he was going out of his way to make things awkward. Was that just typical teenage behaviour or was he deliberately doing his utmost to make me suffer for all the years I hadn't been around?

'That's what I meant,' I said. 'And I'm hoping being here will help.'

'With what?'

'College for a start. It's only a quick bus ride away. You'll be able to get your attendance back up in no time.' I didn't mention the meetings. 'Although I'm still surprised you took the A-level option.'

I'd been mulling that over, and from what I could remember Ryan had always been a practical rather than a studious kid, but perhaps he'd changed.

'I should have been doing an apprenticeship but it didn't

work out,' he said. 'So, I just picked what I thought would keep me out of the house the longest.'

That didn't make sense to me. If he was so keen to stay away from home, why had he stopped going in to college?

'Mum always had some bloke or another staying,' he went on, 'and it made me uncomfortable. I hated it. I've hated the way she carries on for as long as I can remember. She wasn't much different even when she was married to Dad.'

I was sorry he had felt that way but pleased that he had decided to come and stay with me when Mum wasn't in the equation and he could have taken advantage of her absence.

'Well,' I said, 'you're here now.'

'Yeah, well, I was almost out of food,' he said bluntly, 'and she hadn't left me much cash so I didn't have any choice but to come, did I?'

I hoped he didn't mean that, although looking at the stubborn set of his jaw, I think he did. Perhaps my flattered feelings were misplaced. Perhaps the potential sibling solidarity I thought I had just glimpsed was actually wishful thinking.

'Have I got time for another fag before dinner?' he asked, pulling the pouch of tobacco out of his pocket again.

I looked at the now empty plate and wondered if I was going to be able to keep up with his larger than average appetite.

'Yes,' I told him, 'dinner won't be for a while yet and you might want to have an early night. We have a busy day ahead tomorrow.'

Ryan looked at me and frowned.

'We're going to the community garden across the road,' I told him. 'There's lots of planting to do.'

'But it's Sunday tomorrow,' he said, his chin raised in what looked like a challenge.

'Church then?' I suggested, trying to raise a smile.

'I always sleep through Sundays.'

'Not here you don't.'

'Seriously?'

'Seriously,' I said, more firmly. 'My house, my rules.'

'I thought it was your mate's house, Polly,' he said, lighting up again.

This was harder than I thought it was going to be. I didn't want him to walk all over me but I didn't want him heading straight back to Wynmouth because I'd put my foot down too firmly either.

'Let's just start by getting the basics right, shall we?' I suggested. 'It's Poppy, remember? Not Polly.'

'Right,' he said, blowing smoke straight out of his nostrils in one long stream, 'Poppy it is then.'

Things felt a little tense between us after that and I couldn't wait to get to bed, relax and drop the responsible adult act for a few hours. Colin might have thought I was being a wonderful big sis, but I couldn't help thinking that Lou and Jacob's take on the situation was far more accurate. I probably was mad and yes, I was definitely in for a rough ride.

If only Ryan could be the helpful and considerate version

of himself, the one who had helped the woman off the train. I had picked up on intermittent flashes of loveliness throughout the evening, but he was a far more complex character than that. He was a simmering cauldron of emotions with a large pinch of anger and suspicion thrown into the mix, and I knew that his presence in the house, and his ever-changing moods, were going to take some getting used to.

'You all set then?' I asked, when he finally emerged from his room the following morning.

It was nearer lunchtime than breakfast and I had frustratingly watched a steady stream of neighbours leaving the square and heading to Prosperous Place. I was itching to join them but could hardly abandon my brother on his first morning in my care, especially as I'd told him Sundays weren't for sleeping through.

'If you want to jump in the shower,' I urged, 'I'll make you some breakfast and we'll get going.'

'What, now?' he yawned.

'Yes, now,' I answered. 'It's almost lunchtime.'

'All right, Ma,' he tutted, 'keep your wig on. And don't worry about breakfast. I never bother.'

For someone who never bothered he soon made short work of three of the four bacon rolls I cooked up while he was taking his time to get ready to go.

'Enjoy those, did you?' I smiled.

'They were all right.' He shrugged.

'Your turn tomorrow,' I told him.

'To do what?'

'Make breakfast for me,' I said, throwing him the tea towel. 'I think that's only fair, don't you?'

Everyone was well stuck into the planting by the time we arrived, even Jacob, but I was pleased to see that they had saved plenty for us to do.

'What is this place?' asked Ryan when we stepped into the garden and were met with a hail of hellos and warm welcomes.

'This,' I said proudly as I steered him past Lisa's eldest, Tamsin, who was clearly already smitten, and on towards the bothy, 'is the reason I moved to Nightingale Square.'

Ryan looked at me as if I was talking another language, one that he didn't understand at all.

'It's a community garden,' I elaborated, 'for the residents of the square. We all garden here together and share the harvest. We also throw some pretty amazing parties.'

Given the expression on both Tamsin's, who had followed us, and Ryan's faces, my idea of what made for an 'amazing party' didn't match theirs at all.

'Don't knock it until you've tried it, Ryan,' said Jacob, coming to my rescue. 'I had no intention of getting roped in until your sister dragged me here, and look at me now.'

He held up his soil-encrusted hands to prove that he was part of the gang and Ryan looked suitably unimpressed.

'Well, I'm not getting my hands dirty.' He scowled. 'I'm only here because you made me come, Poppy. I'm not joining in.'

Tamsin looked ready to swoon.

'There's chickens,' she said, 'and cats. Wanna see?'

Ryan didn't appear to care either way, but trailed off after her anyway.

'How's it going?' asked Jacob, the second the pair were out of earshot.

'All right,' I said. 'I think.'

I wasn't sure really. Perhaps I should have just left him in bed.

'Last night he said he'd only come because he was running out of money, but I hope he was just saying that to get a rise.'

'Did you give him one?' Jacob asked, reaching round me for a hand trowel and another tray of plants.

'No,' I said. 'It was all a bit fraught though. I feel as if I'm walking on eggshells most of the time, trying not to say the wrong thing.'

'You'll soon get used to each other.' Jacob smiled.

I hoped he was right.

'Come on then,' he said, 'come and show me how to plant these beans.'

I made a point of keeping track of where Ryan was throughout the day, but I didn't keep asking if he was all right. He disappeared a couple of times, back over to the green to smoke, but I tried not to clock-watch all of the time he was out of sight. Tamsin was a more than capable shadow anyway.

By late afternoon we had finished planting everything out and John had fired up the barbecue. Everyone was pleased with our combined efforts and as the plant pots slowly emptied and the beds and troughs began to fill up, I had been mentally running through all manner of recipes I was hoping to try out.

'Are all of your pots made out of plastic then?' Ryan frowned as he watched me rinsing some off and setting them out to dry.

'Pretty much,' I told him, pleased that he had noticed. I liked the thought that for all his prickles my brother was environmentally aware. 'But we reuse what we've got and we've been trying out alternatives, like sowing directly into empty cardboard loo rolls and then planting the whole thing out to biodegrade as the plant grows.'

Ryan appeared to have lost interest and scooped up Dash, one of the cats Luke and Kate had adopted when they were found as kittens in the bothy. Both Dash and his sister Violet seemed as keen on my brother as Tamsin and I remembered that he'd always had a way with animals. He had acquired quite a menagerie by the time I left home. It used to drive Mum mad. Clearly, he hadn't lost his Dr Dolittle tendencies.

'I think you've got a friend there,' I commented, nodding at the tomcat, who was usually harder to handle than his sister and nowhere near as affectionate.

'Yeah,' said Ryan, as he wandered off again. 'He's all right, isn't he?'

We all gathered round the tables to eat together and even though Ryan tried to keep a low profile, Carole and Lisa's questions proved a bit much.

'Would you mind giving me a hand moving some of these

pots, Ryan?' Jacob asked when it became apparent that almost everyone's attention was focused on my brother rather than their second helpings.

'I'll help too,' I said, pushing back my chair.

'Thanks,' said Ryan when he realised that we were shuffling the pots around to nowhere in particular.

'You're welcome,' said Jacob. 'I got the same treatment when I first came here, so I know what it's like. A lot of it came from your sister actually.'

'Hey,' I objected.

'Don't panic,' Jacob rushed on. 'I know now that it was all well-intentioned.'

'That's all right then,' I huffed.

'But it was also pretty full-on,' he added.

Ryan snorted.

'But don't you feel better about life as a result of my pushy ways and full-on interference?' I asked, feeling confident of his answer.

'Not really,' he said, 'but at least I'm occupied.'

Ryan snorted again.

That was not the answer I had expected. So much for me being the Belle to his Beast. Undoubtedly, my work with Jacob still wasn't done. I hoped my little brother wasn't going to be such a tough nut to crack.

'Well,' I said, straightening up and ignoring Ryan's obvious amusement, 'I'll just have to try even harder then, won't I? For both of you.'

# Chapter 13

Even though I had been reluctant to fall in with the suggestion, I was pleased Harry had insisted that I took the week off. It turned out that my brother hadn't been acquainted with how to run a house, or indeed look after himself, at all. He was a stranger to the laundry bin and beyond tipping half a packet of cereal into a Pyrex bowl and slopping almost a full pint of milk on top, his culinary skills were woefully lacking.

He soon realised that I wasn't going to accept ignorance as an excuse for not pulling his weight and by the middle of the week he was as capable of setting the washing machine, drying dishes and adding Marmite to spaghetti, Nigella-style, as I was.

One thing that did need more working on, however, was the time he chose to get out of bed in the mornings.

'I wouldn't be too tough on him about that,' said Lou when she rang to see how things were settling down and to tell me she was still working on the Reading Room makeover plans for Colin. 'When you head back to work next week, you might be grateful to know that he's sleeping the day away.'

'That's a fair point,' I told her, 'but it won't be much of a comfort on the days when he's supposed to be in college, will it?'

'No,' she agreed, 'I guess not, but I might be able to help with that.'

'How?'

'I've just taken delivery of some old-style clocks,' she said, and laughed, 'you know, the wind-up ones with Mickey Mouse on the face and bells on the top for the alarm. Set one of those going in every room in the house and he'll soon get his butt out of bed!'

'It might come to that,' I laughed back.

'I have to go to the market tomorrow,' I mentioned to Ryan towards the end of the week. 'I thought you could come with me.'

'Thrilling,' he sighed, sounding thoroughly fed up.

'I bet you'll be glad to get back to college next week, won't you?' I asked. 'I wouldn't mind if you wanted to have a mate or two round here, you know.'

I hadn't thought about it before, but Ryan's friends from college would probably be local lads.

'No,' he said, looking aghast at the idea, 'you're all right.'

'I promise I wouldn't cramp your style,' I told him. 'I won't ask if they want to stay for tea.'

He still didn't look impressed.

'Well,' I said, shrugging, hoping that a trip to the market might cheer him up a bit, 'the offer's there.'

Ryan's reaction to the market didn't turn out to be quite the one I expected.

'I've never been in here before,' he said, as we criss-crossed our way beneath the striped canopy maze of permanent stalls. 'It's a bit disorientating, isn't it?'

I stopped at one of my favourite stalls, which sold dried herbs and spices, to stock up on a few ingredients for my larder.

'Not really,' I said, not paying him much attention.

'Well, I think it is,' he puffed. 'It's making me feel a bit breathless.'

'It's fine,' I murmured, working my way along the counter to find what I wanted.

Ryan nodded but didn't comment, and when I looked up at him he did look a bit peaky.

'If you walk to the end of any of these rows,' I told him, 'you'll find your way out. It's just like a big square really—'

'I'll see you in a minute then,' he said, striding off before I had even finished.

When I found him, sitting on some steps, he looked deathly pale and his hands were shaking.

'Are you all right?' I frowned. 'You could have picked a better place to stop.'

The public conveniences weren't the nicest the city had to offer.

'I'm fine,' he said, shoving his hands in his pockets as he stood up. 'I'm just not great in enclosed spaces, that's all.'

'I daresay it feels a bit different when you're so tall,' I said, looking back at the warren of stalls and knowing he would resent it if I made a fuss.

'It's not that,' he mumbled.

'How about we go somewhere and get a coffee?' I suggested.

His face had a bit more colour by the time we had wandered over to the café in the Forum, paid for our drinks and found a table with a modicum of shade outside.

'Are you sure you don't want anything to eat?' I asked.

It wasn't like him to miss out on an opportunity to snack and the glazed pastries had looked tempting.

'I'm good,' he said, shaking his head, 'thanks.'

'So, what was all that about then?' I asked. 'Back there in the market, you seemed really shaken up.'

I kept the question as gently phrased as I could. I had no desire to annoy him, but it would be handy to know what pushed his buttons. A big sister should know stuff like that, shouldn't she? A big sister who had been there wouldn't have had to ask, my mind uncharitably reminded me.

'Enclosed spaces,' he eventually croaked with a shudder. 'I hate them.'

I hadn't thought the market was particularly enclosed, but then there was more of Ryan to fill it than me.

'Ever since one of Mum's blokes used to lock me in my bedroom,' he went on, 'I've had a thing about being shut in.'

'What?' I gasped.

This was news to me and unwelcome news at that.

'Given my age I should have been able to handle it, and it wasn't like it was a small room.' He shrugged. He was trying to sound offhand but failing. 'But it was knowing I couldn't get out if I wanted to. It freaked me out and I've haven't been able to cope with confined spaces since.'

'When was this?'

Ryan looked thoughtful.

'Not long after Dad left,' he told me. 'The bloke said I was a pain in the arse and he didn't want me disturbing him and Mum, so he used to lock me in my room.'

'Did Mum know?'

'Dunno.' He shrugged again.

He stirred his coffee, keeping his eyes on the table rather than looking at me.

'I really am sorry about your dad, Ryan,' I said softly. 'He was a good bloke.'

'He was the best.' Ryan sniffed. 'I used to stay with him as much as I could. He used to take me to work with him. It was brilliant.'

Ryan's dad had been an extremely successful business-man. He had worked in the building trade all his life and specialised in renovation projects. He could turn his hand to pretty much any job and I realised my brother could have had a career for life thanks to him, had things turned out differently.

'Was your apprenticeship going to be with him?' I asked, the penny only just dropping.

'No, one of his mates,' Ryan explained. 'Dad said it would be good to work with someone else in the trade. Broaden my horizons a bit.'

'Couldn't you have carried on with that?' I asked. 'Surely your dad's mate . . .'

'I would have done, but she made us move, didn't she?' he said bitterly. 'So, I thought fuck it and enrolled for A levels.'

I didn't know what to say.

'And what a waste of time that's been,' he barked.

'Don't say that,' I said, reaching out and grabbing his hand. 'I'm going to talk to the college. I'll sort it out. We'll sort it out. Maybe you could switch to a different course. Get this term out of the way and start fresh in September.'

Being a summer baby meant that Ryan had finished school at fifteen, so starting over shouldn't prove too complicated.

He sniffed again and pulled his hand away.

'Maybe,' he said. 'We'll see. Can we talk about something else?'

'Okay.' I nodded, a lump forming in my throat. 'Yeah.'

We talked about my return to work the following week and how I hoped he hadn't been too bored during half-term.

'I know the garden isn't really your cup of tea.' I smiled.

He had trailed over with me a few times but hadn't joined in with anything.

'It's all right,' he said, 'and hanging out with Jacob has been okay. He's about as keen on the place as I am.'

I hoped that wasn't true but was grateful that my neighbour had stuck to his word and been on hand to talk to

Ryan when it became obvious that he'd had enough of my company. Ryan's arrival coinciding with Jacob's holiday had certainly helped ease the transition from living alone to sharing my life with my little brother. It was a relief to hear he liked my neighbour, even though they weren't anywhere near the same age, because talking to another guy might be just what Ryan needed. It was then that I remembered Jacob's offer to take him to the youth centre.

'Jacob is a good bloke,' I said, trying not to sound as if I was leading up to something.

Ryan grinned.

'What?' I demanded, caught off guard.

'Nothing.' He carried on smiling but didn't elaborate.

'He was wondering if you might like to help out at the local youth centre,' I said. 'It's having a bit of a makeover and they could do with some more help with the decorating and stuff. You'd be perfect.'

'Maybe.'

'He volunteers there,' I added, feeling somewhat encouraged that he hadn't dismissed the idea.

'I suppose I could give the place a look.'

'Excellent.' I smiled.

I didn't want to push my luck so didn't mention the potential counselling. I thought it best to leave that to Jacob.

'So,' I said, 'I've been meaning to ask if you've got a girlfriend back home? Or a boyfriend,' I quickly added, not wanting to be presumptuous.

'You must be kidding.' Ryan snorted. 'Do you really think

I'm interested in relationships after being exposed to Mum's idea of one?'

'Point taken,' I said, 'but don't let her example stop you—'

'You can talk,' he butted in. 'You're probably as screwed up about it all as I am.'

'No, I'm not,' I told him. 'I have nothing against relationships.'

That was perfectly true. I'd had my share of dates and I enjoyed being one half of a couple. I just hadn't found the person who I wanted to be with for longer than a few months, that was all.

'And when the right chap comes along . . .' I went on.

'You'll know, will you?' Ryan laughed, but I didn't know what at.

'Yes,' I said, 'I will. Now, drink up. We're on watering duty tonight and you promised to cook me dinner.'

After another pasta-based meal I took a leap of faith and left Ryan home alone while I went to meet up with everyone in The Dragon. Initially I had been expecting him to want to tag along, but after another day in each other's company he said he was happy to 'just chill' (his words, not mine) and have an early night.

'So,' said Lou as we moved our glasses to make room for her mood board and piles of paint charts. 'What do you think?'

'Wow,' gasped Colin, as he took in the details of what she had sketched. 'Are you sure this is my shop?'

'It could be.' Lou smiled.

'I thought you were just going to slap some paint about,' said Mark, who had now been told all about the potential Reading Room renovation. 'This must have taken you ages, Lou.'

'Well . . .' Lou paused, and as I looked up I caught her staring fondly at the back of Colin's bent head, 'if a thing is worth doing . . .'

'It's worth doing properly,' finished Jacob.

'This is amazing,' Colin sighed.

So in awe of his beloved's creative talent he had missed the expression on Lou's face; but I had spotted it. It was more than obvious that she wanted him to like what she'd come up with.

'And the colours?' she asked huskily. 'Are they what you had in mind?'

'I honestly don't know what I had in mind,' Colin laughed. 'But this is perfect. I can't wait to get started!'

Lou was clearly delighted and the rest of us were in complete agreement. The only eyes at the table that didn't look impressed belonged to the dog, Gus, who Colin then passed between us as Lou told us about a trip to France she was planning and Mark extolled the delights of a new rye flour he had tracked down. After the chatter died down, the little dog still didn't look any happier.

'So,' said Colin as he tried to settle Gus comfortably on his lap. 'How are things with you, Poppy? How's Ryan?'

'Good,' I said, thinking back over the week, 'really good.

He's sorting his washing and can cook a bowl of pasta, so it's all heading in the right direction.'

'You're obviously teaching him some valuable life skills.' Colin smiled encouragingly. 'Have you been into the college yet?'

'No,' I said, 'not yet. There's no one about during the holidays so we've just spent the week settling in.'

I didn't mention the conversation we'd had about his dad, but I couldn't shake off the sad stuff Ryan was having to deal with as well as the downright horrible.

'Here's Neil,' said Mark, draining his pint. 'Finally. What time do you call this?'

'Sorry,' said Neil, holding up his hands, 'I didn't realise it was so late.'

'Do you want a drink?' Jacob offered.

'No thanks,' said Neil, 'I've just come to collect the Mrs.'

'Cheek,' said Mark, standing up. 'I can find my own way home.'

'I know you can, but I thought it would be nice to go to bed together for once.'

'Too much information!' Lou laughed.

'What I mean is' – Neil blushed – 'I finish work late and he gets up early so I thought—'

'It's all right,' I interjected, 'we know what you meant. I don't suppose you noticed music thumping over at my place, did you? Or gangs of teenagers marauding about?'

'Nope,' said Neil, 'all quiet on the Preston Front. In fact, I don't think there was even a light on.'

Ryan must have opted for that early night.

'Right,' said Mark, kissing us all as he edged his way round the table, 'night night, boys and girls.'

'I wish you wouldn't do that,' said Colin, quickly wiping his cheek.

'I know you do,' said Mark with a wink, 'that's why I do it!'

'And there was me thinking the troublesome neighbours had moved out,' Jacob said laughingly as the couple finally left.

'You look relieved, Pops,' said Lou. 'Did you think Ryan would be up to no good?'

'No,' I said, 'of course not.'

She raised her eyebrows and I felt my temper bristle a little. I knew that she had a brother who had been an absolute ratbag throughout his teens but I didn't want her judging Ryan based on her experiences. What my brother had had to deal with in the last couple of years and what her brother had got up to were poles apart.

'What's that look supposed to mean?' I snapped.

'Nothing,' she replied.

'You have no idea what he's been through,' I told her, my voice rising as I jumped to Ryan's defence. 'I'm only just beginning to realise the full extent of it myself.'

'I really didn't mean anything, Poppy,' she said again.

'Oh, never mind,' I muttered, 'I better get home.'

'It wasn't my intention to piss you off,' Lou said, sounding tearful. 'Don't go.'

'I know you didn't,' I conceded, feeling sorry for snapping.

'It's just that Ryan told me some stuff today and it's knocked me for six. I really should get back.'

'I'll come with you,' said Jacob. 'I could do with an early night ahead of the weekend you've got planned for me.'

I had suggested that all the Nightingale Square residents should get together to have an elderflower gathering over the weekend and then have an en-masse cordial-making session after. The weather looked as though it was going to be perfect and there was plenty to harvest. The elements had been behaving themselves beautifully since the late snowstorm and everything seemed to be celebrating with an early abundance as a result.

I told Lou I loved her plans for the Reading Room and we hugged before Jacob and I left. As we walked back to the square it became increasingly difficult to stave off the tears that had been threatening ever since Ryan had talked about his dad and how different his life had been since his death.

'Are you all right?' asked Jacob, when it became obvious that I wasn't.

'No,' I sniffed, 'I'm not. It's been one hell of a day.'

Had I not been narky with Lou back in the pub I would have made it to my bed before I blubbed, but the brief bout of tension between us had pushed me over the edge.

'Here,' said Jacob, passing me a bundle of tissues.

'Thanks,' I said, stopping to wipe my eyes and blow my nose. 'You don't strike me as the tissue-carrying type.'

'You're forgetting I'm a teacher,' he reminded me, 'of little ones.'

That was something I did quite often forget. I thought of him sitting in the garden and at the May Day celebration on the green, surrounded by youngsters as he reeled off one story after another and held them, and their mothers, enraptured right up until the end.

'Of course,' I said, throwing him a wobbly smile, 'and I would imagine that quite often requires a whole heap of tissues.'

'You'd be amazed what it requires,' he laughed.

He looked nothing like the bear I had encountered the day I moved into the square.

'You love your job, don't you?'

It was more of a statement than a question because the change in his expression at the mere mention of it was confirmation enough.

'I really do.' He grinned.

And I would lay my last pound on him being brilliant at it.

'Do you have any ambitions to move into school management?' I asked. 'Become a head teacher or something?'

I didn't really think that he would have. His love of grassroots teaching was obvious and I couldn't imagine that he would want to do anything that would take him out of the classroom, but questioning him was helping me set aside my sadness about Ryan and so I carried on.

'It's quite unusual to have a chap teaching really young children, isn't it? Or is that just an assumption I've made?'

It was a long time since I'd been in or at school; perhaps things had changed. I was so wrapped up in my thoughts,

I hadn't noticed that Jacob had all but stopped and that the change on his face was warning enough that he wasn't going to answer my questions.

'What?' I asked, taken aback by the sudden switch in him. 'What have I said?'

'Nothing,' he snapped, chewing furiously on his lower lip. 'It's nothing.'

'Sorry,' I said, 'I didn't mean anything—'

'I know,' he interrupted, 'I know you didn't. It's not your fault. It's mine. This is what happens when folk don't know . . .'

'When folk don't know what?' I asked, walking the couple of paces back to him and reaching for his hand. 'You know you can talk to me, Jacob, don't you?'

He looked down at my hand wrapped round his and took a step away, but I didn't let go. As well as both being in need of haircuts, my neighbour and my brother clearly both had secrets, and if I was going to be of any support to either of them, then it would probably help if I knew what they were.

'Jacob,' I said again, closing the gap between us, before cupping his face in my hands and forcing him to look at me.

'Don't,' he whispered, 'please.'

Had I gone too far? I went to move away but he moved a split second before me, grabbing my waist and pulling me closer. His eyes bored into mine and suddenly we weren't standing on a street on the outskirts of Norwich, we were teetering on the edge of somewhere much higher.,

Right up until that moment I had only felt a fleeting

attraction, but with his warm hands firmly planted on my bare skin, courtesy of where my shirt and jeans had parted company, and with my eyes locked on his, I could suddenly see exactly what everyone had been talking about.

'Poppy,' he groaned, his voice as thick as treacle, as he began to lower his head.

I knew he was going to kiss me. Part of me wanted him to and I was in absolutely no doubt at all that I would have kissed him back, but there was something unfathomable in his eyes, some emotion that I couldn't decipher at all, which made me pull away. But that wasn't the only thing. 'Sorry,' I said, jerking myself free to break the spell. 'I'm sorry.'

Jacob was a troubled man, a friend who didn't need to start up anything with a neighbour, someone who was supposed to be just a pal, so, as hard as it was, I forced myself to rein in my suddenly lustful feelings.

'Sorry,' I said again.

'It's okay.'

'That new guest beer must have befuddled my brain,' I joked. 'It was pretty potent.'

'Yeah,' he said, shaking his head, most likely to rid his own brain of whatever it was that had almost just happened between us. 'I probably had a pint more than I should.'

'I need to get back for Ryan,' I croaked.

'Yeah,' he said again, falling smoothly into step, 'I'll come with you.'

# Chapter 14

When we reached my door and I put the key in the lock, I expected Jacob to head for home but he stuck fast to my side.

'Do you want to come in?' I felt obliged to ask.

I didn't particularly want him to. Our almost-kiss had been a surprising end to what had been an emotional roller-coaster of a day and, Ryan aside, I really just wanted to be on my own.

'Just for a minute then,' Jacob said, as if I was forcing him over the threshold. 'Just to make sure everything's okay.'

I didn't know if he meant between us or with my brother, but I stepped aside to let him in and closed the door. The house was in darkness, so we walked quietly along the hall to the kitchen.

I busied myself filling the kettle and sorting mugs while Jacob looked around, his eyes drawn to the spice- and herb-filled containers and rows of neatly lined-up Kilner jars that glistened in the artificial light.

'Did you make these?' he asked.

'Yep.' I nodded. 'They're chutney and pickles and a few different relishes.'

'Nothing sweet?'

'No,' I said, wrinkling my nose. 'My baking skills are crap and I still haven't mastered a successful jam. Although I'm hoping to get in plenty of practice now I have access to all that fruit in the garden.'

'Perhaps it's because you're sweet enough already,' said Jacob, before rolling his eyes in what looked like a mixture of apology and embarrassment.

'What a line,' I guffawed. 'Did you *really* just say that?'

'Shh,' Jacob said laughingly, pointing at the ceiling, 'you'll wake Ryan.'

'Look,' I said, handing him a mug and thinking that we should clear the air, 'about what just happened, out in the street, I really think we should talk about it.'

Jacob shook his head and half-turned away so I couldn't see his face. I knew he wouldn't want to, but I didn't want to leave things as they were. I opened my mouth to get the ball rolling but then I realised something.

'What's wrong?' Jacob frowned as I suddenly banged down my mug and rushed back into the hall.

'No shoes,' I gasped, my heart thumping even harder than it had been earlier. 'He always leaves them in the way.'

I raced up the stairs and flung open the door to Ryan's room. 'Is he there?' Jacob called after me.

'No,' I shouted back, 'no, he's not.'

I tripped back down again, my hands shaking as my brain conjured up all manner of horrific and far-fetched scenarios about what could be happening to my baby brother out in the city streets.

'He told me he was having an early night,' I said. 'He said he was staying here.'

Jacob didn't comment.

'Where the hell is he?' I sobbed. 'He's my responsibility. If anything has happened to him—'

Jacob put up a hand and I stopped, one ear cocked to listen to the sudden noise beyond the front door. I wrenched the door open and found Ryan, looking decidedly worse for wear and about to fall inside.

My relief at seeing him was quickly tempered by the state he was in.

'I was hoping you'd still be up,' he slurred, his breath stinking of fags and booze, 'I think I forgot my key.'

'I didn't give you a key,' I snapped. 'Where the hell have you been?'

'Hello, Jacob,' he said, knocking me to one side. 'What are you doing here at this time, mate? I hope you haven't been taking advantage of my lovely sister.'

'Oh God,' I groaned.

'Ignore him,' said Jacob, sounding every bit as furious as I felt, 'he's drunk.'

'Oh, is he?' I asked, wide-eyed. 'I hadn't realised.'

Ryan began to laugh and I mouthed 'sorry' to Jacob, who steered my brother towards the kitchen.

'I'd really rather like to go to bed,' he said, 'my head's a bit whooshy.'

'Where have you been?' I demanded. 'Who have you been drinking with?'

It was pointless, of course. He was in no state to answer.

'Let's get you some water,' said Jacob – 'and a bowl,' he added in an aside to me – 'and then we'll get you up to bed.'

'You're a good mate,' said Ryan, sounding tearful. 'Isn't he a good mate, Poppy?'

Ordinarily I would have felt a spark of happiness when he got my name right, but all I could feel was hopeful that he'd hurl in the plastic bowl I was going to dig out from under the sink rather than all over Kate's lovely carpet.

'Yes,' I said, 'he's a good mate.'

'I'll get him upstairs,' Jacob said to me, draping Ryan's arm round his shoulder.

'I can manage,' said Ryan stoically, 'I can do it.'

He made an attempt to walk but his legs buckled.

'Oh, would you look at that?' He giggled. 'I don't think I can.'

Jacob grabbed him again and they shuffled off, looking like some wobbly overgrown three-legged pairing.

'I'm sorry, Pops,' Ryan called back to me, 'but I don't think I'll be able to make the elderflower thingy you've got planned for tomorrow.'

'Oh, you will,' I told him. 'In fact, I'll make personally sure that you're one of the first there.'

*

Ryan should have been grateful for the thick covering of cloud that saved him from being blinded by the sun when I sent his curtains rattling back along their pole and threw open the window bright and early the following morning.

'Oh my God,' he yelped, pulling the pillow over his face. 'What are you doing?'

'Getting you up,' I said brusquely. 'Come on.'

'I can't,' he whimpered. 'I'm dying.'

'Painkillers are on the side and there's a fresh glass of water,' I told him sternly. 'Get your shades on and get your arse in the shower. We're leaving in half an hour.'

No one was more surprised than I was when he appeared in the kitchen, washed, dressed and walking as if the ground beneath his feet was made of marshmallows rather than oak.

'I suppose you want to talk about what happened?' he asked, wincing as he lowered himself into a chair and I plonked a plate in front of him before getting up to make toast.

'Not really.'

'Oh,' he said, sounding slightly more perky. 'Okay, cool.'

'Not cool at all,' I said calmly. 'But as you lied to me about staying at home, I can't imagine you're suddenly going to have an attack of conscience now and tell me the truth, so there's no point discussing it.'

I added a thin covering of spread to the granary toast and put a slice on Ryan's plate. I can't say he looked particularly impressed, but given the state of him that was hardly a surprise.

'You abused my trust,' I told him, 'and if it happens again,

I will report Mum to social services and, given your age, you'll probably be taken into care.'

It felt mean saying it, especially given everything he'd been through, but he needed to know I meant business. Not that I ever would have got social services involved.

'But—'

'No buts, Ryan. You can't just come here and take advantage. Now hurry up and eat that because I'm not leaving without you and as this was my idea, I can hardly be late. I have a problem letting people down, even if you don't.'

It might have been a harsh telling-off, but I wanted to let him know that I wasn't a pushover and that I wouldn't tolerate being messed about. The thought had already crossed my mind that I should have taken Lou's cautionary attitude a bit more seriously, but I hoped that my disappointment had touched my brother far more deeply than if I had bawled him out like Mum would have done. Had she even noticed him coming home roaring drunk, that is.

I'd told Jacob that Ryan and I would walk to the garden with him, but he was already halfway round the green by the time I had locked the front door.

'Jacob!' I called. 'Wait up.'

He stopped, but didn't look round, and I got the distinct impression that had I not shouted he would have carried on.

'Come on, Ryan,' I scolded, 'don't dawdle.'

'How's he feeling this morning?' Jacob asked as we walked on together with Ryan trailing behind.

'About as hung over as you'd expect,' I whispered. 'I've kept my cool with him though, and let him know that I won't tolerate it happening again.'

'Good,' said Jacob, 'I daresay you're beginning to think that you should cut him some slack because of everything he's been through.'

The thought had crossed my mind.

'But don't. The last thing a lad in Ryan's position needs is mixed messages, okay?'

'Okay,' I agreed.

I could see the sense in what he was saying, but I was also a little disconcerted that he had read my mind so adeptly. I would have to watch that now that I could see him both as my troubled neighbour in need of a shoulder *and* my dishy neighbour with strong warm hands.

'Come on, Ryan,' Jacob called sharply over to my brother, 'look alive.'

'I can't,' he whinged. 'I'm dying.'

Looking at his pasty complexion and shaky gait, I wouldn't have been surprised if he was.

The grounds of Prosperous Place, combined with the green back in the square and the surrounding side roads, had more than enough elderflowers for us to harvest and everyone agreed that it would be lovely to make their own orange- and lemon-infused batches, rather than pitching in for one communal effort. That way, we could share and swap, to see if there were any differences or preferences when it came to using more or less zest and including or omitting the citric acid that was an optional ingredient.

The beautifully refurbished and well-equipped bothy meant that there was plenty of room for everyone to take turns and even space to store the bottles, along with the associated equipment, should we decide to repeat the experience again next spring.

'Coming?' I asked Ryan, once the buckets and secateurs had been handed out.

'Would it be all right if I stayed?' he asked, sounding almost meek. 'I promise I won't wander off again.'

I was about to say I didn't have a problem with him wandering off, as long as it wasn't too far, as long as he didn't smoke, drink or ingest anything he wasn't supposed to, but Graham got in first.

'If you're not helping with the harvesting, Ryan,' he said keenly, 'you could clean the hens out, if you don't mind? It'll save me a job later.'

'What a kind lad,' said Carole, joining her husband and liberating the bucket they had been assigned from his grip. She then whisked me off before I had the chance to either gloat or commiserate.

The abundant crop of elderflowers meant the buckets filled up fast and there was plenty left over; good foraging practice so that neither us nor Mother Nature went short.

'How's it going with Ryan?' Kate asked as she and Luke snipped their way over to where I was helping Harold fill his bucket.

'All right.' I nodded, smiling at the sight of baby Abigail. She was sound asleep, snugly strapped into the carrier on Kate's chest. Heather's twin boys, cocooned in their buggy, didn't sound quite so content, but she was happy to let them grizzle while she carried on with the job in hand.

'Just all right?' Kate questioned. 'You seemed to be getting along famously last week.'

'Oh, we were,' I told her, 'we are. It's just taking some getting used to, having him around, and I'm sure if you asked him he'd say much the same.'

'He looked a bit under the weather when I saw him earlier,' commented Lisa wryly. 'Our Tamsin has stayed behind to keep him company, so if the poor chap is feeling below par he'll be done for by the time we get back. She can talk the hind legs off a donkey, that one. I've no idea where she gets it from.'

She stopped to draw breath and Kate and I exchanged a look.

'Oh, all right,' said Lisa, 'point taken.'

We decided not to rush the process and spent the rest of the day pottering in the garden and taking our turn at the grater, filling bowls with the zest of the oranges and lemons. The air was soon filled with a strong citrus tang and the addition of boiling water only served to intensify the delicious scent.

'Having fun?' I asked Jacob, who had hung around with everyone else for the entire day.

He might not have noticed but I had been keeping an eye on him. Not because I liked looking at him of course, just because I wanted to make sure he was okay. I had got used to seeing the sunnier side of my neighbour, but since our close encounter the previous evening he seemed to have regressed somewhat. He was fine with everyone else, but I couldn't shake off the feeling that he had been avoiding me.

'Yeah,' he said with a shrug, smiling tightly and avoiding my gaze. 'More than Ryan, anyway.'

I looked over to the hen run where my brother was slumped in a chair feigning sleep in an attempt to throw Tamsin's attention off, and laughed. I turned back to carry on talking but Jacob had gone.

'Is that it?' asked Heather, pulling my attention back to the job in hand.

'That's it,' I said as I set about arranging the bowls of stewing elderflowers on the bothy bench. 'All ready for decanting tomorrow.'

'It was so easy,' she said with a laugh. 'I had no idea.'

'And easy to photograph,' said Lisa, scrolling through the shots she had taken of the beautiful flowers. 'These will be perfect to add to the portfolio for the council.'

'I can't help thinking we're on to a winner with this place,' said Heather, crossing her fingers.

'Me too,' Lisa giggled.

I was about to ask the pair if they'd be interested in taking part in a similar session later in the year, when we could make some relishes and chutneys – I was all for spreading the homespun and home-made love – but I was interrupted by Jacob and Ryan's raised voices from over near the hen run.

'What on earth?' Heather gasped as Tamsin left Ryan's side and rushed back to her mother.

I sped over, keen to keep the argument, if that's what it was, quiet. It had been a wonderful day spent in the company of my friends and neighbours and I didn't want it spoiled for anyone. I didn't want Jacob and Ryan falling out either. I was relying on Jacob to become my second pair of eyes, ears and helping hands when I went back to work on Monday. I knew he would be at school for a lot of the time, but he had still offered to be about whenever he could.

I had almost reached them when Jacob stepped forward and muttered something under his breath that I couldn't make out.

'Do you know what, mate,' Ryan shot back, the last remaining dregs of his hangover miraculously forgotten and his voice nowhere near as quiet as Jacob's. 'If that's what you really think, then I'll just leave, shall I?'

'What?' I stammered. 'Leave and go where?'

Ryan jumped back in surprise. I don't think he'd realised that I was right there.

'Jacob thinks I shouldn't be here,' he said, striding across the garden and disappearing through the gate.

'What?' I said again, heading in the same direction. 'Ryan, wait up!'

I was out of breath and almost as far as the green when I eventually caught up with him.

'What the hell did he say to you?' I demanded.

Ryan spun round. His expression was a mixture of aggression and anguish.

'He said' – he swallowed, taking a breath – 'he said that I don't deserve to have a sister like you, he said that I should go home and let you get on with your own life.'

I couldn't believe it. What on earth would have prompted Jacob to say anything like that? Ryan must have got the wrong end of the stick.

'Are you sure you didn't misunderstand?' I asked, desperate to get to the bottom of what had gone on before it became too awkward to put right.

'Of course I didn't!' Ryan shouted, letting out a strangled sob. 'He couldn't have said it any clearer.'

'I'm sorry.'

'No.' He sniffed, wiping his nose on his sleeve. 'I'm sorry. I should never have come. You've got a great life here; you could have a great life with someone like him. You don't need me hanging around messing things up and stopping you getting on. Mum was right, I do ruin everything.'

In that moment I didn't want any sort of life with someone like Jacob. I hated him for making my little brother feel that he was no better than the waste of space our mother always said he was. To my mind that was both a despicable and an unforgivable thing to do, and coming from someone who I thought had Ryan's best interests at heart made it all the worse.

'No,' I said, pulling my distraught brother into a tight hug, 'you don't, Ryan, you really don't. You're a good guy and you haven't ruined anything and until I've found a way to prove that to you, you're aren't going anywhere.'

# Chapter 15

Jacob's cruel words to Ryan had awoken the protective tigress in me and, needless to say, after I had settled him back at the house, calmed him down and made him promise not to disappear, I went back to the garden to seek out the friend who had now turned into prey. I wasn't expecting to find him still there, but he was.

'What the hell is wrong with you?' I demanded, making sure we were out of earshot of everyone else.

'Look, Poppy—'

'No,' I hotly interrupted, 'you look. You told me you were going to help out with Ryan, but for some reason you've gone out of your way to knock him down, just as I was trying to build him up. I can't believe you'd do that. You know he's a mess at the moment and that I'm doing my best. If telling him to stop wasting my time and that he doesn't deserve my support is your idea of helping then you can keep it, thanks. I'll handle things on my own.'

'Is that what he said?'

'Yes,' I shot back, 'and a whole lot more besides. I suppose you're going to stand there and tell me he's lying now on top of everything else.'

Jacob chewed his lip and took a deep breath.

'No,' he sighed. 'No. I'm not going to say anything of the sort.'

'Good,' I said. 'I think it best if you just leave us both alone from now on. Go back to being the moody, miserable bugger you were when you moved here. You were better at that.'

Not surprisingly, I didn't catch much sleep the next two nights. I'd gone back to the bothy to help with the elderflower bottling on Sunday and was unsurprised that Jacob had chosen to stay away.

I dragged myself out of bed just after six on Monday morning, and felt a mix of anger and relief when I tripped over Ryan's trainers as usual. I made my way to the kitchen, the smell of coffee growing stronger with every step.

'I hope this is all right?' Ryan asked sheepishly as he pulled out a chair and steered me into it. 'After all the trouble I seem to have caused, I thought it was the least I could do.'

The table was set for a breakfast that included orange juice, a variety of cereals and a rack of slightly overdone toast.

'Right.' I nodded, wondering if I was actually still in one of the strange dreams I'd been having. 'I didn't expect you to be up.'

I had been thinking about what Lou had said, about Ryan's love of lie-ins being a blessing when it came to work and non-college days, because I would know where he was, but he sounded and looked so contrite, wringing the tea towel in his hands and looking hopeful, that I didn't mind that he had got up extra-early. I didn't mind at all.

'And just you remember,' I told him so he knew that his effort really meant something, 'Jacob caused far more trouble than you on Saturday, so please stop worrying about it all and certainly don't dwell on what he said.'

'Okay,' said Ryan, pouring us both coffee. 'You know, I don't set out to make a mess of things, it just sort of happens.'

'I think being a teenager is a guarantee of messing some stuff up,' I told him. 'I know I did and given the circumstances you're operating under, I think you're allowed the occasional slip-up.'

Ryan looked a little more cheerful.

'Just don't make a habit of it,' I quickly added. 'And we'll be fine.'

Ryan was washing the breakfast dishes when I set off to work.

'I'll text you later this morning,' I told him, 'to let you know what time my lunch break will be and then you can walk down to meet me. I'm going to ring college to arrange these meetings too, but you can inform them of your change of address.'

'Okay,' he agreed. 'I haven't got to be in until later this afternoon and then only for an hour.'

'In that case,' I said, 'we'll grab a sandwich from Blossom's and you can tell me what you've been up to all morning.'

'It won't be anything bad,' he promised.

'I should think not.' I smiled, banishing my bad dreams. 'Not even you could get into mischief first thing on a Monday morning.'

At least I hoped he couldn't.

'And if there's time I'll introduce you to my friends Lou and Colin,' I carried on. 'But that will depend on how busy work is.'

Lou, Colin and I had talked about my brother but they had yet to meet him.

'They don't live in the square but they have their own shops along the same street as Greengages.'

'What sort of shops?'

'Colin has a second-hand bookshop.'

Ryan feigned a yawn, which I ignored.

'And Lisa has a retro, vintage place called Back in Time.'

'Cool.' He nodded.

Clearly the allure of eighties video games and the like was more appealing than the written word.

'Right,' I said. 'Okay. I'll see you later.'

'I suppose I've blown it as far as going to the youth centre's concerned, haven't I?' Ryan blurted out.

'I don't see why,' I told him.

'Because of Jacob. I can hardly go if he's going to be there. Can I?'

I was still furious with Jacob. The words I'd thrown at

him hadn't purged my temper at all. The youth centre was potentially going to help my brother far more than I could, but now that Ryan had been bawled out by the guy who held the key to the professional support on offer there, I could understand his reluctance to go.

'Maybe we could go together,' I suggested. 'Ask if anyone knows when Jacob is likely to be there, and you can just avoid those times.'

I wasn't sure how the centre managers would take to knowing that Jacob had had a falling-out with just the sort of kid he was trained to support. Not that I would be telling them, but it wasn't an ideal situation to find ourselves in.

Ryan looked horrified by my suggestion of going together and when I thought about it I supposed it would look a bit tragic.

'Actually,' I said, to save him the embarrassment of finding the words to ditch me, 'what I meant was, you could head down there on your own; I know you don't need me holding your hand. You could go when Jacob is at work. That way you definitely won't run the risk of bumping into him.'

The relief on his face was instantaneous.

'Perhaps I'll do that some time this week,' he said, turning his attention back to the dishes. 'On one of the days when I don't have to be in college.'

'Yeah,' I said, gathering up my bag and checking I had my phone, 'that'd be good. Oh,' I added, 'I'll have to lock the front door now and leave you the key for the back otherwise you won't be able to leave.'

'Okay, thanks.'

'And don't forget to shut the windows.'

Ryan looked at me again and rolled his eyes.

'I won't,' he tutted.

There was no sign of Jacob as I set off but, given everything that had happened, all I felt was relief.

Pushing open the door of Greengages was a full-on assault on the senses and as I breathed in the fresh scent of the fruit and vegetables lining the shelves and arranged my new batch of recipe cards along the counter, I realised just how pleased I was to be back at work and how much I had missed the routine, as well as Harry and the customers.

'What have you got there then?' Harry asked with a nod to the cards when he came through from the back carrying two steaming mugs of tea. 'And how's that brother of yours settling in?'

'These are for elderflower cordial,' I explained, showing Harry one of the cards. 'We had such a great time making the stuff in the community garden,' I went on, forcing myself not to think about how the day had ended, 'and there are still so many flowers about that I thought I'd see if anyone else might fancy having a go.'

'Sounds like a good idea to me.' He beamed. 'Now come on, drink this tea and we'll get on. It would be nice to get some work out of you considering you've hardly been here for the last goodness knows how long.'

Fortunately, I knew he was only pulling my leg.

The morning was busy and as my lunch hour drew closer I began to watch the clock. I had texted Ryan to ask him to come over early so I would have a chance to introduce him to Harry before we went down to Blossom's, but there was still no sign of him.

'Don't look so worried,' said Harry, chuckling. 'He'll be here.'

I had told him a bit about Ryan's first week, but I hadn't shared the details of the night he had gone out and got drunk, so as far as Harry was concerned my furrowed brow and rolling stomach were completely unnecessary. Thankfully, it turned out that they were.

'Here he is,' I said, relief coursing through my entire body as I spotted him through the window and rushed out from behind the counter. 'What the . . .'

The words died in my throat as he pushed open the door and leant inside but didn't actually come in.

'What's your policy on dogs?' he asked, grinning from ear to ear.

My gaze travelled from his happy face back to my boss.

'Come in, lad,' Harry said welcomingly, 'it's all quiet so I think we'll risk it.'

'Is that . . . ?' I said, the words trailing off as I realised that it was.

'I take it you know Gus?' Ryan asked, still beaming.

I knew him very well, but this perky, bouncy, vocal little chap was a complete stranger.

'I do know Gus,' I said, kneeling down to fuss him, 'but I don't think this can be him.'

'Isn't he great?' Ryan laughed as the dog looked up at him with what I could only describe as unadulterated adoration.

Gus's soppy expression reminded me a bit of Tamsin's. Or should I say Tamsin's up until the moment Ryan and Jacob had their falling-out. Her loyalties had clearly been torn between her two favourite people.

'Yes,' I said, stroking Gus's silky ears. 'But how come you've got him and what have you been feeding him to make him look so happy?'

Ryan explained that he had left the square early, after locking up at home, to see if he could find either Lou or Colin's shop before the two of us went for lunch. Evidently, he had found the Reading Room.

'You didn't tell me what it was called,' he said, 'but I didn't think there could be that many second-hand bookshops around here so I thought I'd just go in and introduce myself.'

My face must have been a picture.

'That was all right, wasn't it?' Ryan asked. 'I know you said you might be pushed for time.'

'Yes,' I quickly answered, 'of course.'

I was amazed he had the confidence to do that. I certainly wouldn't have at his age.

'I'd only made it as far as the desk at the back where your mate Colin was sitting – looking bored off his tits by the way,' he added in an aside.

I shook my head but I knew it was an accurate description of what my brother would have seen.

'When this little fella leapt on me and he hasn't stopped fussing since.'

I'd never seen Gus so animated. Not even when Colin's uncle was alive. He'd always been a sedate and somewhat withdrawn little character – Gus, not the uncle – but this chap was indulging in what was more puppy than fully grown pooch behaviour. There was obviously something about my brother that had been responsible for the unexpected transformation.

'So,' I asked again as I still hadn't had a proper answer, 'how come you've got him?'

'I told Colin who I was, obviously,' Ryan continued, 'and asked if he would mind me bringing Gus to have lunch with you. I'm going to take him back before I go to college. That was all right, wasn't it?' He frowned. 'I forgot you said we were going to eat at the bakers.'

'Don't worry, lad,' Harry reassured him, 'they've got tables out the front.'

During lunch, I explained that I had left a message at the college, what Lou had planned for Colin's shop and a little of Gus's sad history. Ryan was very keen on the makeover plans but it was Gus who captured his imagination.

'Well,' he said wisely, 'perhaps that was it then.'

'What?'

'Perhaps poor little Gus realised that we're kindred spirits.'

'In what way?'

'Well, we're both grieving, aren't we?' he said huskily, scooping the little dog up and lifting his chin as Gus tried to lick him. 'Perhaps he spotted some of the sadness in me that he feels himself.'

'Oh, Ryan,' I said, tears misting my vision. I still felt guilty for not doing more to help after Mum had finally told me what had happened. 'I'm so sorry.'

'It's all right,' he said, his gaze moving from me to somewhere over my shoulder, 'it's fine.'

I hated that word. When someone said they were fine it generally meant anything but; however, a tap on my shoulder denied me the opportunity to say anything further.

'Hey, you.'

It was Lou.

'Hey.' I smiled. Have you shut the shop?'

She was usually so busy that she opted to eat *in situ* rather than close the place up.

'I have,' she said, shuffling into the empty seat between Ryan and me. It had been Gus's but now he was ensconced on my brother's lap and being fed wholly unsuitable titbits from his plate. 'Colin phoned. He said there'd been a miracle and if I wanted to see the person responsible then I better get my butt down to Blossom's. And here you are,' she said, beaming, turning her kohl-rimmed eyes on Ryan.

Ryan slurped at the straw of his Coke and began to choke. I'd seen my beautiful friend have this impact before. Not usually on someone as young as Ryan; but a figure like hers, coupled with her ready smile and confidence, never went unnoticed.

'Hi,' said Ryan, ducking his head and turning a shade redder, 'I'm Ryan.'

'Lou,' she said, holding out a hand for him to shake, but Gus began to enthusiastically lick it before he had the chance to reach for it. 'Crikey,' she said laughingly, 'it really is a miracle!'

After lunch Ryan went to check out Back in Time with Lou and Gus, and I went back to work. It was obvious that my brother had been a hit with both my friends, which, given Lou's initial misgivings about me inviting him to stay, was a relief.

'He's a lovely lad,' said Harry, when Ryan messaged at five to say that he'd meet me at the Reading Room and we'd walk home together.

'Thanks,' I said, feeling proud. 'He's a good kid.'

'I've got a job,' Ryan exclaimed the second I arrived at Colin's.

'Only a temporary one,' said Colin, 'but it's his if he wants it.'

I was thrown. Colin's lack of customers and footfall certainly didn't justify the services of an assistant and, given Ryan's response that morning when I'd told him the shop sold second-hand books, I couldn't imagine he'd have the wherewithal to shift any more titles than Colin.

'Isn't that brilliant?' Ryan beamed.

At least I couldn't moan about his work ethic – he was certainly keen to get stuck into whatever it was that Colin had in mind.

'I'm going to be helping out with the makeover. Lou says I can do the donkey work while Colin sorts the stock and she faffs about with the finishing touches.'

I couldn't help but laugh at the thought of how Lou would react if she heard Ryan describing her very honed and highly skilled shop-dressing services as 'faffing about'.

'I'm going to be pulling the bookcases apart,' Ryan went on, 'and sanding and painting them before repositioning them. The place could do with an update, don't you think? No offence,' he quickly added.

'None taken,' said Colin, pushing his glasses back up his nose. 'I can't wait to get on with it but until today—'

'Fortunately for me,' Ryan cut in.

'. . . I haven't been able to find anyone willing to help out,' Colin carried on. 'I want it all to happen as quickly as possible once I make a start and,' he looked over to where Ryan was now rolling about with a panting Gus, 'your brother has energy in abundance, Poppy.'

'Not to mention the skills,' Ryan added. 'Thanks to Dad, I can do this sort of thing standing on my head.'

'Brilliant,' I said, smiling, because it was.

This was just the sort of project to keep my brother mentally and physically occupied when he wasn't hitting the books. I'd read somewhere that it was called 'thinkering'.

'This'll show Jacob,' I said in an aside to Ryan, 'won't it?'

'What's wrong with Jacob?' Colin frowned.

'We'll tell you later, won't we, Ryan?' I said, but Ryan didn't answer.

He'd turned an interesting shade of red and gone back to playing with Gus.

# Chapter 16

The rest of the week passed without incident and settled into a satisfactory routine that saw Ryan attending all his lectures as well as making a start on Colin's shop makeover. It wasn't for want of trying, but I still hadn't heard anything back from the college. I was beginning to wonder if the problem was as bad as Mum had made out. By Friday afternoon, I was almost back to my former chilled self. Almost.

'You're early,' I said as my brother appeared in the shop a little after twelve. 'What's up?' I frowned when he didn't answer. 'What's going on?' I persisted.

Even Gus, usually so excitable and full of high-energy bounce these days, was looking a little apprehensive as he sat at my brother's side. I hoped Ryan hadn't missed an assignment deadline or sold one of Colin's precious first editions for the price of a car boot bargain.

'I've done something,' Ryan said, biting his lip, 'bit

of a spur-of-the-moment thing really, and I'm not sure I should have.'

Oh God, he had. He'd practically given away one of Colin's treasured tomes.

'Well, out with it, lad,' said Harry. 'What have you done? I can't imagine it's anything too terrible.'

I could. My brain was encouraging me to imagine it was something very terrible indeed.

'What have you got there?' I asked.

Ryan looked down at his hand.

'The keys to the Reading Room,' he said huskily.

'Have you locked your boss in or out?' Harry chuckled.

'Neither.' Ryan swallowed, looking deadly serious.

'Whatever's happened?' I asked again.

Seeing his unchanged expression, I was really beginning to worry.

'Colin had a phone call,' he explained, sounding choked. 'About his dad. He's had a stroke or something and his sister asked him to go back home straight away.'

'Oh, my goodness,' I gasped. 'Poor Colin.'

'He's locked up the shop and has asked me to take the keys to Lou,' Ryan carried on. 'That's where I'm heading now.'

'So,' I said, thinking that didn't sound like Ryan had done anything bad at all. I looked uncertainly down at Gus. 'Has Colin gone already?'

'Yes,' said Ryan, following my line of sight, 'he's just going back to his place to pick up a few things and then he's driving straight down.'

'So how come you've got Gus?' I frowned.

'Well, that's the thing, you see.' Ryan winced, shuffling from one foot to the other. 'Colin was in such a state and in such a rush that I offered to take care of Gus until he comes back.'

I nodded as the penny began to drop.

'It seemed like a good idea at the time, one less thing for Colin to worry about, and being around the family at such a difficult time was obviously not the best environment for Gus to be in.' The little dog's ears pricked up in response to hearing his name. 'But as I began to walk down here I realised that I shouldn't have offered to take him without talking to you first.'

'But what else could you do?' said Harry, looking from me to Ryan and back again.

'Exactly,' I said, smiling.

'But what if Kate has a no-pet policy,' said Ryan, looking genuinely worried in spite of my smile. 'I'll have to hand him over to Lou and I'm not sure he'd like that.'

I wasn't sure *she* would either.

'I'm pretty certain,' I said reassuringly, 'that given the circumstances, Kate won't mind us having a house guest at all, especially such a well-mannered and house-trained one.'

'Colin wouldn't trust that dog with just anyone, you know,' said Harry. 'You should be proud of yourself, lad. I'm sure your sister is.'

'I certainly am,' I agreed. 'Now, you go and tell Lou what's going on and by the time you get back we'll be able to go for lunch.'

As soon as Ryan had gone, I fired off a text to Colin. I knew he wouldn't see it for a while because he was driving, but I wanted to reassure him that I was happy for Ryan to look after Gus and that we were all here should he need us to do anything else.

'You aren't still worrying about having Gus in the house, are you?' I asked Ryan when he and Lou came back. He did look rather flushed.

Lou shook her head behind my brother's back and gave him a nudge. Ryan just looked at the floor.

'It's not that,' said Ryan. 'It's something else. I've done something else I shouldn't have and now I feel even worse about it.'

Good grief. Was that not the same line he'd turned up with less than an hour ago? Would we ever manage a completely stress-free day?

'Well,' I said, trying to rally him, 'you came in here earlier and said something similar and that turned out to be okay, didn't it?'

Ryan shrugged.

'I'm sure that whatever it is, it can't be that bad.'

Lou's expression was now set to grim. Clearly she didn't agree with my optimistic take on the situation at all.

'Why don't you finish up for the day?' Harry kindly offered. 'We're closing at three today anyway so I can go and check out that new wholesaler. You'd only be back for an hour after your break, so it's hardly worth it.'

'That sounds like a good idea,' said Lou. 'We can pick up

Gus's basket and stuff from the Reading Room and I can check Colin shut everything up properly.'

'All right,' I agreed.

Had it not been for the creases furrowing Ryan's brow I wouldn't have let myself be talked into taking yet more hours off, but clearly whatever was worrying him now was far more serious than having an impromptu sleepover with his canine companion.

'We'll go to The Dragon,' I said, collecting my bag from the back room. 'Something tells me I might need a drink to go with this confession, Ryan.'

'And chips,' added Lou, trying to lighten the moment. 'Definitely more chips.'

But as we settled ourselves at our usual table, though not at our usual hour, I thought a stiff drink and a bowl of chips probably weren't going to cut it. The fact that Ryan hadn't put a foot wrong all week, and the knowledge that everyone, even Lou, had been singing his praises, weren't enough to convince me that this was going to be a fuss over nothing.

'So,' I said once the food had arrived, drawing in a deep breath, 'what's up? What else have you done that you're feeling so woebegone about? I can't imagine it's anything too horrendous, Ryan. You're the talk of our little row of shops this week and all of it has been good.'

I knew I was rambling. The way Lou raised her eyebrows left me in no doubt of that. I stuffed a too-hot chip in my mouth to shut me up.

'That's what's made it all even worse,' Ryan choked, directing his words at the top of Gus's head rather than at me. 'The fact that everyone's been telling me how helpful I am and how good I've been to carry on at college has made me feel like even more of an arse today than ever before.'

'And quite rightly so,' Lou agreed.

'Lou!' I scolded.

'You don't know what he's done yet,' she said sagely.

'It's Jacob,' Ryan blurted out before my brain had a chance to try to imagine.

'What about him?'

I'd managed to avoid my opinionated neighbour all week. Not only had I timed my walks to work to miss him but I'd also been pretty eagle-eyed on the garden front. My curtain-twitching could have given Carole a run for her money, but I had been determined not to turn up at the garden for watering duty when Jacob was anywhere in the vicinity.

'The row we had—' Ryan continued.

'I've already told you,' I interrupted, 'I don't want you worrying about any of that. He was bang out or order and—'

'Will you just shut up and listen,' Lou hissed.

I reached for another chip.

'I *might* not have told you the whole truth about what really happened,' said Ryan, looking more than a little shamefaced.

Lou tutted loudly.

'All right,' he relented, 'I *definitely* didn't tell you *any* of the truth about what happened.'

My stomach turned and I pushed my glass away, bracing myself for whatever came next.

'Go on,' I said.

Ryan wriggled a little in his seat, his eyes still looking anywhere but at me.

'I was talking to Tamsin,' he began.

I could picture him and the girl, who was smitten with him, standing next to the hen run deep in conversation. That was when Jacob had gone over to them and begun bawling my brother out.

'And it was stupid really . . .'

'Go on.'

'I don't know why,' he said, mystified by whatever it was that he had done, 'but I was trying to look hard, I suppose. Putting on a bit of an act.'

'For Tamsin?'

He nodded.

'What did you say to her?'

I hoped it wasn't anything inappropriate. He was older than her, after all.

'First off' – he swallowed nervously – 'I said that I hated the garden and the square and wished I'd never come here.'

I couldn't believe it. I knew he had been feeling resentful that I'd pulled rank and made him join in with things when he was suffering with a hangover, but hate was a strong word to bandy about.

'I also said that you were actually no better than Mum. That you were treating me like a kid and that you were being a right bitch,' he said in a gabbled rush, 'and that if things stayed as they were then I'd be packing up and moving on.'

My mouth fell open, but no words came out. I didn't know what to say.

'I didn't mean it,' Ryan hurried on. 'Not any of it. It was all crap. I admit I was pissed off that you'd put your foot down after the drinking, but I did get why you'd done it. I suppose I was just spouting off to make myself sound like the moody guy that Tamsin was so obviously crushing on. I had no idea that Jacob was right there, listening to every word. I had no idea anyone could hear me. Not that that would have made it all right,' he quickly added.

The thought of Ryan saying those things, regardless of whether he meant them or not, made me feel sick.

'So afterwards,' I said, the words sticking in my throat as I tried not to show him just how hurt I was feeling, 'when I chased after you, when you ran off and then told me what Jacob had said . . .'

Ryan nodded.

'Was all that a lie as well?'

I couldn't bear to think about how I'd spoken to Jacob back in the garden. The realisation that Ryan may well have lied about what my neighbour had said was turning the tigress in me back into a kitten.

'Had he said those things to you or not, Ryan?'

Part of me wanted him to have said them, if only to justify my own harsh words and behaviour. I had missed Jacob more than I would care to admit, and the thought that I hadn't needed to – well, it didn't warrant thinking about.

'Sort of,' he croaked. 'But not in the way I made out. I twisted it all to get me off the hook and I've been avoiding him in case the real story came out ever since.'

He slumped back in his chair and I wondered if Jacob had actually been avoiding us rather than the other way round. Had it been anyone else in his position I was pretty certain they would have dropped Ryan in it to save themselves, but Jacob hadn't done that. He'd listened to what I had to say and let my brother get away with it for some reason.

'I can't believe you did that.' I swallowed.

'I'm so sorry,' said Ryan, finally raising his eyes to meet mine. 'I know it was a stupid thing to do but I was so angry at being called out that I just did what I could to save face. It was a stupid knee-jerk reaction and I let it go too far. I really am sorry.'

'And in the process, you've hurt me and Jacob and probably upset Tamsin.'

'I'm sorry,' he said again.

'You do understand that we're trying to help you, don't you, Ryan?'

'Yes,' he whispered, 'I do and I really didn't mean any of what I said, not a word of it. I've been trying to make amends ever since.'

'So, everything you've done this week has been because you've had a guilty conscience,' I said, my voice rising, 'none of it, not my breakfasts, not taking on Gus, going to college or helping Colin has been genuine at all?'

'It has,' Ryan insisted. 'It has. I admit it started off that first morning because I was feeling guilty but since I walked down to the Reading Room and met Colin and Gus, I've really got into it. I've enjoyed helping everyone. Even my studies haven't felt such a chore. It's all made me feel better.'

'But not better enough to tell me the truth.'

'He's telling you the truth now,' Lou said gently.

'But only because . . . why are you telling me now?'

'Because I couldn't stand it any longer,' Ryan said, his eyes filling with tears. 'Everyone has looked at me differently this week and it's been brilliant. It's felt so nice to be valued and to do things for other people, but at the back of my mind I've known all along that it was tainted because I'd done Jacob a disservice and it's all come to a head today. I know I should have told you sooner. I've wanted to, but I just didn't know how.'

I was so angry with him, but I could see that he was genuinely upset and telling the truth. Finally.

'I've been an idiot.' He sniffed, rubbing his nose on his sleeve. 'And I've messed things up between you and Jacob.'

'There was nothing between us to mess up,' I said quickly.

'Well, whatever,' he said, sitting up straighter and looking as if a great weight had been lifted off his shoulders, 'I'm going to go round to his tonight and apologise. I want to make it up to him and make the two of you friends again.'

'Friends?' questioned Lou, her eyebrows shooting up.

I ignored her.

'No,' I said to Ryan, 'let me talk to him first. You can see him tomorrow.'

'I think that sounds like a good idea,' said Lou before Ryan had the opportunity to contradict me.

I knew it was a good idea. I wanted to find out why Jacob had let Ryan get away with causing so much trouble and whether he really considered our friendship trivial enough to throw away on an unruly teenager's temper.

# Chapter 17

I sent Ryan and Gus ahead on the pretence of wanting to talk to Lou about what we should do with the Reading Room while Colin was away, but in truth, I just needed a few minutes to get my head round what had just happened. Out of all the crazy and far-fetched scenarios my imaginative brain had conjured, the reality of what Ryan had said was far, far worse.

'Why would he say that?' I groaned, forcing the words over the lump that had lodged itself firmly in my throat as I ran my hands through my hair.

'Which bit?'

'All of it,' I said. 'Does he really hate it here? Does he really hate me?'

'No, of course not, you numpty,' Lou tutted, grabbing my hand and giving it a squeeze.

'Then why did he say it?'

'He told you why,' she said, dropping my hand again as she reached for her bag. 'He thought no one else was listening and he was just trying to sound tough. Haven't you ever done something like that?'

'What, tried to impress a young girl?' I asked sarcastically. 'Er, no.'

'No, you idiot,' she said, pulling out her phone as the *Raiders of the Lost Ark* theme tune began to blare out, 'said something to impress someone, embellished a tall tale to big yourself up?'

I thought back to the lengths I'd gone to during my early years at high school, trying to impress the so-called 'populars' so I would fit in. I'd doubtless said far worse than Ryan and with not even half his excuse.

'I guess,' I relented. 'Maybe. Jesus, Lou, are you going to answer that?'

'No,' she said, stuffing the phone back into her bag to muffle the sound. 'It's the guy who took the pinball machine. He's making a bit of a nuisance of himself.'

'He's not the action hero you're holding out for then?'

A couple of years ago, just before Big Ben chimed in the new year, Lou had downloaded the iconic movie tune as her ringtone and vowed not to change it until she had bagged herself a hero fit enough to rival Harrison Ford as Indiana Jones. Apparently being her own hero, and a successful, independent businesswoman and entrepreneur, wasn't enough and she'd been scouting for her equivalent other half ever since.

'No,' she said, looking wistfully at Colin's set of keys, 'absolutely not the hero I'm holding out for.'

*

As it turned out, Ryan ended up arriving home at the exact same moment as I did.

'Where have you been?' I said, frowning.

'I went to see Kate,' he said, quashing my suspicion that he might have sloped off to Jacob before I had the chance. 'I thought I should be the one to ask her about Gus, as it was me who said he could stay.'

'And what did she say? Did she mind?'

'She didn't mind at all,' he told me, his voice full of relief. 'She said he could stay as long as was necessary and asked if you would please pass on their love when you speak to Colin.'

I said I would, feeling thankful that the situation was now above board and properly sorted, and delighted that Ryan had seen fit to take the initiative and arrange things himself.

'Come on then,' I said, opening the front door. 'I'll cook us some dinner and then I'll go and find out if Jacob is feeling as amenable as our landlady.'

I knew it was completely illogical to be standing on Jacob's doorstep with a bottle of wine in one hand, a portion of boxed home-made korma in the other and a massive chip on my shoulder, but I couldn't shake off my disappointment that even though this entire situation was my brother's fault, Jacob had been willing to sacrifice our newly formed friendship off the back of a few angry words. Not that any of them, as it turned out, had actually come from him.

'Poppy,' Jacob said, exhaling, when he eventually opened the door, 'hi.'

It was such a good feeling, seeing him again in all his crumpled and slightly unkempt glory, that my annoyance suddenly felt completely misplaced and unnecessary and I had no idea what to do with it.

'Is there any chance I could just come in for a minute?' I asked.

'Okay,' he said, looking behind him into the hall as he held the door open a little wider to allow me inside, 'sure.'

The house was far from tidy and as he led me along the hall to the kitchen I kept my eyes on my feet, lest I trip over the jumbled collection of shoes and trainers that made Ryan's haphazard attitude towards the shoe rack look meticulous.

I knew I should say something really, but it was a struggle to find the right words.

'I cooked too much korma,' I blurted out to fill the silent void, 'and I thought you might like some.'

'Oh,' he said, turning back to me again as we arrived in the kitchen. 'We've just eaten, but thanks, I'll keep it for tomorrow.'

The kitchen table was littered with a variety of takeaway cartons and containers and sitting on one side of it was a petite and extremely pretty blond-haired woman.

'Oh, right,' I said, startled. The words came out a little too loudly. 'I didn't realise you had company.' I thrust the box and bottle into Jacob's hands and turned to leave again. 'I'm so sorry. I'll go.'

Jacob looked at me and frowned.

'No,' said the woman, standing up and smiling, 'don't go

on my account. I really should be going myself. I didn't mean to stay this long anyway.'

I stopped in the doorway, not knowing quite what to do.

'That smells better than our takeaway,' she said, nodding at the box of korma, completely oblivious of my awkwardness. 'We can carry on with these plans next week, Jacob.'

'All right,' he said.

She gathered up her bags and a bundle of papers and I stepped aside to let her pass.

'It was nice to meet you,' she said. 'It's Poppy, isn't it?'

'Yes,' I said, looking from her to Jacob and back again.

'Don't look so worried' – she laughed – 'he's talked about you in the staffroom at school, and you fit his description perfectly.'

She was a colleague then. My heart thumped and skittered at the realisation. I dreaded to think what he had said about me during the last few days.

'Apparently you're the queen of preserves.' She grinned.

'Okay, thanks, Hannah,' said Jacob, as he rushed forward and ushered her into the hall. 'I'll give some thought to the Year Three trip and we'll discuss it again on Tuesday.'

I would have bet my best preserve pan on him panicking that she was going to say something rather less complimentary in the next breath.

'Sorry about that,' he said, when he came back from letting her out.

'No,' I said, 'I'm sorry for interrupting.'

He nodded and rocked back on his heels.

'Amongst other things,' I added.

He nodded again and began piling the plates and left-overs together.

'How about I tidy this lot up,' he suggested, 'and you open that wine?'

As it was still so warm we sat outside in Jacob's slightly overgrown garden and I looked at him, wondering where to begin. As lovely as the evening was, I was here on a mission and I didn't want to leave Ryan alone for too long. I wanted to get back and check that he and Gus were following the ground rules I had set out during dinner to govern the dog's stay.

'Look,' I said, putting my glass down on the table, 'there's no point beating about the bush, is there? I've come to say how sorry I am about what happened last weekend. Ryan told me the truth this afternoon and, well, I don't know what to say really . . .'

'There's no need to say anything,' Jacob began.

'Of course there is. I said some terrible things to you and all on the back of some angry and untrue words my brother had spouted off.'

Jacob looked at me and smiled.

'What's so amusing?' I frowned. 'Is this all some kind of joke to you?'

'No,' he said, 'not at all.'

'What then?' I demanded. 'Why didn't you say anything when Ryan started lying? Does our friendship really mean so little to you that you were prepared to lose it because of some silly teenage tantrum?'

I had decided I wouldn't say any of that but Jacob's infuriating expression had knocked me off guard.

'Of course not,' he said, finally looking a little more serious. 'But I knew it *was* just a tantrum. I could see how angry Ryan was. I'd caught him talking rubbish to Tamsin and he retaliated, aggressively, just as any teenage boy trying to save face would. Me demanding that he told you the truth there and then would have only escalated the situation even further and so I decided to back off.'

I supposed that made sense.

'I knew the truth would come out in the end,' he continued, 'I just had to wait it out.'

'But what about the things I said,' I reminded him, blushing at the thought.

'They were just proof that you're an amazing sister.' He smiled.

'What?'

'You were like a coiled spring,' he said, laughing, 'ready to jump to Ryan's defence without stopping to question what was really going on.'

That was true. I had been pretty feisty.

'You were like a lion with her cub,' he carried on. 'Ryan's very lucky to have you on his team.'

My face began to almost burn with heat and it had nothing to do with the evening sun.

'So,' I said, skirting around the compliment and the unexpected turn the conversation was taking, 'what did you *really* say to him?'

'I told him what I told you just now: that he's lucky to have a sister like you and that he should be grateful that you were prepared to open up your new home and alter your life to accommodate him. I just wanted to give him a bit of a wake-up call and make him think a bit. I know he's been through hell, is still in it some of the time, but that doesn't give him the right to talk like that.'

Thinking back over Ryan's subsequently impeccable behaviour, I had to accept that Jacob's words had more than hit their mark. My brother had been the model student, employee, dog-sitter and sibling.

'I see,' I said, 'thank you.'

Jacob raised his glass and clinked it against mine.

'Cheers,' he said, clearly pleased the strategy had worked.

'So, was it all some cunning plan on your part then?' I asked. 'Leaving him to stew.'

'Something like that.'

'It was a bit risky though, wasn't it?'

'Not really.' He sighed. 'Anyone can see that Ryan's a good kid at heart. He's had a far rougher time than most and just needs a guiding hand every now and again to show him the right path and remind him there are folk in the world who really are on his side.'

'I suppose that's what parents are for,' I said bitterly.

'And older siblings,' he reminded me. 'You'll see him right.'

In that moment it felt like one hell of a responsibility and one heck of an ask. I only hoped I was up to the job.

'So,' I said, 'am I really forgiven?'

'There's nothing to forgive,' he said, leaning forward to refill my glass. 'I'm pretty certain we're all of us equally guilty of saying things we don't mean when we're hurt or cornered.'

'I guess.'

'I know I've said some pretty harsh things in my time and had far worse thrown back at me.'

'From your brother?' I asked.

'Yeah,' he said, his voice thick in his throat, 'amongst others.'

We were getting on so well I decided it would be foolish to force the issue.

'Families are hard work,' I said, trying to sound more generic than specific.

'They can be,' he agreed, 'but I just know that you and Ryan are going to be fine and if you want me to, I'm still happy to help out.'

'Really?' I gulped. My heart was hammering again.

'Really,' he said. 'In fact, I'm heading down to the youth centre tomorrow. Tell Ryan I'll call for him at ten in the morning and to dress in clothes he won't mind getting covered in paint.'

This time I leant forward to clink my glass against his, grateful that the week had ended with everything jumping tidily back into place and relieved that our almost-kiss had apparently been forgotten. Jacob seemed far happier in my company than he had at the elderflower gathering, so there was little point risking his good mood by reminding him about it.

'Thank you,' I said, really meaning it.

'That's what friends are for.' He smiled.

I was certainly relieved to have this particular one back again.

Despite my constant reassurance, Ryan was a bag of nerves the next morning.

'And you're sure he was all right about everything?' he asked me for what must have been the hundredth time as he looked out of the sitting room window again.

'Stop worrying,' I told him, 'you'll get Gus in a panic if you carry on like this.'

It was a cheap trick but it worked. Ryan scooped the little dog – who, in spite of my strictest instructions, had somehow made his way into my brother's room last night – up into his arms.

'Sorry, pal,' he said, kissing the top of his head. 'Are you sure you'll be all right with him today, sis?'

'Of course,' I said, an internal little glow sparking into life on hearing the endearment, 'he's going to help me in the kitchen.'

I was going to spend my day off cooking up a storm with Gus for when the lads came back from their day of sanding, priming and painting.

'Oh God,' said Ryan, transferring the dog to my arms, 'he's here. I'll see you later.'

He didn't wait for me to answer the door but rushed out into the Saturday sunshine and straight into a hug from my neighbour, who beamed at me over his shoulder and gave me an encouraging thumbs-up.

I knew everything was going to be just fine.

Jacob and Ryan came back at the end of the day tired, grubby and hungry. Jacob headed back to his for a quick shower and, after running about with Gus for a manic twenty minutes of playful re-bonding, Ryan followed suit. He didn't say much about the centre, but his clothes were testament enough that he'd got stuck in with the paint-brush. If only I could get him to pick up a garden trowel with as much enthusiasm.

It took us all far less time to lay waste to the Italian feast than it had taken me to prepare it. We sat out in the garden replete and satisfied that our Saturday had been so well spent.

'Crikey, Poppy, you can cook,' Jacob sighed appreciatively.

'She can't cook cakes,' Ryan quickly added, shattering my moment of indulgent self-satisfied smugness. 'Can you, sis?'

'Thank you, brother,' I said, sticking out my tongue. 'It would be arrogant to be brilliant at everything, so I've sacrificed cakes, buns and pastries to maintain equilibrium.'

'I won't ask you to donate anything for the school bake sale we have coming up then,' Jacob laughed.

'Mark's your man for sweet treats.' Ryan sighed wistfully, in spite of his full belly. 'His cream slices are to die for.'

'How are things at school?' I asked Jacob. 'Hannah seemed very nice.'

'Yeah,' he said, smiling at the thought of his Miss-Honey-perfect co-worker, 'she's lovely. We're sharing a class at the moment.'

I didn't much like the thought of them sharing anything.

'But by the time the September term rolls round I'll be flying solo.'

'How come?' I asked. 'Is she leaving?'

Ryan looked at me and raised his eyebrows and I wondered just how the question had come across. Had my tone been loaded with hope? I hoped not.

'She'll be on maternity leave,' Jacob explained. 'Her third little one will be coming along soon.'

I hadn't noticed a bump but that could be because I had homed in on her perfect features and shining hair.

'How exciting,' I said enthusiastically.

'I'm not sure her husband would agree with you,' Jacob laughed. 'Three kids under eight wouldn't be my cup of tea.'

'Nor mine,' I agreed with a shudder.

It was on the tip of my tongue to ask Jacob about his views on kids in general, but with Ryan listening in I didn't want my interest to be misinterpreted, so I bit the query back.

'And how are your class?' I asked instead.

'Bonkers,' he told me, 'but brilliant.'

'Tell her what happened yesterday,' insisted Ryan, sneakily opening a bottle of beer, which I instantly relieved him of.

'Oh, good grief,' said Jacob, shaking his head at the memory. 'It was mad. Over half the class turned up in PJs and onesies with teddy bears tucked under their arms.'

'What?' I asked. 'Why?'

'Apparently one of the kids was talking in the playground about us having a cosy day, whatever the hell that is, one of the parents overheard and by the end of the day, thanks to the joys of a Facebook group, word had got round that it was happening Friday, that the letters about it had been misplaced and that the kids would be spending the day reading, cuddling soft toys and generally lazing around on beanbags.'

'No way!' I gasped.

'I know.' Jacob joined in, laughing. 'So, half of the kids turned up at eight thirty in their nightwear and the other half were in tears before the bell went because they knew nothing about it.'

'Because there was nothing to know,' I chuckled.

'Exactly, and they were stuck in their *boring uniforms*,' he sobbed, mimicking what I imagined was supposed to be a sulky child.

'So, what did you do?' I asked, laughing all the harder.

'Well,' he explained, now in his own voice, 'as much as I loved the idea of a cosy day, I couldn't have half of them lolling about and the rest of them in tears, so I sent them all to get changed into their PE kits and lectured the parents about the dangers of social media.'

'Brilliant!' I erupted in laughter, clapping my hands together.

'Another example of what happens when a few overheard words get taken out of context, isn't it?' said a rather embarrassed Ryan.

'We've been through that,' said Jacob, leaning over to pat Ryan's shoulder.

'I know,' he said, 'but I still feel a bit of a prat about it.'

'Never mind,' I said, not wanting the conversation to take such a serious turn, 'it's all done with now.'

'That's what I keep telling him,' said Jacob.

'Why don't you take Gus for a wander round the green,' I suggested to Ryan, 'and Jacob will help me clear up?'

'Excellent idea,' said Ryan, jumping up, his misdemeanour soon forgotten as he realised he was getting out of the washing up. 'And I'll go straight up when I come in, give you two some peace,' he added with a wink before darting out the door.

# Chapter 18

Over the next couple of weeks, my life in Nightingale Square settled back to the perfection I had just been beginning to enjoy before Mum's call about Ryan. In fact, with the addition of my brother and my friendship with Jacob deepening, I would say it was actually better.

I had finally had a response from the college and was embarrassed to discover that Mum had, in her customary fashion, completely over-egged the Ryan absenteeism situation. Yes, they had been in touch to say that his attendance record was borderline problematic, but it was nowhere near as bad as Mum had made out. The fortnightly meetings were pure fabrication on her part and I kicked myself for not having talked it all through properly with Ryan when he first arrived. It was a lesson learned though; from then on in, I decided, I would face any hiccups head-on.

Even Colin's prolonged absence from our patch of

Norwich was bearable now that we knew his father's stroke hadn't been anywhere near as serious as initially feared, but I still couldn't wait for him to come back and see what we had done to the Reading Room. The makeover, which had still gone ahead, carried out almost entirely by Ryan under Lou's clever guidance, was nearly complete and nothing short of miraculous. The paper covering the front windows had been a masterstroke; what was going on behind it was all the locals could talk about.

In fact, the only person who didn't seem to be enjoying the excitement was the lady behind the new look, Little Miss Changing Rooms herself.

'What is up with you?' I asked, handing her a burger from the community garden barbecue when she turned up unannounced on a sunny, Sunday afternoon.

She looked sadder than I'd ever seen her and it didn't suit her one little bit. She opened her mouth to answer my brusque question but was interrupted by Lisa, who was noisily clearing her throat, and Neil, who was banging on the table with his cutlery.

'Sorry, everyone,' said Lisa, looking unusually jittery, 'we won't keep you from your food for many seconds. It's just that there's been a development with the competition that we need to tell you about.'

She turned to Neil, who was holding the competition file. He had been elected as Lisa's second in command on the grounds that he worked from home, so was on hand more often than not, and didn't have any dependants clamouring for his attention. However, with Mark feeling broodier than ever I wasn't all that sure how long that particular scenario would last. When I looked along the table I could see he was cooing over baby Abigail while happily holding one of Heather's boys.

'We've had a letter from the council,' Neil explained. 'I won't read the whole thing, but basically, as there have been more than the predicted number of entries to the competition, the council have decided to check them all out before drawing up a shortlist—'

'There'll be a representative visiting here,' Lisa couldn't resist interrupting, 'in the next few days. They won't be judging the place at this point. Just checking the application meets the requirements.'

'But the visit will determine whether or not we'll be put forward,' Neil carried on. 'The decision will be made public fairly soon after the inspection and representatives from each garden going forward will then be asked to attend a local radio slot one Saturday morning to explain why their garden is so special and a little about its history.'

A quiet murmur rippled round the table. I was surprised there had been so many entries, but delighted. Clearly Norwich residents were very much on board with the benefits of gardening and growing.

'In that case,' said Graham, 'could everyone please make sure they fulfil their allotted tasks on the rota. I know we're all very good about it, but now more than ever we need everything to be perfect.'

'We're not being judged on the garden just yet, Graham,' Lisa reminded him.

'But even so,' he said importantly. 'It will be good to get on top of things.'

Everyone nodded in agreement and Lou gave a little squeal as her phone began to bleat and vibrate.

'That's it, folks,' said Neil, raising his voice as the cacophony cranked up a notch. 'Enjoy your afternoon, everyone.'

I waited until Lou had taken the call before pouncing.

'What happened to Indiana?' I demanded.

'Yes,' said Jacob, who had been brought up to speed on the hero-hunt and her unusual choice of ringtone. 'Unless I'm very much mistaken, that was a tune from *Grease*, wasn't it?'

'"You're the One that I Want",' confirmed Ryan as he wandered past, turning puce as we all raised our eyebrows. 'Or something like that.' He coughed, rushing off.

'So,' I said, pulling at Lou's shirt-sleeve, 'does that mean you've finally found your hero?'

'Of course I have,' she said with a sniff. 'I can't believe I didn't see it for so long, but with him being away, I've really missed him and it's made me think . . . maybe Colin is the one.'

I looked at her, my mouth falling open.

'Do you really mean that?' I eventually dared to ask.

I'd had my suspicions that her feelings for him had changed ever since the day she unveiled the makeover plans, but what with one thing and another I hadn't found the right moment to talk to her. Looking at the state of her now, I knew I should have. I had been a little too absorbed in my own affairs recently. Good friends were hard to come by and I felt guilty for neglecting one of mine.

'Yes,' she said, biting her lip. 'I haven't been able to stop thinking about him since he left.'

'But your feelings for him had changed before he went, hadn't they?'

'Was it that obvious?' she gulped.

'Only to me,' I said, rubbing her arm and feeling excited that Colin was going to come back to embrace a happy-ever-after.

I didn't tell Lou that he had loved her for ever. I thought that he should decide when and if she needed to know that.

'Relationships are tricky, aren't they?' I said to Jacob once Lou had headed back to her flat to try to Skype Colin. She'd been trying every day but had little success. The internet at his parents' place was sketchy at best.

'God, yes,' he agreed.

'And I think you know that better than most, don't you?'

'What do you mean?'

'Well,' I went on, 'I know you've had a falling-out with your brother and that you aren't currently in touch with your family, so you know for yourself that *those* kinds of relationships are tricky, but was there ever a Mrs Grizzle? Or at least someone who came close to being a Mrs Grizzle?'

Jacob looked at me and raised his eyebrows.

'You did tell me, not all that long ago,' I forged ahead, 'that you don't do promises and you don't do trust. I can't possibly imagine that's all down to falling out with your brother. Something tells me there was a woman involved.'

'You're always going to wonder about this, aren't you?' said Jacob, narrowing his eyes.

'Afraid so.' There was no point in lying. 'You hated everything when you moved here camping out in an empty house: you didn't talk to your neighbours; you weren't working, even though you love your career; you wouldn't set foot in this place . . .'

'Come on then,' he said with a sigh, 'let's go over to the green. It'll be quieter there.'

I couldn't believe he was going to finally open up and tell me. After checking Ryan was still happy chatting to Mark, I grabbed a couple of bottles of cider and headed to the green – ahead of my neighbour to ensure tongues weren't set wagging for the wrong reasons.

'Okay,' said Jacob, his hands straying through his untidy hair. We were settled in the shade of a tree on the green. 'I'm going to tell you the whys and wherefores, Poppy, but only because I know I can trust *you*.'

'Wow,' I gasped. 'Thank you, Jacob.'

For a man who had recently told me he didn't do trust this really was a declaration, and I felt honoured to be considered worthy of his confidence.

'I can't tell you how much it means to hear you say that.' I smiled.

He let out a long breath while I tucked my hair behind my ears and fiddled with my drink, waiting for him to begin.

'Ever since Daniel and I were born,' he eventually started, 'we've been compared and measured against one another.'

'I'm guessing Daniel is your twin then?'

'Yes, sorry,' said Jacob, smiling wryly, 'twin thing. As much as I hate it, he's still an extension of me and I just assume everyone knows.'

I nodded and handed him a bottle to help lubricate proceedings.

'I suppose,' he continued, 'that comparing us to one another was only natural really.'

I wasn't sure about that. I think if I'd had twins I would have gone out of my way to treat them as individually as possible so that one never felt pressured to be like the other, but I didn't feel qualified to say as much, so I stayed quiet.

'We are—' Jacob stopped and corrected himself. 'We *were* so similar in every possible way, with our lives running along parallel tracks, and that continued as we got older and both decided that we wanted to pursue a career in education.'

'Did you study at the same university?'

'Yes, our lives were still identical at that point, right down to our exam grades. It was spooky sometimes. I wondered if anyone would realise if one of us disappeared. It was like life had provided a spare in case anything went wrong with the prototype.'

'I can see how that would freak you out.'

'It did . . .' Jacob nodded, stopping for a second to take a swig from his bottle, 'and as we worked our way through uni, I became more and more aware of it. I talked to Daniel about it but he just shrugged it off. He reckoned all twins felt that way at some time or another but once I had acknowledged it I couldn't shake the feeling off.'

'So, what did you do?'

It was obvious that he had done something. I was certain that was the point where Jacob's life had changed from duo to solo.

'I jumped off the track,' he said, looking right at me as he confirmed my thoughts. 'We both of us had great postgrad jobs lined up but I decided not to take mine. On the day we graduated I announced I was taking time out to travel instead and off I went.'

'That was brave.'

For someone who had lived a life running in perfect synchronicity with his brother, it was incredibly daring.

'That's not how my parents saw it,' he said with a short laugh, 'or Daniel. Everyone thought I was mad. We had our future, our entire lives plotted out and suddenly I was telling them I was going to, quite literally, follow a different map.'

'Wow.'

'I know. I thought it would be liberating, and after a few months it was, but in the beginning I was as scared as hell. Being on my own, rather than one half of a whole, took some getting used to but I stuck it out, and once I began to relax, enjoy myself and trust my own decisions, I decided to stay away for as long as I could.'

'How long?'

'Over five years.'

'Crikey.' I almost choked. 'Five years. What did you do for all that time? How did you fund it?' I didn't have him down as some rich kid and was fairly certain his parents, given their annoyance that he had gone in the first place, wouldn't have paid for a gap year that lasted half a decade even if he was. 'Did you come back to the UK during that time at all?'

Jacob took another gulp of cider.

'Sorry,' I said, reaching for my own and picking at the label. 'Too many questions.'

'No,' he said, 'it's fine. I spent quite a lot of time teaching in India. I revelled in the freedom and once I'd earned enough to move on a little way I did. The pay was practically pennies, but it was enough to live on and no, in all that time I didn't come back.'

'And what was Daniel doing while you were away?'

'Exactly what he, I mean we, had always planned to do,' he explained. 'He was zipping up the management ladder, happily running up every rung of it. He never gave up trying to get me to come back though.'

'So, what made you return in the end if it wasn't your brother?'

Jacob shook his head and I sensed that we were getting to the heart of the matter.

'I met a girl,' he told me. 'Rebecca. She was younger than me but had also been travelling around since graduating and was heading back to the UK to take up a teaching post of her own near to where my family lived. She'd satisfied her wanderlust far faster than I had and . . .' he sighed, stopping to take a breath. 'And I know this probably sounds ridiculous, but it felt as if my own thirst for adventure couldn't be quenched until I'd found her. She was the missing piece my life had been looking for ever since I'd cut the umbilical with Daniel.'

Jacob shook his head, but I got it. He had found the person I still hadn't. The one person in all the world that he knew he would be able to commit to, for life.

'It was meant to be,' I said, trying to help him out.

'Exactly.' Jacob nodded. 'That was *exactly* how it felt. It was a whirlwind romance played out on white sandy beaches and before I knew it we were flying home. I made amends with my family – they adored Rebecca, which helped things considerably, of course, and then we rented a flat and both settled into the comforting rhythm of the school routine.'

'And were you happy?'

'Happier than I had ever been,' he said huskily. 'I'd seen something of the world and I'd broken free of the twin thing. Daniel was his own man, as was I, the family idolised Becky, I loved my job and, at the risk of sounding smug, everything was pretty damn perfect.'

'So, what went wrong?'

Jacob looked at me and shook his head.

'Well something obviously did,' I pointed out, 'otherwise you wouldn't be living here, on your own, would you?' I waited while he collected his thoughts.

'Daniel,' he eventually carried on, 'as expected, had

streaked miles ahead of me on the career ladder in the time I'd been away.'

'I can't imagine you cared much about that,' I said.

'No,' he said, 'I didn't. In fact, when he called us all together for a celebratory family lunch to announce he had been awarded a headship, I was the first to congratulate him.'

'He was young to become a head, wasn't he?'

'Very,' Jacob agreed, 'but his dedication and determination have always been second to none. His ambition,' he said, sighing heavily, 'only just outstripped Becky's by the tiniest of margins.'

That took me by surprise. I hadn't imagined Rebecca as someone looking to get ahead at all. I envisaged her as a tanned, toned beach beauty. A free spirit with sun-bleached hair and an abundance of shell jewellery – but clearly I had mistaken her for someone else.

'I know exactly what you're thinking,' Jacob said, looking at me again, 'and I hadn't seen it either. I had thought that she'd be as happy with a regular teaching post as I was, but within a year or so of returning to the UK she was looking to further her career, just like Daniel.'

'I see.' I swallowed nervously.

'We started to argue. One time she even asked me why I couldn't be more like Dan. She seemed in awe of him, seduced by his success, and it was at this damn meal,' Jacob said with a frown, 'that I realised . . .'

He stopped and shook his head and I guessed what was coming.

'That she had fallen for him,' I whispered.

Jacob nodded.

'It was just a look, a two-second glance between them, but I knew.'

'I'm so sorry.'

'I had been going to propose that Christmas,' he said grimly, 'but when I tackled them about what I'd seen, they didn't deny it. They'd already—' He stopped and took a breath. I didn't need him to spell it out. 'So,' he went on, 'instead of ring shopping I found myself working my notice and buying this place.' He tipped his bottle towards his house. 'I left everything behind, including my car, and managed to get through the winter with the bits and pieces the previous owner was happy to include in the sale.'

No wonder he had shut himself away. With hindsight it was probably the best thing he could have done. He had hidden away from the world and worked through his trauma. Surely that had to be better than pretending everything was all right and powering through with a brave smile?

'Anyway,' he said, sitting up straighter and clearing his throat, 'they're welcome to each other. I'm moving on. I've put hundreds of miles between us and now I have this place and the garden and a new job and you, Poppy.'

I met his gaze, unsure as to what he meant.

'But there's just one snag, of course,' he carried on before I had time to work it out.

'Which is?'

'Every time I look in the damn mirror, I see Daniel staring back at me.'

Part of me wanted to laugh when he said that, but it wasn't funny. This wasn't some made-for-TV drama, it was real life, Jacob's life. I wondered if that was why he still hadn't had a haircut.

'I don't know what to say,' I croaked.

'Of course you don't,' he replied. 'Who would?'

I shuffled over and reached for his hand.

'No wonder you were Mr Grumpy when you moved here,' I said sympathetically, 'and no wonder you don't do trust.'

'But I do trust you, Poppy,' he said for the second time, squeezing my hand back. 'I told you that. I really do feel as though I can trust you and that's hit me like a bolt out of the blue because I never thought I'd be able to trust anyone ever again.'

I nodded, delighted that he felt that way, had the capacity to even consider feeling that way after everything he had been through.

'And this spark between us,' he shocked me by adding, 'that's another surprise.'

'Spark?' I squeaked.

'Don't embarrass me by denying it,' he tutted. 'I know you feel it too.'

I nodded again but couldn't look at him. The way my heart had fluttered when our hands had touched, the pain in the pit of my stomach when I had first seen Hannah sitting at his kitchen table. Those uncontrollable physical reactions were all about the spark. They were things I'd never felt before. For anyone.

'Yes,' I admitted, 'I feel it.'

But feeling was one thing and acting on those feelings was something else entirely.

'But—' I began.

'But,' he interrupted, 'given my recent heartbreak, we aren't going to let that spark burst into flame, are we?'

'No,' I said. 'I don't think that would be a good idea just now.'

'That's all right then,' he said, giving me back my hand, 'because right now what I really need, more than anything, Poppy, is a true friend.'

'Me too,' I whispered.

# Chapter 19

Having unburdened himself, and feeling safe in the knowledge that I wouldn't let the heartbreaking details of his past go any further, Jacob was a changed man. He was often to be heard laughing, swapping silly jokes with Ryan, who thought the world of him, and he'd even braved a trip to the barber.

The tidy-up wasn't particularly dramatic, and his fringe still flopped when he ran his hands through it, but he was delighted with the results nonetheless and it was nice to be able to see his eyes for a change. Even if I did have to endure more than my fair share of tummy butterflies whenever I caught them looking in my direction.

'I even managed a couple of glances in the mirror,' he told me as he stood scratching at his hair-filled shirt collar immediately after the event. 'I couldn't have done that six months ago, Poppy, or even six weeks, come to that.'

I could well believe it. Ryan aside, I had no close family

connections to compare with, but I was having a hard time getting my head round how Jacob's brother and Rebecca had treated him. I had always thought there was some sort of unwritten rule, some extra-special twin code of conduct, forged as a result of shared amniotic fluid, which somehow guaranteed against this sort of fuckwittery – but obviously I was wrong.

'Don't forget the meeting in the garden later,' Jacob reminded me. 'I'm going home for a shower and a change of clothes first, so I'll meet you there.'

We'd all been on the lookout for the council rep but, in spite of our meerkat sentry set-up, we hadn't seen or heard a thing. Weeks had flown by rather than the days suggested when Lisa and Neil had explained what was going to happen and I couldn't help thinking that we had failed. If the garden had been inspected at least one of us would have known about it because we would have had to let them in. This sudden summoning was no doubt going to be a 'better luck next time' announcement.

'Thank you all for coming,' Lisa said with a nervous smile, once we were all gathered. 'I know it was short notice so thanks for turning out. The heavens look fit to burst, so we'll keep this brief.'

The clouds were indeed gathering. I hoped that wasn't a bad sign. A portent predicting our failure. A downpour would get me out of watering duty, but I'd rather spend an hour exercising my arm muscles if it meant we were in the competition.

'So, it looks like we have some news,' said Neil, holding up a white envelope bearing the council stamp.

'Is it good?' asked Graham.

He sounded every bit as edgy as the rest of us were feeling.

'We haven't opened it yet,' Lisa explained. 'We thought we should wait until we were all together.'

'Well, get on with it,' urged Carole. 'My nerves can't cope with the waiting.'

We looked on as, with shaking hands, Neil tore the envelope open and handed the letter over to Lisa. Her eyes skimmed across the contents and then her face split into the biggest grin.

'We're through!' she shouted, joyously waving the letter. 'We've made the shortlist!'

She went back to reading as the rest of us clapped and cheered. Even Jacob, once so convinced that he wouldn't be having anything to do with the place, looked delighted.

'But when did they come and look?' asked Colin, scratching his head.

'About a week ago,' said Luke, turning red. 'I had to be here to let them in and they asked me not to mention it. Sorry, guys. I didn't want to risk breaking the rules.'

No one looked particularly upset that he had been hanging on to the secret.

'Is this going to mean you'll have double duties?' Ryan nudged at my side. 'Even more deadheading and potting on?'

'Afraid so,' I said with a laugh and he rolled his eyes.

'Just as well I've almost finished at Colin's shop then, isn't it?'

'Will you help?' I gasped.

'I suppose.' He beamed. 'If I must.'

I was delighted. I couldn't imagine there were many sixteen-year-old lads who would allow themselves to get roped in to something like this, especially if their older sister was involved.

'What about the radio spot?' asked Mark. 'Does it say anything about that?'

Lisa handed the letter back to Neil.

'Yes,' she said, 'and we're going to need some help from you lot there. They want two of us to go in on Saturday.'

'What, this Saturday?' asked Luke.

'Yes,' said Lisa, biting her lip. 'I can't do it. I'm going to be in London, promoting my book at a blogger event. I can't miss that.'

'Of course you can't,' said John.

'And I'm going to be on site with a tricky client,' explained Neil. 'It's taken weeks to get our diaries to coincide.'

Luke was the obvious choice as the owner of Prosperous Place, but he was eschewing anything to do with the media now he'd given up his modelling career, and Heather, Glen and John would have their hands full with their little ones. Harold declared he was too old for messing about on the wireless, and Carole and Graham had booked a coach trip to the coast. Carole looked gutted, whereas Graham appeared relieved. I couldn't blame him.

'So,' said Lisa, turning to Jacob and me. 'That just leaves you two.'

'No way,' said Jacob.

'Yes,' said Neil, 'you guys would be perfect. The two newcomers.'

Everyone's eyes swung to us.

'You'll be able to explain how inclusive the place is, Jacob,' said Lisa, smiling at him. 'How coming here has helped you settle in and get to know everyone.'

'And you could talk about how you've been making use of all the produce, Poppy,' added Neil.

'I've barely started,' I reminded him.

'You could even mention your recipe cards,' suggested Mark. 'That's bound to give us an edge! I bet none of the other gardens can boast having a champion pickler on their premises.'

I'd never been a champion at anything, but I didn't have the chance to point that out.

'You'll be the perfect pairing to promote the place,' said Kate. 'Don't you think, Ryan?'

'Absolutely,' my cheeky brother joined in, no doubt encouraged by my look of dismay.

'That's settled then,' said Lisa, sliding the letter back into its envelope and handing it to Neil so he could add it to the file. 'What a relief.'

Jacob looked every bit as dumbfounded as I felt and I was just poised to form further objections when Gus let out a bark and ran across the garden.

'Hey, Colin!' called Ryan as he came into view through the gate and scooped up his overexcited pooch. 'You're back!'

*

Within seconds of Colin's arrival, a deep rumble of thunder could be heard in the distance and fat heavy raindrops began to fall.

'Let's call it a day, folks,' announced Lisa, 'thank you, guys. Oh, and if we can come up with a name for the garden by Saturday that would be even better. An official title would help the place stick in people's minds. Isn't that right, Luke?'

'Absolutely,' he agreed. 'Great idea.'

'And' she added, now addressing Jacob and me, 'if you could be at the radio studio by three on Saturday, that would be great.'

'But I'll be at work,' I told her, thinking it might be worth having one last-ditch attempt at getting out of it. 'I don't finish until five on Saturday.'

Jacob didn't look at all impressed that I was bailing on him, but I couldn't do it. I'd get tongue-tied and make a total twot of myself, I knew I would.

'And Harry won't be able to spare me again,' I pushed on. 'I've had so much time off recently . . .'

'Don't worry, sis,' said Ryan, throwing a heavy arm round my shoulder, 'I'll cover for you. I'm sure Harry won't mind. It's only for an hour or so.'

I could have brained him.

'That's settled then,' said Lisa, smiling at Ryan before rushing off to get out of the rain.

I still couldn't look at Jacob.

'Thanks for that,' he tutted. 'You were going to leave me high and dry.'

'Come on,' said Colin, before I could defend myself, 'let's get down to The Dragon before it really starts to pour.'

'Great idea,' I said, reaching for a couple of the umbrellas we kept in the bothy and which would be just the thing for blocking Colin's view of his shop as we ducked by. 'We better take these.'

As we walked to the pub I had fired off a quick text to Lou, letting her know her recently identified hero was finally back in town, but as I listened to what he had to say, I wasn't sure that had been a wise move.

'So,' he said with a sigh, as he came to the end of telling us exactly what had happened to his dad and how his recovery had been slow but positive so far, 'he's being discharged from the convalescent home next week. I've helped Mum get as much sorted as I can. He's going to have some pretty intense therapy to help get him better, not to mention some fairly major lifestyle changes.'

'Well,' I said, 'it certainly sounds as if you're on top of things, Colin.'

'I've done what I can,' he said, his cheeks turning slightly pink, 'but I couldn't have managed even half of it without Natalie. She's been amazing,' he added wistfully.

Ryan looked at me and raised his eyebrows. I knew exactly what he was thinking. The name Natalie had come up at least half a dozen times since we'd arrived at the pub and I clearly wasn't the only one who had noticed.

'So, this Natalie,' Jacob began, venturing where I, in view of what I now knew about how Lou was feeling, didn't dare, 'she sounds . . . nice.'

'She's the best,' Colin cheerfully agreed. 'We were at school together, but she was in the year below me. She works for the care agency I called hoping to find someone reliable. We knew she was going to be perfect straight away.'

'You've known each other for a while then,' Jacob carried on.

'Not really,' Colin replied. 'We used to go to the same reading group after school but we weren't what you would call close, or even friends really. To be honest, I was surprised she even remembered me.'

'But she did.' Ryan grinned. 'You sound well in there, Col.'

'Well,' said Colin, laughing, 'I don't know about that but we have been out a couple of times and she's been really great helping us get the house sorted and drawing up a care plan. The agency couldn't have sent anyone better—'

'I daresay she's just doing her job,' I interjected, trying not to think how Lou was going to react to the news that Natalie the nurse was tending to more than Colin's dad's needs.

'Perhaps,' Colin said, looking at me, 'but Dad isn't the only one feeling better for having her around—'

He broke off as his phone began to ring, and fished around in his pocket for it before heading to a quieter spot in the bar. 'It's her,' he mouthed, pointing at the phone and grinning.

'Bloody hell,' I groaned.

'Ironic, isn't it?' muttered Jacob.

'Just a bit.'

I had been so excited that Colin was going to come

back and discover that Lou had finally acknowledged her feelings for him that I hadn't considered the fact that while Colin was away he might fall for someone else. He was supposed to be looking after his parents, for goodness sake, not falling for the carer. It was all very First World War love story, only the nurse was looking after his father, not him.

'What is?' Ryan asked. 'What's ironic?'

'Never you mind,' I said tersely, handing him a five-pound note and asking him to get some crisps so I could have a moment to think what to do next without his chatter.

'Do you think you should call Lou,' Jacob asked as soon as Ryan was out of earshot, 'give her a quick low-down on the situation?'

'That might not be a bad idea,' I agreed, reaching for my phone. 'If I can head her off and set her straight before she . . .'

The words died in my throat as the pub door was flung open and Lou rushed in, forcing her way through the crowd at the bar and enveloping Colin in the biggest bear hug imaginable.

'Ah,' said Jacob, 'too late. Time to initiate plan B.'

'Which is?'

'I have absolutely no idea.'

Lou didn't look at all happy when Colin eventually prised himself free from her clutches and pointed first at his phone and then to where Jacob and I were sitting.

'Hi,' I said nervously as she came over.

'Hey,' she harrumphed, ripping into one of the bags of

crisps Ryan had just dumped on the table. 'Apparently he'll be over in a minute, he's just talking to his dad's carer.'

'That'll be Nurse Natalie,' nudged Ryan, throwing in a cheeky wink for good measure.

Lou sat up a little straighter in her seat.

'I'll get another round in,' said Jacob, jumping up. 'Give us a hand will you, Ryan?'

'And who is "Nurse Natalie"?' Lou demanded.

'She's an old friend from school,' I said lightly. 'Apparently,' I forced myself on, 'they've been out for a couple of drinks.'

Lou blanched. She knew as well as I did that that wasn't usual Colin behaviour at all. Yes, he headed to The Dragon with us and Mark most weeks, but that was different.

'I'm sure there's nothing in it,' I blundered on even though I didn't know anything of the sort.

'Right,' she said, chewing her lip and looking over to where Colin was still talking animatedly into his phone. 'I see.'

We could hear him laughing, even though the bar was pretty crowded.

'Well,' she said, rallying, 'he looks happy. That's the main thing, isn't it? I mean, he's been through a shitty time of it recently. He's entitled to have a bit of a laugh, isn't he?'

'Absolutely,' I said, relieved that she seemed to be taking the unexpected turn of events in her stride. 'You're right. This is a good thing, and it's great news that his dad's getting on so well.'

'Exactly,' she agreed, 'and I can't wait to see how he'll react when he sees what we've done with the shop.'

'I'm just grateful it was raining as we came along and I was able to use the brolly to shield his view of the papered windows. I suppose he'll want his keys back now.'

'No way,' she said. 'Ryan and I won't be handing them over until we're completely ready.'

'You can't stop him going into his own shop, Lou.'

'Just you watch me,' she said firmly. 'Ryan and I have worked bloody hard to turn that place round and we'll be giving it the launch it deserves. A little earlier than expected, I know, but it's happening nonetheless.'

'That was Natalie,' said Colin, beaming, rejoining us at the table at the same time as Jacob and Ryan. 'I left some books at her place and she wanted to know if she should send them on.'

'Nice.' Ryan sniggered.

The rest of us didn't comment.

'And talking of books,' said Colin, taking the chair next to Lou and stretching his arm across the back of hers in a relaxed gesture that wasn't like him at all, 'I suppose I better have the keys to the shop back. Maybe we'll pick up where we left off with the makeover next week, Ryan? That is, if you're still up for helping out?'

'Oh blast,' said Lou. She was clearly better at subterfuge than my brother, who had turned bright red and looked about to give the game away. 'I've left the keys at mine.'

'Never mind,' said Colin, 'I'll come back with you when we're done here and pick them up, if you like.'

Lou winked at me and I wondered if she was planning some sweet seduction using the keys to the Reading Room as bait.

'You're more than welcome to come back to mine,' she said, leaning back onto Colin's arm, 'but why not leave the shop until Saturday?'

'But why would I?'

'That sounds like a good idea,' said Jacob, cottoning on, 'why not take tomorrow off, mate? I'm sure keeping the place shut for just one more day won't make any difference, will it?'

'I suppose not,' Colin agreed, stifling a yawn. 'I'm hoping I'll be too busy to take much time off once we've finished the makeover, so perhaps I should make the most of it.'

'Exactly,' said Ryan, 'leave the keys with Lou for now and spend tomorrow bonding with Gus again.'

I knew it was going to come as a wrench for Ryan to have to hand Gus back. They'd been practically joined at the hip from the moment they met and the little chap had been no bother at all. He had the loveliest manners.

'Actually,' said Colin, leaning across to where Gus was sitting on my brother's lap and stroking the dog's soft little head, 'I was wondering if you wanted to hang on to him for a bit. I'm going to be doing quite a bit of travelling during the next few weeks to check up on Dad and see Natalie and Gus isn't great in the car. And besides,' he added, 'look at him. He's obviously far happier with you than me.'

Ryan looked as if he'd won the lottery but poor Lou was suddenly looking as sick as a dog.

# Chapter 20

Saturday morning, I was a jumbled bag of mixed emotions. I was excited about the relaunch of Colin's shop, terrified at the thought of appearing on the radio and frazzled from Lou's seemingly endless and increasingly paranoid babble.

'How am I supposed to compete with her healing hands?' was the most frequently asked question as Colin continued to sing Natalie's praises at every given opportunity. 'I can't possibly best Natalie friggin' Nightingale!'

No matter what answer I came up with, Lou couldn't be calmed and I had my hopes pinned on the extensive work she and Ryan had undertaken in the Reading Room as being enough to help Colin see that her efforts were definitely more than those which could be expected of a *friend*.

'Hey, Poppy,' said the man himself with a frown, when he turned up in Greengages earlier than expected that morning. 'I've just been to Lou's place to pick up the shop keys, but it's all shut up and she isn't answering her phone.

There isn't anything wrong, is there? She never misses a Saturday.'

'Not as far as I know,' I said, my panic kicking up a gear as I realised that if Colin had come down the street the other way the whole plan for a grand reveal would have been scuppered.

'Well, we arranged to meet there this morning,' he said, pulling his phone out of his pocket. 'Perhaps I should give her mobile another—'

'No!' I cut in. 'Let me ring her, just in case she's poorly or something.' I didn't give him the opportunity to point out that he was every bit as capable of talking to a poorly Lou as I was. 'You wait here.'

I ushered Harry into the back room on the pretence of him helping me find my phone.

'You have to go to Colin's shop, Harry,' I urgently whispered, 'and tell Lou that Colin's on his way. I'll hold him here for as long as I can but she might have to let him cut the ribbon early.'

With Harry dispatched I quickly made two cups of coffee and carried them back through to the shop. Thankfully it was a slow start to trading and I happily imagined everyone was gathering further down the street, waiting to finally find out what had been going on behind the papered windows of the Reading Room.

'I thought you might like a coffee,' I told Colin, handing him a mug.

He looked at me as if I was from a different planet.

'What?' I asked, taking a caffeine-packed sip.

'Did you get hold of her?'

'Who?'

'Lou!'

'Oh,' I spluttered, 'no, sorry. She's not answering. But I'm sure everything's fine.'

'Well, I can't just hang about here all morning,' he tutted. 'Saturday really is the only day I have a chance of getting more than half a dozen customers into the shop. Perhaps I should go back and see if she's turned up at her place yet.'

'Have your coffee first,' I encouraged, trying to sound calmer than I felt.

I managed to keep him talking for the next twenty minutes or so. As soon as I mentioned the name Natalie he was off and running and by the time Harry arrived back with Ryan and Gus in tow and had given me a crafty thumbs-up to indicate that everything was good to go, I was every bit as sick of the kind-hearted carer's name as Lou was.

'So *here* you are, Colin,' said Ryan, playing along a little too dramatically. 'Lou's been waiting ages for you down at the Reading Room.'

Colin handed his empty mug back to me and tutted.

'But I told her last night on the phone that we'd meet at her place,' he grumbled. 'I swear she doesn't listen to a word I'm saying half the time.'

It wasn't all that long ago that he'd found that particular flaw in Lou's character endearing, but now he just sounded annoyed. I would have bet my weekly wages that Natalie hung on his every word, never missing so much as a single syllable.

'I better get down there,' he said, sounding more irritated than ever.

'I'll come with you,' said Ryan, rushing off after him.

Harry and I quickly locked the shop and followed on a clandestine few paces behind.

'What's going on?' we heard Colin call ahead of us when he realised that all of the shops were closed and the owners, along with quite a crowd, were gathered around the front of his store. 'What's happened?'

'We have a surprise for you, Colin,' Lou said, smiling, as she stepped away from the masses to greet him.

She quickly took his hand and turned him back round before he saw too much. She glanced over to me and beamed, looking absolutely beautiful in a fifties-styled frock, the fabric of which was covered in books. She was really going all out to impress him. I only hoped her efforts weren't now in vain.

It was amazing to think how quickly and completely the tables had turned on this pair who seemed destined to keep missing each other.

'I'm not a big fan of surprises.' Colin frowned.

'Well,' said Ryan, handing over Gus's lead to Jacob, who was at the front of the crowd and looking every bit as excited as Lou, 'I can guarantee you're going to love this one, mate.'

'Promise you won't look up until we tell you to?' begged Lou.

'If I must,' Colin sighed.

He still wasn't entering into the spirit of the occasion but I was certain he would soon get into the swing of it. My brother and my best friend turned him back round and led him further along the road to stand directly in front of the shop that they had worked so hard to transform.

From the freshly painted exterior alone, the place looked completely different. I couldn't wait to see what they had achieved inside. The layers of paper had been removed from the windows now and everyone strained to see beyond the balloon- and bunting-festooned sills.

'You can look now,' said Lou, letting go of Colin's arm but not moving away.

Slowly he looked up, his eyes travelling from the pavement to the new green and cream colour scheme and then further up to where the Reading Room signage was covered in a swathe of fabric. Ryan held out a piece of cord that was attached to one corner and Colin, looking more than a little shell-shocked, stepped forward to take it from him.

'Pull it,' my brother told him, 'but not too hard.'

Colin pulled as instructed and the fabric fell smoothly away to reveal the name A Good Book, scribed in a flowing font that matched the new exterior perfectly. The crowd began to cheer and Lou stepped up to take her place next to Colin again.

'A Good Book,' mouthed Colin, his eyes wide in wonder.

'That was Jacob's idea.' Ryan beamed.

I looked at Jacob, who shrugged his shoulders and smiled.

I had no idea he had come up with a new name. I didn't even know one had been in the offing.

'There's more,' said Lou, as a guy with a camera rushed in front of them and began to snap away, 'come and see.'

Inside the shop was a revelation. Gone were the dark, dusty, towering shelves that had overpowered the space and created an uninviting ambience. They had all been carved up, painted and replaced with a welcoming, open warmth, tucked-away places to sit, discreet groupings of chairs, a shiny new coffee machine and even a bespoke 'book nook' for young customers.

'But when ... how ... why ...' Colin began to splutter as Mark proudly steered him towards a table next to the counter that was filled with glasses of fizz and a book-shaped cake bearing the shop's new name in exactly the same font as the sign.

'While you were away,' said Lou through tearful laughter, 'with a lot of help from Ryan and because' – she swallowed – 'we love you.'

'I wouldn't go that far,' said Ryan gruffly, 'but Lou thought you could do with a hand, given everything else you've had going on, and it's kept me out of mischief and my sister's hair.'

'Do you like it?' Lou asked, sounding a little breathless. 'Is it all right?'

Her eyes hadn't left Colin's face and I don't think she'd heard a word of what Ryan had said.

'Like it,' said Colin, turning round as everyone filed inside and began filling the seats, thumbing through the newly arranged stock and admiring the coffee dispenser, 'no,' he said, shaking his head, 'of course I don't like it.'

Jacob looked at me and winked, one of the biggest smiles I had ever seen on him lighting up his face.

'I absolutely love it!' Colin shouted, scooping Lou up and spinning her round. 'And I love you for doing it,' he added, planting a kiss on her cheek before putting her back down and bumping fists with Ryan in a more modest show of affection.

Colin's words weren't quite an undying declaration, but they were good enough for Lou, who pulled him back into a hug and hung on as if he were a lifejacket and she'd just fallen overboard.

'If I might interrupt for a moment,' asked the guy who I had seen taking photos outside, 'I was just wondering if the three of you might have time for a quick interview?'

Later that afternoon, when Jacob came back to Greengages so we could walk to the radio studio together, he told me the party at Colin's was still in full swing. Harry had told Ryan, who was every bit as popular as Colin and Lou with the journalists reporting the event, not to worry about covering for me in the shop and between us we arranged to meet everyone else back in A Good Book after the radio spot to discuss how our airtime had gone.

'Are you nervous?' Jacob asked as we signed in at the station.

I stole a quick glance at him. His earlier smile had been

replaced by the furrowed brow that had been so familiar when he first moved into the square, and I could see that his hands were shaking every bit as much as mine.

'What do you think?'

'Sorry,' he said. 'Yeah, me too.'

I fiddled with the few recipe cards I had grabbed from the counter in Greengages while we waited to be taken up to meet the presenter. I think it was quite possibly the longest twenty minutes of my life but once we were in the studio, each with a massive microphone in front of us and chatting about the beautiful garden, it all became easy. Talking about fresh tomatoes and the earlier abundance of rhubarb felt fine.

'So,' said Steve Simpson, the station's most popular and longest-serving presenter, after the initial flurry of chat had settled, 'when your garden representative called to tell us who'd be joining me this afternoon, he said the garden still didn't have a name.'

'Oh, that's changed now,' I said, leaning closer to the foam-covered microphone. 'We've decided it should be called the Grow-Well Garden.'

This was another of Jacob's bright ideas. Clearly, he had a knack for names.

'The Grow-Well Garden,' Steve repeated. 'I like it. Is that because everything does indeed grow so well there? Is there some sort of magic in your manure?'

'Something like that,' Jacob explained. 'But it doesn't just refer to the plants. The garden name reflects what happens to the people who go there as well. I think Poppy would agree that we've all benefited from gardening with our neighbours. We've all grown every bit as well as the plants.'

I was delighted he understood that. The name he had come up with matched the sentiment perfectly. Jacob really was a green-fingered convert. I loved that the garden had made such an impact on him, in such a short space of time and against such odds.

'Definitely.' I nodded in agreement, even though the listeners couldn't see the gesture. 'A communal space like the Grow-Well offers company to those who might otherwise be lonely,' I said, thinking of Harold and Kate and Heather, who, for various reasons, couldn't always venture far, 'and there really is something, as you put it, magical in helping something to grow.'

'And then harvesting the results,' added Steve, with a nod to my pile of recipe cards. 'I can see you've come prepared,' he went on, laughing. 'Tell us a bit about what you're hanging on to there, Poppy.'

I explained about the recipes I gave away at work – giving Greengages a mention, which I knew would make Harry's day – and then Steve surprised me by telling me that he already had half a dozen of the cards in his kitchen at home.

'And I can confirm,' he added with a wink, 'that the chuck-it-all-in chutney I made last autumn was an absolute triumph.'

'I'm delighted to hear it.' I flushed.

'Stick with us, folks,' he said, grinning at me, 'and we'll be back after this to take a couple of calls.'

After a quick breather while the listeners were treated to Blur's 'Parklife', the switchboard was alight with callers wanting to know all about the garden, how to successfully grow outdoor tomatoes (a question neither Jacob nor I were really qualified to answer) and whether we had a Twitter account for folk to follow.

Jacob told that particular keen caller that at that precise moment we hadn't but he was certain that by the end of the day we would. We exchanged smiles; he was no doubt thinking the same as I was – that Ryan would be able to help with that.

'And we have time for just one more question,' said Steve, who was clearly delighted with how the interview had gone.

'This is for Poppy,' came a man's voice I vaguely recognised.

'Hi,' I said. 'How can I help?'

'I was wondering if you were ever going to get round to putting your recipes in a book?' he asked.

'They're just a hobby really,' I answered. 'I don't think there's anywhere near enough interest in them to warrant it—'

'Oh, I don't know about that,' interrupted Steve. 'I think it sounds like a wonderful idea.'

'I agree,' joined in Jacob. 'You could publish one for each season and include photos from the garden.'

I shook my head; the idea was ridiculous. But it did sound nice.

'Well,' I conceded, 'I'll definitely think about it.'

'Perhaps you could sell them to raise funds for the Grow-Well,' the caller suggested.

Now that really was an exciting idea.

Back at Colin's shop, which had now closed for the day after a very brisk day of trading, Jacob and I were greeted by a heroes' welcome. Almost everyone from the Grow-Well Garden was there and they all gathered round Colin's laptop to listen to the interview again via the station's catch-up facility.

'You were both fantastic,' said Lou after we had gone through the excruciating experience of listening to ourselves online, thrusting glasses of prosecco into our hands. 'You sounded really good together,' she added with a wink.

The wink was an unnecessary addition to her comment and made me feel grateful that Lisa was in London promoting her book. I knew exactly what Lou was insinuating and in lieu of Lisa I waited for Ryan to comment. Although his loaded comments had been somewhat lacking of late, I was sure he would have something to say. When he didn't I looked around and realised he wasn't there. Gus was enjoying the comforts of his new basket in the shop window, from where he had an uninterrupted view of the street, but my brother wasn't with him.

'Where's Ryan?' I frowned.

'What did you think of my question, Poppy?' called Mark from across the room.

'That was you!' I called back, momentarily distracted. 'I knew I recognised the voice.'

'I thought it was a great idea,' said Jacob, 'I'm sure they'd sell.'

'Me too,' Mark carried on, coming across to join us. 'And if it helps you decide, I'd happily contribute a few simple bread recipes.'

'Really?' I asked.

Perhaps his idea wasn't such a crazy one after all. Working on a collaboration wouldn't be anywhere near as daunting as doing it on my own. Perhaps I could even ask John to share his top-secret barbecue marinades.

'Really.' Mark nodded. 'And I love the seasonal idea, Jacob. I'm sure between us all we could cook enough up, Poppy – no pun intended – to produce four small issues. It could be a little slice of simple country life right here in the heart of the city. Maybe Colin could be our stockist.'

'Hmm,' I said, imagining four prettily decorated books packed full of simple ideas to encourage folk to grow, preserve, barbecue, bake and enjoy produce they had grown, or had at least a hand in growing, themselves. 'Perhaps he could.'

In spite of the fact that Norfolk was a rural county there were, as with most places, plenty of folk who were completely cut off from the countryside and had little idea about where their food came from and how it was grown. Perhaps something like these books Mark was suggesting would provide an opportunity to help them think about that a bit.

'Did I not give you Ryan's message, Poppy?' Colin came over and asked.

He looked a little wobbly round the edges but I couldn't be sure if he was tipsy or simply on a high from the day's excitement. Either way, I wasn't going to broach the book stockist suggestion with him then; I was more concerned about what my brother was up to.

'No,' I said, 'you didn't, what message?'

'He said to tell you that you were great on the radio,' he explained, counting off each comment on his fingers, 'that he's heading into the city for a bit with some lad called Joe and that you aren't to worry because he won't be drinking.'

'Oh,' I said, feeling instantly worried as Colin wandered off again. 'Right. Thanks.'

I'd already had one dose of my brother heading out on his own and I hadn't much enjoyed the result. I abandoned my half-full glass on the shop counter as an immediate ache began to pulse through my head.

'Don't look so worried,' said Jacob, trying to hand me back my glass. 'I'm sure everything will be fine.'

I ignored the glass and raised my eyebrows.

'Look,' Jacob continued, 'there's a lad called Joe who comes to the youth club. He's a good kid.'

'Is he friends with Ryan?'

'I'm not really sure,' he admitted. 'But he's the only Joe I know and it's not as if Ryan has been gadding about the city getting in trouble, is it?'

'I guess not,' I said, biting my lip and trying not to replay the last time he had gone out. 'But he's not really mentioned any friends to me, and certainly no one called Joe.'

'He's your sixteen-year-old brother, Poppy.' Jacob smiled. 'I daresay there's plenty he hasn't mentioned to you.'

As much as I hated that, I knew it was true.

'I think I'll head home,' I said. 'It's been a really busy day.'

'I'll walk you back,' said Jacob.

'There's no need.'

'I know there's no need,' he said, putting his glass down next to mine, 'but I'd like to. Besides, you aren't the only one who could do with an early night.'

It was a warm evening. The weather reports were all warning of unprecedented soaring temperatures for July and that was something I personally wasn't looking forward to at all. I was a sunny-spring and smoky-autumn kind of girl and I didn't mind cosy fireside winters either, but summer heat left me cold.

'Are you okay?' Jacob asked when we arrived back in the square. 'You've barely said a word since we left the party.'

I was feeling a bit rotten for ducking out so early, but the fact that Ryan was out goodness knows where and with goodness knows who had kind of knocked my desire to celebrate on the head.

'I'm not sure I much like this parenting lark,' I admitted, pressing the palms of my hands into my aching temples. 'It's harder than I thought it would be.'

'You're his sister,' Jacob said gently, 'not his mother, and you're doing the best you can. You've more than made up for the years you had drifted apart and I know for a fact that he wouldn't do anything to hurt you or disappoint you, Poppy. Not again. He's learned his lesson now.'

'Really?'

'Really,' he reiterated. 'I'm certain you can trust him to do the right thing.'

I wished with all my heart that I felt as sure of that as Jacob sounded.

'He thinks the world of you,' he carried on. 'We all do.'

I dropped my hands and looked up at him and he gently pulled me into a hug. This wasn't the sort of gesture I associated with Jacob but I allowed myself to relax into his embrace. I realised it had been a long time since I had been held. It felt safe and comfortable and I clung on a little tighter, unwilling to let the momentary sanctuary go.

I'd been single for quite a while now and I realised in that moment that my life was somewhat lacking in physical comforts. I wasn't thinking about sex and passion, but the simple intimacy and reassurance of an all-encompassing hug. The desire to be held, to be held up, if only for a minute, was something I missed far more than a sweaty hour in the sack.

Given the chance I would have stayed there, wrapped in Jacob's arms, all night. I could feel his breath in the crook of my neck, his firm grip holding me close and the warmth of his body meeting and mingling with mine.

I shifted a little to look up at him again. He was staring down at me and I could tell from the size of his pupils that he had more than a hug on his mind. It was a shock to see his expression, but not an unpleasant one, and I remained rooted to the spot.

Very slowly he lowered his lips to meet mine. His kiss was tender and soft and over all too quickly. As I felt him begin to pull away I moved with him, determined not to lose the connection. The kiss deepened as he came back, the tip of his tongue slowly caressing my lips, and I opened my mouth, letting him in deeper as my body came alive and desire took over. So much for only missing the comfort of a hug. My libido had suddenly burst into flame and felt searing hot.

'I'm sorry,' he said, suddenly dropping his arms and stepping away. 'What am I doing?'

He sounded angry rather than aroused.

'Poppy, I'm so sorry,' he said again.

'It's okay,' I said, trying to reach out to him.

'No,' he said, his hands straying to his hair as he took another step back. 'It's really not.'

'It was just a kiss,' I said.

I knew it was way more than 'just a kiss' really, but it clearly wasn't the time to make a song and dance about it.

'Blame it on the prosecco.' I smiled.

I would have blamed it on anything if it meant I could have wiped away the look of horror on his face.

'I didn't really drink any.'

'Well, the stars then.'

'I can't see any stars.'

I was out of ideas.

'Friends don't kiss, Poppy,' he pointed out, still looking stricken, 'especially ones who have acknowledged the spark they don't want to encourage. It's too risky.'

'Stop being so dramatic,' I said, trying to calmly shrug off what had just happened, but he was right; it was a risk.

Jacob was my friend, a good friend, and I wasn't going to allow one heart-stopping kiss, the best kiss I'd ever had, actually, to jeopardise that if that was all he wanted from me.

'I'm going to go,' he said, before I had a chance to make it all right.

He couldn't even look me in the eye.

'Okay,' I called after him, 'just don't make a big deal out of this, Jacob. It doesn't have to mean anything, okay? Jacob?'

He didn't look back and I watched him walk away before letting myself into the house, wondering how such a wonderful and well-planned day could have such an unexpected and spontaneous end.

# Chapter 21

When Jacob and I had left Colin's after-hours launch party I had been determined that I wouldn't go to bed and fall asleep until Ryan was safely home, checked for wear and tear and subtly, but thoroughly, quizzed about what he'd been doing.

Had I known that I was about to be kissed and consequently stirred in a way that I had never been before, I wouldn't have felt quite so preoccupied about the possibility of nodding off, because after my all-too-brief encounter with Jacob's loving lips there was absolutely no way I was going to be able to sleep.

I had no way of knowing if Jacob felt the same way as I did but those thirty or so shared seconds had completely knocked my socks off. I did however know that he had referred once again to The Spark and that if his sack full of damaged relationship baggage was added to it, we could well end up with a lost friendship and awkward neighbourly relations. Neither of us wanted that. This little flame had to be properly snuffed out. We were friends, firm friends, now and we both needed and had welcomed that platonic, uncomplicated togetherness into our lives – but that kiss, though . . .

I was just beginning to think that it was going to be impossible to stop playing it over in my head (and embellishing for good measure) when the sound of Ryan's key rattled in the front door lock and I was thankfully distracted.

I lay quiet and still, hardly daring to breathe as I strained to listen. How he handled taking off his trainers and scaling the staircase would give me some clue as to the state he was in. I waited, fully expecting to hear him trip, giggle, hurl or possibly all three, but from what I could make out he was stone-cold sober and in complete control of his fine motor skills. It was such a relief to hear him moving quietly and competently about that I began to wonder if I really wanted to get into a conversation, that could well descend into a row, at ten minutes to midnight. Perhaps it would be best to wait until the morning and have The Talk over tea and toast in the back garden.

I slipped back under the duvet and tried to get comfortable. I would deal with Ryan, and my feelings for Jacob, tomorrow.

'Morning, sis, good night was it?'

'What?'

'Colin's party! How long did it go on for?'

'No idea,' I muttered, floating up from the depths of sleep and shielding my eyes from the sudden burst of sunlight that filled the room as Ryan flung open the curtains. 'I was actually home before you were.'

All of the events of the evening before came flooding back in an overwhelming rush. Ryan had gone off with some random boy and Jacob had rocked my world and aroused my slumbering libido and I was supposed to be up, dressed and dealing with it all like a responsible adult.

'You're not hung over then?' Ryan grinned as he placed a mug of tea on the nightstand and plonked himself down heavily on the bed next to me.

'No,' I snapped, feeling nettled that he had the upper hand. 'Are you?'

'Hardly,' he said and laughed, making my head pound. 'I've learned my lesson as far as alcohol is concerned, but to be honest I expected to find you feeling the worse for wear.'

'Why?'

'Because you never sleep in,' he said, leaning forward and tapping the top of my alarm clock, 'not even on a Sunday.'

I didn't explain that I didn't usually sleep in because as a rule I wouldn't be lying awake half the night worrying that I wasn't doing a good enough job of taking care of him, before moving on to mulling over how I thought my nearest neighbour's soft full lips would feel caressing other parts of my anatomy. Not that I was supposed to be thinking about that, of course, but during the longest watches of the night the brain was prone to wander off along all kinds of forbidden paths . . .

'It's almost nine,' Ryan nudged, pulling me back to the present and reminding me that I had failed to get up and play the role of concerned sister, with its potential to end in a shouty showdown.

'I know,' I said, sitting up and pushing my hair away from my face. 'I can see that, but I didn't get off to sleep until after four.'

I was annoyed that I felt compelled to justify my slatternly Sunday lie-in.

'Well, I'll leave you to it.' Ryan smiled, handing me the tea he had gone to the effort of getting up to make. 'I'll be back later.'

'No, hang on,' I said, no doubt sounding snappier than I should, but I was none too impressed that he was heading off out again. 'You promised Graham that you'd help in the garden today. You can't go shirking your responsibilities just because you've found something more exciting to go and do, you know.'

'What's that supposed to mean?'

'You still haven't told me what you got up to last night.'

'Jeez, I knew you wouldn't be able to resist starting on about that,' he bit back.

'So, where did you go,' I blurted out, 'and who is this Joe who has suddenly appeared on the scene?'

I had a horrible feeling that I was beginning to sound like a nagging parent. A big sister was supposed to be more of an ally than an inquisitor, wasn't she?

'He hasn't *just appeared*,' Ryan said, mimicking my tone. 'He's a regular at the youth centre and we've been hanging out together whenever I've been down there. Last night was the first time we'd met up outside the club and we just mooched about a bit. He introduced me to a couple of other lads he knows and we wandered down to Chapelfield Gardens and messed about on their skateboards.'

'Right,' I said. 'I see.'

'To be honest, I thought you would have been pleased that I've found a mate my own age. I can't spend my entire time here hanging around with you and your friends, you know.'

I didn't say so, but I wished he could. That way I could have wrapped him up in cotton wool and kept him safe – not that he was really likely to come to any harm, but now I was responsible for him it was my intention to keep him on the straight and narrow.

'Well, I would have appreciated it if you could have let me know yourself,' I told him.

It was a bit much to find something else to moan about given the fact that he'd offered a perfectly satisfactory response to my questioning, but I couldn't seem to help myself.

'I was going to send you a text, but you were at the radio station. I thought you'd be pissed off if your phone started going off in the middle of the interview.'

He was right. I would have been annoyed, especially as I hadn't thought to turn it to silent.

'So, I asked Colin to let you know. I left a message with him and asked him to tell you as soon as you got back.'

'He did tell me,' I admitted.

'So, why the fuss?' Ryan demanded, stomping over to the door. 'You still don't trust me, do you?'

'Look—'

'No. I've got to go.'

'You can't just go,' I shouted after him. 'There are things you promised to do today, Ryan!'

I couldn't believe that he was going to let Graham down. I knew he was annoyed with me, but that was no reason to let everyone else down.

'I'm well aware of that,' he said, with anger flashing in his eyes. 'But first I promised I would go and collect Gus, which is where I'm heading now, and then, if it's all right with you, I'm going to the garden. If you'd waited to hear me out, you'd know I'd never arranged to do anything different.'

'Oh . . .'

'I can't believe you thought I was going to bail,' he said sadly, which made me feel even worse. 'Do you really think I'm still that selfish?'

Not surprisingly, he didn't hang around to hear me apologise but stormed out, slamming the front door behind him and making the windows rattle in their frames. I drained my tea, slumped back down in the bed and pulled the duvet over my head. Given the mess I'd just made of things with my brother, I thought it was probably best if I didn't try to talk to Jacob, not today anyway.

The following week kept me so busy that there was no opportunity to worry about my kiss with Jacob or properly make amends with Ryan. Work was so manic, I barely had time to draw breath, let alone keep tabs on my brother.

'Have you got any of those chuck-it-all-in chutney cards left that you were talking about on the radio?' asked a young woman with a small baby in a pram. 'It sounds like just the thing for our end-of-summer allotment party.'

'This is the last one,' I told her, handing it over, 'and there's a piccalilli one as well if you're interested.'

She took both and I began to think that given the number of customers who had started to take the cards, there wouldn't be any point in producing the recipe books because I'd given so many ideas away for free.

'You were right about this being the way forward,' Harry puffed as he rushed by, 'but I had no idea it would make us this busy.'

'Me neither,' I laughed.

Harry had decided to go ahead and turn Greengages into the first completely plastic-free grocer in the city. Thanks to my research earlier in the year, the produce was now packed into paper bags, or bags the customers came in with, and nothing was unnecessarily wrapped. It hadn't been easy finding a wholesaler who would go out of their way to deliver loose, but Harry had stuck to his principles. He said the look of the place, and the people holding open their jute bags and baskets to be filled, reminded him of his grandfather's old shop, but I knew that what we were working on now was the future.

'Here's Andy,' he said with a smile as a horn tooted outside. 'He's here for today's orders.'

As well as going plastic-free, Harry was also trialling a

new delivery service. The delivery charge was waived if the order was worth a certain amount or if there were enough properties in a certain proximity prepared to take delivery at the same time. It was a logistical challenge but was working well so far.

'Hey, Poppy,' Ryan muttered as he unexpectedly turned up just as Harry and I were getting ready to close the shop.

'Hey,' I said back, bending to greet Gus. 'What's up?'

Ryan had been every bit as busy as I had over the last few days. If he wasn't at college or doing his bit in the garden, he was helping Colin in A Good Book, which had seen a definite upturn in trade, especially now Colin had decided to sell online as well as directly from the shop.

My clever brother had proved most useful when it came to setting up both the Grow-Well Twitter account and a website and newsletter for Colin, and I knew the book club and some author events were also in the pipeline. I wasn't sure the cheeky tweets referring to Mark's tasty baps and the like were entirely appropriate, but the Grow-Well followers were lapping them up.

Ryan and I hadn't talked about his evening with Joe or the subsequent trips out and I daresay my brother was wondering, just as I was, if we were both keeping busy to avoid having to talk through anything meaningful at all.

'I've had a message,' he told me, 'from Mum.'

'No way,' I gulped, standing back up. 'I take it she's back then?'

'Yeah.'

'She hasn't said you've got to move back, has she?'

Ryan gave me a withering look.

'What about college? Did she ask about that?'

'She's barely acknowledged the note I left about coming here,' he huffed. 'So, she's hardly likely to ask about lessons, is she?'

'Sorry,' I apologised, 'stupid questions. So, what did she want then?'

I had checked my own phone earlier when I was making Harry tea, so I knew she hadn't bothered to message me.

'To moan.'

Ryan shook his head and handed me his phone. I wrinkled my nose as I read.

'So, she's come back to find you gone,' I said, 'and the only thing she's worried about is the state of the outside bin.'

'Maggots though' – Ryan gagged – 'and flies.'

'Even so,' I said, handing back the phone and trying to dismiss the image of the photo she had attached from my mind. 'You'd think that would be the last thing she'd be concerned about.'

I had secretly hoped that her coming back and finding Ryan gone would have given her a jolt. Not necessarily kick-start her maternal instincts, because I knew she didn't have any, but perhaps prompt her to question her priorities. Clearly, I had been wrong. She hadn't even broached the subject of him going home – but then, given how quickly I'd got used to having him around, that was a relief.

'Don't forget this is our mother we're talking about,' Ryan

reminded me. 'She's nothing like your average everyday mum, is she? She wouldn't be out of place on Jeremy Kyle's couch.'

'That's true,' I conceded, bowing to Ryan's more recent experience of life with her, 'but even so, she could be at least a *little* bit grateful that you were responsible enough to lock up.'

'Do you think I'm responsible then?' he asked, looking up from his phone screen.

'Of course, I do,' I said, pulling him into a sisterly hug before he'd had a chance to see it coming.

'But after the row last Sunday . . .'

'We're brother and sister, Ryan,' I said, letting him go before I reached up to ruffle his hair, which I knew he absolutely hated, 'we're supposed to row, remember?'

'I guess,' he said, knocking my hand away and smoothing his hair back down. 'So, we're all right then?'

'We're fine,' I said, wishing I'd had the sense, in spite of how busy the week had been, to clear the air sooner. 'We're good.'

It was true. I did feel better now the subject had been broached. Life had got heavy going enough all of a sudden. Dragging around the additional weight of extra worries was one burden I didn't need right now. Perhaps it was time to bite the bullet and face my neighbour after that sweet seductive kiss?

'In that case,' said Ryan, 'shall we go to The Dragon together? Colin said everyone was meeting down there for dinner.'

There was no time like the present.

# Chapter 22

It was still early enough in the evening for The Dragon to be relatively quiet. In fact, it was so early, Ryan and I were the first of our little crew to arrive.

'Let's see if there's a table outside,' he suggested, heading for the door next to the bar that led to the pub's little garden. 'It's been so hot today but it's supposed to be cooler this evening. If we wait for the others, we won't stand a chance of getting anywhere to sit out there.'

He had a point. The heat, as predicted, had already begun to build and we were only one week into the month.

'Wow,' gasped Ryan, not long after we had picked a spot in the furthest corner, which was shaded by the overhanging branches of a silver birch tree. 'She always looks good, but she's scrubbed up even better tonight, hasn't she?'

I turned to see who had drawn his attention.

'Blimey.' I smiled. 'Hey, Lou. You look amazing. Have you been home to change?'

'No,' she said casually, carefully picking her way across the grass to join us, 'I've just come straight from the shop.'

'In that case I wish I'd called in.' Ryan grinned.

Lou flashed him a dazzling smile and sat herself in the seat best positioned to see the pub door. I was fairly certain she didn't usually go to work wearing heels and such a low neckline, but forbore to comment. I wasn't all that sure about the comments Ryan had made about her appearance either. Was I going to have to broach a conversation with him about objectifying women, on top of everything else?

'Aren't the boys here yet?' Lou asked, pulling an old-fashioned gold-plated compact out of her bag and lightly powdering her nose.

'Not yet,' I said, looking at her sophisticated outfit and then down at my creased T-shirt-and-combats get-up.

No one could ever accuse me of getting dressed up to go to work, but then, humping sacks of spuds around really didn't lend itself to wearing posh frocks and shoes I would no doubt break my neck in.

Ryan looked at me and smirked. I knew he was thinking exactly the same thing.

'I'll get some drinks in and grab some menus,' I said, before he had a chance to comment.

'I think I'll have a G and T,' said Lou as she snapped the compact shut and returned it to her bag. 'For a change. And I don't think I fancy anything to eat. It's too hot. Ask for plenty of ice, won't you?'

'And don't get me anything,' Ryan said quickly, having just read something on his phone.

'I had no intention of buying you gin,' I told him.

'No,' he said. 'I meant anything to eat or drink. I'll have something when I get back.'

'Back from where?' I asked.

'Luke's just messaged and asked if I can go to the garden,' he explained. 'Will it be all right if I leave Gus here?'

'Of course,' said Lou, holding out her hands to take hold of the little dog.

Gus promptly wriggled himself free from her grasp and threw himself down in the shade under the table with a disgruntled huff. Clearly it was still too warm for being fussed over.

'He'll be fine,' I reassured my brother as we walked back into the pub together. 'I'll get someone to refill the doggy water bowl and I'll keep an eye on him, don't worry. Do you know what Luke wants to see you about?'

'Not a clue.' He shrugged. 'I'll see you in a bit.'

Ryan headed off. I was pleased I hadn't snapped and launched into another lecture. Perhaps I was learning something as I blundered my way along after all, I thought as I waited in the queue to order drinks and a few bags of crisps instead of asking for menus. Lou was right, it was too hot to eat. In the few minutes we had been outside the place had started to fill up and I was pleased we had managed to get seated outside.

'Need a hand?' said a voice behind me.

It was Jacob.

'Hey, Jacob,' I squeaked. What had happened to my voice? 'Yeah, thanks. That'd be great.'

I cleared my throat and stared ahead, ostensibly admiring the optics.

'So,' he said, sounding every bit as awkward as I was feeling, 'how's your week been? I heard the shop's been really busy. I've been meaning to come along but . . .'

His words trailed off as I reached the front of the queue and ordered our round, remembering to ask for plenty of ice for Lou's G and T.

'You were saying,' I said, turning to look at him while the guy behind the bar began to pour and fill.

'Sorry?'

'You said you were going to come to the shop, but didn't get to tell me why you hadn't.'

'Well—' he began again.

'You haven't been trying to avoid me, by any chance, have you?' I interrupted with a smile.

There was no point in beating about the bush. If we didn't at least give a nod to how our last encounter had ended we were going to face an evening of furtive glances and disjointed chat that the others would, no doubt, pick up on. After the week I'd had I didn't think I could cope with that. Best to have the conversation now, while we were out of earshot.

'No,' he said, looking a little flustered, 'no, of course not.'

'That's all right then.' I nodded. 'It's just that I noticed you've been getting a lift in to work with Hannah and I wondered if that was because you didn't want to walk with me.'

'No,' he said again, more firmly this time. 'No, nothing like that. It's just that it's almost the end of term and I've had loads of extra stuff to ferry backwards and forwards. We're putting on an end-of-year performance, the class that is, not me, and I've been working on the props and stuff in the evenings.'

'Right.' I smiled. 'I see.'

'Although,' he added, dropping his voice, 'I have been feeling really rotten about what happened, but that's not why I haven't been around.'

'Well, that's all right then,' I lied.

It really wasn't all right at all but I could hardly say as much, could I? I didn't want him feeling rotten about it; I wanted him so overcome with desire that he had made a point of avoiding me for fear of finding the urge to kiss me again irresistible. I know I had told myself I didn't want to jeopardise our bond, that the spark had to be snuffed out, that his baggage would help ensure I kept him at a friend-appropriate arm's length, but actually standing there next to him for the first time since our lips had met, I was flabbergasted to realise that I *was* prepared to risk our friendship.

It was finally time to accept what I had, without comprehending it, been feeling for weeks. Jacob was the man who I wanted to go the distance with.

'There you go, Poppy,' said the barman.

'Thanks,' I stuttered, fumbling to hand over the cash. 'Thanks very much.'

I took my change and the crisps and Jacob carried the tray out to the garden.

'Evening, Lou,' he said with a grin. 'You're looking very lovely this evening. What's the occasion? Are you going on somewhere later?'

I sat back down, trying not to feel niggled that he hadn't commented on my appearance, but then given that I'd had a sweaty day working in the shop there was nothing he could compliment me on anyway.

'Thank you, Jacob,' said Lou, shooting him a friendly grin as she sipped her ice-packed glass, 'how lovely of you to say so.'

It wasn't all that long ago that they'd met and fallen out within a matter of minutes. It was mind-blowing to think of how much had changed, for all of us, in such a short space of time.

'I have no plans to go anywhere else,' she added, 'but the night is still young.'

Jacob laughed as Colin appeared, framed in the pub doorway, and I realised that his and Lou's relationship wasn't the only thing that had altered. Colin looked more relaxed than I had ever seen him, in spite of everything he'd recently been through with his father.

'Sorry I'm late,' he said, rushing over as Lou ushered me out of my seat to ensure that Colin had no choice but to sit next to her. 'Mark popped in to say that he was bailing on us because Neil had finished work on time for once and Natalie called just as I was about to leave.'

The smallest sigh escaped Lou's lips and I wasn't the only one to notice it. Jacob caught my eye and I realised that he too was well aware of why Lou was going out of her way these days to look even more stunning than usual. Of course, the irony was that the only person who hadn't realised was the one who had thought she was perfect however she looked for the last goodness knows how many years!

'Is everything all right with your dad?' Jacob asked.

'Yes,' said Colin, reaching under the table to make a fuss of Gus. 'He's doing really well, thanks. This was more of a social call.'

'Right,' said Jacob, looking at me again. 'You and Natalie seem to be getting on well.'

I raised my eyebrows in a *what the hell are you doing* kind of way and he shrugged back at me, indicating that he had no idea but felt he had to say something. I looked at Lou, who had suddenly become more interested in something on her phone than the conversation going on around her.

'Yeah,' said Colin, his face flushing as red as Lou's, 'we are. I'm hoping to go and see her next weekend. And to check up on Dad of course,' he hastily added.

'But what about the shop?' Lou asked, tuning back in as quickly as she'd allegedly zoned out. 'It would be a shame if you shut for the weekend and missed out on all the extra trade the makeover is bringing in, wouldn't it?'

'You're right,' he agreed. 'And there's no way I'd do that. I've arranged cover.'

'Oh,' she said, 'right.'

'I take it things are still going well, Colin?' I asked, keen to move the conversation on to safer ground. 'With the shop, I mean.'

'Really well.' He smiled. 'I know a certain amount of footfall is down to curiosity and that it will tail off a bit at some point, but so far so good. Lou and Ryan have really turned the fortunes of the place round. And Jacob with the new name, of course.'

Jacob raised his glass.

'We were pleased to be able to help out,' said Lou, sounding somewhat appeased. 'Have you had many comments about the window display?'

The current display depicted a beach scene, complete with sand, flamingo-themed accessories and a variety of popular beach and summer holiday reads.

'Loads,' said Colin, 'so many people have come in and said they didn't realise I sold those sorts of books. I think because of the dark paintwork and gloomy interior folk assumed it was all non-fiction and musty second-hand atlases and encyclopaedias.'

That didn't surprise me at all.

'I sent Natalie a picture of the window earlier in the week and she's made me promise to keep three of the books for her to take away with her on her holiday next month. Do you think you'll be ready to change the display by then, Lou?'

I could feel my shoulders slumping almost as low as Lou's had just dropped.

'I'll see what I can do,' she said through gritted teeth.

'Or I suppose I could swap the three titles that Natalie wants for three different ones, couldn't I?' he suggested brightly. 'That way you wouldn't have to change it and the customers would have some different books to look at.'

'Great idea,' Lou agreed.

We all jumped as Jacob's phone suddenly began to vibrate across the table. He looked completely taken aback but didn't pick it up.

'Aren't you going to answer that?' Lou asked.

'Yeah,' he said, finally snatching it up and glowering at the screen. 'Sorry. I'll take it out front. It'll be quieter there.'

'I wonder who that was,' commented Lou, her eyes trained on his retreating back. 'Did you see the colour drain from his face?'

'Do you talk about everyone behind their backs?' asked Colin.

There was no real sting in his tone, but Lou obviously felt one nonetheless.

'Well excuse me,' she bit back, 'it was just an observation.'

I couldn't remember a time when the pair of them had ever been so prickly with each other. Lou might have made a career out of teasing Colin and winding him up, but he usually just took it on the chin. I wasn't sure their friendship was going to survive the changes Colin's acquaintance with Nurse Natalie had instigated.

'I'll just go and ask for some fresh water for the dog bowl,' I told them. 'I forgot before and Gus looks as though he could do with a drink.'

There was no sign of Jacob out along the road and I hoped he hadn't gone home. I didn't much fancy playing referee to the pair I could now see, through the window, sitting with their backs to each other.

'Can I have a pint of water for the dog bowl, please?' I asked at the bar.

'And how about a drink for your brother and his mate?'

'Ryan!' I jumped, turning round. 'You're back quick. Was everything all right?'

'Better than all right actually.' He grinned. 'Poppy, this is Joe, Joe this is my sister Poppy.'

'Hi,' said Joe, flicking his hair out of his eyes. 'Ryan's told me a lot about you.'

'Yeah,' I said, looking back at my brother, 'I'll bet he has.'

'Nothing bad.' Joe smiled, revealing dimples that made him look more boyish than bloke. 'Not that bad, anyway.'

'Well,' I said, feeling relieved that Joe didn't look like the type of lad who would lead my brother astray. 'That's something I suppose. Ryan, why don't you take that water out for Gus and I'll get you two drinks. Will Coke be okay?'

'Yeah,' said Joe, 'great, thanks.'

No request for rum and he had lovely manners. The lad was ticking all the right boxes. I was pretty certain that Ryan had asked his friend along to prove to me that he hadn't hooked up with someone I wouldn't approve of and I was grateful for that. I had enough on my plate at the moment without having to worry about whether his friendship group was as harmless as he made out.

'So,' I asked, as I turfed my brother out of my seat and he and Joe made themselves comfy on the grass. 'What did Luke want? Is everything all right in the garden?'

'Graham was there too,' he said and grinned, 'they had a favour to ask and yes, everything is absolutely fine in the garden.'

'The place looks amazing,' joined in Joe. 'There's no way you won't win the competition.'

I was liking this lad more and more.

'I hope you're right, Joe,' I told him. 'We're all working really hard to make sure it's as perfect as possible in time for the judging.'

'When exactly is the judging?' asked Colin.

'No one knows for sure,' I explained, 'that's why we're keeping on top of everything now. It will definitely be done before the end of the month though. We're supposed to get a bit of warning so it'll be all hands on deck then, but keeping everything in order now will mean there's less to do when the time comes.'

'It doesn't look as if there's a leaf out of place to me,' said Joe. 'My grandad has an allotment south of the city but it's nothing like your place.'

'Well,' I said, feeling proud, 'I daresay there are more of us to keep it ticking over.'

'Hey, Jacob,' said Lou, 'everything all right?'

'Yep,' he said, sliding into the seat next to mine. 'Fine.'

He didn't look fine. Lou had commented on his pallor when he went to answer his phone but now he looked positively ashen, and he'd been gone a while. I hoped it wasn't bad news.

'So,' I said, trying to divert everyone's attention, 'what was the favour Luke and Graham wanted, Ryan?'

'Yes,' said Lou, 'don't keep us in suspenders.'

Both Ryan and Joe went bright red, but Colin seemed not to have heard and Jacob looked to be away with the fairies.

'Well,' said Ryan, kneeling up, 'I think I have Jacob to thank really—'

'Not at all,' he cut in, looking up at the mention of his name. 'This is down to you, Ryan.'

So he was listening then, and he knew why Ryan had been asked to go over to Prosperous Place.

'Go on,' I encouraged my brother.

'Graham and Carole are going away for a few days,' he said, 'so he's asked if I would be happy to look after the hens while he's gone. Just me,' he said proudly, 'no one else is going to be on the rota.'

'That's wonderful!' I exclaimed, resisting the urge to give him a hug.

Not only had my brother stopped smoking and learned that alcohol didn't agree with him, he'd also rediscovered his passion for birds and animals. I was delighted that Graham, having no doubt seen how well he was looking after Gus, considered him responsible enough to look after the Grow-Well girls too.

'And that's not all,' Ryan went on.

'Go on,' I said again.

'Luke and Kate are taking a trip to Wynbridge before the summer holidays and Luke has asked if I would be happy to look after the cats while they're away. He says he'll give me a set of keys to Prosperous Place so I can let myself in and out.'

'Wow, Ryan.' I swallowed, a lump forming in my throat. 'That's amazing. That house means the world to Luke. He wouldn't trust just anyone to come and go, you know.'

'That's what I said,' agreed Joe, slapping Ryan on the back. 'That guy must really think a lot of you, mate.'

Ryan looked fit to burst. I knew that to most people this wouldn't mean all that much but to my brother, who had been made to feel more or less worthless for as long as he could remember, it was the ultimate accolade. Knowing that my friends and neighbours trusted him without question would hopefully prove to him that he wasn't a nuisance, as our mother's many fellas had suggested, or a noose, as Mum herself had told him on more than one occasion.

'Didn't you know?' Ryan asked me. 'Hadn't they mentioned it to you first?'

'No,' I said, 'I had no idea.'

'And I only know because Graham told me about the hens,' Jacob added. 'He didn't ask me if I thought you'd be interested or if I thought it was a good idea, he just said that was what he was going to do.'

Ryan nodded and ducked his head.

'And acting as keyholder for Prosperous Place is news to me,' Jacob went on. 'I hadn't heard anything about that at all.'

'And don't forget you're covering some hours with Andrew for me in the shop next weekend,' put in Colin.

'You really are Mr Indispensable,' praised Lou, making Ryan's colour flare again. 'I don't know what we'd all do without you.'

I had to agree with her there. We had all grown to love having Ryan around and I tried not to think of how quickly the time was ticking by and how soon it would be that he had to decide what he was going to do next. I knew that our mother's lack of interest in having him home meant he was hardly likely to go back to Wynmouth, but given the life he was carving out for himself in Nightingale Square, even though he wouldn't want to stay living with me for ever, I also knew that it wasn't going to be easy for him to leave there either.

# Chapter 23

Ryan and Joe didn't hang around for long after Ryan had made his exciting announcement. They were heading back to the youth centre, where Joe was hoping to give Ryan a run for his money at the pool table. I hadn't been aware of it but apparently my brother, as well as being the most responsible teenager within a two-mile radius, was also a wizard with a cue.

'Can you believe it?' I said once the boys had gone, beaming.

'I know,' said Lou, pulling her phone back out of her bag again. 'I didn't think people played pool these days, especially teenagers.'

Colin looked at me and rolled his eyes.

'I didn't mean that,' I scolded.

'I know you didn't.' She laughed. 'But yes, I can believe it. I'm not at all surprised that Graham and Luke have put their trust in him. Don't forget I worked with him on Colin's shop makeover. He's a hard worker, Poppy, with some amazing skills for a sixteen-year-old.'

I knew they were the result of the time he'd spent working with his dad.

'If he had been poised to tip off the rails when you invited him to stay,' Lou continued, 'I think it's safe to say he's firmly back on track now.'

'I have Jacob to thank for that, really,' I reminded her. 'You're the one who has really helped him, aren't you?' I added, giving him a nudge.

'Sorry,' he said, 'what?'

He looked dog-tired and although he had been pleased with Ryan's news, he hadn't jumped up and down nearly half as much as I would have expected.

'What's up with you tonight?' asked Lou. 'You've not been right since you took that call. I thought the original Mr Grizzle had been packed in your attic since Poppy signed you up at the Grow-Well. Did you have some bad news? Is that what's turned you back into Mr Grumpy?'

'Lou,' Colin tutted.

'Colin,' she shot back, mimicking his tone.

'You two,' I tried to interject.

'I'm only trying to make light of the situation,' she snapped at Colin, standing up. 'At least I've bothered to ask.'

'But it's *how* you ask,' said Colin.

'Well, excuse me for coming straight to the point,' she said bitterly, 'I daresay precious Nurse Natalie has all manner of speaking and listening skills at her disposal, doesn't she?'

'What are you talking about now?' Colin frowned while Jacob and I tried to pretend we were invisible.

'I bet,' Lou raged on, her voice catching in her throat, 'I bet if she was here tonight asking Jacob who took the jam out of his bloody doughnut she'd be making a far better job of it than me, wouldn't she? Of course, she would,' she rushed on, 'because she's so sodding perfect!'

'Lou!' Colin called after her, standing up.

'I have to go!' she called back. 'I've got a date.'

Colin flopped back down in his seat and looked from me to Jacob and back again.

'What the hell was that about?' he asked. 'What did I say?'

'Work it out for yourself, mate,' said Jacob, gathering glasses, 'I'm not going to spell it out for you. Another?'

'Yeah,' I said, 'just a half though, thanks.'

'Not for me,' said Colin. 'Has she really got a date?' he asked me.

'No idea,' I said as my phone began to bleat. 'She didn't say anything earlier.'

The text message lighting up my screen was from Lou and I read it out of Colin's view. No, she didn't have a date. She was going home for a bubble bath and a good cry and no, I wasn't to let on to Colin.

'I think I'll head home,' said Colin sadly. 'This evening hasn't quite turned out how I thought it would.'

'And why do you think that is?'

'Beats me,' he said. 'I was on cloud nine when I arrived. Are you still happy for Gus to go home with you?'

'Of course,' I told him, 'I don't think you'd be the best company for him really, Colin, do you?'

It appalled me to think that he was every bit as dense about recognising that Lou had fallen for him as she had been for so long about picking up on how he felt about her. If they didn't get their acts together soon I was going to have to bang their heads together. That is, assuming Natalie didn't rush in to tend to Colin's bump and kiss him better.

'I take it Colin's gone home then?' asked Jacob when he came back with our drinks.

'Yes,' I answered, 'and Lou hasn't got a date—'

'I didn't think she had.'

'. . . she's gone home for a good cry.'

'Jeez,' he muttered before taking a pull at his pint. 'This just goes to prove everything we said, doesn't it?'

'About what?'

'Relationships between friends being a bad idea.'

'Yeah,' I glumly agreed, 'I suppose it does.'

'Because when they go belly-up,' he carried on, 'which they inevitably will, you end up losing a friend as well as a lover.'

'Uh-huh.'

'Not that relationships between adults who weren't friends first necessarily turn out any better, of course.'

I didn't say anything.

'And I'll tell you something else,' he said, turning to look me in the eye, 'you won't ever catch me jumping into another relationship, short-term or otherwise.'

'Given everything you've been through,' I said gently, 'I'm not at all surprised that you feel that way.'

I yearned to suggest that he might feel differently in a few months' time. After all, if I was in the midst of, dare I say it, falling in love, then perhaps one day he might find himself there too?

'You don't know the half of it,' he said, draining his glass. 'Same again?'

I'd barely started mine.

'No,' I said, 'I'm still on this one, thanks.'

I guessed that Lou had been right; the phone call had been bad news.

'I'll be back in a sec.'

'Jacob,' I said, laying my hand on his arm as he stood up again, 'I think I'm going to go home. It's been a long week and I could do with an early night and a chilled day tomorrow before I'm back to work on Monday.'

'Oh, right.'

'And I daresay you've got loads to do for school, haven't you?'

'Yeah,' he said, running his free hand through his hair and making it stand up in all directions. 'Yeah, I have got quite a bit to do.'

'Why don't you come with me?'

'To your place?'

'Yes,' I said, 'come on. Let's go back to mine and if you want to, you can tell me the half that I don't know.'

*

We walked slowly back to the square with Gus padding quietly alongside. The evening was still early and it was light and warm, with just the faintest breeze rustling the leaves of the trees on the green.

'Thanks for stopping me,' said Jacob, as he breathed in a lungful of fresh air.

'From doing what?'

'Making a fool of myself in the pub.'

'You didn't make a fool of yourself,' I said.

'But I would have,' he replied huskily, 'had you not been there, and how would that have looked? A local teacher drinking himself senseless on a Saturday night because his ex still has the ability to tear his heart in two.'

I unlocked the front door, buying myself a few seconds as I bent to unclip Gus's lead and let him go in ahead of us. If Jacob's ex of what must be getting on for ten months now could still do that to him, did that mean he was still in love with her? If he was, even after all this time apart, then it was probably a good thing that I'd kept my thoughts to myself back in the pub.

'Come on,' I said, 'let's have a coffee.'

Jacob didn't want to sit outside, so we made ourselves comfortable in the little sitting room at the front of the house. I closed the curtains, just in case any of the neighbours happened to be taking an evening stroll. We each had enough going on in our lives without having to contend with adding speculation about the parameters of our relationship to the list. A rumour about that would, I knew, spread itself like bindweed through everyone's conversations.

I handed Jacob his mug and sat on the armchair next to the fireplace, curling my bare feet beneath me as was my usual habit. Jacob stretched out on the sofa, then sat forward again. He put his mug back on the coffee table and rested his elbows on his knees, looking down at the carpet.

'She's pregnant,' he blurted out. 'She's fucking pregnant.'

I stared at the top of his head, not knowing what I could possibly say. No wonder he was feeling so bad. Out of all the things he could have told me had happened this was perhaps the most unexpected. He'd painted Rebecca as a high-flying career-driven character, just like his twin brother Daniel, so it was a complete surprise to hear that she was planning to put her professional advancement on hold for parenthood.

'Oh Jacob.'

I wondered if it was Rebecca herself who had called to tell him, or his brother or perhaps one of his parents. Would it have been any more bearable to hear it from one rather than the other?

'It was Dad who phoned,' he said, looking briefly up at me.

I could see his eyes were filled with tears and rushed to kneel next to him, dumping my mug next to his on the table. It was hardly any wonder he had seemed a bit off when he came back from taking the call. He hadn't even had time to properly take it in yet.

'I'm so sorry.'

He sniffed and nodded and took a deep, shuddering breath. My heart was thrumming in my chest as I moved to lay a hand on his leg. He grabbed it before it came to rest and pulled me up on to the sofa next to him.

'Apparently they're telling everyone now because she's just reached three months. It wasn't planned or anything.'

Given Rebecca's career ambitions, that I *could* believe.

'Dad didn't want me to hear about it from anyone else.'

'That was kind of him.'

I wasn't sure if that was the right thing to say.

'Yeah well,' Jacob said. 'Dad is kind. Him and Mum are still reeling from everything that's happened almost as much as I am.'

I shook my head. There really were no words.

'And do you know what the worst of it is?' Jacob asked, looking right at me, the anguish in his eyes unbearable.

I shook my head.

'She's carrying twins.'

'Oh God.'

'Yep, she's just had the scan to confirm it. No idea of the sex yet, but God help the little mites if they're boys. I wouldn't wish a twin brother on anyone.'

I squeezed his hand tighter.

'But things might be different for them,' I suggested, 'Daniel might—'

Jacob shook his head and I stopped.

'Sorry.'

'It's all right,' he said, lifting my hand and pressing his lips against the back of it. 'In your position I wouldn't know what to say either.'

I certainly didn't know what to say now as his firm lips skimmed my hand. I repeated the *'I'm his friend'* mantra over in my head a few dozen times, just to remind myself that this evening needed to be about making Jacob feel better, not looking forward to going to bed so I could lie staring at the ceiling, thinking about where his lips had lingered.

'Here,' I said, leaning forward and reaching for his mug so he had to let me go, 'drink this. I daresay you could do with the caffeine.'

'Thanks,' he said, taking it from me and sitting back again. 'I could do with something.'

I stayed next to him on the sofa.

'This is the thing I've been dreading,' he said after we had sat in silence for a minute or two. 'I knew it was bound to happen at some point, but I wasn't expecting it to be so soon.'

'Well,' I said, wondering if it had taken Rebecca the three months to come to terms with the idea, 'perhaps it's a good thing.'

'A good thing?'

'Yes,' I said, turning to face him. 'Maybe it's no bad thing that you're having to deal with it now. If this is the most difficult thing you could imagine happening, then surely it's better to face it and get it all over and done with while everything else is still so raw.'

'Maybe,' he said, 'but in a year or two I might have moved on. The news might have hurt me less.'

'And it might not,' I batted back. 'It might have just opened up old wounds all over again. At least now you're at rock bottom and can establish a firm foundation to build on.'

'Thanks.' He smiled. 'Is that supposed to be the silver lining?'

'Yes.' I smiled back, pleased with his reaction. 'That's exactly what it is. At least now you aren't waiting for it to happen. Right now, things are as crap as they can possibly be so the only way for you to go is up.'

'Maybe.' He frowned.

'You only have to think about everything you've achieved since you've moved here to know that you can do it,' I rushed on, encouraged that he hadn't dismissed my take on the situation.

'What have I achieved?'

'Well, for a start, you have more friends here now than you can shake a stick at, you've settled into a job that you love, you have a lad who thinks the world of you and you've developed a passion for gardening—'

'Woah.' He laughed, holding up his hands. 'I wouldn't go that far.'

'Yes, you have,' I insisted, knowing that it was the gardening bit he was objecting to. 'No one can tie in beans like you can, Mr Grizzle. You've got the most dextrous hands out of all of us.'

I felt my cheeks start to burn as I imagined those hands being put to a very different use.

'When I first moved here,' I carried on, 'you told me you weren't interested in joining in and helping out.'

'I wasn't.'

'And later you said you'd never trust a living soul again.'

'I didn't think I would,' he said softly.

'Well there you are then,' I said, slapping his leg, 'all that just goes to prove that you can change and that you're more than capable of dealing with this latest blow. I have every faith in you, Jacob.'

'Bloody hell, Poppy,' he said laughingly, 'how do you do it?'

'Do what?' I smiled, stopping to take a breath.

'You know what.'

'No,' I said, 'what do you mean?'

'How do you always manage to talk me down and make me see the best of a bloody awful situation?'

I wasn't sure that I did always manage it, but I was pleased he was willing to acknowledge my efforts.

'Is that what I do?'

He raised his eyebrows.

'You had a rough time before you came here,' I said simply, 'and I wanted to help. I'd had a rough time myself when I first started work at Greengages and Harry helped me through it. I was able to turn my life round and become a part of this community and I always maintained that if I could do the same for someone else, then I would.'

'So, I'm your pay-it-forward project, am I?' Jacob grinned. 'If you aren't careful you'll use up your kindness quota on me and there won't be enough of you left to go around.'

'Don't be silly.'

'I'm not.' He laughed again. 'I mean it.'

'Well,' I said, 'living here in Nightingale Square has been a long-held dream come true for me and I just want everyone else who moves here to enjoy it as much as I do. I want to share my recipe for life far and wide.'

'Including with your brother.'

'Of course,' I agreed.

'You're doing a great job with him, you know.'

'It's not all down to me though, is it?' I reminded him. 'You're paying it forward now by looking out for him.'

'He's doing well.' Jacob nodded. 'He probably hasn't told you, but he's been seeing the counsellor at the youth centre. He says it's helping.'

Ryan hadn't told me that, but I didn't mind. I was just pleased a professional ear was listening to him.

'See,' I said, as if that proved Jacob's influence. 'You've done that.'

'It's teamwork,' he said, 'we're a great team, Poppy.'

'A formidable team,' I agreed, thinking of everything Ryan had achieved since he had moved to Norwich. He was another one whose kindness was creating ripples throughout the square.

'It's a shame we can't be more than teammates,' Jacob added.

I couldn't believe he'd said that.

'Yes, well,' I reminded him, 'we've already discussed, on more than one occasion, that it would be foolish to risk ruining what is already a very beautiful friendship, and now you have this most recent family development to contend with on top of everything else—'

'But that kiss, though,' he interrupted, his voice husky and seductive.

'What about it?'

'Don't tell me you haven't thought about it?'

I'd thought of little else but I wasn't about to admit that, was I?

'I thought we'd agreed that we were going to forget all about it.'

'We did.'

'So why are you bringing it up now?'

'Because I can't get it out of my head!' he burst out, jumping up and striding over to the door. 'I don't want to keep thinking about it but I can't stop myself. It just won't leave me alone.'

This was a thrilling development – and a complete disaster.

'So, what are we going to do about it then?'

'I'll show you what we're going to do,' he said, rushing back and pulling me to my feet. 'We're going to play fast and loose with our precious friendship and see where it takes us.'

He pulled me close, his mouth finding mine, his arms pinning me down as we fell back on to the sofa.

'This isn't a good idea,' I gasped, my hands and lips moving in such a way that left him in no doubt that I didn't really want him to stop.

'It's a terrible idea,' he groaned as I wrapped my legs round him, pulling him down harder.

'No good will come of it,' I gasped again as he ran his hands under my T-shirt, his fingers finding my breasts.

We both froze as the front door slammed shut and Gus skittered along the hall.

'Hey, Gus,' Ryan said, laughing, 'let me get my shoes off, mate.'

Jacob and I scrambled to sit up, smoothing our hair and rearranging the cushions as we tried to calm our breathing.

'Ryan,' I said, picking up the mugs, as his head appeared round the door. 'I was just making us another coffee; would you like one?'

'No thanks.' He scowled, looking from me to my dishevelled guest. 'I think I'll go straight up.'

'Night then,' I called after him.

He didn't answer.

'Oh God,' I mouthed to Jacob once Ryan had gone.

'I know,' he puffed as my brother slammed his bedroom door.

# Chapter 24

Given the looks Ryan was shooting me across the garden the next day, I knew he wasn't happy about what he had come home to last night.

I tried not to let his death stare get to me. After all, I hadn't done anything wrong; that said, his disapproval was palpable and hard to ignore. It was a relief when Jacob showed up and took some of the heat off me.

'What's with Ryan?' he surreptitiously asked, having also been on the receiving end of my brother's glare as he made everyone a drink in the bothy.

I was staying well out of the way, working right at the other end of the garden, tidying and weeding the cut flower bed.

'He hasn't said anything,' I confided, ducking down behind the patch of cornflowers, 'but I think he's still cross about last night. He was hardly thrilled to find us together, was he?'

'Thank God he came back when he did. Can you imagine if he'd been a minute or two—'

'Don't,' I interrupted, 'don't even go there.'

Jacob looked at me and smiled.

'I can't decide' – he sighed heavily – 'if it was divine intervention or just supremely unfortunate timing.'

'I don't understand.'

'What I mean is, given what I'd just discovered about Daniel and Rebecca, I can't be sure if the way I behaved was a result of Dad telling me their news.'

'Oh,' I said, 'right.'

He hadn't found me irresistible then. Shock, rather than lust and longing, had been his motivation for risking our friendship – but he had said our kiss had been quite something.

'I'm not usually prone to spontaneous passionate outbursts,' he went on, making the situation even more awkward.

'So, you're telling me that what happened was simply your way of trying to block out bad news?' I demanded.

I needed to be clear about this. If he was simply using me to take the strain then I needed to put the brakes on, because that wasn't the sort of relationship I had imagined having with him at all. This was the first time I had ever been able to picture myself in a committed long-term situation, one that wouldn't compromise my independence, of course, but nonetheless something very different to what I had experienced before.

'Playing fast and loose with our friendship, as you put it last night, was worth it if seducing me made me feel you feel better for a few minutes, is that it?'

'Seducing you!' Jacob laughed, drawing the attention of Heather, who was working closest, weeding a bed with one hand and rocking the twins' stroller with the other. 'Seducing you,' Jacob said again more quietly. 'The seduction felt pretty equal on both sides if you ask me.'

I felt my face begin to colour.

'I did say that no good would come of what we were doing and that it was a bad idea,' I primly reminded him.

'Yes,' Jacob agreed, 'you did. Right before you wrapped your legs round me and pulled me down on top of you.'

'Oh, all right.' I flushed. 'You don't need to give me a blow-by-blow account. I was there. I can remember what happened.'

Jacob nodded. He was looking a little rosy himself now.

'So, what you're saying is that it was a good thing we were interrupted because you were only risking our friendship off the back of the news about your brother. You don't actually want to take things between us . . . in a different direction?'

Jacob looked at me and chewed his bottom lip, his eyes taking me in. It was some seconds before he spoke again.

'Oh, who am I kidding?' he breathed, reaching out and gently running a finger along my jawline.

'What?'

'I'm talking shit, Poppy. Using my dick of a brother and my ex as an excuse. Of course I want to take things in a different direction. I've been kept awake half the bloody night imagining taking you in all sorts of directions.'

I was pleased I wasn't the only one who had succumbed to playing out the scene in my head.

'So, why have you just gone on about us being interrupted last night as the best thing that could have happened?'

He really was infuriating, not to say confusing. I wasn't sure I could cope with much more of this emotional back and forth.

'Because I wanted to give you the opportunity to agree with me. I needed to know if you were regretting what we'd started.'

The only thing I regretted was not being able to finish it.

'But you haven't given me a chance to agree with you,' I reminded him. 'You just changed tack again before I'd said a word.'

'So, do you regret it?'

Now it was my chance to make him wait, but I couldn't.

'No,' I said shyly, suddenly unable to meet his gaze, 'of course not.'

'You really want to give us a chance,' he went on, 'to be more than friends?'

At last, a straight-out question that I could respond to with a straightforward answer.

'Yes.' I nodded. 'Yes, I want us to see if we can be more than friends. I know you're still dealing with everything that's happened to you but I think you might be worth the risk.'

'I can't believe this is happening.' He grinned, his hands straying, as they always did in times of heightened emotion, back to his hair. 'First the square, then the garden and now you.'

'And Ryan,' I reminded him. 'We come as a pair, I'm afraid.'

'Of course you do,' he laughed. 'And that's fine with me.'

It might have been fine by Jacob, but at the end of the day Ryan was still looking less than happy. He had worked hard all afternoon, roping an unwilling Tamsin in to helping him thoroughly clean the henhouse and douse each of the girls in mite powder. He was obviously going all out to impress Graham and prove that he was worthy of the responsibility that had been bestowed upon him.

'I didn't know the girls had mites,' said Lisa as she told her daughter to go home with John for a thorough wash before we sat down to enjoy a picnic lunch together.

'They don't,' Tamsin huffed, 'Ryan said it was just a precaution. Better to be safe than sorry.'

Lisa looked at me and rolled her eyes.

'I think the novelty's wearing off,' she confided in me as John and Tamsin headed off. 'Ryan's not the bad boy she thought he'd be.'

'I can't say that I'm sorry about that,' I laughed. 'I don't think I could have coped had he fallen completely off the rails.'

'He might have done had you not stepped in.' She smiled kindly. 'He's a credit to you, hon, and he had better watch out or he might find himself filling the pages of my next book!'

As always with Lisa, I couldn't be sure if she was joking. Her debut novel was selling well and receiving rave reviews, so I knew she would be going all out to make the next one even better.

There weren't many of us eating together that day. Graham and Carole were away and the heat had sent Heather and her family into Prosperous Place with Kate, Luke, Jasmine and Abigail. They were going to picnic indoors while the rest of us tried to find the shadiest spot outside.

I had tried to call Lou a few times throughout the morning to ask her to join us but she wasn't picking up. I had thought about going round to her place, but didn't think I could trust myself not to tell her about me and Jacob, and that was probably the last thing she needed to hear. Perhaps it was best to leave her to herself for today.

'Will you be all right here, Harold?' I asked, once I had settled him next to Neil and Mark in the shade of the massive oak tree. The tree was planted some way over the wall in the adjoining part of the garden, but the welcome shade offered by its branches was far-reaching.

'We'll look after him,' said Mark, pouring him a glass of squash while Neil loaded a plate with sandwiches and cheese straws.

'You can fill me in on this baby business you were talking about before,' said Harold. 'Have you decided what you're going to do yet?'

'I think we can all squeeze in here,' said Lisa, who was being followed by the rest of her clan and Jacob and Ryan carrying rugs, cool bags and plastic boxes. 'And yes, you two, what have you decided?'

The simple meal had a celebratory feel as our friends shared their news.

'We've decided to go for it.' Mark beamed. 'We're going to adopt.'

'We don't want to put it off any longer,' added Neil. 'We'll be starting the process in the autumn and you never know, we might have the best Christmas present ever!'

'I don't think it will happen that quickly,' Mark laughed.

'I didn't say which Christmas, did I?' Neil laughed back.

'Well, as disappointed as I am not to be acting as a surrogate,' said Lisa, raising her glass, 'I'm thrilled for you.'

'You'll make wonderful parents,' Harold agreed. 'I wish you both every happiness. It's going to be a very lucky little one who has you two as parents.'

'Thank you, Harold,' said Mark, sounding slightly choked, 'and if you're still thinking about writing that recipe book, Poppy, you'll have to get a move on. I'm still keen to contribute but once we have a little one, I won't have spare time to fill.'

With everything that had been going on since the idea had been suggested, I had completely forgotten about it. I made a mental promise to take some time out and do some planning. Things in Greengages were bound to settle back down soon and with Ryan all sorted as well, I felt certain I would be able to dedicate some time to the project.

'Leave it with me, Mark,' I said, raising my cup. 'Cheers you two, and congratulations.'

We all toasted the guys' decision and got stuck into our lunch.

'Luke has told me that you're going to be looking after the cats while he and Kate are away next weekend, Ryan,' commented Harold.

'That's right,' Ryan confirmed. 'He's giving me keys to the house so I can go in and feed them. Not that they seem to be spending much time indoors at the moment.'

That was true. Ever since the temperature had started to soar both Dash and Violet had been out in the garden most of the time, nights included. They had a slightly feral look in their eyes, but I was certain that it wouldn't take many autumnal frosts to drive them back inside to the warmth of the open fire and the comfort of their bed next to the big range in the kitchen.

'Even so,' said Harold, sitting up straighter in his chair, 'I hope you're feeling proud of yourself, lad. It's quite an honour.'

'That it is,' agreed John.

Ryan appeared pleased that they thought so, but he still didn't seem to be back to his usual self.

'You're quite the Dr Dolittle these days, aren't you?' Harold chuckled.

'Who?' Ryan frowned.

'Dr Dolittle,' Harold repeated.

'You know,' said Tamsin, 'the bloke who can talk to animals.'

'The Eddie Murphy film,' Lisa explained, 'about the guy who can hear what animals say.'

'It was Rex Harrison in my day,' Harold muttered.

'I don't understand,' Ryan said.

'What I think Harold is getting at,' said Jacob, trying to come to his rescue, 'is that you've taken on a lot of animals—'

'And poultry,' interrupted Mark, pointing at the hens.

'. . . since you've been here,' Jacob finished.

'Yes, Ryan,' I agreed. 'It all started with Gus and now you've acquired an entire menagerie.'

'I like looking after them,' he said, colouring slightly.

'You always have.' I smiled. 'Do you remember that corn snake your dad got you for Christmas when you were about ten? Mum was furious, wasn't she?'

'Hell yeah,' he said and laughed. 'I've still got him.' Then he quickly added, 'He's with a mate at the moment. My friend Ant loves snakes. He's looking after him.'

'That's all right then,' I said, feeling relieved. 'I wouldn't have fancied his chances if Mum had come home and found him slithering about the house.'

'Not after that Boxing Day morning.' Ryan sniggered.

'What happened?' asked Tamsin, edging closer to where Ryan was sitting. The tale had obviously refreshed her interest in him.

'Let's just say she was none too pleased to wake up and find she was sharing her bed with a snake she hadn't invited.'

Everyone gasped and Ryan looked at me and smiled. I knew exactly what he was getting at but there was no need to elaborate for everyone else's benefit. I remembered that Ryan had told her she should be used to waking up and finding a snake asleep next to her. It hadn't been the cheeriest of Christmases after that.

'That's awful,' said Lisa with a shudder, 'your poor mother.'

Another conspiratorial glance passed between us and I knew he was feeling all right again.

'Given your love of animals, birds and reptiles, Ryan,' I said, 'I can't help thinking you must wish you'd taken a City and Guilds in animal care or something instead of your A levels?'

'Yeah,' he said, 'maybe.'

I knew he had been rushed into deciding last autumn and with no support, so it was hardly surprising he hadn't nailed it first time round, but it wasn't too late.

'Maybe,' I suggested, 'you could change courses in September. Now would be the perfect time to start thinking about it, what with having almost finished your AS year.'

I hadn't made a fuss about revision and coursework, which had helped him knuckle down of his own accord.

'You could even look at another apprenticeship.'

'But that will mean I have nothing to show for this year.'

'You'll still have your AS levels,' said Jacob wisely. 'And in my experience, nothing that happens in life is ever wasted. Horrible things sometimes turn out to be the catalysts that lead you to something even better. Something you didn't expect.'

He looked at me and smiled. Aware of Ryan's gaze, I began to busy myself tidying the empty plates and containers.

'Which reminds me,' said Lisa, 'you never did enlighten us as to what it was that happened in your life, Jacob, that meant you ended up buying your house in the square.'

'No,' he said, with a smile, 'I didn't, did I?'

Lisa waited but Jacob didn't say anything else.

'Well done, lad,' wheezed Harold, 'that's the way. Don't give in to her or you'll never hold on to any secrets!'

We all laughed and Lisa shook her head.

'It's no good,' she said, tutting, 'I'm losing my touch, and right when I need to keep topping up the well of inspiration.'

'I'm going to rinse these dishes off in the bothy,' I said, hoping to distract her further, as everyone began to stretch and decide whether to carry on working in the garden or nip home for a siesta and come back again when it was cooler.

'I'll give you a hand,' said Ryan.

I had thought it wasn't going to be necessary to explain what my brother had almost walked in on the night before, but given how silent he became once we were alone, I didn't think I had much choice.

'About last night,' I began.

'It's none of my business.' He shrugged.

'I know it isn't, but I want to explain.'

'I just don't want you to fuck things up,' he blurted out, throwing down the tea towel and dumping himself heavily on a bag of compost that doubled up as a makeshift seat.

'Fuck what up?'

'Whatever it is that you've started with Jacob, I don't want you to balls it up.'

'I haven't really started anything,' I told him honestly, 'yet.'

'No,' he said, 'but you're going to. It's obvious the pair of you are into each other.'

Was it? I hoped no one else had noticed.

'And is that a problem?'

Ryan shrugged.

'I seem to remember you assumed we were a couple the day you arrived,' I reminded him. 'When we came to pick you up from the station you thought we were together.'

'Yeah, but that was then.'

'I don't understand.'

'I didn't know Jacob then, did I?' he sniffed. 'I didn't know you really either. The pair of you didn't mean anything to me.'

'But now . . .'

'But now,' he said, beginning to sound angry, 'he's my mate.'

'I see.'

'And if you mess this up then I won't have him. If you start going out with him and then it goes wrong, it'll be bound to change things between him and me.'

'Why are you assuming it will end in disaster?'

'Let's just call it a hunch,' he said, 'something to do with our crap genetics perhaps.'

'Oh Ryan,' I sighed, laying a hand on his shoulder.

He shrugged it off. It hurt me to think that he was convinced that it could only be me who would mess things up. Jacob, apparently, was without fault and if the relationship ended it would be because of something I said or did. It was hardly fair – but I knew this was more about our mother than me.

'I know it sounds shit,' he went on, 'and I know it's completely selfish, but it's how I feel.'

'And I'm sorry you feel this way, I really am.'

'So, you won't start seeing him?' he asked hopefully.

'What?'

'You won't start going out with him?'

'Are you serious?' Jacob said later, once I had explained Ryan's concerns.

'Watch it!' I gasped, jumping out of the way as he spun round, spraying the ground at my feet with the hose. 'You're supposed to be watering the veg, not me.'

It was late in the evening and everyone else had gone home. Neither Harold nor Lisa's lot had come back after their afternoon naps but I didn't mind. As far as I was concerned, the more time I could spend alone in the garden the better. It kept my mind occupied. Most of the time.

'He really thinks I'd dump him if you dumped me,' muttered Jacob, shaking his head.

'It sounds really harsh when you put it like that,' I said, 'but you can't blame him. The only adult relationships he's ever witnessed are those our manipulative mother has orchestrated, so he's hardly got the best point of reference.'

'But to think that,' Jacob carried on, 'about me.'

He sounded genuinely upset.

'Please don't take it personally,' I pleaded. 'Surely you should be feeling happy that he thinks so much of you that he can't cope with the thought of losing you.'

'I guess.'

'That's why he's saying all this. He told me he's been happier living here these last few months than he has in a long time and I think he's terrified of anything changing in case it gets spoiled.'

'But things in life do change.'

'I know that,' I said, 'and you know that, and deep down so does Ryan, but given everything the poor lad has been through, don't you think he deserves this time to shine in his life like a beacon of happiness when nothing went wrong, the sun always shone and everything and everyone was perfect.'

'Bloody hell,' Jacob said with a smile, 'you don't need to lay on the hard sell. That little speech had more cheese than a triple-loaded from the pizza place.'

I grabbed the hose and turned it on him.

'Hey,' he said, snatching it back. 'I don't think that's a game you really want to start playing, is it? That dress would turn pretty see-through if I soaked it, and how would that look to the world when you walked home?'

'All right,' I said, laughing, 'sorry.'

'God, I'd love to see you soaked to the skin,' he groaned, 'that thin fabric clinging to those beautiful—'

'Hey!' I broke in, 'now who's being cheesy?'

'That wasn't cheese,' he said, turning back to the courgette bed, 'that was pure lust.'

Damn Ryan and his relationship veto. I wondered if it covered a shared steamy moment in the back of the bothy.

'So, what are we going to do?'

I raised my eyebrows.

'About what Ryan said,' Jacob clarified. 'Do you think we should cool it?'

'Do you?'

'Yeah,' he said, 'I guess. I don't want to,' he added forcefully, 'believe me, cooling it is the last thing I want to do, but I don't think we have any choice.'

'You're right,' I reluctantly agreed. 'We'll just have to carry on as before and see what happens. If he keeps seeing us together he might decide that actually everything could be okay.'

'*Will* be okay,' Jacob insisted. 'And in the meantime, we'll have to make sure we aren't alone, because I don't know about you but I can't vouch for my self-control.'

'We're alone now,' I reminded him.

'Exactly,' he said, glancing about him and giving the hose one final blast, 'and look how that just almost turned out.'

# Chapter 25

With the following week turning out to be almost as busy as the one before, I had very little time to worry about finding myself alone with Jacob, or opportunity for that matter. Giving in to lustful temptation was the least of my concerns because we hardly saw each other. He was busy with his hectic end-of-term schedule and I was rushing about making the changes in Greengages happen as smoothly as possible and moaning about the heat.

We were all on extra watering duty in the garden, Ryan included now he had finished college for the year, and it was impossible to sleep properly at night. Everywhere had sold out of electric fans and self-contained air-con units and tempers were beginning to fray.

'Haven't you finished yet?' groaned Harry as we were closing up, one day towards the end of the week. 'It hasn't been that busy. I can't believe there's all that much to tally up.'

'There isn't,' I said, dumping the change back in the till

and starting to count again, 'but my brain is fried and I keep miscounting. I'm so bloody tired.'

'Oh here,' said Harry, waving me away. 'Let me. You get home and have a nice cool shower.'

'Are you sure?'

'Yes,' he said, 'go on, it might perk you up a bit.'

I didn't need telling twice. The shop was stuffy and dusty and I wanted some fresh air. Not that the air was particularly fresh at the moment. Stepping outside was like opening an oven door. There was nothing refreshing about being outside at all.

'All right,' I said, stepping aside. 'Thanks, Harry.'

Unusually, I was in no rush to head home. Since the sun had started to beat down the place had become something of a teenage hangout. Ryan and Joe had been constantly hanging around and, at the beginning of the week, I had arrived home to find lads I didn't recognise sprawled all over the garden. There was an aroma hanging around one of them that smelt a little too like weed for my liking.

'I don't mind you and Joe being here,' I told Ryan out of earshot of the others, 'but not this lot.'

I had expected him to have a bit of a moan, but he seemed relieved.

'I didn't even invite them,' he confided. 'Kyle just turned up and the others trailed in after him.'

'What, Kyle as in the lad who was at the house in Wynmouth when I tried to ring you in May? That Kyle?'

'Yeah.' Ryan swallowed, looking nervously over his shoulder. 'That's him. Apparently, he'd spotted my photo in his dad's paper after Colin's party and then Mum told him about me staying with you. He just sort of tracked me down.'

As furious as I was that he had let the lads in, there was something disconcerting about Ryan's behaviour and hushed tone that suggested his friendship with this Kyle wasn't quite as I had imagined. When I had spoken to him on the phone I had shoved him in the 'cheeky chappie' category where most adolescent lads I've known end up, but now I wasn't so sure that was the right place for him after all.

'Well, get rid of them all,' I told Ryan sharply. 'Except Joe, of course. And make sure they know they can't come back.'

The last thing I needed was to be worrying about what was happening back in the square when I was supposed to be working.

'All right,' he agreed, 'I'll tell them you want them out. Is it all right to say that you're kicking them out, not me?'

'Of course it is,' I told him, 'because I am.'

Not fancying the company of Ryan and Joe this evening, I headed to Colin's instead. A Good Book was always a couple of degrees cooler than everywhere else for some reason and it would be a treat to peruse the cookbook section. I was feeling a bit frustrated that I hadn't managed to spend much time in my kitchen working on potential recipes for the book, but given the thirty-plus temperatures we had been subjected to, not even I was up for standing and stirring, bottling and boiling in front of the stove.

'Hey, Poppy! Wait up!'

I spun round to find Lou a few paces behind me.

'I've been calling you all the way along the street,' she panted as she reached me, 'didn't you hear?'

'No,' I said, 'sorry. I was miles away.'

'Not thinking about Jacob by any chance, were you?' She winked. 'Are you two going to get it on or what? We're all waiting, you know.'

'And what about you and Colin,' I shot back. 'How are things going with you two? I'm waiting to see if he'll bin off Nurse Natalie for you, you know.'

I knew it was mean, even as the words were tripping off my tongue, but I hadn't been able to bite them back once they'd started to flow. Not surprisingly, Lou looked more than a little hurt.

'Oh God, ignore me, Lou,' I said, 'I'm sorry. This heat is really starting to get to me. I didn't mean it.'

'I suppose I deserved it really,' she said, giving me a wobbly smile, 'it's none of my business, but the pair of you have seemed to be getting closer recently and, even though you didn't get off to the best of starts, I can't help thinking you'd be perfect together. If only you'd get your acts together and realise it.'

'Oh Lou,' I groaned, 'we have realised it, but it's not going to happen.'

'What?' she cawed. 'Why ever not?'

I shook my head.

'Come on,' she said, linking arms and pulling me along,

'let's go to Colin's. It'll be cooler in there and you can tell me all about it.'

I didn't particularly want to talk about it, but she was right, the shop would be cooler than the pavement, and maybe if she and Colin listened to the troubles Jacob and I were having then they might see how straightforward their own relationship could be.

'So, let me see if I've got this straight,' said Colin with a frown as he handed me an ice-packed glass of lemonade. 'You and Jacob both really like each other, you've decided that you want to be more than friends, but because Ryan is afraid that if the relationship doesn't work out he'll lose Jacob, the pair of you aren't going to get it together.'

'Succinct as ever, Colin.' I nodded, taking a chilled, refreshing sip. 'You've summed it up beautifully.'

'But what about when Ryan goes home?' Lou asked. 'Will it be all systems go then? I mean, Ryan wouldn't even need to know, would he? Not to begin with anyway.'

'To tell you the truth,' I said, 'I haven't thought that far ahead.'

I didn't much like the idea of sending Ryan back to Mum but there was a certain inevitability about it, even if none of us had mentioned it. It simply wasn't feasible for him to stay with me for ever. Ryan really needed to get his brain in gear and think about what he wanted to do next with his life. He'd been looking at his options and told the college he might not carry on with his A levels, but he hadn't got round to deciding what he would do if he dropped them.

'It's some sacrifice you're making, Pops,' said Lou, her gaze resting on Colin's back as he busied himself sorting through a pile of books.

'Family first,' he muttered.

'I know family comes first, Colin,' she carried on. 'You've told us often enough, but it's not always as simple as that, is it, Pops?'

'No,' I agreed, thinking of mine and Jacob's first kiss and our subsequent more passionate embrace on the sofa, 'it's definitely not.'

'Isn't it?' said Colin, looking up and pushing his glasses further back up his nose.

'No,' Lou said with a sigh, 'it isn't. When you find the one, the thought of having to give them up for any reason, family included, is heartbreaking, especially when it's taken you so long to find them.'

Colin nodded and went back to his sorting.

This wasn't working out how I had hoped it would at all. Perhaps I needed to make a more direct assault on the pair of them.

'So, Colin,' I said a little louder, 'are you all set for the weekend? What are your plans for Nurse Natalie?'

Lou looked at me and shook her head. The scowl etched on her face could have given Ryan's from Sunday a run for its money.

'I'm not sure yet,' he said.

'Not sure!' I laughed. 'I thought you'd have it all well planned out by now.'

Colin was methodical if nothing else.

'A romantic candlelit dinner for two,' I said dreamily, 'followed by a stroll somewhere secluded—'

'Maybe,' he interrupted. 'We'll see.'

'Do I detect a lack of enthusiasm all of a sudden?' I pounced. I hoped so. It would make what I was going to do next so very much easier.

'No,' he said, his eyes flicking momentarily to our mutual friend, 'maybe . . . perhaps.'

Lou sat quiet and still, staring down at her sandals. I was sure she was holding her breath.

'She's just not . . .' he stammered. 'Oh, I don't know, she's just not—'

'Lou?' I cut in.

'What?' she said, looking back up.

Colin was suddenly looking more like a startled fawn than the owner of a second-hand bookshop.

'No,' I laughed. 'I was talking to Colin.'

'What?' the pair said together.

'You said Natalie wasn't, and then you stopped, so I said Lou. Natalie isn't Lou.'

The pair looked at each other and then back to me.

'All right,' I said, standing up and pulling Lou to her feet. 'Let me spell it out for you.'

I walked her over to Colin, grabbed his hand and placed it in Lou's.

'Lou,' I began, 'Colin has been in love with you since the very first moment he set eyes on you.'

Colin began to splutter but didn't let go of her hand.

'And Colin,' I said, turning to look at his red face and bulging eyes, 'Lou is in love with you too. She didn't realise it until you went away and then you came back singing the praises of your father's carer and she hasn't felt able to tell you because she thought your affections lay elsewhere.'

Now it was Lou who started to choke.

'There,' I said, clapping my hands together and feeling pleased with my minute's work. 'Doesn't that feel better?'

I walked back to the window, picking up my glass on the way. I needed a drink after that. I didn't know about Lou and Colin's hearts but mine was fair hammering away.

'Perhaps,' I said turning back to face them, 'now you'll—' There was no need to finish the sentence because the pair were wrapped in each other's arms, passionately kissing as if they had years' worth of missing moments to make up for, which of course they did.

I couldn't wait to fill Ryan in on how I had spilled the beans to Lou and Colin about how they were both crazy for each other but too dense to realise it, but when I got home, he wasn't there. Then I remembered that he had said he was going to the youth centre and then popping to Prosperous Place to run through the security system with Luke ahead of looking after Violet and Dash at the weekend.

I took advantage of the fact that, for the first time in what felt like ages, I had the house to myself, and did absolutely nothing. Aside from taking a cool shower, ordering in a takeaway and flicking through the pages of my grandmother's recipe book, that is. The key to keeping even slightly cool, I had worked out, was to move as little as possible. I wondered wryly if Lou and Colin were managing to adhere to that theory.

It had been a few hours since I left them, so I decided to send them a quick text to each to check all was okay. I wasn't going to apologise for what I had done, though. If anything, I was certain they would be thanking me soon enough.

'Hey, Ryan!' I called out as the front door slammed and I heard the familiar tapping of Gus's claws on the hall floor.

That little dog was going to be heartbroken when he had to go back to Colin. If it was down to me I would have proposed some kind of equal custody arrangement but I was sure my mother wouldn't go for that, so I wouldn't even be suggesting it.

'How did you get on?'

'All right,' he said as he came into the room.

He didn't sound very enthusiastic.

'What's up?' I frowned.

'What are you doing?' He frowned back.

'Looking for my phone,' I said, rifling through the upturned contents of my bag, which were spread out across the sofa. 'You haven't seen it, have you?'

'No,' he snapped, 'why the hell would I know where your phone is?'

'Hey,' I said, stopping to look at him, 'there's no need to bite my head off. I was only asking.'

'Sorry,' he mumbled, reaching for the takeaway menu. 'Did you have a Chinese for dinner?'

'Yes,' I said, going back to my search, 'I saved you some, it's in the fridge.'

'How did you order it?'

'What?'

'The takeaway, how did you order it?'

'Oh,' I said, realising that he was actually trying to help rather than wanting to fill his belly (an impossible task). 'I used the landline.'

'Maybe you left your phone at work then,' he suggested.

'Perhaps,' I said, trying to think where I'd last seen it. 'Given the way I've been feeling today, it wouldn't surprise me, but I was sure it was in my bag.'

'Well, perhaps I've pinched it then.' He snapped again. 'Is that what you're getting at?'

'Of course that's not what I'm getting at!' I gasped, shocked by the sudden change in him. 'Why would you even suggest that? What on earth has got into you?'

He didn't say anything, just shrugged, looking as sulky as hell. He was all sharp edges and tension.

'You're probably right,' I said, taking a deep breath, 'my phone is most likely, as you suggested, at work somewhere. No one is accusing you of anything. Why are you so tetchy?'

Having lived with him for a while now, I was pretty much used to his hormonally charged mood swings, but this was completely different. This was off the scale of anything I'd experienced before. He was aggressive, defensive and nothing like my lovely brother at all.

'I dunno,' he said gruffly, 'I'm probably just tired. It's so fucking hot. It's really getting to me.'

It was getting to us all but there was definitely more to his temper than that. Heatwave or no heatwave, he had started the week full of excitement about how well his stint as hen-keeper had gone and he was desperate for the weekend, when he could prove his worth as keeper of keys for Prosperous Place. So, what had happened in the interim? This explosive outburst just didn't add up.

'I'm going up,' he said, before I could quiz him further.

'But what about your dinner?' I called after him.

'I'll have it tomorrow.'

In a foul mood *and* off his food. Something was definitely wrong.

# Chapter 26

Not even the combination of hints from the local TV team that the weather would break over the weekend and Ryan's imminent cat-care duties were capable of lifting his spirits or lightening his mood. He was just as grumpy on Friday morning when he lumped down the stairs for breakfast as he had been the night before.

'You found it then,' he said, slumping down on a chair in the kitchen and pointing at my phone, which was on the worktop.

'Nope,' I said, 'the fairies did.'

'What?' He frowned, pouring himself a glass of orange juice.

'Last night when I went to bed it wasn't there and this morning it was.'

'Weird.'

'Very,' I agreed.

I was certain my phone hadn't been there when I had

given up the hunt and gone to bed, so the fairy folk were the only feasible explanation for it turning up.

'What are your plans for today then?' I asked. 'Do you fancy meeting up for lunch?'

'Can't,' he said, peeling himself out of the chair again. 'I've got extra stuff to do in the garden. Lisa's convinced we're going to be judged any day now and if the weather breaks with thunderstorms we'll need to make sure we've got as much protected as possible.'

I'd been feeling so excited about the prospect of some cooling rain, I hadn't thought about the potential damage it could cause. One big storm could wreck everything.

'Dinner then?'

'I'm at the youth club tonight.' He yawned, traipsing out again and taking his glass with him.

'Right,' I said, 'good. Well, maybe I'll see you tomorrow then.'

He didn't answer and my phone began to ping, distracting me from trying to get him to commit to spending some time with me over the weekend. I hoped it *was* just the weather that had put him in such a strange mood. Everything had been going so well and, what with sacrificing my potential relationship with Jacob to keep everything jogging smoothly along, I wanted it to stay that way. At least he was willing to help out more in the garden now the competition pressure was cranking up. Yes, I told myself, it was just the weather. And perhaps an influx of tempestuous teenage testosterone.

*

That Friday was, without doubt, one of the longest and one of the quietest I had ever worked.

'Where is everyone?' I groaned, rearranging the soft fruit display for the umpteenth time.

'Will you leave that?' Harry scolded. 'If you keep fingering it all like that it'll be too bruised to sell.'

'Well, I'm bored,' I whined, sounding more Ryan's age than mine. 'There's nothing to do.'

'Are you going out for lunch?'

'In this heat?' I laughed. 'Are you kidding?'

'There you are then,' said Harry, sounding satisfied.

'There I am what?'

'Don't you think our customers are feeling exactly the same?' he said, wiping his forehead with a large white cotton handkerchief. 'Everyone's had enough. Didn't you see those pictures of the park on the news last night?'

'No.'

'All those deckchairs the council invested in and put in the park for folk to enjoy during the fine weather.'

'I remember,' I said, thinking of the recent story.

'Every single one empty,' Harry explained. 'There wasn't a soul in sight. No one wants to be out in this now. The novelty's worn off.'

He was right. Over the last few days I'd heard far more customers moaning about the sunshine than embracing it. The only person who I knew still enjoying it was Blossom, and that was because she said it reminded her of her childhood in the Caribbean. She was loving the fact she was harvesting decent crops of her Jamaican favourites from her beloved allotment. She had promised me some callaloo seeds to sow at the Grow-Well next year.

'You're right.' I nodded. 'Let's hope the rain comes soon and cools us all down a bit.'

'It better,' said Harry with a nod to the shelves, 'otherwise you're going to have one heck of a marathon jam-making session on your hands.'

I didn't say as much but I still didn't fancy standing in front of a hot stove, even if it would be the ideal opportunity to work on my technique.

The shop got a little busier later on, but not until well after four.

'I thought you might have shut up early for the day,' said one customer as he filled an old ice cream container with strawberries for me to weigh, 'but I just couldn't face coming out this morning.'

'We had a rush of people in at nine,' I told him, as other customers began to trickle in, all puffing and red in the face, 'but after that it settled right down. There have been a few deliveries to get out, but beyond that practically nothing.'

'Folk were no doubt trying to beat the heat at opening time,' he said wisely as he paid, 'and now everyone's venturing back out again. There's quite a breeze getting up,' he told me, 'but it's not made any difference to the temperature.'

In the end it was almost half six when Harry and I closed up.

'Look at that,' I said, indicating the display I had been so intent on fiddling about with earlier, 'we've hardly anything left. Customers will be moaning tomorrow.'

'Typical.' Harry sniffed. 'I don't think we've ever stayed open so late. Not even at Christmas.'

'It was worth it though,' I said as I began cashing up, 'it's made up for the slow start.'

'Leave that,' said Harry, 'you get off.'

I handed him the bundle of notes I was counting out and stepped away from the till.

'That way you can have a slow walk down to the pub.'

Earlier I'd had texts from both Colin and Lou asking me to meet them in The Dragon and I was looking forward to finding out if they had forgiven me for revealing their love for one another. Had they not been entwined in a passionate embrace when I left them the evening before I would have turned their invitations down, but seeing them kissing like that had left me in little doubt that my brazen declaration had been the right course.

'Okay,' I said to Harry, 'I'll just sort out the front and then I'll get off.'

'Thanks, love,' he said, pulling out a fistful of change from the till. 'If these thunderstorms are going to be as bad as the reports are suggesting then we won't want to risk leaving anything out.'

My mind tracked back to the Grow-Well. We didn't have much option other than to let our beloved garden fend for itself, but at least Ryan was going to go along and help give what could be moved and protected some sort of shelter.

'There now.' I smiled, pulling my T-shirt away from my skin, as I arrived at the pub and found Lou practically sitting on Colin's lap at our usual table. 'Don't you two look cosy together.'

To be honest, I didn't know how they could bear to be so close, given the heat. The short walk had left me feeling pretty dehydrated. I was convinced every drop of fluid that should have been on my inside had leaked out.

'Sit down for a minute,' said Lou, pushing a chair out for me with her foot, 'you'll cool off after you've been sitting down for a bit.'

'And here,' said Colin, handing me a glass of lemonade, 'this has just been poured, although I'm afraid there's not much ice left.'

'Thanks,' I said, gratefully gulping half of it straight down, 'I really needed that.'

I eyed the pair of them over the rim of my glass.

'So,' I said, 'I take it I'm forgiven, then?'

'There's nothing to forgive.' Colin grinned.

He kissed Lou's cheek and put a hand round her waist, giving her a squeeze.

'Thank goodness,' I laughed. 'God, I'm so happy for you both.' I swallowed.

'Me too,' said Lou, sounding a little breathless.

'And how did poor Natalie take the news?' I asked. 'I take it you've told her, Colin?'

'I called her this morning,' said Colin, his grin still in place.

'And?'

'And,' he carried on, 'she told me that she hadn't for one second thought there was anything serious between us because every time we were together I spent the whole time talking about a certain someone else.'

I began to laugh.

'She said she was under no illusion that I would start dating her because I was clearly so in love with Lou.'

'So, the only people in the entire world who weren't aware of what was going on were the pair of you?'

'Apparently,' said Lou, sighing contently. 'To be honest, Pops, I don't know how you've put up with us both for all this time.'

'To be honest,' I replied, 'I don't know either.'

Our conversation was interrupted as the door opened, letting in another blast of hot air and the distant sound of rumbling thunder.

'Jacob,' I gasped, looking up.

His arrival was a surprise.

'I didn't expect to see you tonight,' I told him.

'Lou sent Ryan to my place with a message' – he frowned – 'asking me to meet you all in here. Is everything okay?'

He slid into the seat next to mine, his leg pressed close, the heat between us even more intense than the outside temperature.

'Colin and Lou have some news,' I told him, assuming that was why Lou had invited him along.

'We're a couple!' she announced. 'Colin and I have finally got our acts together.'

'Thanks to Poppy here,' Colin added.

'That's fantastic.' Jacob smiled. 'Congratulations, guys, but what did Poppy have to do with it?'

Colin began to relay some of the details of what had happened the evening before and I took the opportunity to slip away and order us all another round of drinks. Lou was hot on my heels.

'I'm hoping our little bit of matchmaking works out as well for you as yours has for us,' she hissed in my ear, plucking keenly at the sleeve of my T-shirt.

'What do you mean?' I frowned.

'Inviting Jacob.' She beamed, surreptitiously looking back to where the two men were deep in conversation. 'We wanted to get him here to see if we can work things out for the two of you.'

'Oh Lou,' I groaned.

'What?' She giggled, turning her attention back to me.

'We already know that we like each other,' I reminded her, 'and left to our own devices we would be going out.'

Her smile faltered but she didn't say anything.

'I know you've asked him here tonight with the loveliest of intentions, but neither of us are prepared to act on our feelings knowing how concerned Ryan is about what may or may not happen if things didn't work out. I told you and Colin that only yesterday.'

'I know,' she said, biting her lip. 'But I thought, what if I had a word with Ryan. What if I—'

'No,' I interrupted, 'please don't do that. He would be mortified if he knew we had talked about the situation.'

'But you and Jacob should be together!'

'I know that,' I told her. 'I'm well aware of that but, for now at least, we're happy as we are. If Ryan has a change of heart at some point then we'll take things from there but for the time being,' I said, looking right at her and sounding as determined as I could to make sure that she really understood there was no wriggle room for her to interfere, 'we'll keep things as they are. For now, our friendship is the most important thing.'

'I just want you to be happy,' she murmured, 'as happy as I am.'

'I'm fine,' I told her, 'really. I've never been happier.'

'As long as you're sure.'

'One hundred per cent,' I reiterated. 'Absolutely no matchmaking required.'

She nodded and left me to carry on at the bar, returning to her seat next to Colin.

'How's the weather looking out there?' I asked Jacob as I deposited the fresh tray of drinks. 'I thought I heard thunder when you came in.'

Talking about the weather wasn't particularly inspired but I thought it best to steer us all a little way away from love and all its connotations and potential complications, for the time being at least.

'You did,' he confirmed, 'but it's as hot as hell and there's still no rain. The lightning is pretty impressive though.'

'It better rain soon,' panted Lou, fanning herself with a menu. 'Otherwise we'll all go mad. Ryan said he was going to help move some stuff at the Grow-Well. Just to be on the safe side if the storms do hit.'

'That's not a bad idea,' said Jacob, gulping down the Coke I had collected for him. 'The judging will have to happen soon and it would be such a shame if the weather shredded all our hard work.'

'Are you going to the youth centre tonight?' I asked.

'Yes,' he said, looking up as the lights flickered on and off and the thunder rumbled again, closer this time.

It had grown so dark that the bar lights had been turned on, but given the storm that was beginning to build, I wasn't sure how long they'd be working for.

'I'm heading down there in a bit,' he carried on. 'Weather permitting.'

'I hope Gus will be all right,' I said to Colin, suddenly remembering how sensitive the little dog could be.

'That's the funny thing with Gus,' Colin said cheerfully, 'he doesn't bother about storms at all.'

Another boom cracked through the air, making us all jump.

'Just as well.' I smiled. 'I hope Violet and Dash aren't giving Ryan the runaround.'

I didn't much like the thought of my brother trying to round them up in the middle of the storm that we could hear starting to rage.

'I think I'll just call and make sure he's okay.'

Lost in each other's eyes, Colin and Lou didn't answer, and Jacob was busy with his own phone, which had just gone off.

'Bloody hell,' he groaned, stuffing it back in his pocket and draining his glass. 'I have to go.'

'What's up?' I asked while waiting for Ryan to pick up.

'It's the youth centre,' he sighed. 'Some bother between a couple of the boys. I need to get down there.'

Ryan hadn't answered, so I hung up.

'You don't know who the culprits are by any chance, do you?' I asked.

'No,' he told me, 'why, what's wrong?'

'Ryan isn't answering his phone.' I swallowed. 'And I'm not sure if he'll be at the garden or the youth centre right now.'

'It won't be anything to do with him, Poppy,' said Lou, coming back out of her trance. 'He's a good lad. I daresay he's still at the Grow-Well.'

'But even so,' I said, reaching for my bag and purse, 'I think I'll come with you, Jacob, just to be on the safe side.'

'No,' he said, laying his hand over mine. 'Don't do that.'

'But—'

'Look,' he said, 'if it is anything to do with Ryan I'll text you straight away, but I'm certain it won't be.'

'So, where's the harm in me coming with you?'

'How's it going to look if you tag along?' said Jacob, trying to make me understand. 'If Ryan is there and you turn up, he'll assume you thought he was one of the lads causing trouble, won't he?'

'I guess . . .'

'It'll annoy the hell out of him,' said Lou, 'especially if it is nothing to do with him.'

I supposed they had a point. It would look a bit odd, me going down there for the first time ever, with Jacob, who had just happened to have received the text saying there was trouble afoot. Given the mood Ryan had been in this week, it probably wasn't a good idea to wind him up even more.

'All right,' I relented. 'I won't come.'

'But why would you even think it has anything to do with Ryan?' Colin frowned.

I felt guilty for even entertaining the idea, especially when my friends were all so certain that it wouldn't be anything to do with him, but I knew something was amiss with Ryan. I just couldn't put my finger on what it was.

'It's just that he's been in a funny mood this week,' I said, trying to justify my suspicion. 'Not himself at all.'

'Along with everyone else,' said Jacob. 'This weather hasn't exactly made any of us feel like the life and soul, has it?'

'Oh, I don't know,' I said, nodding back to Colin and Lou, who were kissing, again. 'Some have definitely coped better than others.'

# Chapter 27

I followed Jacob to the door as he left. The electricity between us felt even more highly charged than that which was racing through the dark clouds hanging over the city.

'Promise you'll ring if it's Ryan,' I begged, hardly daring to look up at him.

'Promise.' He smiled, lowering his head and lightly brushing his lips against my warm cheek.

This whole business of keeping our relationship platonic, now we had acknowledged we both wanted it to be anything but, was hard work and it took every ounce of strength not to turn my head and meet his lips.

'Okay,' I whispered, 'thanks.'

I was ready to leave The Dragon a little while later and, as I hadn't heard a word from Jacob, I knew I could head straight home. I was relieved that my fears about Ryan were unfounded but felt more than a little ashamed that I had jumped to the wrong conclusion. Colin, Lou and I stood on the pavement and looked up at the sky. The storm, which had been threatening us with rain all evening, had moved off without shedding a single drop and, if possible, the air felt even hotter and heavier than before.

'I'll catch up with you two over the weekend,' I said to the pair before we parted. 'I'm so pleased everything has worked out for you both.'

'Me too.' Lou sighed dreamily. 'Now all we need to do is make Ryan see sense about you and Jacob and we'll be double-dating before you know it.'

Colin shook his head.

'Don't worry,' he told me, 'I'll keep her under control.'

'Thank you, Colin,' I said with a smile, 'that will be much appreciated.'

I headed back to the square and found Gus contentedly curled up in his bed in the kitchen. Colin had been right; the little dog didn't appear at all concerned about the thunder and trotted happily enough into the garden when I opened the door before making myself a cup of tea and going up for a shower.

I knew Ryan wasn't at home because of the absence of discarded footwear in the hall for me to trip over, but out of habit I checked his room anyway. Everything looked much as it always did, and I carried on into the bathroom, hoping he wouldn't be too late. It was going to be hard enough to sleep as it was; if his bed remained empty for too much longer I knew I'd never nod off.

*

I was surprised to see when I woke up that it was almost half four, the sound of thunder pulling me out of the slumber I hadn't expected to succumb to. I opened the bedroom curtains and leant out of the window, hoping to take in a lungful of fresh air, but it was still stiflingly hot and there was no sign of the promised rain. Everything was every bit as parched as it had been the night before, me included.

I quietly made my way to the bathroom for some water, but I needn't have worried about slipping into stealth mode because Ryan's door was still open, and his bed was untouched.

'I know it's early,' I found myself saying to Jacob a couple of hours later as I stood on his doorstep, wringing my hands and fighting back tears, 'but I'm going out of my mind and didn't know who else to ask.'

'Poppy.' He frowned. 'For God's sake come in. Whatever's happened?'

'Nothing probably,' I said, stepping into his hall and trying to sound less anxious than I felt, 'but Ryan hasn't come home and I'm at my wits' end.'

I knew he wasn't the only sixteen-year-old in the world who may well have decided not to come home on a Friday night, but right now he was my responsibility and he was the current keyholder for Prosperous Place. That alone was enough to crank up my concern. Ryan had been taking his responsibilities very seriously of late and he had been looking forward to caring for Violet and Dash, so this sudden disappearance was frighteningly out of character.

'Was he at the youth centre last night?' I asked Jacob. 'You never called, so I thought everything was all right.'

'It was,' said Jacob, rubbing his hands through his messy hair and leading the way along to the kitchen. 'He was there when I arrived, but as he was nothing to do with the trouble, I didn't ring you.'

'Good,' I said, feeling relieved.

That was something.

'And then, by the time I'd helped calm things down, he'd left. I assumed he was going to check on the cats and would then head home.'

I was annoyed that he hadn't let me know that Ryan had left, but then he'd only promised to text if my brother was in trouble and he hadn't been. Not then, anyway.

'Maybe he's at Joe's,' Jacob suggested, sloshing milk into two mugs. 'Perhaps he decided to stay at his place. The pair are as thick as thieves these days.'

'Maybe,' I said, pressing the tips of my fingers into my temples to relieve some of the pressure I could feel building.

A headache would be most unwelcome, but given the heavy air and the worry it felt inevitable.

'But if he was going across the road to see to the cats,' I said, wincing as I stopped massaging and the pain began to pulse, 'then why would he go to Joe's, rather than come home? Given the weather warnings it would have made more sense for him to come over to the square, even with Joe, rather than to trek across the city to his place, wouldn't it?'

Jacob shrugged.

'Was Joe even at the youth centre?'

'I'm not sure,' he admitted, putting a mug of tea on the table in front of me. 'I didn't take much notice of who was hanging around beyond those involved in the disturbance.'

I wondered if he thought I was making too much of it all. But I wasn't, was I? Ryan deciding to disappear now of all times, when he had so much going on, really was something to make a fuss about. I felt certain my fears were more than justified.

'Look, Jacob,' I said, growing angry, 'I know you're probably thinking I'm being completely over the top about this.'

'I'm not thinking anything like that,' he said softly.

'But this isn't like him, is it?' I carried on, ignoring his denial.

'We'll find him,' said Jacob, pulling out the chair next to mine so he could sit close. 'I'll help you. I promise.'

'Thank you,' I whispered, the words catching in my throat.

He lifted my chin as two fat tears made a bid to escape and rolled down my cheeks. He brushed them away and leant in to kiss me. I turned my face and my lips easily found his, the caress firm and reassuring, even though it was forbidden, and I gave in to it, finding comfort as the remains of my anger melted away.

As much as I loved my independence and was in no hurry to compromise it, not having to bear the weight of this current problem on my own was a relief. The physical comfort Jacob was offering was kindly shared rather than sexually charged and it felt heartening in the face of the current crises.

'What's that?' I asked, pulling back. 'Can you hear sirens?'

Jacob took a moment to listen before he answered.

'Ryan has the place rigged.' He smiled. 'He's seen us kissing on some spyware he's secretly installed and called the cops on us.'

'That's not funny,' I said, jumping up, 'they sound really close.'

I rushed from the kitchen, along the hall, and pulled open the front door. They were close. They were just across the road.

'What's going on?' I called to Graham, who was talking to a female police officer just outside the gate to the garden. 'What's happened?'

'Poppy!' Jacob called after me. 'Wait up, will you?'

I had rushed across the road while he grabbed his trainers and locked his front door.

'There's been a break-in,' said Graham, as the officer started talking into her radio and then strode off into the grounds.

He explained how he had come over to the garden extra-early to check yet again that everything was in its rightful place in case the predicted downpour hit and, once finished, took the longer path, which led along the side of the house, back to the gate.

'Violet and Dash,' he told me, 'were play-fighting in the bushes next to the back door. I knew straight away that something was wrong because Ryan had locked them in the house last night after we had finished up in the garden.'

I was relieved to hear my brother had done his duty before he disappeared.

'I know he's an early riser these days,' Graham continued as Jacob caught up, 'but I didn't think he would have let them out yet and I was right. When I went to check on the house the back door was wide open.'

'Oh no,' I gasped. 'Did you go in?'

'No way,' said Graham, 'I could see from the hall into the kitchen that someone had been inside. Everything looked upside down and I wasn't going to risk going in in case they were still in there. I came straight out here and called the police.'

'Very wise,' said Jacob, chewing his lip and frowning as he studied the gate. 'This doesn't look as though it's been forced.'

'It hasn't been,' Graham confirmed. 'It was locked as usual when I arrived. I had to use the code to get in. Whoever broke in must have scaled the wall.'

My mind began to race, flitting through the potential possibilities that might explain how this had happened.

'You don't think Ryan might have made some sort of mistake locking up the house, do you?' I swallowed.

'Of course I didn't,' snapped an angry voice behind me.

'Oh, Ryan!' I exclaimed, spinning round to face him, my cheeks burning. 'Thank God. Where the hell have you been?'

'What's going on?' he asked, ignoring my question. 'What's happened?'

'There's been a break-in—' Jacob began, but he didn't get the chance to elaborate.

'Are you Ryan Radcliffe?' asked a male officer who had just rushed back along the path to the gate. 'Mr Ryan Radcliffe?'

'Yes,' said Ryan, stepping forward. 'That's me.'

'Can you come with me, please?'

Ryan joined the officer under the strip of police tape that had been tied either side of the gate.

'Can I come with him?' I asked. 'I'm his sister.'

'That won't be necessary,' said the officer, striding off with Ryan at his side.

My brother didn't look back and I couldn't believe that I had even hinted that what had happened might be down to his negligence. He and Luke had worked through the locks and alarm system at least a hundred times in the run-up to Ryan taking charge. But with that in mind, why hadn't the alarm gone off when someone broke in?

'The back door had been hacked at with a crowbar, Poppy.' Graham hastily explained. 'It didn't look as if it had been left open to me.'

I wish I'd known that before I opened my mouth.

'So why didn't the alarm go off then?' I asked anyway. 'If the alarm was set it should have started blaring out as soon as someone got inside and then didn't key in the code to deactivate it, shouldn't it?'

'What are you suggesting?' Jacob frowned, looking every bit as horrified as Graham now did.

'I'm not suggesting anything,' I said, 'I'm just trying to work out how this happened, that's all.'

From what I could decipher, whoever had got inside the house had managed to bypass both the code to the gate *and* the alarm system once they had forced their way inside. The only thing they hadn't had, which would have made gaining entry even easier, was a set of keys. Keys that my brother had, thankfully, been keeping safe.

'What's happened here then?' asked John as he crossed the road to join us, with Neil, Mark and Carole hot on his heels. 'Is everyone all right?'

I took a step back as Graham filled them in on the details. I wondered why the police officer had been so keen to identify Ryan and then take him with him. I would have felt easier about it all had I known where my brother had spent the previous night, and who with, but for now I would just have to wait for the answers to those and the dozens of other questions buzzing about my head.

'Don't you think you should call Harry and let him know you'll be late for work today?' Jacob suggested, as the minutes ticked by and neither Ryan nor the police officers came back out of the grounds.

'Yes,' I sighed. 'I suppose I should.'

It was still early, but I couldn't imagine there was going to be a resolution to what had gone on within the next couple of hours. I only hoped the place wasn't in too much of a state and that there wasn't anything of value missing. Or anything missing at all, for that matter.

'I'll have to go home to ring,' I told Jacob, 'I didn't think to bring my mobile to yours.'

I should have done, though. If Ryan had been trying to get in touch he would have been more likely to send a text than call the house.

'If he comes out while I'm gone, please tell him to come straight home.'

'I will.'

'You won't let him disappear again?'

'Of course not.'

The community grapevine being what it was, even in our part of the city, had ensured that Harry had already heard that something was afoot.

'Come in when you can,' he said once I had filled him in on the finer details, or what I knew of them anyway, 'and if you can. Don't worry if you can't make it and don't even entertain the idea that this had anything to do with Ryan,' he went on firmly, sounding like the father figure neither my brother nor I had. 'It won't be anything to do with him. I daresay he's just helping the police with their enquiries.'

I ended the call thinking that, given Ryan was the current keyholder, Harry was probably right. It just wasn't possible that he could have played any part in breaking into the house. I might not have known him as well as I did now for all that long, but I knew he was a good lad, with a heart of gold, who had settled into our little community and enjoyed the love and respect his behaviour and helpfulness had earned him.

But there was something, some fear, I couldn't completely

set aside. Perhaps it was only natural given that I was responsible for him. Had I given him too much freedom lately? Had I been too preoccupied with my feelings for Jacob to spot the signs that Ryan might be heading for trouble?

I jumped as the front door was flung open and then slammed shut. Heavy footsteps pounding up the stairs told me it was Ryan.

'Ryan?' I called.

He didn't answer.

'Hey!' I called again.

'I can't believe you thought I hadn't locked up properly,' he shouted down.

'I'm so sorry,' I called back. 'It was a stupid thing to say.'

'Yeah,' he said, thudding back down. 'It was.'

'I'm really sorry, all right,' I said again. 'I didn't know the door had been forced then,' I added, unwittingly making the situation even worse. 'What did the police want?'

'It doesn't matter.' He sniffed. 'But as you can see, I'm not under arrest, so *they* didn't think I'd done anything wrong.'

'It wasn't like that,' I told him. 'I didn't think you'd done anything wrong.'

He didn't look as though he believed me and had I been in his position, I probably wouldn't have believed me either.

'I don't want to talk about it,' he said huskily, striding into the kitchen and filling the kettle.

I was desperate to ask where he'd been all night, but knew I wouldn't stand a chance of getting an answer.

'I've let you down, haven't I?' I said instead, the words

catching in my throat. 'After all I said about being an adult you could rely on, after promising I'd always be there for you, I've messed up, haven't I?'

'Forget it,' he said, glancing up at the kitchen clock. 'Isn't it about time you were getting ready for work?'

He didn't say anything else. He didn't have to.

# Chapter 28

I got ready for work, as Ryan had suggested, and left the house without another word. I had lingered for a few seconds outside his bedroom door, wondering if perhaps I should have been more like Jacob; less generous when it came to handing out promises, especially if I ended up not being able to keep them. I had promised to be there for my brother and right when he needed me most, I had let him down by doubting his ability to competently carry out his responsibilities.

'Where's Ryan?' asked Jacob when I arrived back at the gate to see if there was anything I could do, or whether there was any more information to be had. 'Have you seen him? My God, you look terrible, Poppy. What's happened?'

The others were chatting to the female police officer, so Jacob left them to it and moved away a little, taking me with him so we could talk without being overheard.

'Yes, I've seen him.' I sniffed, doing my best not to cry. 'He hates me, Jacob.'

'Of course he doesn't hate you,' he said, pulling me in for a hug. 'He's just a bit pissed off about what you said, that's all. He'll come round once he's had a chance to think it all through.'

I shook my head and pulled away.

'I don't think he will,' I told him, blowing my nose on the bundle of kitchen roll I had stuffed into my pocket before leaving the house. 'He's really angry.'

'Teenage boys often are.' He smiled, trying to jolly me along.

'No,' I said, 'he's really angry and I can hardly blame him.'

I thought back over the last few days, how his enthusiasm for looking after Prosperous Place had all but evaporated and how he had been surlier, far less smiley.

'And there's something else . . .' I began.

'What?'

'I don't know,' I said. 'I wish I did, but I don't.'

Jacob's poor hair didn't look as if it could cope with much more manhandling and I was disconcerted to see him running his fingers through it yet again. That sort of follicle abuse could only mean one thing: Jacob was really worried too. I stuffed the shredded ball of kitchen roll back into my pocket.

'He has seemed different this week, hasn't he?' he admitted.

'Oh God,' I groaned.

I had wanted him to tell me I was being paranoid rather than perceptive.

'Look,' he said, 'you don't think—'

'Poppy!' called Mark, beckoning me over to where the group were still talking to the policewoman.

'Yes,' I said, nervously stepping forward, Jacob's potential question forgotten.

'I was just telling your neighbours here,' said the officer, 'what a help your brother was when he came with us into the house earlier.'

'Oh.'

'He was pretty cut up about what had gone on.'

'I know.' I nodded.

'He kept saying he felt responsible that it had happened on his watch.'

'It's certainly unfortunate timing for the lad,' Graham agreed with her, 'but perhaps the thieves had been watching the place and waiting until Luke and Kate weren't here before they made their move.'

'That is a possibility,' the officer said. 'And if that does turn out to be the case then it really was bad luck for Ryan because he's obviously highly thought of and well trusted by the owner,' she went on, glancing back at the house. 'We spoke to Mr Lonsdale and he told us that Ryan would be the only person who could give us all the information we needed about locks and codes and where the most valuable things are kept in the house.'

'Wow,' said Neil, whistling under his breath, 'that's quite something.'

'It is,' said the officer, smiling, without so much as a

hint of suspicion. 'I can't imagine there are many people who would trust such a young lad with that sort of information.' She turned to me again. 'You must be very proud of him.'

'I am, yes.'

I knew she wasn't trying to make me feel even worse, but she was managing it nonetheless. Her kind words were making a fine job of tightening the knot of pain that had lodged in the pit of my stomach. Had this been an ITV police drama I knew that my brother would have been suspect number one, but this was reality rather than fabricated fiction and the only person who had put my brother in the frame was me. I looked at Jacob for some moral support, but he didn't appear to be listening.

'That brother of yours will probably need a bit of reassurance that this wasn't his fault,' said the male officer, who had rejoined his colleague and also picked me out. 'I take it he's living with you at the moment?'

'That's right,' I confirmed, 'he's been with me for a while now.'

'And we're really going to miss him when he leaves,' said Carole. 'He's a credit to you, Poppy.'

I couldn't bear to hear any more.

'If you don't need me for anything,' I said, 'I think I'll head off. I need to get to work.'

'I'll walk with you,' said Jacob. 'I'll pop in and see Colin on the way.'

'Okay,' I said, 'perhaps you could bring him and Lou up

to speed about what's happened. I don't think I could cope with having to go through it all again.'

Harry was surprised to find me already setting up the shop when he pulled up in his van just before nine.

'Give me a hand with this, will you?' he asked, jumping out and opening the back doors. 'And then you can give me an update.'

'Where did you get this?' I gasped. 'They're rarer than hens' teeth.'

Harry tapped the side of his nose and between us we manhandled the pedestal fan into the shop and set it to full speed. It didn't cool the air much, but it did waft it about a bit, easing our discomfort during what was set to be yet another ludicrously hot day, as well as sending the pile of paper bags skittering across the counter and fluttering to the floor.

I gave my boss a few more details about what had happened, carefully omitting the part where I had all but accused Ryan of leaving the house unlocked, and we settled ourselves in for another quiet day of trading. I did feel guilty about not telling Harry everything, but I didn't think I could bear to be on the receiving end of yet another accusatory stare. Those I had endured in the square had been tough enough to take.

'I've had enough of this,' Harry harrumphed as the clock finally reached three. 'We'll give it until half past and then we're closing.'

I couldn't believe the weather could have such an impact, but the heat was certainly making everything ten times harder. The few people who were out and about were all carrying umbrellas, not to take refuge from the rain, which still stubbornly refused to pour, but to protect themselves from the searing sun.

'If this doesn't break tonight,' Harry grumbled as he lumbered through to the back and I spotted Jacob across the road, 'I'll . . . well, I don't know what I'll do.'

'Jacob,' I said, rushing to open the door and ignoring Harry's half-finished threats against the sun, 'is everything all right?'

'Of course everything's all right,' he said, taking down his umbrella to come inside, 'stop panicking. You'll dehydrate ten times faster if you keep flapping about, won't she, Harry?'

'What's she got to flap about?' Harry frowned.

Jacob looked at me and I inclined my head just enough, hopefully, to imply that I hadn't explained absolutely *everything* that had happened.

'I take it you didn't tell Harry what Ryan heard you say then?' Jacob asked as we walked back to the square together.

I kicked at a stone on the dusty pavement and Jacob linked his arm through mine, more to keep us both in the shade than to feel close.

'And risk being made to feel even worse,' I croaked. 'I've been beating myself up about what I said all day. I didn't need to hand Harry the baton to carry on the assault.'

Jacob nodded, but didn't comment. He obviously thought I should still be giving myself a hard time about what I had said too.

'Anyway,' I said, 'I've decided what I'm going to do. When we get back, I'm going to sit Ryan down—'

'Poppy—'

'And I'm going to make him listen.'

'Poppy—'

'I know you'll say I should just leave him, but—'

'Pops!'

'What?'

'There's something I need to tell you.'

'There is?'

'Yes.' Jacob nodded, his croakiness matching mine. 'Let's get back to the square and I'll explain.'

Ryan's trainers weren't in their usual spot and the house was quiet. The light throughout had taken on a surreal underwater feel because I had been keeping the curtains and shutters all firmly closed. Stepping inside felt marginally cooler than outside, but only for a moment.

'So,' I said, once I had kicked off my shoes and poured us both a glass of water from the bottle I had kept chilling in the fridge, 'what is it that you have to tell me?'

'Okay,' said Jacob, digging around in his pocket for his phone.

'Where's Gus?' I frowned. 'I hope Ryan hasn't taken him out. It's far too hot; his little pads will sizzle.'

'Gus is with Colin,' Jacob told me. 'Ryan took him to the shop earlier.'

'But why?'

'Because your brother has decided to go away for a couple of days.'

My head snapped up.

'What do you mean? Why? Gone where? He's sixteen years old, he can't just take off.'

Jacob waited until I had finished bombarding him with questions.

'He messaged me,' he said, holding up his phone. 'He wanted me to tell you that you're not to worry and that him leaving is nothing to do with what you said earlier. My guess is, he's with Joe,' he carried on. 'The message was sent from someone else's phone. He doesn't say why he isn't using his.'

'So how do you even know it's from him?' I demanded, a sob rising in my throat as I began to panic. 'Anyone could have sent it.'

'He says he's left you a note in his room.'

I belted up the stairs and into Ryan's room. Nothing looked different but his canvas bag was missing from the bottom of his wardrobe and there were a few empty hangers.

'It's here,' I said, grabbing the piece of A4 that had been torn from a pad. 'I've got it.'

There was no denying the note was written in Ryan's hand and the words, imploring me to listen to what Jacob had to say, were definitely his. There was no mention of his phone, though.

'So, what am I supposed to do?' I said, flopping down on to a chair. 'He's sixteen, Jacob. I can't just pretend this isn't happening. Can't you access the files at the youth centre and get Joe's address? If that is where he is, we could go and get him back.'

'It doesn't work like that,' said Jacob patiently. 'We don't have that information on file and even if we did—'

'But—'

'Even if we did,' he said louder. 'I couldn't do that. You know I couldn't.'

'So, you're saying I should do nothing? Surely I should report his disappearance to the police?'

'I can't make that decision for you, Poppy,' Jacob said gently. 'But he hasn't technically disappeared, has he?'

I was about to argue back, but was interrupted by the house phone. I dashed into the hall to answer it.

'Hello,' I said, snatching it up.

'Is that Poppy?'

'Yes,' I said. 'Who's this?'

'My name's Sandra. I'm Joe's mum.'

I seriously hoped she wasn't phoning to check that Joe was staying with me. That would be the ultimate double twist.

'Ryan has asked me to call,' she went on. 'He's staying with us for a few days and was concerned that you would be worried about him.'

'I see.'

'Is that all right, him being here?' she asked. 'It's no problem for us. Great company for Joe actually.'

'Yes,' I said, feeling somewhat relieved.

Perhaps it was something the boys had already planned, after all.

'Yes, that's fine,' I said again. 'Tell him I'll see him soon.'

'Will do,' said Sandra. 'He's a lovely lad, isn't he?'

'Yes,' I said, imagining her to be an equally lovely mum. 'He really is.'

'Who was that?' asked Jacob as I walked back into the kitchen and his mobile began to ping.

'Joe's mum,' I told him. 'Happy to have Ryan staying for a few days, apparently.'

'And this is another message from him.'

'What does it say?'

'He says he knows you love him, and . . .' He faltered.

'And what?'

'He loves you too.'

'He actually said that?'

'Well,' Jacob said, smiling, 'he typed it, but you get the gist.'

'So why hasn't he messaged me?' I whispered. 'And why isn't he here?'

'I think he just needs a bit of space.'

'Some time away from me, you mean.'

'Didn't you ever feel like that when you were his age?' Jacob asked. 'I know I did. I couldn't wait to get to uni and then, as you know, I went much further after that.'

He was right, of course. I had left home the moment I had somewhere else to go. I hadn't been focused on my studies at all, I could see that now; I was merely using the degree route as the most plausible way out of a shitty home life. I could hardly blame my brother for feeling the same need for freedom. Although, the fact that he had run away from the life at Nightingale Square that I had worked so hard to create did grate a little. But then, why should my version of perfection match his?

'Does he say anything about when he'll come back?'

'No,' said Jacob, tucking his phone away again, 'but my guess is, he'll be home soon enough.'

I didn't think there was much else I could do now. Reporting Ryan missing was definitely out of the equation.

'And has everything here been okay today?' I asked, thinking of Prosperous Place.

'Yes,' said Jacob. 'Luke and Kate arrived back this afternoon. They dropped the girls off with Carole while they went to assess the damage and talk to the police.'

'Of course. They wouldn't want to take the little ones back with them, would they?'

'No,' Jacob agreed, 'but as it turned out, it was nowhere near as bad as it could have been. The kitchen had been turned upside down but whoever was in there couldn't get any further because Ryan had set the internal locks. To access the rest of the house they would have had to go back out and start smashing windows, and they obviously didn't think that was worth the risk.'

'I wonder if they trashed the kitchen out of frustration, then?'

'Maybe.' Jacob shrugged. 'Who knows? But that's not for you to worry about, Poppy, you need to relax.'

'Ha!' I laughed. 'Chance would be a fine thing.'

I didn't think there was anything in the world capable of distracting me from my head full of thoughts and worries.

'And I happen to know just the thing to help.'

'Well, it better not be alcohol-related,' I told him. 'After everything that's happened today and this bloody heat, the last thing I feel like doing is drinking.'

There was a certain amount of drinking involved with Jacob's relaxation therapy, but it wasn't the alcoholic kind.

'Right,' he said, throwing open the back door and carrying one of the kitchen chairs outside. 'This will be about the right height,' he added, having taken a step back to appraise it.

'For what?' I questioned, following him out with our replenished glasses, which were now filled with tonic water, lemon and ice.

He took his glass and, after we had drunk deeply, he relieved me of mine and set the pair down together on the bistro table, then sat me in the chair.

'Close your eyes,' he instructed.

'Yeah right,' I muttered, 'I've heard that one before.'

'Don't be silly,' he said firmly, 'and try to relax.'

My silliness was nothing more than a defence mechanism. It was my way of settling my thrumming heart and stomping out the tingling feeling that had started after our fingers touched as I passed him his glass. Perhaps there was something that could distract me from my woes after all.

'Come on,' he said, 'I'm trying to help, and I've been told I happen to be very good at this, and don't,' he rushed on, 'use that as an excuse for another smart-arse comment.'

I didn't say another word but did as I was told and closed my eyes.

'Right,' he said, a distant deep rumble of thunder providing a dramatic backdrop to his words, 'that's better.'

'Do you think it might rain this time?' I asked, my voice cracking a little as I felt him move behind me.

'Yes,' he said softly, 'I think it might.'

The tingling feeling was intensified tenfold as he moved my ponytail to one side, my hair caressing the back of my neck and making me shiver.

'You aren't cold, are you?' he asked.

I could hear the smile in his voice.

'I wish.' I smiled back.

I sat quiet and still as his hands moved across the back of my neck, his fingers deftly and purposefully working their way along the series of little knots that had been responsible for making me walk around with my shoulders almost touching my ears all day.

'How's that?' he asked. 'Is it helping?'

'Yes,' I whispered, 'it's definitely helping.'

He carried on as a slow pitter-patter of gentle rain began to fall and the thunder moved a little closer. I bent my head, amazed that Jacob's hands on my neck could be having such an arousing effect on parts of my body that couldn't have been much further away.

'Are you okay?' he asked, his mouth so close to my ear he was almost touching it.

'Yes,' I answered, lifting my head again and laying my hands over the top of his. 'Yes.'

He didn't resist as I gently pulled them down until they

were cupping my breasts. I arched my back as his thumbs began to caress them with the same pressure he had applied to my shoulders.

'Jesus, Poppy,' he groaned, as it began to rain a little harder. 'We can't . . .'

The words died in his throat as I arched further, and his mouth met my collarbone and then my throat as he moved round the chair to kneel in front of me.

'Your turn,' I said, standing up and moving him onto the chair before hitching up the skirt of my dress and slowly lowering myself down until I was sitting astride him.

I looked into his eyes and then we began. His hands were in my hair, my fingers were tearing at the buttons on his shirt, my dress was over my head and we were kissing, searing kisses as the rain began to pour, the sting of it sharp and deliciously cold on our bare skin.

As one we moved into the house, him carrying me with my legs wrapped round him, and the thunder raged on. We somehow made it up the stairs and into the bedroom, falling heavily on to the bed, where we stayed, slaking our thirst for one another as the long-awaited rain continued to pour.

# Chapter 29

My first thought the next morning was that the storm was still raging, but as I drifted up from the depths of the deepest sleep I had enjoyed in weeks, I realised that it wasn't thunder at all, but someone hammering hard on the front door. Jacob, sound asleep on his front next to me, didn't stir and I slipped quietly out of the bed, pulled on my dressing gown and closed the bedroom door behind me.

'Whatever is it?' I gulped, taking in Lisa's tear-stained face and Mark's glowering one as I opened the front door. 'What's happened?'

'It's the garden,' Lisa sobbed, 'can you come over, Poppy? I don't know what we're going to do.'

Mark stepped forward and draped an arm round her shoulders, kissing the top of her head.

'Come as soon as you can love, will you?' he said to me.

He sounded more serious than I had ever heard him and

that, coupled with Lisa's despair, undid all the good work Jacob had put in on my shoulders.

'Everyone's making their way over,' he said, nodding over to Prosperous Place. 'We're going to go and see Jacob and then we'll be going back.'

'Don't worry about him,' I said, thinking that whatever had happened, no one needed to discover that Jacob wasn't home at this time on a Sunday morning and then start wondering where he was. 'I'll get dressed and then go and get him. You two head back now.'

Perhaps I was being a little paranoid, but I didn't think it would be that big a leap, for an enquiring mind like Lisa's or Carole's, to start wondering if my neighbour and I had spent the evening together; and the last thing I wanted was word somehow getting back to Ryan, especially as Jacob and I had promised to keep things between us platonic. If my memory served, and I was certain that it did, then we had more than crossed that line, at least three times, during the last few hours.

'All right,' said Lisa, sniffing, 'but hurry, won't you?'

'I will,' I promised.

I raced back up the stairs and found Jacob awake and sitting up in bed.

'Well, good morning.' He smiled.

His hair was its usual mess and there were dark smudges under his eyes betraying the fact that he'd had nowhere near the recommended hours of sleep. He looked extremely content and relaxed though, and I wanted nothing more than to crawl back under the covers with him and snuggle down for the rest of the day. The guilt I had been feeling about betraying my brother's wishes just seconds before was momentarily forgotten, but I knew there would be a reason, an important reason, why Lisa and Mark had looked so devastated.

I hurriedly shed my dressing gown, letting it puddle around my feet, and Jacob pulled back the sheets.

'No time for that,' I said, pulling a clean T-shirt over my head. 'We need to get to the garden.'

'What, *now*?' He frowned, looking at the clock on the nightstand. 'But it poured all night. No one will be expecting you to be on watering duty this morning.'

I had been so distracted by the sight of my neighbours that I hadn't noticed whether the rain had cooled the outside temperature. It was certainly still hot in the bedroom.

'It's not that,' I said, tutting, 'didn't you just hear Lisa and Mark?'

He shrugged, and I guessed not.

'Something's happened,' I said, 'at the Grow-Well. Everyone's going over.'

'Oh no,' Jacob groaned, throwing back the sheet and treating me to a sight of his beautifully toned body, 'it'll be the storm, won't it? I bet it's done no end of damage.'

It was certainly cooler, but muggy with it, as we walked over wondering what we were about to face. As we stepped through the gate it felt as though every bit of air had been suddenly squeezed out of my lungs.

'This wasn't the storm,' I stammered, my eyes taking in the scene of destruction and devastation before us. 'Thunder and rain couldn't do this.'

'You're right,' said Graham. 'We've been vandalised.'

We all huddled together under the dripping branches of the old oak tree, waiting while the police, different officers this time, strode about assessing the damage, asking questions and scribbling notes.

'They didn't take long to get here, did they?' commented Jacob.

'Probably because of what happened at the house,' said Graham reasonably.

Their response time might have been speedy, but they didn't hang about long and I didn't see any of them sweeping the scene for fingerprints; but, given the amount of rain that had fallen, there probably wouldn't have been any left.

Once they had gone to the house with Luke and Kate, the rest of us worked together to clear up the worst of the mess, round up the hens, repair their run and cut away what couldn't be salvaged. No part of the garden had escaped the unwanted attentions of whoever had broken in. Even the elderflower cordial in the bothy had been smashed and spilled.

'There's just one crate left,' I said, carrying it out and putting it on the table.

'In that case,' said Luke, who had rejoined us and was, with good reason, looking wearier than the rest of us put together, 'I think we should open it, don't you?'

'Yes,' rallied John, 'let's not let the bastards get the better of us.'

'Dad!' scolded Tamsin, her eyes red from crying.

'Sorry, love,' he said, giving her a squeeze and setting her off again.

'I can't believe we didn't hear anything,' said Kate, as she shifted the sling holding Abigail into a more comfortable position across her chest.

'It was the storm,' said Harold, 'you couldn't hear anything over that wind.'

We raised our glasses and stared at the sorry mess before us. Jacob had put his hands to good use, repairing the bean-poles and tying in the plants that were left, and the hens were having a wonderful time gorging themselves on some of the fruit and veg that had come their way because it had been torn out of the soil or off its vines and bushes and trampled.

'I'll make up some veg boxes,' said Carole, her voice cracking. 'We can eat most of what's been damaged. There must be something we can salvage from this.'

Graham reached for her hand and I wished I felt able to do the same with Jacob. No one had commented on us arriving together, but that wasn't surprising. Everyone was too pre-occupied with the clear-up mission, plus I had told Lisa and Mark that I would be going to get him.

'I know no one wants to hear it,' said Neil, bravely broaching the subject that was on all our minds, 'but we do need to have a think about the competition.'

'Yeah,' said Heather as she and Glen got ready to take their little brood home for lunch, 'that's a good point, Neil. We can't possibly win now, can we?'

'But after all our hard work!' sobbed Lisa.

'Very little of which is left,' pointed out her husband.

'Let's all go home for a rest,' suggested Luke, 'and have a think about it.'

It was with hanging heads and heavy hearts that the sad little party broke up. I took one last glance at the state of the place before ducking through the gate to go back to the square.

'I can't believe it,' said Jacob, falling into step next to me. 'After all our work. I know I hated even the thought of it when I first moved here, but I can't be without it now. I love that place as much as I love—'

'Hey, you two,' said Neil, pushing his way between us and cutting Jacob off, 'do you want to come back to ours?'

'Thanks, Neil,' I said, thinking of the kitchen chair I needed to salvage from my own garden, along with the glasses, 'but if you don't mind I'm just going to go back to mine for a bit.'

'No worries,' he said, nodding, 'we'll see you later though, yeah?'

'Yes,' I promised. 'In a while.'

Jacob didn't pick up his train of thought once Neil had gone and as I put my key in the front door I realised that his sentence wasn't the only thing that had been left hanging and unresolved. No one had made any suggestion as to who might have been responsible for wrecking our beloved

Grow-Well and no one had asked why Ryan wasn't helping with the clear-up operation either.

'Why do you think no one asked where Ryan was?' I asked Jacob as he helped me dry off the kitchen chair. 'I know we were all getting on with things, but not a single person asked where he was. You don't think—'

'No,' he interrupted sharply. 'I don't. No one would entertain the idea that Ryan was in any way responsible for what's happened over there.'

'I wasn't going to say that,' I snapped back.

'Oh.' He flushed. 'Sorry.'

'I was going to say' – I swallowed, the thought tearing into my heart – 'that he'd probably spoken to them rather than me. Maybe he told them he was going to Joe's.'

It was a horrid thought and, if that was the case, why had no one warned me?

'It wasn't like that that,' said Jacob, his face turning even redder as he set the chair down in the kitchen on the newspaper I had spread over the floor in case it dripped as it dried out.

I didn't think I would ever be able to sit on it again without experiencing the tingly feelings Jacob had elicited from me while I was sitting on and then astride it last night.

'But how can you be sure?' I frowned. 'If no one knows he's gone to Joe's, then why didn't they ask where he was?'

'They do know.' He sighed. 'I told them. Before I came to meet you at work on Saturday, I gathered everyone together on the green and told them that Ryan was staying with a mate.'

'You spoke to everyone before you told me about his text message?' I said, the glasses slipping a little in my grasp.

Jacob carefully took them from me.

'Yes,' he said, reaching for my hands. 'I know you probably won't thank me for it, but I was worried about how you were going to react and I didn't think you'd want to be faced with extra questions. I gave Graham back the keys to Prosperous Place and told everyone that Ryan would be back again soon.'

'Right,' I said, 'I see.'

'I knew you were going to be upset, and I wanted to make sure that no one started asking you about it.'

'And that's why they haven't asked after him today?'

'Yes,' he said, looking sheepish. 'I hope I wasn't out of line. I just didn't want you to be feeling worse about it all than you probably still are.'

'And what about you?' I asked him. 'How are you feeling?'

I was relieved that his answer proved that he knew exactly what I was talking about.

'The same as you,' he said, dropping my hands. 'Guilty as. We promised to keep things platonic, didn't we? And the second Ryan's not here . . .'

'We did promise,' I said, nodding, 'and we've failed. If he finds out,' I added, feeling teary again, 'it'll be a miracle if my brother ever comes back.'

We all congregated back in the garden later that afternoon and Lisa took charge of overseeing the vote that would decide whether we withdrew from the competition we had all worked our backsides off for; but before it got underway she had something she wanted to say to me.

'Poppy,' she said, 'we weren't going to say anything . . .'

'. . . but in view of this most recent disaster . . .' added Carole.

'We don't want you to think that any of us have assumed,' Lisa carried on, 'that because he's isn't here right now, your wonderful brother has had anything to do with what's happened here.'

'Or with the house, for that matter,' Luke quickly added.

'Jacob told us he's gone to stay with a mate for a few days,' Lisa continued, 'and that he's feeling more than gutted that the house was broken into while he was in charge.'

'It was rotten timing.' Carole smiled kindly.

'As is what's happened here,' muttered some of the others.

'But that's all it is,' said Luke stoutly, 'bad timing.'

'And we know you're probably wishing he hadn't decided to go at all,' Lisa finished up, 'so we're not going to go on about it, we just want you to know that we're not blaming him for any of this.'

Jacob looked at me and winked and I knew I couldn't be cross that he had told them. He only had my best interests at heart; they all did.

'Thanks, everyone,' I said, blushing under their attention. 'I really appreciate that, and I know Ryan would too if he was here, but he isn't and that's my most pressing concern right now. If he hears about what's happened here overnight he might well assume that we're thinking he did have something to do with it.'

'He wouldn't think that,' said Neil, stepping up and rubbing my arm, 'he knows we think the world of him.'

'But if you're that worried,' suggested Mark, stepping up to my other side, 'why don't you ring him or send him a text? Get in first and explain everything?'

'Yes,' said Neil, 'before he hears about it on the news or something.'

'I can't,' I said, shaking my head, 'I have a feeling he's lost his phone.'

'And the one he used to get in touch with me,' said Jacob, holding up his own mobile, 'is switched off.'

'Well don't worry,' said Mark stoutly, 'we'll think of something, won't we, guys?'

Everyone promised to think the problem through and then the vote got underway.

'So,' said Lisa, her voice wobbling as she made the announcement, 'that's decided then. We're pulling out of the competition.'

There was barely a dry eye amongst us.

'I still can't believe it,' she said again. 'After all our work.'

We all looked over the garden. It was marginally tidier thanks to our earlier efforts, but it was still wrecked. I didn't think I'd ever seen a sorrier sight.

'What's that noise?' Graham said suddenly, cocking his head the better to listen.

'I can't hear anything,' Carole answered.

'Shush,' he urged, earning himself one of her steeliest stares. 'Over there.'

As one our eyes swivelled to where he was pointing, and Tamsin ran across to the mangled courgette bed.

'Tamsin,' Lisa called after her. 'Be careful.'

'It's coming from here!' she shouted, plunging her hands into the tangle of broken and twisted leaves. 'It's a phone,' she added, pulling it out as her father rushed over to retrieve it.

We crowded round to take a look.

I swallowed. 'It's Ryan's.

# Chapter 30

Luke put off making the call to the police to tell them that a phone had been found at the Grow-Well, along with who it belonged to, for as long as possible. When they turned up to collect it, depositing it into a plastic bag and sealing it inside, Jacob made sure he told them that Ryan had been in touch via someone else's phone, so he couldn't have been anywhere near the garden when it was trashed, but I'm not sure it helped.

'So, my guess is that this was lost, or perhaps stolen, a few days ago,' he insisted. 'Ryan hasn't had this phone since the house was broken into,' he added. 'I'm certain of that.'

'Thank you, sir,' said the policeman. 'We'll be the judge of that.'

It was the same guy who had been to the house, but he didn't sound quite so sure of my brother's glowing reputation and innocence now.

'And you say you haven't seen him since he took off after the break-in?' he said, turning his attention to me.

'No—' I started huskily.

'He didn't take off,' Jacob interrupted, eliciting a raised eyebrow from the officer. 'It's not like he's run away or anything. He's just gone to stay with a mate.'

'In that case, you'd better tell us all about this so-called mate and where we can find him, hadn't you?'

As the time ticked by and Monday nudged towards Tuesday, I began to think my brother was never coming back. The police hadn't been able to track down either Ryan or Joe. Joe's mum, Sandra, had said they'd gone off camping somewhere but she didn't know where. She wasn't unduly concerned as they were both good lads.

'They'll turn up when they run out of food,' she had told the police.

My own mother wasn't worried either, but that was because she didn't care.

'She didn't seem all that bothered,' the officer in charge, the one who had taken the phone, told me when he popped into Greengages late on Tuesday afternoon.

'Yes, well, I'm afraid she's not that sort of mother,' I said, mouthing an apology to Harry that the police had turned up at the shop. 'She's actually the reason why Ryan's been staying with me.'

'I can well believe it. When someone called round to see her in person, she was positively rude.'

I had been wondering whether I should call her myself, given the seriousness of the situation, but her reaction to the police was enough to reassure me that I needn't bother.

'Anyway,' said the officer, picking up a couple of bananas. 'If Ryan gets in touch . . .'

'I'll call you.' I nodded. 'Straight away.'

'Any news?' asked Harry once the shop had emptied a bit.

'No,' I said. 'Nothing.'

'And you're sure you want to be here?' he asked, concern etched across his kind face.

'Yes,' I said, releasing a long breath, 'definitely. I'd be going stir crazy at home, just sitting about and waiting.'

'All right,' he said, waving to Lou, who had just come into view outside. 'But if you change your mind . . .'

'I won't,' I told him. 'This place is set to save my sanity.'

'And not for the first time.' He smiled, reminding me that it had been a refuge as well as my workplace on more than one occasion. 'But you get off now for the day,' he said. 'Go and see how the lovebirds are faring.'

The lovebirds were faring very well, but both were concerned about Ryan's continued absence, and Gus was positively miserable.

'Here,' said Colin when Lou and I arrived at the bookshop, 'you sit with him.'

He dumped the little dog on my lap.

'He might be able to pick up on your genetic connection to Ryan or something,' said Colin, standing back and shaking his head as Lou made us all coffees. 'He can't carry on like this.'

'None of us can,' said Lou. 'How are you coping at home?' she asked me. 'It must be so quiet.'

It was strange to think that the peace and quiet of Nightingale Square was one of the things that had drawn me there and something I had been so reluctant to give up. I had known that inviting Ryan to stay with me while he got his life into some sort of order would mean sacrificing the simplicity I had worked so hard to create and yet, now I had it again, I couldn't bear it. I had hardly spent any time in the house at all since Ryan had gone. Thankfully Jacob's door was always open, but I wasn't in the mood to share that particular bit of information with my two friends, who might well read just the right amount into the admission.

'It is,' I said, focusing on Gus's silky head, 'it's horribly quiet and I miss tripping over his trainers and moaning about him leaving piles of wet towels all over the bathroom floor.'

'I'm sure he'll be back home soon,' said Lou stoically.

I knew she was trying to reassure me, and I wished I could feel as sure as she sounded, but I had already fallen to wondering how much worse I would feel when Ryan went back to Mum for good. Would home still feel like home without him living in it long-term?

'And what about your book?' asked Colin. 'Have you got any further with that?'

'No,' I said, 'I haven't even given it a thought.'

'Perhaps now would be a good time to start planning,' he suggested. 'It might take your mind off things.'

'Yes,' Lou agreed, 'it's always good to have a project on the go.'

'Perhaps,' I said, sitting up and trying to pull myself together a bit. 'Maybe.'

As I walked home a little later I wondered if perhaps the pair of them were right; perhaps a project would help focus my mind and stop me fretting quite so much.

'Jacob,' I said, rushing up the path when I spotted him sitting on the step, 'is everything all right?'

'Yes,' he said, jumping up, 'don't panic. I thought you might not be in the mood to cook tonight, so I thought I could instead. I popped to Greengages and stocked up. I thought I might try out that vegetable curry recipe card you gave me.'

'And you want me to be your guinea pig?' I smiled.

'Something like that.' He smiled back. 'And I want to talk to you.'

He sounded serious and he looked exhausted. I didn't envy him one little bit; trying to squeeze the last few pieces of scheduled learning into a class who had one eye on the calendar and the six weeks of freedom that were now tantalisingly close must have been nigh on impossible. As a child I used to dread the long summer break, but I knew that not everyone hated being at home as much as I did.

'In that case,' I said, opening the door, 'you'd better come in.'

Having shown Jacob where he could find the utensils and pans he was going to need to cook up our vegetarian supper, I settled myself at the table and tried not to interfere. It wasn't easy.

'Haven't you got anything else you could be doing?' Jacob suggested, prising the wooden spoon from my grasp after I'd interrupted him for the umpteenth time. 'Go and have a shower or something.'

'I thought you wanted to talk,' I reminded him.

'I do,' he said, 'but not yet. I want to concentrate on getting this right for now.'

'Sorry,' I said, feeling suitably chastened. 'I'll let you get on.'

I didn't much feel like showering, not on my own anyway, so I gathered together my recipe notes, along with Gran's more impressive tome, and started flicking through the pages, trying to work out which recipes might prove most practical, and complement Mark's bread suggestions, if they ever did end up in a book.

'What have you got there?' asked Jacob as he peered over my shoulder, just minutes after I had finally agreed to leaving him alone.

'It's my recipe collection,' I told him, 'and my gran's. Now don't worry about what I'm doing, that pan will catch if you don't keep stirring.'

We ate outside as it was such a wonderful evening. Jacob's curry was a mouth-watering and fragrant triumph. I'd soon finished my bowlful, mopping up the last of the sauce with soft naans and washing it down with a bottle of Indian Pale Ale.

'I don't think I've been eating enough,' I hiccupped when I realised Jacob still had a few mouthfuls to finish and at least a quarter of his naan to go.

'Do you want some more?' he asked, making to stand up. 'There's easily another serving, if you'd like it.'

'No,' I said, patting my slightly rounded tum, 'I'm good, but thank you. It was delicious. Thank you for thinking to do it. Left to my own devices it would have probably been a round of toast again for me.'

'That's not like you, Poppy.' He frowned, reaching for my hand and kissing the back of it.

'I know,' I told him. 'I just can't seem to make the effort at the moment. I'm in a daze, worrying about my blasted brother.'

It was unfair to turn my concern into annoyance but I couldn't help it. This continued non-appearance was taking its toll and I had thought Ryan would have realised that and at least made some effort to let me know he was still in the land of the living.

'Anyway,' I said, squeezing Jacob's hand and forcing myself not to carry on walking down that particular path, 'tell me, what is it you wanted to talk about?'

'Your blasted brother, actually.' Jacob smiled. 'But let me get us another beer first.'

I gathered our dishes together and waited while Jacob stacked them in the kitchen and cracked open two more bottles.

'I've been wondering,' he began, 'what's going to happen to Ryan when he comes back.'

'If, you mean.'

'No,' he said firmly, 'when.'

'Well,' I said with a sigh, 'he'll go back to Mum, I suppose. I can't imagine after everything that's happened that he'll want to hang around here for much longer, can you?'

'I don't know.' Jacob shrugged.

'That's assuming he is still round here somewhere.'

For all any of us knew, he and Joe could have set up camp in another county by now. Joe's phone was still turned off and with no access to the Grow-Well Twitter account Ryan wouldn't know any of what had happened since he left.

'I'm sure he is,' said Jacob. 'He and Joe won't have ventured far. They haven't got the money to go anywhere too far-flung, have they?'

I hoped they hadn't been relying on hitchhiking to move around. Best not to think about that.

'But what's he going to do once he's gone home?' Jacob persisted. 'What are his options?'

'I don't know.' I frowned, 'I haven't thought that far ahead, although I'm certain he won't be carrying on with his A levels. He never wanted to take them in the first place.'

'Then how about—' Jacob began, but stopped suddenly. 'Was that the door?'

'Yes,' I said, as the sound of someone knocking reached my ears. 'I'll be back in a sec.'

The unmistakable silhouette of two police officers filled the glass panel on the front door and I felt my heart jump. I took a deep breath and prepared myself for bad news; I didn't know what sort of bad news, but every time I had had a visit from the police since the Prosperous Place break-in they had come alone. A brace of them couldn't be good, could it?

'Good evening, Poppy,' said the one I recognised as I opened the door, my mouth filling with saliva.

'E-evening,' I stammered.

'We have someone here we think you'll be rather relieved to see.'

The pair parted to reveal Ryan, dishevelled and dirty, standing between them, his rucksack at his feet and his expression more miserable than I'd ever seen it.

'Oh my God!' I gasped, pushing between the officers and pulling my brother into a non-negotiable hug. 'Thank God you're all right.'

Relief flooded through me and I began to cry. The realisation that he was actually there, wrapped in my arms, hit me straight in the heart.

'Thank God you've come back.'

'Hey, Jacob,' said Ryan over my shoulder as he awkwardly hugged me back.

'Hey,' Jacob replied, 'are you going to let him in, Poppy?'

'Yes,' I said, loosening my grip a little and pulling him by the arm over the threshold. 'Of course. Thank you both so much for bringing him back.'

'He found his own way back,' said the younger officer with a smile, following me and Ryan inside. 'We'll just come in for a quick chat and then we'll get off.'

Jacob made us all tea as we stood crowded in the kitchen, Ryan lingering at the back.

'I'm sure Ryan will fill you in on the finer points,' said the older officer after helping himself to two heaped spoons of sugar. 'We just wanted to reassure you that he had absolutely nothing to do with either the break-in at Prosperous Place or the vandalisation of the Grow-Well.'

'We knew that already, didn't we, Poppy?' said Jacob, smiling at Ryan as he handed him a mug. 'No one thought you had anything to do with any of it, Ryan.'

Ryan nodded but didn't say anything.

'I can't go into too many details,' the officer continued, 'but the culprits have been arrested and charged with both crimes.'

'Thanks in no small part to your brother here, miss, and his friend, Joe,' said the younger officer, beaming.

I'd never seen him before, and his older colleague was looking as though he regretted bringing him along.

'Er yes, thank you,' he said sternly, making the young guy blush.

'Sorry,' he said, turning red and taking a swig from his mug.

'Well,' the older officer continued, 'I don't think we need to say any more. I'm sure Ryan will want to tell you at least a bit about what's happened, won't you, lad?'

'I guess,' he said, 'if I have to.'

'I'd like to know.' I smiled at him. 'It sounds to me as if you've been quite the hero, Ryan.'

'I wouldn't go that far,' he muttered.

'Don't keep beating yourself up about it, lad,' said the older officer, 'it's done now and your actions have ended up helping us solve a couple of other crimes that have been outstanding for a while. It's all turned out all right in the end.'

Ryan still didn't look too pleased about whatever it was that had happened and what he had played a part in. I was bursting to find out what those 'actions' were but my brother didn't look in any way ready to answer any of the questions I had buzzing about in my brain.

'Well done, Ryan,' said Jacob before I had a chance to open my mouth. 'I'm sure you'll tell us when and if you're ready, but for now I can imagine you just want a long hot shower and an early night.'

'You're not wrong,' said Ryan, picking up his bag.

'Don't you want anything to eat?' I asked, keen to keep him in sight for as long as possible.

'I had something at the station,' he said, making for the stairs. 'Thanks for everything,' he said to the police officers as he slid his trainers off and kicked them almost out of the way. 'I appreciate you bringing me home.'

I watched him run up the stairs, the lump in my throat forming again as I thought about him considering my home as his.

'We'll get off then,' said the younger officer.

'And don't worry,' the older one said to me, 'your brother hasn't done anything wrong. He's a fine young man, with a decent head on his shoulders. I'd leave him alone for tonight. Let him get his head straight before you start asking him questions.'

'I will,' I told him, as much as it pained me to do so.

# Chapter 31

'Do you think I should go and check he's okay?' I said to Jacob once we could hear that Ryan had left the bathroom and was moving about in his room.

'No,' he said firmly. 'Absolutely not. He won't thank you if you do and you won't get anything out of him until he's ready to tell you, so I'd just leave him if I were you.'

He was right, but I was itching to get it all out in the open, deal with it and then forget about it. The last few days had really taken a toll on me and I wanted to put them behind me as quickly as possible – but, I reminded myself, this wasn't about me.

'All right,' I relented. 'I'll ring Harry and tell him I might be a bit late in tomorrow. For a change.'

'And I better get home,' said Jacob, pulling me into a hug and kissing the top of my head. 'The next couple of days are going to be busy at school, but after that I'll be able to help you out if you need me. You'll soon be the focus of my undivided attention for a month at least, assuming you want to be, of course.'

Now Ryan was back the fragility of our relationship was even more apparent. There was nothing I wanted more than to be the focus of Jacob's attention, but I knew my brother would notice the shift in our relationship without even trying. As I stood on tiptoe to return Jacob's kiss with a light touch of my own, I couldn't help wishing that my brother hadn't been quite so fixed in his thoughts about what my connection to our wonderful neighbour should be.

'I'll see you soon,' Jacob said to me in the hall as I pushed Ryan's trainers further aside with my foot.

It was a familiar gesture and one that caused my eyes to fill with tears.

'He's back now.' Jacob smiled. 'Everything's going to be fine.'

I nodded.

'I know,' I croaked, 'I'm just relieved.'

Jacob quickly kissed me again.

'See you later, Ryan!' he called up the stairs.

There was no answer.

Harry insisted that I took the day off and that we'd work something out if I needed more time after that. It was my day off on Saturday, so at least if I did go back in on Thursday and Friday it wasn't going to be the longest working week imaginable.

'Is it true?' Lisa blurted out when I opened the door to her after she'd been on the school run the next morning. 'Is Ryan back?'

'He is,' I told her. 'He's home. Currently non-communicative, fast asleep I'm guessing, but he is back.'

'Oh, thank God,' she cried, beaming and looking relieved, 'can I tell the others?'

'Of course,' I said, looking around the square. 'I'm sure everyone will be as pleased as I am.'

Truth be told, I was fairly certain they would know already. I couldn't imagine the arrival of a police car in the square would have gone unnoticed, by Carole at least.

'They will,' Lisa enthusiastically agreed. 'They definitely will.'

I was wrong in my assumption about the car being spotted but Lisa, with little Archie, her son, in tow, must have sprinted round the square because the floodgates opened within minutes of her visit and I was inundated with neighbours and phone calls all day. Unfortunately, nothing and no one had been able to tempt Ryan out of his room; however, every time I had replenished the tray outside his bedroom door with hot drinks and snacks it had disappeared within minutes, only to reappear, as if by magic and covered in crumbs, a short while later.

Kate and Luke popped over from Prosperous Place with the girls. Luke insisted on going upstairs to talk to Ryan through the still-closed door while I took Kate and the little ones out into the garden.

'I hope you don't think I'm talking out of turn,' Kate said to me as we watched Jasmine rearranging some of the pots in my little herb area, 'but I can't help wondering whether Ryan might benefit from some more specific counselling to help him come to terms with the loss of his father.'

'I don't think you're talking out of turn at all,' I reassured her. 'In fact, I'm sure you're right, but I haven't had a chance to even think about where I can go or how I can get him that extra level of support. I had thought talking to the counsellor at the youth centre would be enough, but now I'm not so sure. I suppose there must be somewhere more specialised here in Norfolk. I'll have to look into it.'

'I know somewhere,' she said, pulling a leaflet out of her pocket, 'but it's in Cambridgeshire, not Norfolk. This place, Wynthorpe Hall, is on the outskirts of Wynbridge, my home town. It offers a bereavement counselling service for under-eighteens. I'm certain they would be able to help.'

I turned the leaflet over in my hands. From what I could make out from a quick scan, the charity was all for getting youngsters outside, out of a formal environment, and into what looked like some woods and pretty dramatic country-side, to talk through their experiences and problems. I felt certain it would suit Ryan far better than four walls.

'This looks great,' I said, smiling, 'thank you, Kate. Once things have settled down a bit and the time's right, I'll suggest it.'

I only hoped that Ryan was going to be with me long enough for us to get to that time.

'Ready?' said Luke from the kitchen door. 'We'd better get back.'

'Did he speak to you?' I asked, careful to keep my voice low, as Ryan's room overlooked the little back garden.

'No,' Luke said, 'but that's fine. I wasn't expecting him to. I just wanted him to hear directly from me that I didn't blame him for any of what's happened. That none of us do.'

'Thank you.' I nodded. 'I appreciate that. And if you could work out a way to get him to come out of his room, I'd appreciate that too.'

'I know,' said Jasmine, skipping up and taking Luke's hand. 'I know how you can get him to come out.'

And she did.

Jasmine's idea was a true stroke of genius and one that I managed to set up for the end of the day.

'Do you really think this will work?' whispered Lou as she crossed the threshold behind Colin and Gus, who was already straining to get off his lead.

'There's no doubt in my mind.' I smiled as Colin set the diminutive pooch free.

He raced up the stairs, at a speed you wouldn't have thought his little legs were capable of, and began crying and scratching at Ryan's door. I only hoped the scuffed paintwork would be easy to touch up.

'Let's leave him to it,' said Colin, ushering us towards the kitchen.

We had barely made it along the hall before I heard Ryan's

door open and the little dog's cries were replaced by yappy barks of excitement.

'Well, that's all well and good,' said Lou, 'but he hasn't come out. He's taken Gus in.'

'That's all right,' I said, reaching for the kettle. 'Trust me, Lou, this will definitely work.'

Colin and Lou didn't stay for long and Colin was happy to leave Gus with Ryan. I think it was a weight off his shoulders to hear the little dog tearing about above him and I hoped his presence was doing my brother just as much good.

A little while later I heard the bedroom door open and strained my ears to work out if there were two sets of feet padding down the stairs or one.

'Do we have any of Gus's food left?' Ryan asked. His voice sounded hoarse, as if it hadn't been used for a while. 'And I think he might need to go out.'

I let Gus outside and then handed Ryan the bag of food and assorted bits and pieces that Colin and Lou had dropped off.

'I think Colin would appreciate it if you could take care of Gus for a few days,' I told him as the dog rushed back in and started circling around our feet, having spotted his food bowl. 'Us humans aren't the only ones who have missed you, you know.'

Ryan didn't say anything and, as hard as it was, I kept Jacob's words of wisdom at the forefront of my mind. If I messed this conversation up, Ryan would go scurrying back upstairs and we'd be back to square one. I didn't think the hens would be up to the task of tempting him out again in quite the same way as Gus had managed. Violet and Dash might have been worth a shot though.

'Do you want some dinner?' I asked. 'I don't feel like cooking, so I thought I might order a takeaway.'

'Chinese?' Ryan asked, sounding hopeful.

'If you like,' I said, reaching for the menu. 'What do you fancy?'

A few light spots of rain had started to fall by the time our dinner was delivered, so we elected to sit inside and eat in front of the TV with our plates on lap trays. The television was only on quietly, but it provided a comforting drone of background chatter that stopped the silence turning awkward.

'Do you want some more?' I asked after Ryan had polished off his second plateful in record time. 'There's a spoonful of rice left and some of my chicken in vegetables, if you want it?'

'Better not,' he said breathing out and readjusting his waistband, 'I think I've reached my limit.'

'I'll get rid of it then.'

'Don't waste it,' said Ryan, reaching across to spear the last prawn ball. 'Just put it in the fridge and I'll have it for breakfast.'

'How about you put it in the fridge?' I said, raising an eyebrow, 'as you're the one who wants to keep it.'

'Yeah,' he said, 'sorry.'

Between us we sorted the dishes and the leftovers and Ryan let Gus out again.

'I'll walk him tomorrow,' he said, 'when everyone's gone to work. I don't think I can face them yet.'

'They don't blame you, you know.'

'I know,' he said, 'Luke told me and I've heard most of what's been said here today. The soundproofing in this place is non-existent.'

My mind flitted back over the conversations that had taken place and I wondered if he had heard more than I would have wanted him to of my exchange with Jacob.

'That Wynthorpe Hall place sounds interesting,' he said, his cheeks colouring slightly.

He really did have supersonic hearing if he'd caught the gist of that while Luke had been talking to him through his door, I thought. But it turned out that Luke had mentioned it. 'He said Kate had a leaflet about it that she was going to leave with you,' Ryan said now.

'That's right,' I said, trying to temper my enthusiasm. 'It's above the fireplace.'

'I might have a look in a bit.'

I nodded.

'I thought Jacob might have come over tonight,' Ryan carried on.

'I think he's a bit snowed under at the moment,' I said, 'what with it being the end of term and everything.'

'Oh yeah, I'd forgotten about that.'

'Ryan—'

'I don't want to talk about it, Poppy,' he cut in, 'not yet anyway. I will soon, but for now, I just want to get my head straight. I'm thinking about what I'm going to do after the summer, amongst other things, but I'm not going to talk to you about any of it until I've got it all in order. Is that all right?'

'I guess.' I smiled. 'I was just going to ask you to pass me the tea towel.'

Ryan snatched it up, threw it at me and started to laugh. It was the best sound I'd heard in a long time.

'Now,' I said, 'if it's all right with you, I'm going to have an early night. I have to go back to work tomorrow. You can lock up before you and Gus turn in, can't you?'

The next couple of days were extraordinarily ordinary compared with those which had gone before and I for one was grateful for that. Greengages was as busy as it had been before the heatwave and there were plenty of enquiries, about both what was happening in the Grow-Well and whether I had secured a publisher for my recipe book. I managed to answer them all without giving too much away and was more than ready for my day off and lie-in on Saturday morning.

However, it was not meant to be and I wasn't the only one who was up with the lark.

'What's going on?' I asked Jacob, who arrived at his gate at the same time as I was pulling my front door shut. 'I thought you'd be making the most of the first day of your summer hols by sleeping in.'

'That was the plan,' he said yawning, 'and what about you? I thought you had a date with your mattress until at least lunchtime.'

'I did,' I said, waving my mobile in his direction, 'but

Ryan's not in his room and I've had a message from Luke, asking if I can get to the garden.'

'Snap,' said Jacob, 'I've had the same. Perhaps Ryan is there already? I hope the vandals haven't been back to finish the job off. I thought the police said they'd caught and charged whoever was responsible.'

'Morning, Poppy, morning, Jacob!' called Harold as he zipped up to us on his mobility scooter. 'Where's the fire?' He tutted. 'What's going on now?'

'I've no idea,' said Jacob, as we spotted Carole and Graham crossing the road to Prosperous Place ahead of us, 'but something tells me we're about to find out.'

Almost everyone was assembled when we arrived at the garden and in varying states of undress, due to the early hour. Heather was missing, but Glen was there and Mark, Neil explained, would be joining us as soon as he'd finished the early morning bakes and Blossom could spare him.

'What's going on?' John asked Luke. 'You said it was urgent.'

'That was me actually,' said Ryan, stepping out of the bothy with Gus at his heels. 'I borrowed Luke's phone to message you all because the police have still got mine.'

'Ryan has something he wants to tell us,' said Luke, 'don't you, mate?'

'Yeah,' he said, looking awkward, 'yeah I do.'

'Well come on then, lad,' said Harold, 'spit it out. I haven't had my first brew yet.'

'It's all in hand,' said Kate, 'if someone could just help me with the trays.'

Lisa and Carole rushed off to help and Jacob and I took the opportunity to ask Ryan if he was all right.

'I will be in a minute,' he said quietly, 'don't look so worried, Pops. Everything's fine.'

We all sat round the large wooden table, helped ourselves to mugs of tea and bacon rolls and waited for Ryan to explain exactly why he had thought it was a good idea to drag us from our beds at such an ungodly hour.

'I know that none of you blame me for what happened at the house and in here,' he began, his voice wobbling a little, in spite of his insistence that everything was fine. 'And I really appreciate that, but I am actually responsible and I want to explain why.'

We all looked up at him, holding our breath. Even the birds had fallen silent.

'Ryan—' I began but Jacob shook his head and I stopped.

'When Poppy asked me to come and live here and you guys treated me like one of you,' Ryan began with a swallow, 'it meant the world to me.'

'That's because you are one of us,' said Graham.

Ryan nodded.

'Thank you, Graham,' he went on, 'but I'm not sure I deserve to be. You see, I had a bit of an ulterior motive for taking up my sister's kind offer.'

'Go on,' I said gently.

Ryan dipped his head.

'When Mum moved us to Wynmouth last year,' he said, 'I was in a bit of a state. I was still getting over losing Dad and

I was angry all the time. Especially angry that she'd made us move. And I was determined to make things as difficult for her as possible.'

'What did you do?' asked Jacob.

I couldn't imagine that anything my brother had done would hold Mum's attention for long or make her think she'd made a mistake.

'Nothing that bothered her,' he confirmed, 'as it turned out.'

I was right.

'I made a point of falling in with the wrong crowd,' he said, shaking his head. 'There were a small bunch of locals who loved making a nuisance of themselves and there was this one lad—'

'Kyle,' I interrupted. 'You're talking about that Kyle, aren't you?'

Ryan nodded again.

'Yeah,' he said, 'he was the ringleader. I knew he was trouble right from the start but at the time I didn't care. He got me smoking the odd joint and when I enrolled at college he thought I'd be the ideal person to ferry his dope from Norwich for him.'

There was a sharp intake of breath from Carole.

'I knew I was really in deep then,' said Ryan, rushing on. 'I'd enrolled with the intention of getting away from Mum and Kyle for as long as possible during the week, but my plan backfired.'

'So, when I called and offered you the chance to move here . . .' I said.

'I jumped at the chance.' He nodded. 'I thought it was the perfect way of getting out of the mess I realised I'd got myself in.'

I hated how he blamed himself and wanted to point out that he was the one who had been taken advantage of, that someone had latched on to his vulnerability and used it to get what they wanted, but I didn't. There would be time to say all that once Ryan had told us everything.

'And it was great to begin with.' He smiled. 'Better than great. You guys actually made me believe in myself again. You made me feel like I was worth something and I was stuck into my studies, helping out here and loving life, until Colin's party at the bookshop.'

'What happened at the party?' Lisa asked. 'I don't remember anything going on.'

'It was after,' Ryan explained. 'My photo made it into the paper and Kyle saw it.'

'Of course,' I said, thinking back to when I had found him and some others at the house. 'He tracked you down. I knew you weren't happy about him turning up. Why didn't you say anything?'

And more to the point, why hadn't I? I should have followed my gut instinct, but I'd let the moment pass. I'd assumed the lads had gone and that was that.

'Because I was scared you'd find out I'd been transporting weed, Pops,' said Ryan. He looked horrified now the worst of it was all coming out. 'I was afraid that you all would. Kyle said that if I didn't get back on board with his plan he'd make sure everyone knew. I was so ashamed. I didn't want any of you thinking of me as a lad who did that.'

'So, what did you do?' asked Jacob.

'I tried to stand up to him,' said Ryan. 'I told him to go to hell, and that's when all this started. He said he needed money and that Prosperous Place would be full of stuff he could flog. He pinched Poppy's phone and made a note of the gate code and then when I wouldn't let him into the house he took my phone. He was so pissed when he couldn't find the house codes that he just smashed his way in.'

'Why didn't you say anything then?' I asked.

'Because I thought that would be the end of it.' He choked. 'I thought that as he hadn't got anywhere he'd leave it but' – he looked around him – 'I was wrong. I'm so sorry.'

'He tried to use your phone to frame you, didn't he?' said Jacob.

Ryan nodded.

'Joe thought it might not be a bad idea to disappear for a bit, so that's what we did.'

'What made you come back, Ryan?' asked Neil.

'We got a lift with this lorry driver,' Ryan said, rubbing his nose. 'He had his radio blaring out and when the news came on there was a story about this place. I knew that it was down to Kyle and I knew he had my phone. I had to come back to clear my name and say sorry to you guys.'

He stopped for a second, his eyes filling with tears as he looked at the destruction.

'Oh Ryan.' I sniffed.

'Don't,' he said, wiping his eyes. 'Let me finish.'

I nodded and put my head down.

'So,' he carried on, 'I went to the police. They'd already found Kyle's prints on my phone and worked out most of it. They know him pretty well and when I told them how I'd got involved with him it confirmed everything. It's not the first time he's done something like this. I'm just so sorry I let you all . . .' he started saying, but no one would hear of it. Everyone crowded round to hug and kiss him and pat him on the back.

It was such a relief to see everyone rallying round my brother that I found it impossible to stem the tears he had asked me to hold back.

'It's all right,' said Jacob, wrapping me in his arms and kissing my cheek, 'it's okay.'

'I know.' I nodded, sniffing. 'I know it is, but I just wish he'd talked to me.'

'I'm so sorry, Pops,' Ryan stammered, his bottom lip wobbling as he walked around the group to me.

'And I wish Kyle had left this place alone,' I said.

'But he didn't,' Ryan carried on.

Jacob loosened his grip but stayed close. I hoped Ryan would interpret our brief embrace as nothing more than friendly.

'And that's the other reason why I've asked you all here,' Ryan carried on, raising his voice. 'There's no way I can cope with the guilt if we pull out of this competition now,' he said. 'I know it's nowhere near as good as it was before, but we owe it to the Grow-Well and I owe it to all of you to at least give it a shot. Don't I?'

A second silence fell across the garden as everyone exchanged glances, clearly not knowing what to say.

'We can't let him win,' said Ryan, sounding choked again. 'This place deserves a chance to shine and if we all pull together, I really believe that we can make it happen. Who's with me?'

# Chapter 32

That weekend we worked harder than we ever had in the Grow-Well. Thankfully the searing temperature of the few weeks before hadn't made a return, but by the end of Sunday we were still all hot, tired, grubby and in need of a relaxing Radox soak.

'There's nothing else we can do now,' said Ryan, as we all stood back and looked at what our long hours, aching muscles and blistered hands had achieved. 'And whatever happens, at least we can say we've tried.'

Both the break-in at the house and subsequent trashing of the garden had meant interest in the place had soared, and our phones were all abuzz with encouraging Tweets and good wishes. Lisa had roused the council worker responsible for processing the competition paperwork and convinced them to let us withdraw our withdrawal and everything was as firmly back on track as we could get it.

'Yep,' said Luke, stepping up to stand next to Ryan, 'that's it, folks. Let's all go home. We'll soon find out whether we've done enough.'

Jacob, Ryan and I walked back to the square together. Well, I say walked – my legs were so stiff that it was more of a shuffle really. How I was going to get up the stairs and into the bath was anyone's guess, but it didn't matter because there was a car parked outside my house. I clearly had company to see to first.

'That's Mum,' my brother gasped when he spotted the car.

'*What*?'

'It's Mum,' he said, 'that's her car.'

'Are you sure?'

'Of course, I'm sure,' Ryan tutted. 'That's her tacky private plate.'

'What the hell is she after?' I frowned. 'Hey, Jacob, I don't suppose you fancy coming in to give us some moral support, do you?'

'I would,' he said, pointing to his own driveway, which I saw now had an unfamiliar car parked on it, 'but by the looks of it you aren't the only ones with visitors.'

We crossed the green and parted company, promising to catch up later. I held my breath as Mum's car door opened and a pair of slender mahogany legs appeared.

'Jesus,' said Ryan, tutting, 'she'd give that old bird on *Benidorm* a run for her money, wouldn't she?'

I couldn't help but smile.

'Mum,' I said, protectively stepping in front of my brother. 'What are you doing here?'

'Neither of us have got any money,' said Ryan, stepping round me and taking his place at my side. 'So if it's cash you're after you've had a wasted trip. I daresay Poppy hasn't recouped the last lot you had.'

'How did you know?' I gasped.

'It didn't take a genius to work it out, Pops,' he told me.

Mum ignored us both and reached into her car for a large and gaudy handbag, which had no doubt cost the earth, and a bulky manila file.

'Are you going to ask me in then, or what?' she snapped.

As much as I would have liked to make her stand on the street, I didn't think it fair to subject my neighbours to her overexposed bronzed cleavage, so I ushered her over the threshold.

'Tea?' Ryan muttered. He filled the kettle and then set about organising mugs and milk.

'Yes, please,' I answered. 'Better make mine camomile, I think.'

'Not for me,' said Mum, wrinkling her nose in disgust. 'I'm not stopping.'

'Oh no,' said Ryan sarcastically. 'That's a shame. I thought you'd want to hear all about how I've been getting on, and you and Pops must have loads to catch up on? I'm sure we could make a bed up on the sofa if you wanted to make a night of it.'

'Ryan,' I said, 'don't.'

'Well,' he said, crashing the fridge door shut. 'She brings out the worst in me.'

'I am here, you know,' Mum suddenly burst out. 'I can hear you, Ryan.'

I was beginning to think I should have left her on the doorstep after all. If this was a taste of what life in Wynmouth had been like, then it was no wonder Ryan had ended up making some bad decisions.

'So out with it then, Mum,' I said bluntly. 'Why are you here?'

I wanted to get her gone as quickly as possible.

'It's Tony's will,' she said, thumping the file down on the table. 'It's finally been sorted. He's left you rather a lot of money, Ryan.'

'Has he?' Ryan gasped.

'Yes.' She sniffed. 'But you can't touch any of it until you turn eighteen and some of it has to stay in trust until you're twenty-one.'

Ryan burst out laughing.

'No wonder you're looking more sour than usual.' He grinned. 'I daresay you were hoping to help me spend it.'

She did look a bit like she'd swallowed a lemon.

'It's not easy being a single parent, you know,' she choked. 'There are all sorts of expenses. You don't seem to understand that, Ryan.'

'He might not,' I said, 'but I do and you haven't been a single parent for more than five minutes, so don't start with the waterworks because they won't work on us. When Tony was alive he always paid for everything, and Ryan's been my responsibility for the last few months so you haven't had to shell out at all. You haven't even sent me his child benefit!'

'I'm sorry, Pops,' said Ryan, turning red, 'I've never thought how hard it must be for you financially.'

'Don't you worry about that,' I told him firmly. 'I'm saying this for her benefit, not to make you feel bad.'

Ryan nodded and I hoped he knew I meant that.

'Give it a couple of years,' he said to me, 'and I'll be able to treat you.'

'That money is for your future,' I said, even more firmly than before. 'I'll be making sure you won't be frittering it away on takeaways and chew toys for Gus!'

Ryan smiled and Mum looked disappointed. If she thought that turning up in person would soften our hardened hearts then she was in for a rude awakening. I would be doing everything in my power to make sure she wouldn't see a penny of Ryan's inheritance.

'Tony put down in the paperwork that he wanted you to act as trustee, actually,' Mum said to me. 'If you agree, you'll be looking after things on Ryan's behalf until he's old enough.'

'Of course I'll agree,' I said, pulling the file towards me and thinking what an astute man Tony was, 'but why am I only hearing about this now? Tony's been gone for over a year.'

Mum shrugged.

'Well,' she said, 'there have been complications.'

'You mean you've been stalling the solicitor,' said

Ryan, 'to see if there's any way you can get your mitts on the money.'

I wasn't sure that a solicitor would fall for her theatrics, but clearly something had been going on to stop them getting in touch. Thank goodness Tony had known what Mum was really like and had decided to leave the administration to me.

'Don't worry,' I told Ryan. 'I'll ring the solicitor first thing tomorrow and straighten everything out.'

'And if they need me for anything,' said Mum, standing up to deliver her parting shot, 'then they'll have to email or Skype.'

'Why?' Ryan and I asked together.

'Because I'm going back to Spain,' she said haughtily, 'and this time I won't be coming back.'

Mum's grand exit from the house was somewhat ruined as she collided with the lanky frame of Joe in the hallway. I wasn't sure who was more startled, but Mum recovered enough to untangle herself and drive off at speed. She hadn't even mentioned what was going to happen to Ryan. Not that either of us were worried about that.

'Fancy coming down to the youth centre?' Joe asked Ryan. 'They're supposed to be announcing their summer schedule in a bit.'

Ryan looked at me.

'You can go if you want to,' I told him.

'But haven't we got stuff to talk about?' he asked.

'Yes,' I said, smiling, 'lots, but it'll keep.'

I watched the two boys slope off out of the square and then looked across at Jacob's house. The car that had been on his drive had gone, so I figured it was safe to call round. I was bursting to tell him that Mum was leaving again, and this time hopefully for good.

The front door was slightly ajar so I slipped inside, along the hall and into the kitchen, where I could see him standing at the sink with his back to me. I stepped close behind, reached round and covered his eyes with my hands.

'Guess who?' I breathed, leaning into him.

Mum's departure, coupled with Ryan's good fortune, had revived my earlier flagging spirits and I was feeling in a playful mood, ready to capitalise on my brother's absence even though I knew it was taboo.

'I have absolutely no idea,' said a voice that sounded something like Jacob's, but was very definitely not.

'Shit,' I said, jumping back as I realised my mistake.

'Jesus,' said another voice behind me. This time the one I had been expecting all along. 'What is it with my women, Dan, you just can't keep your hands off them, can you?'

I stood, frozen, between the two men, who appeared identical in every possible way.

'It's all right.' Jacob suddenly laughed, leaning forward and pulling me to him. 'I'm joking.'

I let go of my bottled-up breath and thumped him on the chest. My heart was hammering.

'You must be Poppy,' said the man who could only be Dan. 'I'm Dan.'

'The one I was telling you about,' Jacob whispered theatrically.

'And he's Jacob,' said Dan, pointing at his twin, 'the one with the sick sense of humour.'

It turned out that spending time with Ryan had made Jacob miss his brother more than he thought he would ever be capable of given everything that had happened between them. So when Dan sent him a text to test the water, Jacob responded and the pair had been messaging ever since. Jacob hadn't been expecting Dan to turn up unannounced, but one twin missing the other clearly worked both ways and Dan knew he was the one with the making up to do.

'I was going to tell you,' said Jacob to me, 'but Ryan disappeared just as I was about to and I didn't want to give you anything else to think about.'

'Brothers eh?' Dan smiled. 'What are they like?'

'Quite.' I smiled too. 'More trouble than they're worth half the time.'

It was strange looking at Dan because he looked like Jacob, but at the same time he didn't. Jacob was rougher round the edges; Dan was smooth and sleek. Just like the car I'd seen earlier.

'Did you drive here, Dan?' I asked, wondering how I was going to break the news that his car had disappeared.

'No,' he said, 'I had a taxi from the station. I came on the train. And actually,' he added, looking at his watch, 'I better go and see if it's back. I need to go if I'm going to make it to the station on time.' This was only a flying visit.

I busied myself with the dishes while the pair said their goodbyes, and when Jacob came back I explained what Mum had turned up to say.

'It's been something of a red-letter day all round then, hasn't it?' He smiled, pulling me on to his lap.

'Just a bit,' I agreed. 'Do you think everything's going to be all right now?' I asked. 'With you and Dan, I mean. It can't have been easy for you, letting him back into your life.'

Jacob took a moment before answering.

'It's actually been easier than I expected,' he said seriously. 'When I moved here last year I was all set to face a future without any of my family in it at all, but seeing you with Ryan, and taking the time to get it all sorted out in my head without the pressure of anyone trying to force me into doing anything, has made all the difference.'

'That's good,' I said, planting a kiss on the end of his nose, 'better than good, because you've dealt with it all properly. If only Ryan could find it in his heart to change his mind about us.'

'If only,' Jacob agreed, squeezing me tighter.

# Chapter 33

Two weekends later we were back in the garden and Luke was once again standing in front of us, with Ryan at his side, along with three of the judges who had scrutinised our efforts.

'Having had a preliminary look around this garden when we drew up the shortlist,' said one of the women, 'we were amazed to see what you had achieved in such a short space of time.'

'It was obvious to us,' said another, 'that the watchword here was community. This garden was lucky enough to have you all on board and as a result you were all benefiting from it in many different ways.'

'Needless to say,' carried on the first woman, 'we were devastated to hear that you had withdrawn from the competition, but having seen the photographs of what had happened we could understand why.'

Those photographs, which, unbeknown to us at the time, Luke had snapped, had recorded the carnage and were still hard to look at even though we had all worked so hard to repair the damage.

'What we see around us now,' the judge continued, 'in terms of the crops and plants at least, is a mere shadow of what was here before, and that's such a shame.'

We all hung our heads, knowing the competition was lost.

'However,' she said, smiling, 'what we can also see, and it shines through stronger than any row of chard or juicy red tomato, is your community spirit, your resilience in the face of adversity and your determination to keep the Grow-Well alive. This garden, in its current state, isn't the most polished of the entries we've received, but it's packed full of heart and soul and that's why we are delighted to award it, and you, first place in the community garden competition!'

As one, we looked back up again and then at each other.

'Congratulations, Grow-Well team!' said the other woman, laughing, as the man stepped forward to present Luke with a silver cup and large envelope. 'You're this year's competition winners!'

It was only then that the noise erupted. Cheers, whoops, tears and the odd shocked expletive rang out, along with popping corks and the clicks of cameras from local journalists we hadn't noticed loitering around the bothy.

'We did it!' shouted Ryan. 'We did it!'

He pulled me in for a hug, jumping up and down and making me jump with him.

'My God, Poppy,' he said, laughing, his eyes smiling, 'can you believe it?'

'You did it, you mean,' said Luke, slapping him on the back.

'Yes, Ryan,' said Lisa, rushing over and passing round plastic cups filled with fizz, 'if it wasn't for you, we wouldn't have even been in the competition, let alone in with the chance of being awarded first place. You were the one who wouldn't let us give up.'

Marshalled together by the journalists and the judges, we posed for photographs and were briefly interviewed about our reaction and the roles we played in the garden. We were all in agreement that the prize money would be well spent creating another garden at the youth centre, which had an ample though neglected plot. I didn't think I'd ever seen so many smiles in one place and as neighbours and friends from further afield began to arrive, I knew the party was going to go on long into the night.

When no one was watching, Jacob and I slipped behind the bothy, out of sight, to where we stacked the empty pots and trays.

'I know we can't be long,' I said a little breathlessly, 'but I just wanted to grab a minute with you.'

'I know.' Jacob smiled, slipping his arms round my waist as I draped mine round his neck. 'I've been wanting to kiss you all afternoon. The look on your face when we were announced as the winner' – he sighed – 'I just wanted to grab you right then.'

He lowered his mouth to mine and as we kissed I imagined there were going to be innumerable snatched moments in the future. I hoped that having to sneak around wasn't going to impair our relationship. My simple life was complicated enough these days and even though we had agreed to take things slow, I wasn't sure how we were going to manage the logistics of such a clandestine association—

'I thought I saw you two sneaking down here.'

'Ryan!' yelped Jacob, dropping his hands as if I were a hot potato and taking a step back that almost upset an entire stack of pots. 'It's not what it looks like, mate.'

Ryan raised his eyebrows.

'Just wait before you jump to any conclusions,' I pleaded.

'No,' he said. 'You wait. I've known for weeks now that the pair of you weren't going to be able to keep your hands off one another. Right from when we talked about you not taking your relationship further, Poppy, it was obvious to me that you wouldn't be able to resist.'

'Bloody hell, Ryan,' said Jacob, his hands all but pulling his hair out in tufts.

'I'm sorry,' I said, my voice catching with emotion. 'I'm so sorry.'

'So am I,' said Ryan, shaking his head. 'I'm sorry I've made you sneak around.'

Jacob and I looked at him, amazed to see a smile lighting up his face, and then at one another.

'And I'm sorry I ever thought I had any right to dictate to either of you about what your relationship should be.'

'Really?' I tentatively asked.

'Really.' He beamed. 'It's obvious to everyone that you should be a couple and I've no right to tell you that you shouldn't be. All I ask is that you don't bump uglies when I'm in the house.'

'Ryan!' I scolded, heat flooding my face.

'Deal,' Jacob said, stepping forward and holding out his hand.

'Jacob!'

'What?' He laughed, gripping my brother's hand and turning the full strength of his sunny smile on to me.

It warmed me to my very toes.

'What's going on here then?' said Lou, when she came up and spotted us all hugging.

Ryan opened his mouth to answer her but I cut him off, neatly changing the subject before he had a chance to share with everyone at the Grow-Well team the sex veto he had just imposed. No one knew Jacob and I were even a couple yet, so they certainly didn't need to be better acquainted with the intimate details of our private life.

'We were just talking about Ryan's plans,' I blagged, 'weren't we, Ryan?'

Ryan grinned and let me off the hook.

Yes,' he said, 'I've finally made up my mind what I'm going to do.'

Once the judges and journalists and most of the neighbours who had popped in to offer their congratulations had gone, we all sat together round the table, squeezing close to make room for Harry, Lou, Colin and Blossom.

'Did I hear you say that you've decided what you're going to do, Ryan?' asked Graham.

The fact that he had overheard that part of our conversation made me blush all over again and thank my lucky stars that Ryan had allowed me to steer talk away from the ground rules he had been keen to establish when it came to my more private moments with Jacob. Sitting close, Jacob reached for my hand under the table and gave it a squeeze. I giggled in response. Clearly, he was thinking exactly the same thing.

'Yes,' said Jacob, to cover my reaction, 'isn't it about time you told everyone, Ryan?'

My brother and I had spent long hours since Mum's visit working out what he was going to do when the summer came to an end.

'Well,' he said, smiling at me, 'I'm definitely staying here with Pops.'

'You mean, you're going to be living here permanently?' gasped Tamsin.

'Yep,' he nodded, 'you're stuck with me, Tam.'

Tamsin turned even redder than I had been and John rolled his eyes, but a nudge from Lisa stopped his teasing in its tracks.

'Are you going to look for a job?' asked Colin, 'because I could do with an extra pair of hands in the shop from time to time.'

'And so could I,' agreed Lou.

I was delighted that both their businesses were thriving.

'Thanks, guys,' said Ryan, 'that would be great, thank you. As long as we can work around my college course, I'll happily work for both of you.'

'What are you going to be doing at college?' asked Heather.

'You aren't going to carry on with your A levels, are you?'

'No fear,' said Ryan, his body emitting a shudder at the mere mention of them. 'I'm going to Easton.'

Everyone smiled and nodded at the mention of the local agricultural college. Clearly, they all thought Ryan's change of academic direction was a good one. As he had to be in education until he was eighteen, he needed to be doing something he enjoyed, and working towards a qualification that would really mean something to him.

'I know I'm pretty handy with a paintbrush and I might think about following in my dad's footsteps one day, but for now my heart is set on looking after birds and animals,' he said, lifting Gus up on to his lap. 'I'm enrolling on an animal care course and I can't wait to get started.'

'That'll be perfect for you, lad,' said Graham fondly, 'you've certainly got a way with them. I think you'll do very well there.'

Everyone agreed and raised their drinks to toast my brother, who had changed almost beyond all recognition since his arrival in the square – and he wasn't the only one. The man sitting next to me, caressing my fingers under the table, was pretty altered too.

'And what about our recipe book, Poppy?' said Mark once everyone had finished quizzing Ryan about his course, turning the attention to me. 'Have you got any further with that?'

'I have, actually,' I admitted. 'In fact, I had a folder all ready to show you with some ideas in, but I've left it at home.'

'Go and get it then,' Mark urged, 'chop, chop!'

'I'll give you a hand,' said Jacob, pushing back his chair and following me across the garden.

'Don't be long, guys,' my cheeky brother called after me, 'and remember, I could come back at any moment!'

A loud cheer went up behind us and I guessed that my secret association with Jacob wasn't quite as clandestine as I'd thought. Jacob slipped his hand into mine.

'No point keeping us quiet from now on, by the sounds of it,' he laughed, kissing the back of my hand.

'No.' I smiled. 'I guess not. Do you mind?'

'God, no,' he sighed. 'I've had more than enough secrets to last me a lifetime. I'm proud of our relationship, Poppy, and I don't care who knows about it.'

I mulled his words over as we crossed the road to the square.

'That's all right,' he asked, when I didn't say anything, 'isn't it? You're happy for everyone to know, aren't you?'

'I'm more than happy for everyone to know,' I said, stopping to face him as we reached the green. 'In fact I've never been happier.'

'Really?'

'Really.'

'Me too.' He laughed, sweeping me into his arms. 'When I first moved here I thought I was destined to be a miserable bugger for the rest of my life, but you've woken me back up, Poppy. I thought my life was over but you, and the garden, you've revived me, you've bought me back from the brink.'

I knew what he meant. When I had moved into

Nightingale Square I had thought that my life was complete, but adding my brother and Jacob to the mix, two additions I hadn't been at all sure about in the beginning, had ended up enriching it beyond all belief.

'It's all part of my recipe for a happy life,' I told him, planting a kiss firmly on his lips.

# Acknowledgements

It's incredible to think that it has been less than a year since I took you all along with me for that first walk around Nightingale Square and into the garden at Prosperous Place. Another festive trip to Wynthorpe Hall has happened in the interim but I knew the Square had another tale to tell and I'm delighted to have had the opportunity to share Poppy's story with you all.

As always, writing a book is a collaborative effort and the list of those involved from conception to completion is steadily growing!

Huge and heartfelt thanks go out to my fabulous agent, Amanda Preston (she's Agent of the Year don't you know), who always has exactly the right words for every occasion. The incredible Books and the City Team – there really are too many of you to mention and I'm always worried about missing one of you out so here's a massive collective hug and a kiss for you all.

That said, my wonderful editor, Emma Capron, who will find her name at the front of this book gets a special mention. In the immortal words of Fatboy Slim, we really have 'come a long, long way together', Emma, and I am incredibly grateful to have had you by my side for this exciting part of my writing journey.

The more books I write, the more blurred the lines between best friends, supportive bloggers and loyal readers become so I'm saying thank you for your continued support en masse on this occasion. It's wonderful to know that if I don't pop up on social media for a day or so then you're all messaging to find out where I am. I feel very blessed.

Special thanks to Laura (@GrumpyGirlie) for keeping the baking tin stocked with delicious home-baked fare and for the festive bunting. And thanks also to Mr Dingle for supplying one of the funniest school anecdotes I've ever heard. Oh, how I wish I could have been there!

Last, but by no means least, thank you to my wonderful family for your continued support. I really am striving to 'Be More Milly', my darling girl!

All that remains for me to do now is to wish you all a wonderful summer! I hope you enjoy this latest trip to Nightingale Square and perhaps feel inspired to cook up your own Recipe for Life! May your bookshelves – be they virtual or real – always be filled with fabulous fiction.

H x

# Reading Group Questions

1) Why do you think the author chose to give the community garden such a central role in the novel? What do you think she is trying to convey about the act of gardening?

2) What do you think of Poppy and Jacob's decision to try to accommodate Ryan's feelings in their relationship? Do you agree with their choice?

3) The importance of family is emphasised throughout the novel, particularly concerning damaged or broken relationships. How does the theme of family develop in different ways throughout the novel?

4) Poppy rearranges her whole life to help her brother and spends a good portion of her time trying to aid others around her. Why do you think this is so important to her? Do you think it is a strength or weakness in her character?

5) How does the setting of Nightingale Square influence the themes of the novel, and why does it have such an impact?

6) How is mental health addressed in the book, especially in reference to Ryan? Why do you think it is portrayed in such a way and do you agree with it?

7) What do you think the novel is saying about independent shops and businesses and their ability to adapt to the times, especially in concern to Harry's grocery store and Colin's book shop?

8) Ryan faces some difficult decisions about his future at a rather young age. What do you think the novel is saying about the societal pressure on teenagers to always have their lives figured out? Do you agree with this expectation?

## *Snowflakes and Cinnamon Swirls at the Winter Wonderland*

**'The most delicious slice of festive fiction: a true comfort read and the perfect Christmas treat to alleviate all the stress!' Veronica Henry**

**'Full of Heidi's trademark gentle charm. Lock the door, pour some mulled wine and settle into this wonderful Christmas treat!' Milly Johnson**

Moving into Wynthorpe Hall to escape the town's gossip, Hayley finds herself immersed in the eccentric Connelly family's festive activities as they plan to host their first ever Winter Wonderland. But Hayley isn't the only new resident at the hall. Gabe, a friend of the Connellys' son Jamie, has also taken up residence, moving into Gatekeeper's Cottage, and he quickly makes an impression on Wynbridge's reformed good-girl.

Under the starry winter skies, will Gabe convince Hayley to open her heart again once more? And in doing so, will he convince himself?

**Available now in paperback, eBook and eAudio**

SIMON & SCHUSTER

## *Sunshine and Sweet Peas in Nightingale Square*

Kate is on the run from her soon-to-be ex-husband, who still desperately wants her back, when she stumbles across a cosy nook in Norwich – Nightingale Square.

What Kate doesn't count on is being pulled out of her perfect little hiding place and into a community that won't take no for an answer. Before long, Kate finds herself surrounded by friends. But when developers move in on the magnificent Victorian mansion on the other side of the square, the preservation of their community's history is challenged.

As all hope seems lost, will the arrival of a handsome stranger turn things around for both Kate and Nightingale Square? Or have their chances for a happy-ever-after finally run out . . . ?

**Available now in paperback, eBook and eAudio**

SIMON & SCHUSTER

# *Summer at Skylark Farm*

Amber is a city girl at heart. So when her boyfriend Jake Somerville suggests they move to the countryside to help out at his family farm, she doesn't quite know how to react. But work has been hectic and she needs a break, so she decides to grasp the opportunity.

Dreaming of organic orchards, paddling in streams and frolicking in fields, Amber packs up her things and moves to Skylark Farm. But life is not quite how she imagined – it's cold and dirty and the farm buildings are dilapidated and crumbling . . .

Even so, Amber is determined to make the best of it and throws herself into farm life. But can she really fit in here? And can she and Jake stay together when they are so different?

**Available now in paperback, eBook and eAudio**

SIMON &
SCHUSTER